Seductive Scoundrels
SERIES BOOKS 4-6

COLLETTE CAMERON

Blue Rose Romance®
Portland, Oregon

Sweet-to-Spicy Timeless Romance®

Collette
Cameron

Other Collette Cameron Books

Daughters of Desire (Scandalous Ladies)
A Lady, A Kiss, A Christmas Wish
Coming soon in the series!
No Lady for the Lord
Love Lessons for a Lady
His One and Only Lady

The Honorable Rogues®
A Kiss for a Rogue
A Bride for a Rogue
A Rogue's Scandalous Wish
To Capture a Rogue's Heart
The Rogue and the Wallflower
A Rose for a Rogue

The Blue Rose Regency Romances:
The Culpepper Misses
The Earl and the Spinster
The Marquis and the Vixen
The Lord and the Wallflower
The Buccaneer and the Bluestocking
The Lieutenant and the Lady

Highland Heather Romancing a Scot
Triumph and Treasure
Virtue and Valor
Heartbreak and Honor
Scandal's Splendor
Passion and Plunder
Seductive Surrender
A Yuletide Highlander

Castle Brides
The Viscount's Vow
Highlander's Hope
The Earl's Enticement
Heart of a Highlander (*prequel to Highlander's Hope*)

Seductive Scoundrel's
A Diamond for a Duke
Only a Duke Would Dare
A December with a Duke
What Would a Duke Do?
Wooed by a Wicked Duke
Duchess of His Heart
Never Dance with a Duke
Earl of Wainthorpe
Earl of Scarborough
The Debutante and the Duke
Wedding her Christmas Duke
Earl of Keyworth
Coming soon in the series!
How to Win A Duke's Heart
Loved by a Dangerous Duke
When a Duke Loves a Lass

Boxed Sets
Lords in Love
Castle Brides Collection: Books 1-3
The Honorable Rogues® Books 1-3
The Honorable Rogues® Books 4-6
Seductive Scoundrels Series Books 1-3
Seductive Scoundrels Series Books 4-6
The Blue Rose Regency Romances:
The Culpepper Misses Series 1-2

Contents

What Would a Duke Do?

Prologue

December 1809
Ridgewood Court, Essex England

Humming beneath her breath, Gabriella Breckensole practically skipped down the stairs on her way to meet the other female houseguests to make kissing boughs and other festive decorations. The past few days had been a whirlwind of activity, as her hostess, Theadosia, the Duchess of Sutcliffe and one of her dearest friends, hosted a Christmastide house party, the likes of which Essex had never witnessed before.

The event was made all that much more enjoyable by the presence of Maxwell Woolbright, the Duke of Pennington. Since Gabriella and her twin sister had returned from finishing school almost two years ago, she'd encountered him at a few gatherings. He was quite the most dashing man she'd ever met, and despite being far above her station, she thrilled whenever he directed his attention her way.

Descending the last riser, she puzzled for a moment. Where were the ladies to meet? The drawing room, the floral salon, or the dining room? Forehead scrunched, she pulled her mouth to the side and started toward the drawing room. Halfway there, she remembered they were to meet in the slightly larger dining room. She spun around and marched the other direction, passing the impressive library, its door slightly ajar.

"Harold Breckensole will pay for what he's done," a man declared in an angry, gruff voice.

Gabriella halted mid-step, her stomach plunging to her slippered feet. She swiftly looked up and down the vacant corridor before tip-toeing to the cracked doorway. Who spoke about her grandfather with such hostility?

Breath held, she peeked through the narrow opening. The Dukes of Sutcliffe, Pennington, and Sheffield stood beside the fireplace, facing each other.

Pennington held a glass of umber-colored spirits in one hand as he stared morosely into the capering flames. "I shall reclaim Hartfordshire Court. I swear."

"You say the estate was once part of the unentailed part of the duchy?" Sutcliffe asked, concern forming a line between his eyebrows.

Pennington tossed back a swallow of his drink. "Yes. It belonged to my grandmother's family for generations, and after what I've recently learned, I mean to see it restored to the ducal holdings, come hell or high water. And I'll destroy Breckensole too."

Slapping a hand over her mouth, she backed away, shaking her head as stinging tears slid from the corners of her eyes.

Oh, my God. She'd been halfway to falling in love with a man bent on revenge of some sort. Gabriella jutted her chin up, angrily swiping at her cheeks. The Duke of Pennington had just become her enemy.

Late March 1810
Colechester, Essex, England

"Miss Breckensole, what an unexpected...pleasure," a man drawled in a cultured voice, the merest hint of laughter coloring his melodious baritone.

Unexpected and wholly unwelcome.

Gabriella froze in her admiration of Nicolette Twistleton's adorable pug puppy, and barely refrained from gnashing her teeth. She knew full well who stood behind her. The odious, arrogant—*annoying as Hades*—Maxwell, Duke of Pennington. His delicious cologne wafted past her nostrils, and she let her eyelids drift half shut as she ordered her heart to resume its regular cadence.

He didn't know what she'd discovered about him. That he was a dishonorable, deceiving blackguard behind his oh, so charming demeanor. And he meant to destroy her grandfather. That knowledge bolstered her courage and settled her erratic pulse.

One midnight eyebrow arched questioningly; Nicolette threw her a harried glance before dipping into a curtsy. "Your Grace."

Gabriella hadn't confided in Nicolette. Hadn't confided in anyone as to why she disliked him so very much. Quashing her irritation at his appearance and his daring to greet her as if they were the greatest of friends, she schooled her features into blandness before turning and sinking into the expected deferential greeting. "Duke."

He bowed; his strong mouth slanted into his usual half-mocking smile.

"What brings you to town?" He glanced around. "Your sister or grandmother aren't with you? Or an abigail either?" A hint of disapproval edged his observation. "Did you come with Miss Twistleton?"

Beast. Who was he to question her conduct? She wasn't accountable to him.

"No, I am here with my mother." Nicolette cast Gabriella another bewildered glance. "She's in the milliner's."

Surely, he was aware, as was the whole of Colechester, that a lady's maid was an unnecessary expense, according to Gabriella's grandfather. That the duke so offhandedly and publicly made mention of the deficiency angered and chagrined her.

Pennington turned an expectant look upon her. As if he were entitled to have an answer, because, after all, *he* was the much sought-after Duke of Pennington.

Edging her chin upward, Gabriella clutched her packages tighter, one of which was her twin's birthday present. She saved for months to be able to surprise Ophelia with the mazurine blue velvet cloak.

"Grandmama is unwell, and Ophelia stayed home to care for her." She wouldn't offer him further explanation.

"I am truly sorry to hear that. May I have my physician call upon her?" he asked, all solicitousness, even going so far as to lower his brows as if he truly cared. A concern she knew to be feigned given what she'd overheard at the Duke and Duchess of Sutcliffe's Christmastide house party last December.

"That's not necessary. She was seen by one only last week." My, she sounded positively unaffected. The epitome of a self-possessed gently-bred young woman.

Inside, she fumed at his forwardness.

How she wanted to rail at him. To tell him precisely what she thought of his nefarious scheme. Why did he—*conceited, handsome rakehell*—

4

have to be in Colechester today too? He promptly turned her much-anticipated afternoon outing sour. Freshly cut lemon or gooseberry face-puckering, attitude-ruining sour.

And why he insisted upon trying to speak to her at every opportunity, she couldn't conceive. Three months ago, and the few unfortunate occasions they'd come across each other since, she'd made her feelings perfectly clear—to-the-point-of-rudeness-clear.

She'd heard him vow to the Dukes of Sheffield and Sutcliffe that *come hell or high water*—Pennington's very sternly muttered words—he'd reclaim the lands that had once been an unentailed part of the duchy. Lands that had belonged to his grandmother's family for generations.

Property, which included her beloved home, Hartfordshire Court. A holding that Grandpapa had purchased, fair and square, from the duke's own degenerate grandfather decades before and which, with hard work and industry, had made the estate prosperous.

"Mama is so very pleased you are to attend our musical assembly, Your Grace," Nicolette blurted. As if sensing the stilted silence and not understanding the reason why, but wanting to defuse the tangible awkwardness.

Unable to contain her disbelief, Gabriella sent him a quick glance from beneath her lashes. *He is to attend? Of all the dashed rotten luck.* He rarely remained at his country seat past mid-March. London held far more appeal to a man of the world like him, and truth be told, she had anticipated—*needed*—a few months' reprieve from his presence.

She and Ophelia were to attend as well, but now she no longer anticipated her first social foray other than tea in two months as she had but a minute ago.

Nicolette shifted the puppy and received a wet tongue on the cheek for her efforts. "No licking, Bella," she admonished whilst rubbing the pup behind her ears. "It's also Gabriella's birthday that day," she offered with an impish twinkle in her eye. "She'll be one and twenty."

Gabriella shot her a quelling glance. The world—*he*—didn't need to know she was practically on the shelf with no prospects, save spinsterhood.

"I quite look forward to the entertainment." Insincerity rang in his tone as he gave a gracious nod and continued staring at Gabriella. "And also, to wish you a happy day, Miss Breckensole." The latter held a note of authenticity. He flicked his gaze down the street, seeming uncharacteristically uncertain. "Ladies, would you join me for a cup of chocolate or coffee?"

The Prince's Coffee House was but four doors down and acclaimed not only for its hot beverages, but ambiance and scrumptious pastries. Not that Gabriella had ever sampled either.

She'd wanted to, but Grandpapa frowned upon eating in the village. A waste of good coin, he grumbled.

Nicolette shook her head, no genuine regret shadowing her face. After being jilted, she bore disdain for every male, save her brother, the Earl of Scarborough. "I fear Mama is expecting me inside. I only came outside for Bella's sake."

"And I must return home straightaway." Gabriella signaled her driver with a flick of her wrist and slant of her head. She'd finished her shopping before bumping into Nicolette and the newest addition to the Twistleton household.

Amid a chorus of creaks and groans, her grandfather's slightly lopsided and dated coach pulled alongside her. Jackson, the groomsman, climbed down and after three rigorous attempts, managed to lower the steps. She passed him her parcels, which he promptly placed inside the conveyance.

"Please allow me." The duke stepped forward and offered his hand to assist her inside.

While she wanted to give him the cut by refusing to accept his offer, Nicolette was sure to interrogate her as to why she'd been so rude the next time they met. A year ago, even three months ago, Gabriella would've been overjoyed at his attention. Now, he was her enemy. A handsome, dangerous, cunning, and unpredictable nemesis.

As lightly as she was able, she placed her fingertips atop his palm and entered the rickety out of fashion forty-year-old coach. Lips melded, she studiously disregarded the alarming jolt of sensation zipping up her arm at his touch. She should feel nothing but contempt for him and most assuredly entertain no carnal attraction.

The duke didn't immediately close the door behind her. His gaze probed hers for a long sliver of a moment, and suddenly the coach became very confining. And hot. She waved her hand before her face, having left her fan at home. "Might I call upon you tomorrow?" *Is he utterly daft?* "Perhaps we might take a ride? Naturally, Miss Ophelia is welcome too."

That latter seemed more of an after-thought. He knew she couldn't ride out alone with him, and he was mad as a Bedlam guest if he truly believed she'd willingly spend time in his company.

Gabriella met his gaze straight on. Something undefinable shadowed the depths of his unusual eyes—one green and one blue. "I must decline, Your Grace. I also must ask you, once again, to direct your attentions elsewhere. I am not now, nor will I ever be, receptive to them."

If she never spoke to him again, it would be too soon.

Did he really think just because he was a duke and she was the lowly granddaughter of a gentleman-farmer, she'd jump at the opportunity to spend time in his company?

You did at one time. And suffered a broken heart when his true character became evident.

Not. Anymore. Never again. Not when she knew his true motivation for seeking her company. How much her feelings had changed for him these past months.

At once his striking countenance grew shuttered, his high cheekbones more pronounced with... Anger? Disappointment? "We, shall see, *cherie.* We shall see."

"What, precisely, do you mean by that?" Something very near dread clogged her throat, and the words came out husky rather than terse as she'd intended.

Instead of answering, he offered an enigmatic smile and doffed his hat, the afternoon sunlight glinting on his raven hair. "Good day."

We, shall see, cherie. We shall see.

His words replaying over and over in her mind, she remained immobile, her focus trained on his retreating form until he disappeared into the Pony and Pint instead of The Prince's Coffee House. At one time, she'd fancied herself enamored of him. She'd been flattered he'd turned his ducal attention on her: a simple country girl without prospects.

Firmly stifling those memories and the associated emotions, she tapped the roof. "Home. Jackson, and do hurry. Grandmama needs her medicines."

And I need to put distance between myself and the Duke of Pennington. Because even though she knew the truth, a tiny part of her heart yet ached for him, and she loathed herself for that weakness.

Two hours later shivering and briskly rubbing her arms, Gabriella bent forward to peer out the coach window again.

Tentatively probing her head, she winced. The knot from smacking her noggin on the side of the vehicle when the axle snapped hadn't grown any larger. Neither did it bleed. Nonetheless, the walnut-sized lump ached with the ferocity of a newly trapped tiger. A superbly large, sharp-toothed, and foul-tempered beast.

"Really," she muttered, exasperated and uncharacteristically cross from hunger, cold, and the painful bump. "Whatever can be taking Jackson so long to return? Hartsfordshire Court isn't so very blasted far."

Less than two miles she estimated after another glance at the familiar green meadow sloping to the winding river beyond. The recent rains caused the brown-tinged water to run high and spill over its banks, as it did nearly every spring. In the summer, the lush grasslands fed Grandpapa's famed South Devon cattle on one side, and their neighbor, the Duke of Pennington's fluffy black-faced sheep on the other.

An uncharitable thought about the distinction between the keen intelligence of cows and sheep's lack of acumen tried to form, but she squelched it. It wasn't the poor sheep's fault she couldn't abide their owner.

After repeatedly assuring her hesitant coachman she would be perfectly fine until he returned with the seldom-used phaeton, Jackson had swiftly stridden away. Not, however, without turning to work his worried gaze over her, the team, and the disabled coach's crippled wheel thrice. Each time, she donned a smile wide enough to crack her cheeks and made a shooing motion for him to continue on.

For pity's sake. She wasn't one of those silly, simpering misses afraid the hem of her skirt might become dusty or who shrieked hysterically upon a cobweb brushing her gloves or cheek. So long as the resident eight-fuzzy-legged spider had *long* since removed itself to a new home.

If it weren't for her impractical footwear, Gabriella would've walked as well. But, she'd no wish for bruised feet or the lecture certain to follow from dear Grandpapa about the cost of replacing ruined slippers. And that would probably produce another discourse about unnecessary trips to Colechester for what he deemed nonsensical fripperies.

Perhaps they were absurd to a man given to wearing the same staid suit and shoes for the past five years as Grandpapa had been. But Ophelia's birthday present wasn't a silly frippery. Neither were Grandmama's medicine nor the chemises for Gabriella and her sister frivolous expenses. It had been three years since anyone had purchased new undergarments.

With her leftover pin money—one half a crown every month—Gabriella had purchased the beloved hunch-shouldered curmudgeon his favorite blend of pipe tobacco. Oh, he'd grumble and grouse over the wasteful spending, but she hadn't a doubt she'd earn a kiss upon her forehead before he shuffled off to enjoy a pipe and a tot in his fusty study amongst his even fustier tomes.

A wry smile quirked her mouth.

Did Grandpapa use the same tobacco five times as he insisted Grandmama do with tea leaves? Anything to save a penny or two. The Breckensoles didn't enjoy neat lumps of white sugar in their tea either, but rather the golden-brown nubs chiseled from a cheaper hard-as-a-blasted-boulder loaf. Since they never—truly never—had guests for tea or for any other occasion for that matter, there was no need to feel a trifle embarrassed at the economy.

She ran a gloved finger over the lumpy parcel containing the umber-brown bottles for her grandmother. A month ago, a nasty cough had settled in Grandmama's lungs, and she couldn't shake the ailment.

Gabriella's current discomfort tugged her meandering musings back to her immediate situation. For all of two seconds—fine, mayhap three—she'd considered riding one of the horses still harnessed to the coach home. But that would've required hiking her gown knee-high and riding astride. Even she daren't that degree of boldness.

Nonetheless, on days she yearned to toss aside society's and her strict grandparents' constraints, she *might've* been known to sneak a horse from the stables and ride along the river: bonnet-free and skirts rucked most inappropriately high. Oh, the freedom was wondrous, though the tell-tale freckles that were wont to sprout upon her nose usually gave her recklessness away.

Her grandparents never lectured, but their silent disapproval was sufficient to quell her hoydenish ways. For a week or two.

The carriage made an eerie noise; the way a vehicle sounded in the throes of death. *If* a vehicle were capable of such a thing. Another juddering crack followed as the damaged side wedged deeper into the dirt.

She let loose a softly-sworn oath no respectable woman ought to know, let alone utter aloud as she grabbed the seat to keep from tumbling onto the floor. A labored groan and a piercing creak followed on the heels of her crude vulgarity, and a five-inch-long jagged crack split the near window.

"Blast and damn."

A new chill skidded down her spine as she mentally braced herself for Grandpapa's intense displeasure. He'd be aggravated about the damage to the coach, but more so about the cost to repair it. A frugal, self-made man, he was as reluctant to part with a coin as he was to leave Hartfordshire Court. Others who didn't know him well called him stingy and miserly.

In the fifteen years since coming to live at Hartfordshire, Gabriella could count on two hands the number of times either grandparent had left the estate. She would shrivel up and die if forced to stay there months on end.

Yet, her hermit-like grandparents had been diligent to assure she and her sister never lacked for company or social interactions. They'd even conceded to send the twins to finishing school. At no little cost either. What a juxtaposition. Her grandparents eschewed all things social, but she and her sister craved the routs, soirees, balls, picnics, musical parties, and all else that guaranteed a superior assemblage.

One troublesome, unignorable fact remained unaddressed, however. Grandpapa had never spoken of a dowry for either of them. They'd never wanted for necessities, but Gabriella suspected his pockets weren't as flush as he'd have his family believe.

Her heart gave a queer pang. It wasn't exactly worry or distress. But neither was the peculiar feeling frustration or disappointment. Nevertheless, it left her unsettled. Discontent and restless. Disconcerted about what her future might entail. Ophelia's too.

As improbable as it was, except for splurging on the matched team and phaeton, her grandfather had been noticeably less inclined to spend money after the twins returned home two years ago. Now, almost one and twenty, their aging grandparents' health beginning to fail, and their neighbor, the mercenary Duke of Pennington, bent on stealing Hartsfordshire Court from them, Gabriella fretted about what would happen to her sister if neither one of them married and soon.

There weren't exactly men—noble or otherwise—scurrying to form a queue to court either of them. Or to dance with them at assemblies or request romantic strolls through opulent gardens. No posies, sweets, or poems found their way to the house's front door on a regular basis either. On *any* basis, for that matter.

Oh, the country gentlemen were kind and polite enough. Indeed, some aristocrats and gentry—even a rogue or two—had been downright charming and flirtatious. More than one had hinted they'd very much like to pursue an immoral liaison. But the simple truth was as obvious as a giraffe's purple tongue sampling pea soup in the dining room. Dowerless, Gabriella's and Ophelia's prospects were few.

Nonexistent, truth to tell.

For one horrid, ugly fact couldn't be overlooked: a woman without a dowry, no matter how refined, immaculately fitted out, or proficient in French, Latin, Spanish, painting, playing the pianoforte—or the violin in Gabriella's case—and managing a household she might be, without the lure of a marriage settlement to entice a respectable suitor, such an unfortunate lady was labeled an undesirable.

And much like other hapless women in the same ill-fated predicament, spinsterhood, dark and foreboding, loomed on the horizon, a slightly terrifying fate for any young woman.

Which made the duke's interest in her all the more questionable. He couldn't possibly have honorable intentions.

She pursed her mouth, drawing her eyebrows into a taut line. Barbaric, this business of bribing a man with money, land, and the good Lord only knew what else to take a woman to wife. Why couldn't love be enough?

Like Theadosia and Sutcliffe? Or her maternal cousin Everleigh and the Duke of Sheffield? Or even Jemmah and Jules, the Duke and Duchess of Dandridge? Once not so long ago, Gabriella had yearned for that kind of love. Had dared to hope she might've found it, but the object of her affections had turned out to be a colossal rat.

Unfortunately, such was the nature of the Marriage Mart. Without dowries, Gabriella and her twin could look forward to caring for their grandparents into their dotage rather than marry and have families. Their lack of suitors could be laid at Society's silk-clad feet. Strictures, along with a goodly portion of greed and hunger for power, dictated most matches. That, regrettably, was an indisputable fact.

Something uncomfortable and slightly terrifying, much like melancholy, turned over in her breast and swirled in her stomach. To distract herself from her somber reflections, she inspected the lonely road once more.

The fading afternoon sun filtering through the towering evergreen treetops on the other side of the deserted track confirmed dusk's dark cloak and chill would blanket the countryside soon. For at least the sixth time in the past hour, Gabriella examined the dainty timepiece pinned to her spencer.

She frowned and gave it a little shake. Was the deuced thing working?

Yes, the big hand shifted just then. She huffed out a small petulant sigh, for she recognized her own impatience.

Where the devil was Jackson, for pity's sake? Had something waylaid him? *Obviously.* Yes, but what? The unbidden thoughts agitated her already heightened nerves. Nerves that had been fraught since departing the village earlier.

Angered anew at Pennington's audacity, she pressed her lips into an irritated line and fisted her hands. Only he had the ability to make her so peeved. *Bloody, greedy bounder. By Jove, didn't he have enough? Why must he covet what we have too?*

Chartworth Hall was an immense estate boasting some two-thousand acres, a mansion—more castle than house—a hunting lodge, a dower house, embarrassingly massive and full stables, and numerous other outbuildings.

Why the duke focused on Hartfordshire's acres and seventeen-room residence, quite desperately in need of refurbishing and restoration, made no sense at all. She didn't know the particulars of the sale. Neither did she understand how the unentailed property came to be adjacent to the entailed lands, but she didn't give a fig.

What she *did* care about was the duke's callousness. His insensitivity and cold-heartedness. He hadn't a thought for any of the Breckensoles, of displacing them from their home. Oh, no. His only concern was how to cheat Grandpapa out of his property and to expand the already enormous ducal holdings.

By God, she wouldn't permit it. She would not.

2

Drumming her fingertips atop her thigh, Gabriella huffed out another frustrated breath. Ophelia was the patient twin. The sensible twin. The good-natured, genial twin. The one capable of tempering tart retorts and painting a benign mien upon her features.

Far too frequently, Gabriella spoke her mind and responded with emotion rather than reason. Alternating tapping her toes on the sloping floor, one foot then the next, she put a hand to her hollow middle and moistened her lower lip. She was rather parched too.

Memory of the meat pies and other savory foods' aromas wafting from the lodging house and The Prince's Coffee House caused her stomach to protest loudly. *We've plenty of food and refreshment at Hartfordshire Court. No sense wasting good coin.* Grandpapa's admonishment replayed through her mind.

She still hadn't informed her grandparents of Pennington's devious plan. She couldn't fathom a legal way he could regain the estate, and therefore, rather than cause the elderly pair an upset, she kept the knowledge to herself.

When the need arose—*pray God it never would*—she'd tell all. But until that time, the tall debonair duke with his shock of midnight hair and unusual eyes beneath slashing brows the same hue as his hair, wasted his time directing his attention toward her. She, alone, must protect her family from that craven's cunning and scheming.

In fact, she'd taken to carrying a small dagger in her boot or reticle.

Just in case…Well, she didn't know exactly what. But far better to be prepared than caught unawares. She also knew how to wield a fan, a hat pin, and even a parasol as an improvised weapon should the need arise. Nicolette firmly believed every woman should be able to defend herself, and Gabriella agreed wholeheartedly.

Her ability to fend off an attacker was another reason she'd been comfortable sending Jackson for assistance. Besides, rarely did anyone travel this isolated length of road. Only Hartfordshire Court, Pennington's palatial country seat, and a seldom used shortcut connecting the main route to London lay this far along the remote track.

Flopping back against the pale blue velvet squabs, she folded her arms and wrinkled her nose.

How could she ever have thought the Duke of Pennington amusing or charming? *Enthralling. Fascinating. Wholly extraordinary*. His black-lashed eyes *were* quite extraordinary. Never before had she seen anyone with two different colored eyes. They enhanced the air of mystery surrounding him. As if he were privy to a secret no one else knew. She'd seen it in the way he observed her through his heavy-lidded, smoldering eyes.

A little rush of exhilaration tingled in her blood.

Heavy-lidded? Smoldering? My God.

What in the world had come over her? Surely it must be hunger or the knock to her head. Either or perhaps both had made her dizzy and fanciful.

What a good thing she discovered his true colors before she'd permitted her schoolgirl *tendre* to foolishly become something more. Now, however, she knew better than to trust his cheerful demeanor and too-alluring-for-her-good smile. All of his attention and murmured compliments had all been a calculated ruse to get near her and use her as a means to rob her grandparents of their home. Oh, how she longed to plant him a facer or challenge him to pistols or swords.

She wasn't such a refined lady that either choice wasn't an option.

Her grandparents would be horrified to know, but she and Ophelia had learned fencing, how to shoot pistols, and even how to deliver a precisely-aimed blow with their fists. All thanks to their many visits and overnight stays with her dear friend, Nicolette.

15

Gabriella tapped her chin with her forefinger. Mayhap she should ask Nicolette how to discourage a gentleman's attention. After being jilted a mere day before her wedding, her friend had perfected snubbing men to a fine art. To the point of cruelty at times. Nicolette also possessed an assortment of naughty romance novels, which she freely shared with her friends.

Or perchance, Gabriella should enlist her cousin Everleigh or their mutual friend Theadosia for help. The duchesses could discretely question their husbands about what types of things were certain to put Pennington off the chase.

What surely must be a crafty smile tipped her mouth.

Why, yes. Why hadn't she considered that sooner?

Shifting uncomfortably, she eyed the wispy ferns and underbrush crowding the tree trunks. Nature called with ever-increasing urgency.

Finally, when another impatient glare to her timepiece revealed ten more minutes had inched past, she could wait no longer. With some difficulty, and only by pressing her shoulder forcefully into the stubborn panel, she managed to shove the door open then hopped to the ground. In the looming twilight, a magnificent stag stood near the river. Ebony eyes wary and ears twitching, he observed her, the tips of his mighty antlers obscured in the gloaming light.

If only she had her pencils and sketch pad, she might've drawn him, and she'd have had something to pass the time as well. She must remember to bring them next time, for one never knew when an opportunity might arise that she'd want to record on paper. Apparently deciding she posed him no threat, the stag lowered his head to the shimmering water.

The horses, a striking matched pair of grays right down to their black manes and tails, flicked those impressive tails and shifted their feet. No doubt they longed for their warm stalls and a bucket of oats to happily munch upon.

She yearned for a hot bath liberally sprinkled with jasmine, lavender, and lemongrass-scented oil—her own creation since perfume was an expense Grandpapa disallowed. A bowl of Mrs. McCandish's sumptuous cock-a-leekie soup, and an equally hot toddy, generously laced with whisky wouldn't go amiss either.

"Brrr."

Shivering, Gabriella rubbed the dark green velvet covering her arms again as she carefully studied the narrow, rutted track first in one direction then the other. When she'd left the house this afternoon, the temperature had been quite warm for March. Since she traveled directly to Colechester and back, she hadn't believed a cloak necessary.

Neither was there a lap robe in the drafty coach. Grandpapa claimed the moths and vermin would feast upon it. One didn't argue with him or point out that the robe might be stored inside the house until needed.

Always the more practical sister, Ophelia's advice from earlier today rang in Gabriella's ears. "Gabby, you really ought to at least take a shawl or mantle. You know how quickly the weather can turn ugly this time of year. We don't need you falling ill as well."

In her typical impetuous way, Gabriella had ignored her sister's warning, more fool she. Especially, if night fell before, she was rescued. It surely appeared as if it would.

That miserable thought coiled in her empty belly. It was one thing to think oneself daring and independent in daylight and another thing entirely when darkness blacker than a moonless night descended upon the countryside... *This* oh, so very isolated particular spot of countryside to be precise.

Despite her impulsive inclinations, she'd never pretended to be an audacious, adventurous sort. With each passing minute, real concern for Jackson grew. As did the unpleasant realization that she very well may have to spend the night huddled in the coach or trod home in the dark.

Alone.

With wild, *hungry* creatures meandering about.

Each alternative held as much appeal as kissing Pennington. *Kissing Pennington?* Good heavens, where did that odious thought come from? *Is it truly odious?*

Yes, she very sternly chided her romping imagination. *Of course it is.* Everything to do with him was disagreeable, the charlatan. Pretending to be her friend and paying her marked attention all the while plotting to steal her home.

She'd sooner pull every hair from her head than touch her mouth to his.

Liar, chided an annoying voice in her mind. Thoroughly vexed, she admonished the voice to shut up.

After giving each gelding a pet on his withers, she adjusted her askew bonnet more firmly upon her head. She retied the ribbons beneath what she considered a too-strong jaw for a female. Grandmama, a twinkle in her eyes, declared it was no such thing. It was merely Gabriella's tendency to jut her chin out in obstinacy that made her jawline appear prominent.

Considering her grandmother's penchant for doing the exact same thing, Gabriella was hard put to argue against her jesting.

Hands on her hips, a frown turning the corners of her mouth downward, she weighed her options. Stay here or walk home? Could she even manage the unharnessing of the hobbled team and to lead them to Hartfordshire? If so, surely she'd meet Jackson on his return.

Nevertheless, indecision beleaguered her.

She'd attend to her personal needs then decide what to do.

Gingerly picking her way through the sparse underbrush, she at last found a well-concealed spot several yards from the road that promised more privacy. Yes, this would do nicely. Just to be on the safe side, she withdrew her dagger. One never knew what other creatures might seek a drink from the river this evening.

A short while later, having restored her knife to her boot and just as she lifted her skirts to step over a broad branch, far-off hoofbeats echoed. A relieved smile bent her mouth. Thank the Divine powers. She'd be home in time for dinner, after all, and a good long soak would take the chill from her bones.

And a toddy. Don't forget the toddy. Abundantly dosed with whisky.

Another luxury the Breckensoles rarely indulged in, but one enjoyed by the entire family on occasion.

A horseman called to the other, and upon hearing his rough Cockney-accented voice, she paused, one foot raised and head canted. These

18

weren't riders from Hartfordshire Court. Wisdom decreed she remain concealed until she learned exactly who they were. Hopefully, the smooth snake that had slithered across her path a few moments ago hadn't lingered.

With stealth and care, Gabriella retreated into the woods until the undergrowth grew denser once more. She crouched behind an ancient oak, her heart banging so fiercely against her breastbone, she feared the men would hear the loud staccato. Settling onto her knees, she flinched as the bruised flesh from being hurled onto the carriage floor objected. Making herself as small and inconspicuous as possible, she silently praised God that her green ensemble camouflaged her to a degree.

Breath held and squinting slightly, she peeked around the trunk, scrutinizing the travelers.

Upon spying the crippled coach, the two rough-looking men cantered to a stop. The portly older fellow slouched in his saddle, whilst a younger, thinner version of him considered the vehicle, a sly grin blooming across his grimy, unshaven face.

The hairs on her arms raised straight up from wrist to shoulder, and she clapped a gloved hand over her mouth to keep from making any noise. *Oh, God.* Had they arrived a few minutes later, she would've already returned to the carriage. From their filthy, scruffy appearances, she'd be bound they weren't honorable sorts. Vagabonds, most likely.

"Well, well. Wot 'ave we 'ere, Wills?" Resting an elbow on his thick thigh, the older man leaned forward.

The younger chap chuckled and wiped his nose with the back of his hand. "An opportunity, Da."

As the men slid from their saddles, Gabriella shrank further to the root-ridden ground and closer to the trunk, scarcely daring to breathe. Fear's vice-like grip squeezed her lungs and cramped her burning throat.

Hitching up his baggy trousers, Wills opened the carriage door. He dangled one of Gabriella's packages in the doorway. "Looky 'ere."

Grandmama's medicine.

In short order, they tore her parcels open, tossing the chemises and Grandmama's remedies into the middle of the road. If that weren't awful enough, Wills stomped on the delicate undergarments before grinding the medicine bottles beneath his heel. The crunch of glass breaking sent a shudder through Gabriella and anger welling behind her ribs. *Damned rotter*. At least try to sell the items rather than destroy them.

He tipped the few coins remaining in her reticule into his grimy palm. The dainty bag, crocheted by Grandmama for Gabriella last Christmastide, met the same fate as the chemises. He crowed anew at discovering the pouch of tobacco and promptly stuffed it inside his coat.

The father held up the blue velvet cloak intended for Ophelia. "Wouldn't Miss Minnie like to prance 'round in dis?" He gave his son a lewd wink and minced around, swinging his large bum and the garment back and forth. "I'm bettin' she'd show 'er appreciation fer somfin' dis fancy." He grabbed his groin, imitating a vulgar movement.

"Do ye s'ppose she let me 'ave one of 'er fancier whores?" Wills bobbed his head and licked his lips. "One o' 'em gels tha' smell an' dresses pretty? And 'av nice teeth an' skin?"

"Not unless they've taken t' swivin' wif swine." His father hooted as he draped the cloak over his saddle. "Ye smell like a pig, son, an' rut like one too."

Sweat trickled a sticky path down her spine, and Gabriella swallowed against the burning nausea throttling up her throat. It was a good thing she hadn't eaten a midday meal, for it might very well have made a violent, noisy reappearance.

The frightened team neighed and pranced nervously, but Wills grabbed their harnesses, and cut the grays free.

They meant to steal Admiral and General. *God curse them. Fiends. Devil's spawns.*

Gabriella's stomach churned anew, and hot tears leaked from her eyes. Grandpapa had only purchased the pair last year, after waiting a lifetime to splurge on one of the few things he had ever wanted.

With gloating sneers curling their mouths, they mounted their horses and galloped away.

Wills's voice carried back to her. "I 'opes we come 'pon t' wench an' she's young. I 'aven't 'ad a good …"

20

Gabriella remained squatted in place for several long blinks. Her breathing ragged and uneven, she sluggishly stood upright using the coarse trunk to steady herself. If she hadn't sought privacy in the shrubberies, hadn't needed to relieve herself, she'd have been inside the carriage.

Wills would've...

Oh, God.

Another flash of icy-cold terror rippled over her.

No help for it now, she'd have to walk home and pray no more strangers ventured down the remote lane. Or that those two blackguards returned this way. She'd nearly reached the road when the unmistakable sound of another rider approaching met her ears.

Those hoofbeats also came from the direction of Colechester.

It had been months since she encountered another person on this isolated road, and today within minutes, she'd done so twice? Well, she hadn't actually *encountered* them because she concealed herself in the woods, but that was beside the point.

Retreating into the deepening shadows once more, she awaited the horseman's approach with bated breath. Friend or foe? A means of sending word to home or another villain to avoid?

As had the other riders, the man—a gentleman from his expensively tailored attire—slowed his horse, and a low whistle preceded his, "Holy hell." Another muffled half-curse, half surprised exclamation escaped him as he stood in his stirrups surveying the conveyance. "What the blazes?"

Gabriella slid her eyelids shut and gave a short shake of her head. *No. No. It cannot be. Please, don't let it be.* Anyone...*anyone, dear God...*but *him.*

The Duke of Pennington was good and truly the last person she wanted to see right at this moment. Covered in dirt and leaves, tears dried upon her cheeks, and frightened half out of her mind she didn't have the strength to match wits with him. Not now. Not when her reserves were spent.

She raked her disbelieving gaze over his polished Hessians to track up his biscuit-colored buckskins stretched over muscled calves and thighs. He sat regal and self-confident. A man sure of himself and his position. She ventured higher still, past his buff-toned coat and brown leather-gloved hands gripping the reins, to his familiar granite jaw, the slashing blade of his nose, and his mismatched green and blue eyes beneath severe midnight eyebrows.

Blast, astride his mount he presented a fine figure of a man, her artist's discernment reluctantly conceded. How difficult would it be to capture the two distinct shades of his eyes on paper?

Just then, she swore he looked straight at her, directly through the greenery and the dusky twilight. Right into her eyes, as if he knew exactly where she stood, frozen in disbelief. A disconcerting jolt zipped to her stomach.

Dash it to ribbons.

Dash it to ribbons?

No, that didn't begin to describe her frustration. She blew a puff of air out her nose in a silent snort. Why did *he* of all people have to come along? After she'd pointedly told him to leave her alone.

The duke scrutinized the coach, then slowly, methodically inspected the surrounding area before his gaze came to rest on her hiding place once more.

He knows. He knew she hid here.

How?

That slow, lazy smile that so annoyed her she yearned to slap it from his handsome face, hitched his well-formed mouth skyward at the corners. He sank back into his saddle, casually looping his reins around one hand.

"Miss Breckensole, it's safe to come out now."

3

"*Merde*." Maxwell swore beneath his breath, examining the disabled coach once more. *What the hell happened here?* Obviously, the axel had snapped and the back wheel shattered, but why were these belongings strewn about? Another systematic sweep down the length of the road confirmed neither the coachman nor the team were anywhere to be seen.

Yet Gabriella was.

Had she opted to stay behind rather than ride one of the horses bareback to Hartsfordshire Court? Her driver ought to be sacked for leaving her here. What could the man have been thinking? No doubt, she had something to do with his absence, stubborn chit.

From beneath his eyelashes, he sliced a covert glance to the shadowy woods. Just there, hovering half-concealed by that large tree, she still refused to come out of the forest. If she'd witnessed this destruction—and she most probably had—terror undoubtedly rendered her immobile.

If it hadn't been for her faint, involuntary gasp when he'd first reined Balor to a stop, he'd not have spied her either. All too familiar frustration and ire stiffened Max's shoulder muscles when he thought of Breckensole residing in the home that had once been in his paternal grandmother's family.

Not now. Soon, but not now.

Despite the sobriety of the moment, his lips twitched upward. She'd been outraged that he'd dared to ask her to go riding. He'd truly wanted her to accompany him on an outing, because despite everything, he liked her. Liked her very much, indeed. For months now, she'd fascinated him. Even before he'd learned of her grandfather's perfidy.

He could almost visualize the proper, but unpredictable, Gabriella Breckensole astride a horse in that green and black confection she'd been wearing in Colechester this afternoon. The image of her shapely legs exposed from ankle to thigh, hugging the horse's sides, created an unexpected but powerful sensual reaction. A response he'd have contemplated further if it weren't so bloody cold and darkness was quickly descending. Not that he was feeling particularly chilled. No, in fact inferior brandy yet warmed his gut.

However, if after her characteristically icy reception in Colechester, he hadn't indulged in two glasses at The Pony and Pint rather than his usual one, he'd have come upon the disabled vehicle sooner. And he might've been able to prevent this.

God's teeth. What if he'd gone beyond his usual restraints and quaffed the third brandy to help buffer the sharp abrasion of her scorn? Who knows what would've happened to her? As it was, even if he immediately took her before him on the saddle, they'd not make the house before night's mantle shrouded them.

What a remarkable idea, holding Gabriella Breckensole before him, his arms wrapped around her lush form, her rounded bum pressed into his thighs... *Egads, enough. She's likely frightened mute, and I'm indulging in lurid imaginations.* Besides, he did have a degree of pride. She'd all but snubbed him in Colechester and demanded he leave her alone. He couldn't though.

A slight movement caught his attention again. Nothing about her rigid, untrusting demeanor suggested she meant to join him on the road any time soon. Did she intend to continue lurking in the trees? All night? Was her loathing of him such she'd risk her safety or health by refusing to leave the concealment?

That knowledge grated, bitter and raw. When had she come to hate him? And more on point, why? He'd asked the question innumerable times. He did not, however, ask himself *why* he kept asking himself that question.

One hand braced on his hip, he swiped the back of the other across his forehead. By God, if the people who'd done this had known she was there… A vicious band tightened about his middle, stalling his breath for a long, gut-wrenching moment. He clenched his jaw against a wave of rage so powerful, the surge caused him pause.

They'd have set upon her. Harmed her. *Or worse*, damn the bloody bastards. Another swell of fury pelted his ribs. Was Gabriella injured? Blast him for a fool for not considering that straightaway. No woman should be subjected to something of this nature. It was ingrained in him to help, even if she didn't want his assistance. He'd do the same for anyone.

"Miss Breckensole?" When she remained silent, tension spiraled up his spine. The air left his lungs in a whoosh.

Christ above. Had she been…?

His eyelids flitted shut for an agonizing blink, and he set his jaw against the godawful thought he ought to have instantly considered. Mindful to keep the alarm from reaching his voice, he gently put forward, "Gabriella, are you…*unharmed*?"

Was there any other way to tactfully ask if she'd been set upon? Despoiled? Violated?

Only a sleepy bird's call punctuated the discomfiting silence.

"Yes. I'm fine." Her answer came as a faint whisper, so soft, he wasn't sure he'd heard her, yet she didn't move from the security of the woods.

Examining the horizon, he heaved a sigh then swung a leg over the saddle and hopped to the ground. "Do you intend to remain in the forest the entire night? There may well be all sorts of wild creatures—bears, wolves, badgers, lynx, and wolverines—hereabouts."

Perhaps not precisely *here*, but surely somewhere in the whole of England, hungry beasts roamed about stalking their next meal.

"Go bugger yourself, you pompous twit." Distinct vexation riddled the vixen's mutinous response.

He'd vow, she didn't think he'd heard her inappropriate comment.

Regardless of the seriousness of the situation, an unfettered chuckle escaped him. *Damn*, but he admired the minx's spirit. In fact, in his seven and twenty years, he'd never met a more extraordinary, frustrating woman. After tying Balor's reins to a nearby branch, Max shook his head in resignation, and with long strides, made directly for her.

Her harsh intake of breath earned her another derisive chuckle.

"Yes, I see you. You're most lucky the miscreants who destroyed your possessions did not." He jabbed a thumb in the sagging vehicle's direction. "I cannot leave you skulking in the greeneries, Miss Breckensole. Nightfall is nearly upon us, and though I confess, I cannot imagine why you are here and neither your coachman nor your team are present, a duke would never desert a lady in need."

"And of course, *you* always do what a duke would do, don't you?" she put forward, rapier sharp sarcasm dripping from each word.

Her accusation stung. As much from the utter contempt she hurled toward him as his lack of understanding why she felt such hostility. He bent into an exaggerated bow, made even more awkward given he straddled a log. Doffing his hat, he only just managing to keep from toppling face first into the dirt.

"Always, my dearest Miss Breckensole. Always."

Always, at least, when it came to her, damn his eyes. Which made the incredulous task he'd set himself equally pleasurable and disagreeable.

A theatrical sigh, followed by what most assuredly was another mumbled curse met his poetic declaration, and as he reached the road's edge, she emerged from her hiding place. Wariness lingered in the gaze she settled upon him. In the vanishing light, her hazel eyes appeared deep green, either a reflection from her gown or her verdant surroundings,

"Now, pray tell me," Max pointedly kept his tone light but empathetic as he gestured casually. "How, might I ask, came you to be here alone?"

"I am here, Your Grace, because as you can clearly see, my coach has a broken wheel and my driver, Jackson, went for help." She flung a gloved hand, the palm dirt-smeared, toward the abused vehicle.

Your coach has a great deal more wrong with it than a broken wheel. Rather than state the obvious, he asked, "How long have you been stranded?"

Frowning down at the timepiece pinned to her spencer, she crinkled her nose adorably.

Were those new freckles atop the bridge? He hadn't noticed them earlier today.

"My coachman left over two hours ago." Pert chin jutted forward and ignoring the hand he extended to assist her onto the road, she swept past him as regally as any of Almacks' elegant patronesses. "I cannot imagine what's keeping Jackson." As she stood in the middle of the road, her arms folded, she gave the slightest, befuddled shake of her head.

A bit of moss drifted to the ground.

Gabriella tracked the movement with her keen-eyed gaze. Her mouth pulled into a prim line before she anchored those arresting, thick-lashed eyes on him with a don't-you-dare-laugh look. Shaking out her skirts, little bits of twigs, leaves, and dirt spilling around her feet, she searched the road again and a bit of tension left her. She relaxed her stiff shoulders and lowered her chin.

Even rumpled, frazzled, her hem soiled, and dirt clinging to her gown, in the fading light she was a radiant jewel. A forest nymph: mysterious and untamed and utterly bewitching.

She squatted and gingerly lifted the shredded remnant of what appeared to be a night shift or perhaps a chemise. A perplexed frowned wrinkled her brow as she spread both hands wide, staring at the destruction. "I don't understand...*this*. Why would anyone do this? Be so despicable? So destructive for no reason? Such vileness is beyond me."

Dropping the mangled cloth, she swallowed audibly, and compassion swelled within his chest. *The darling, brave girl*. Were those dried tears on her face? Impossible to tell in the half-light, but a definite dirt smudge slashed across one porcelain cheek. He'd dipped his hand halfway to his coat pocket to fetch his handkerchief to wipe her face before he stopped himself. Not only didn't he have the right, these tender sentiments toward her muddled his determination.

Nonetheless, he admired her gumption. She was much more affected than she let on. But then, what woman wouldn't be?

If he took her in his arms and comforted her as he ached to do, she'd likely box his ears or punch him in the nose. Or both. She'd probably stomp his foot and elbow his ribs too. He'd not mind all that much if doing so removed the haunted look from her arresting eyes.

27

Max extended a hand again, and this time, after a long, long moment's hesitation where he was certain she meant to refuse his offer of assistance once more, she slid her fingers into his palm. He helped her stand upright. "What the devil happened, Miss Breckensole?"

"You can see what they did for yourself, Your Grace." She promptly withdrew her hand then wiped it on her skirt.

He scowled. Was his touch so unwelcome? "Tell me anyway."

She released a fragile little laugh, spreading both hands wide once more. "Two ruffians came along. They also stole Ophelia's birthday present and the team." Her bravado slipped a notch, and her lower lip trembled the merest bit before she ticked that stubborn chin upward once more. "Grandpapa will be devastated."

Probably because the miser would have to purchase another team. Did the skinflint's coffers creak and groan from infrequent use when he was forced to lift the lid to extract money?

Everyone far and wide knew Harold Breckensole for an uncharitable tightwad. A man who never paid the asking price for anything and a pinchfist misanthrope who rarely gave so much as a groat to those less fortunate. He was also the unconscionable bounder who'd swindled Max's grandfather and purchased Hartfordshire Court and the surrounding five-and-forty acres for a bloody pittance.

He cheated and blackmailed Grandfather.

Max shook loose his morose meanderings. This wasn't the time, but he had a plan, and by God, old Breckensole would pay dearly for his shady dealings. Indeed, the bloody blighter would. And soon. Very soon.

Two fingers pressed to his temple, Max studied the ruined garments and torn wrapping papers scattered about the ground. This act bespoke hatred and vengeance. "Your coachman's been gone for upward of two hours, you say?" More than enough time to walk to Hartfordshire Court and return.

Gabriella responded with a single, terse nod.

She'd behaved this way since this past December. Since that Christmas house-party they'd attended as guests of the Duke and Duchess of Sutcliffe. One day, she'd been warm and welcoming, her sable-fringed hazel eyes sparkling and her kissable petal-pink lips smiling. The next morning, a warrior's practiced scowl upon those same lovely features and thunder darkening her eyes to steely gray, she'd become brusque and cold, avoiding him as if he were covered in oozing sores.

Which made the task he'd set himself—to woo and marry her to gain Hartfordshire Court once more—all the more difficult. He well knew Breckensole's only heirs were the twins. Yes, Max's man of business had done his research. He also knew Breckensole's dirty little secret. A secret he'd most certainly wouldn't want his granddaughters to learn.

Worried Gabriella would think his rage was directed toward her, he lowered his eyelids against the fury he feared glinted there and unrelentingly twisted his gut.

Of its own accord, his attention swept her shapely figure. Mayhap this incident might be used in his favor. She required rescuing, though he hadn't a single doubt she'd deny it with her last breath. And Providence had seen to it that he came along at an opportune moment where she was hard-put to toss his chivalry back in his face.

He rather liked playing the gallant for her.

True, a smidgeon of remorse for what he intended to do poked its unwanted head up. But Max reconciled his guilt with the knowledge she and her sister would be well-cared for after Breckensole's ruination.

His ire wasn't directed at the twins, or even the old man's wife, for that matter. No, the sole recipient of Max's disgust and retribution was Harold Breckensole; the man directly or indirectly responsible for the deaths of four of Max's family members.

His regard sank to Gabriella's tapping toes. *Left foot. Right foot. Left foot. Right foot.* A cadence of annoyance clearly revealing her impatience. Did she know she drummed her feet whenever aggravated? He checked a smile. She was so easy to read. He'd wager at this very moment, she skewed her mouth back and forth in a winsome fashion, something else she did whenever vexed or anxious. A fashion that made him very much want to kiss those lush lips she'd nibbled to a raspberry red in her frustration.

"Do you think the constable will be able to find Grandpapa's horses?"

she asked. After all she'd been through, her concern was for her grandfather.

He wouldn't lift a finger to help Breckensole, but he would for her. "Quite possibly. The team is unusual and not easily forgotten. I can put the word out to sources I know to have them stay on alert."

Her expression contemplative, she continued to torture the soil with her toes.

Given the dainty, thin-soled slippers she wore, he wasn't at all surprised she hadn't walked home as well. Her tramp into the forest had undoubtedly ruined the footwear though. "Most wise of you to conceal yourself in the woodlands until your man returned."

A surprised, discomfited look flitted across her pale features, which she concealed almost instantly. Not meeting his gaze, she cleared her throat. "*Erm*...yes. Exactly so."

Even in the faint light he didn't miss the rosy hue sweeping across her cheeks as she became suddenly fixated on the trees' silhouettes. *Ah*. His mind had stumbled upon the awkward truth, and to spare her further embarrassment, he cupped her elbow. "Come, let's be away from here. I cannot help but feel it's not altogether safe for us to remain."

She trained her gaze on the wreckage and put a slightly unsteady hand to her forehead. Was she hurt worse than she let on? Or did emotion overwhelm her?

He squinted one eye, and for the first time noticed the ugly discoloration on her forehead. "Miss Breckensole, you *are* injured."

Bending slightly nearer, he lifted the edge of her bonnet. Intoxicating and seductive, her perfume wafted upward. Nostrils flared, he breathed in her essence: lavender and something lemony? Mayhap a hint of jasmine as well.

The heady combination sent Max's senses reeling, and it took all of his restraint to keep from nuzzling the slim, ivory column of her throat where the fragrance surely lingered on her satiny skin. Annoyance pelted him. He needed to wrestle his attraction to her under control. She was a means to an end. She couldn't be anything more.

Before I found my grandfather's journal, she could've been.

He'd very much wished her to be.

"You didn't answer. Are you hurt?" He skimmed her from head to toe. She hadn't limped as she exited the woods, and he detected no obvious abrasions.

"Not seriously." She tilted her head, her eyes round with uncertainty. "A slight bump on my head and sore knees. I'm far more worried about my grandfather's reaction to all of this. Grandmama's too. She's not been well."

He'd known that before she made mention of it in the village today. Truthfully, there wasn't much he didn't know about the Breckensoles. He'd made it his business. *Know one's enemy,* Father had drilled into him as had his father before him. And *his* before him.

Head cocked, he combed his gaze over her refined features. White lines of strain bracketed her mouth and crimped the corners of her lovely eyes. Reaching into his coat pocket, he retrieved a flask. After twisting the cap off, he offered the silver casket to her.

A delicate, tawny eyebrow lifted mockingly.

She probably had no idea what the contents were. In general, gentle-bred young ladies didn't go about quaffing strong spirits. Still, a bottle of the stuff was delivered to Hartfordshire Court monthly, so someone imbibed, albeit not heavily.

"It's whisky," he offered by way of explanation, levering the flask up and down.

And as Miss Gabriella Breckensole had done on almost every occasion he'd encountered her, she'd flummoxed him once again. "I am not so very ignorant, Your Grace. I know what it is."

A wry smile tipping her soft oh-so-kissable lips, she accepted the flask and wrapping that rosebud mouth around the opening, took a hearty swallow. Not a dainty, feminine sip. No indeed. She took a gulp worthy of any healthy young buck and didn't cough and gasp afterward as many a gent was wont to do.

Max could almost feel the sharp sting on his tongue and the fiery trail burning to his stomach. A craving to taste the spirit on her mouth, to tease the flavor from her tongue, slammed into him, obliterating his rationale for what he planned to do to her.

4

That stunning hunger, unequal and startling in its potency, set Max back on his heels.

Control. Yourself. He thundered silently. *She's the means to an end. Nothing more. She cannot be.*

He really had become a selfish bastard, all in the name of vengeance for a sin committed decades before he'd been born. Yes, but he'd seen the effects played out and now understood his Grandfather's choosing to drink himself into oblivion rather than face a single day sober.

Eyes closed, Gabriella took another swig and gave a delicate shudder. She swallowed and thrust her arm straight out. "Here. I've had enough, thank you."

"Are you *quite* certain?" Max couldn't prevent the humor filtering into his voice as he topped the case before tucking it back into his pocket.

"Yes. Quite." A heated glower accompanied her pithy retort.

There was the spirited vixen he'd come to expect. The one that had told him to go bugger himself. The one who lifted her nose and thrust her mutinous, dimpled chin upward whenever their gazes clashed. The one who snubbed and cut him at every opportunity.

And yet, his captivation waned not a jot. If anything, her allure grew. Considering his animosity toward her grandfather, and hers toward Max, did that make him perverse? Or mad? Or both, mayhap?

None of that mattered. Achieving his goal was the only thing—*the only thing*—that did.

He untied his horse's reins. "As I cannot in good conscience leave you here to await your coachman's return, Miss Breckensole, you'll have to ride before me on Balor."

Before she could object, he grasped her narrow waist, his hands almost spanning the circumference, and lifted her onto the horse's back, both of her svelte legs dangling over the near side.

Through his gloves, his palms burned from the intimate contact. He might've let his hands linger an instant longer than was completely necessary. Too bad he couldn't encourage her to ride astride. On second thought, that was a bloody awful notion. He'd explode in his pantaloons if he had to watch those creamy thighs flex and ripple as they gripped Balor.

Giving him a fuming glare, she clutched Balor's mane, and before she could slip to the ground, Max leapt into the saddle behind her. Securing her firmly around her slim waist, he lowered his mouth near her ear.

"Don't be foolish, Gabriella. We have but the one horse, and you're wearing slippers. I shall not leave you here to await your coachman. The miscreants who stole your team could very well return." Not likely, but not impossible either. "As much as you dislike me, I am a gentleman, and I shall see you safely home."

She grunted her displeasure and jerked away, in the process bumping his already sensitized groin. He stifled a groan. It was going to prove to be one bloody uncomfortable ride.

Bowing her head in what he could only assume was resignation, she muttered, "I haven't given you leave to use my Christian name, and neither am I fool enough to throw myself from a horse, Your Grace."

"I don't believe you a fool at all, *chérie*."

She stiffened before elbowing him hard in the stomach.

"Oomph," he grunted, not daring to rub the offended flesh, else she slip loose, but he took the opportunity to lurch forward and brush his lips across one dainty ear. *Tit for tat, chérie.*

"I am not now, nor will I ever be *your* sweetheart, you buffoon," she finished rather breathlessly.

We shall see, sweet Gabriella. We shall see.

A stupid grin slashed Max's mouth upward. He'd felt the tremor running through her, recognized the subtle shudder for what it was. Desire. For all of Miss Gabriella Breckensole's protestations of dislike for him, her young body said something much, much different. And he could, and would, use that to his advantage.

Inordinately pleased by the discovery, with a click of his tongue and a nudge to Balor's sides, he directed his sturdy black toward Hartfordshire Court. "Walk on."

Stick straight and just as inflexible, Gabriella rode before him, doing her utmost to keep her behind—any part of her body for that matter—from brushing his.

"Miss Breckensole, you can relax against me. Upon my word, I promise to act the perfect gentleman."

A distinctly unladylike snort met his declaration. "And I'm the Queen of Sheba."

He'd much prefer to address her as Gabriella or *chérie*, enjoying the way the syllables rolled off his tongue, but he wouldn't put it past her to leap to the ground just to prove her point.

Chin tucked, he glowered at the bonnet hiding her luxurious, rich honey-brown hair threaded with golden ribbons from his appreciative gaze. He gave her waist a little prod, and she jumped, rearing her head back and smacking him solidly in the jaw.

That would bruise, he'd be bound.

"It's two miles to Hartfordshire." He nudged her once more. "Relax."

She acted as if she'd sooner ride bald and bare-ass-naked through Hyde Park than allow any part of her body to touch him. Her rejection shouldn't rankle, but it did. And while Max didn't consider himself a rapscallion per se, he wasn't a stranger to the joys of a woman's form or the pleasures that could be found with a willing bed partner.

He'd also evaded his fair share of huntresses in full cry, their title-hungry mamas, directing their eager daughter's every move as they tried to snare a duke. Tried to trap him, to be exact. There hadn't been a ball, soiree, assembly, picnic, or rout that he hadn't been eyed like a prize stallion by debutantes, spinsters, wallflowers, heiresses, and the occasional widow too.

He held no illusions of marital bliss. His parents' union had been less than idyllic.

Of their own volition, his lips kicked up into a sardonic smirk.

But Max's grandfather had adored his grandmother. So much so that after she died, he'd moved the household to London and refused to stay at Chartworth Hall. Grandfather had been an empty shell of a man, given to too much drink, going days on end without bathing or dressing. And in the end, he took his own life, because he couldn't bear living without his beloved wife.

If that was love, Max could well do without the castrating emotion.

It was his turn to snort, and Gabriella sent him a puzzled, sideways look.

Nevertheless, her aversion to him exasperated. He was the highly sought-after Duke of Pennington. Known for his wit and jovial temperament. His vices were few: a fine cognac or whisky, the occasional cheroot, and superior horseflesh. He didn't keep a mistress—not for the lack of offers—and he was honest and fair; judiciously so most of the time.

And yet, the minx grudgingly riding before him couldn't abide him. Mayhap that was why he found her so intriguing. No, if he were honest with himself, he'd found her remarkable, *too remarkable*, before she'd turned her icy disdain upon him. He gave a slight shake of his head, reining in his wayward musings. It mattered not.

She would be his bride and the dowry he'd insist upon was Hartfordshire Court. Nothing else would do. He had no compunction about resorting to extreme measures. His own version of blackmail, if need be. Nothing and no one kept him from something once he'd set his mind to it.

Her grandfather was responsible for Max's grandmother's and grandfather's deaths. Even Father's, though he conceded, that was a bit of a stretch. His father's tendency to drink and gamble to excess, as well as his less than discriminating taste in the women he took to bed had been his downfall. He'd tried to hire a strumpet already engaged with a ship's captain. There'd been a fight and the captain had stabbed the seventh duke in the stomach. The wound had grown putrid, the infection spread, and he'd died a horrifying death.

Breckensole *would* pay.

Gabriella made a little noise—likely involuntary. No doubt her thoughts also tumbled about in her head. Her parents were dead as well. He wracked his brain, trying to remember how old the twins were when they came to live with their grandparents. He'd been at Eton by then.

Recalling her puckered expression at the Christmastide dinner before she swiftly assumed the bland mien she presented to him when she'd found herself seated beside him, a silent chuckle shook his chest. Their hostess, the Duchess of Sutcliffe, might have served vermin in white sauce for all the attention Gabriella had paid to the food that evening. Her ability to answer his questions with clipped one-word responses and to resolutely direct her attention to her other dinner partner surely had to be a feat worthy of recognition.

Why, he supposed he ought to be flattered she'd actually strung more than two words together in conversation with him in the village and since he'd come upon her this afternoon.

Given Max was hell-bent on having her home returned to his family, he had no business—*none whatsoever*—entertaining this perverse interest in her. And yet the more she resisted him, the more she disdained his presence, ignored the tipping of his hat or the extending of his elbow, the more captivated he became. That either made him dicked in the nob, or…

By God, he wasn't sure what that made him.

Stupid? Imbecilic? Pathetic? *A predator?*

That disagreeable thought stuck fast in his craw, mostly due to the degree of truth in the ugly acknowledgement. It gave him a sour taste in his mouth. Nonetheless, he must remain rational at all costs. He couldn't afford to let his emotions become entangled even if she was to become his duchess and the mother of his heir and spare. He'd permit his lust for her free rein, but never anything more.

As much to catch another whiff of her unique perfume as to spare her the sore muscles she would endure tomorrow if she continued holding her unnatural posture, he leaned into her slender back, and pressing one palm into her middle urged her against him. "I said relax," he breathed into her ear.

"Are you always such an arrogant bully?" Even as she muttered the words, a ragged almost wistful sigh juddered her shoulders, and she sank into his chest.

Most women of his acquaintance would've dissolved into histrionics or tears had they been forced to huddle in the forest and witness their possessions destroyed and horses stolen. Not to mention deigning to relieve themselves in those same woods. Not Miss Gabriella Breckensole. She refused to show weakness to anyone.

That was one of the things he most admired about her. Her stubbornness. Her independence. Her I-don't-need-your-help-I-can-do-it-myself bravado. The almost intractable child-like attitude that lit a spark in her eyes and bent her lips into an endearing, mulish slant. It was also what would make his task more difficult.

In the beginning, she might resent their marriage, but with her keen wit and intellect, she'd make an extraordinary duchess. He was confident of the fact. Their desire was mutual, and that was nothing to scoff at. Even if they never claimed the love his grandparents had.

After stumbling upon his grandfather's journal in the study a few months ago, Max had sworn an oath to avenge him. He'd replaced the ancient, scarred monstrosity of a desk with a smaller one. Whilst the four hirelings labored to lift the old piece, a hidden drawer had popped open, revealing the leather-bound book.

The first entry that had leapt out at him—had burned in his mind since.

August 1744

I told Margaret that Hartfordshire Court was sold. How she sobbed when I confessed I'd been forced to sell her childhood home to Harold Breckensole.

The rotter blackmailed me into selling it. He'd vowed he'd have his revenge on me, because he fancied a little tart who climbed into my bed, and now he has. The lying bastard claims he caught me cheating at cards. The bloody sot even went so far as to enlist those insolent pups up from university, Wakefield and Garrison, to act as witnesses. Those two bounders will do anything for a drink, a whore, and a few pounds.

The cards were marked, but not by me. Breckensole must have marked them and then framed me. I cannot prove it, and when he threatened to make the disgrace public, I feared what the scandal and shunning would do to Margaret. Feared she'd quicken early again. And so, in desperation, I agreed to his damnable terms. I couldn't risk her miscarrying yet another heir.

My heir must come before all else. He must. The ducal lineage must continue.

Breckensole's bloody terms included a legal bill of sale and a contract between us that no one could ever know about the marked cards. He thinks he's been so clever. He's the victor for now, but someday, his scheme will come back to bite him in the arse. I've made sure of it.

I only agreed to his extortion for my heir's sake. Margaret's losing three babes in as many years has made me a mad man. Her health is frail and grows more so. She weeps incessantly. That is enough to drive me madder still. I should have married a woman with a stronger constitution, but how does any man know his wife's womb will fail?

While Margaret was with child, she couldn't know I'd sold Hartfordshire Court, so I waited six months until I was sure our son would live.

At long last I have my heir.

Only a few short, terse entries followed, two of which stuck in Max's mind:

Reverend Michael Shaw was killed in a duel.

Egads, what could a reverend have done to find himself challenged to an affair of honor? Preached on adultery? Bigamy? Helped himself to the tithes?

The last entry sent a queer chill up his spine.

Margaret is dead. She was with child.

And Breckensole was to blame, damn his covetous soul to hell. Well, not the particular entry about the reverend, but the rest could be laid at his feet.

The hushed whisper he'd heard once as a child that his grandmother had flung herself down the stairs had been nothing more than gossip from the lower orders, his father had insisted. His own mother had died within two years of giving birth to him, and he had no memory of her except for woeful, nondescript brown eyes in a plump, plain face.

From beneath half-closed eyelids, Max considered Gabriella. Her slim nape and sloping shoulders, the dip of her slender waist and her hips that flared out into luscious curves. Curves he itched to run his hands over.

Yes, she was far better than the simpering misses he was accustomed to having hanging on his arm, batting their eyelashes, and incapable of stringing an intelligent sentence together let alone retrieving their own handkerchief or fan from the floor.

He'd rip his hair out by the roots and run screaming from the room if forced to endure another inane conversation about the weather, who was seen riding with whom in Hyde Park, or the latest *on dit* in the gossip rags.

Only their breathing and the rhythmic *clip-clopping* of Balor's hooves punctuating the peaceful evening stillness, Max and Gabriella rode for several minutes. Unfortunately, no moon illuminated their way, although an occasional brave star peeked from amongst the cloud-ridden sky.

He wasn't concerned, however. Many were the times he'd traveled this road with the heavens darker than this. His estate lay little more than a half mile beyond Hartfordshire Court. Even decades after that bounder Breckensole had cheated Max's grandfather of the manor and grounds, he refused to refer to the estate as Breckensole's.

"Gabriella?" he put forth, even as his instinct warned him to stop.

"Hmm?" she murmured sleepily as she half-turned her head to look into his eyes. Sloe-eyed, her face softened by fatigue and her guard down, her earlier hostility had disappeared and something indefinable held him in thrall.

Another peculiar tightening contracted his ribs.

Why did she of all women have to affect him thusly? The granddaughter of his grandfather's nemesis and by extension, his as well?

He couldn't see her expression clearly in the inky blackness, and his usual confidence wobbled for a moment. Grazing his knuckles along her silky jaw, he asked softly, "What have I done to offend you?"

5

Darkness hid the blush blooming across Gabriella's face at the duke's intimate touch upon her skin. For God help her, the harsh retort hovering on the tip of her tongue evaporated, and—*how could it possibly be?* —she yearned to press her cheek into his gloved hand.

She blamed fear, hunger, and worry about her grandfather's reaction. *Yes, of course, that's it.* Her anxiety and fretting caused her to harbor such uncharacteristic, fanciful notions. Certainly not a desire to have the duke caress her.

But how should she answer his question?

It would be pure foolishness to make him aware she knew about his dastardly scheme to reclaim Hartfordshire Court. Fine, mayhap she didn't *precisely* know what that plot was or how the duke planned to enact it, but she did know he intended to do that very thing.

"Help. Help."

The weak cry saved her from having to answer the duke's prying query. Straightening, straining her eyes, she made out the shadowy rocky contours of the arched stone bridge.

"Help me, please. I'm down here, on the embankment."

As the plea echoed through the darkness once more, the duke slowed his powerful horse. His muscular body taut, Pennington brushed against Gabriella's back as he pulled upright.

"Jackson," she breathed, clutching the duke's forearm and twisting to catch his gaze. Or at least she tried to. In the dim light, she could only make out the edges of his hewn features. "That's my coachman. I know his voice. He must be hurt."

That was why he hadn't returned.

With a short nod—at least she thought the duke nodded. The darkness made it so very difficult to tell—he said, "Stay here. I'll check on his condition."

As soon as he slipped from the saddle and ventured down the embankment, she rolled onto her stomach and slid from the horse as well. She hurried over to the bridge, and one hand holding the rough, rocky edge, leaned over. Only obscure shadowy shapes met her scrutiny. *Curses.* Why couldn't there have been a moon tonight? They hadn't even the convenience of the coach lamp to light the area.

"Jackson, it's Miss Gabriella. Are you hurt?"

A sharp oath met her ears. "Miss Breckensole, I told you to remain on my horse." Flint-like annoyance accented each short syllable the duke rasped.

Yes, he had, and she'd chosen to disregard his directive. He might be accustomed to having his every wish promptly granted, but he wasted his breath ordering her about.

"Your Grace, as I am not your servant, hireling or wife, I don't feel obliged to obey your commands. Most particularly when Jackson is a member of *my* household." Her words rang every bit as pompous and harsh in the quiet of the night, and immediate chagrin for her churlishness sluiced her. She refused to become a harpy, even if he did vex her to next December and beyond.

The duke had been nothing but kind, helpful, and gentlemanly.

She could almost like this considerate man. If only... *If only.* If wishes were horses, beggars would ride, as Grandpapa was wont to quote.

"Jackson, are you badly hurt?" she called, regret softening her voice.

A loud, pain-filled groan met her question. "I fear my leg's broken, miss."

She sucked in an abrupt breath. If the duke hadn't come along when he had... Hanging farther over the bridge's side, she squinted at the two indistinguishable men below. "However did you end up down there?"

"I only meant to have myself a drink of water, but the ground gave way, and I tumbled," Jackson answered. "I'm sorry, Miss Breckensole."

"You've nothing to be sorry for," Gabriella assured him.

However, Grandpapa would chew nails at another unexpected expense, for the servants' care fell to him. A new, most unpleasant, thought struck her. Her grandparents and Ophelia would be frantic that she hadn't returned from Colechester yet. Even as the truth crossed her mind, the rumble of an approaching conveyance rent the night air, overwhelming the crickets' chirps and frogs' croaking.

There, across the old arced bridge, a conveyance came from Hartfordshire's direction. Either Grandpapa or the young groom. No one else knew how to tool a vehicle. She'd asked to learn but had been denied the privilege.

"Someone's coming." She turned, waving her arms up and down in the unlikely event the driver didn't see her.

One arm around Jackson's waist and the other holding the servant's arm across Max's broad shoulders, the men labored up the incline. The carriage lamps sent an eerie glow over the road as the landau drew to an uneven stop.

"Gabriella girl, is that you?" Grandpapa squinted into the night. "Where are the coach and team?"

"Yes, Grandpapa, it's me. I'm afraid the coach lost a wheel, and Jackson's hurt." Best not to tell him the condition of the coach or that his team had been stolen just yet. As an afterthought she added, "The Duke of Pennington is here as well. He came to our aid."

She sensed as much as saw her grandfather go rigid and defensive.

"We don't need or accept help from a Woolbright or any Duke of Pennington," Grandpapa all but growled in a gravelly tone she'd never heard from him before.

The air fairly crackled with enmity, and her jaw hung slack. Never before had she witnessed such hostility from her gentle, eccentric grandfather. Was it possible he was already aware of the duke's plans to try to force them from their home? That certainly would warrant well-earned antagonism. God knew it had caused hers.

To Pennington's credit, he didn't respond in kind but continued to assist the injured coachman to the waiting carriage. That raised him a notch in her estimation—to worm rather than maggot.

"Can you step into the conveyance?" Pennington asked Jackson, covered with muck and grass streaks. "I'll bear your weight and balance you."

She'd never known a peer to expend effort for a commoner, let alone soil his fancy—*expensive*—clothing or muddy his fine—*very expensive*—boots.

"Aye, Your Grace." Muttering a muffled oath, Jackson braced his arms on the open door then giving a tremendous heave, levered himself onto the cushion. With a low groan, he collapsed into the corner, and even in the half-light, Gabriella recognized the strain creasing his pale face.

"Gabriella, take a seat at once," Grandpapa all but snapped, including her in his curmudgeon's glare. "Your grandmother and sister are beside themselves with worry, and I must retrieve the team as soon as I've seen you home."

Oh no. How can I tell Grandpapa?

She raised what surely must be stricken eyes to the duke's. Why she'd look to him for help or reassurance she couldn't begin to speculate. Simply put, it seemed the most natural thing in the world to do.

Something akin to compassion transformed the granite-like angled planes of Pennington's face. His strong mouth softened and tipped up at the corners. "Breckensole, I regret your team's been stolen and your coach has a broken axel." Sympathy rather than gloating tempered Pennington's somber tone. "I came upon the wreckage and found your granddaughter huddled in the woods, terrified for her life."

Eyelids sliding closed, Gabriella gave a whimpering groan. *Bother and blast.* She believed she'd been so stoic and brave—had hidden her fear so well.

"What...? What say you?" Grandpapa brought his aghast gaze up to swing between her and Pennington. He whispered brokenly, "My...my team stolen? My coach destroyed?" His stooped shoulders slumped, and he hung his head.

Gabriella tried to reach up to pat his arm. "I'm so sorry, Grandpapa. Maybe if I'd stayed in the coach…"

She'd have been despoiled, for certain.

"No, Miss Breckensole. You were wise to hide." In an instant, flint-like censure turned Pennington's speech ruthless and unforgiving. "I should think you'd be more concerned with your granddaughter's wellbeing, Breckensole. A coach and team are replaceable. Something as precious as her cannot ever be."

An odd inflection roughened his last words.

She caught his eye and gave a small shake of her head. He'd only make things worse, pointing out the obvious truth to her grandfather. She was still trying to come to terms with the loss herself. It was easier for a man as wealthy as the duke to consider acquiring a new matched pair and commissioning another coach a minor inconvenience. Not as true for her family.

Her grandfather's head snapped up, and she almost gasped at the loathing contorting his lined face. "How dare you imply I don't care for my granddaughter?"

What had happened to cause such visceral enmity between him and the Dukes of Pennington? He'd been remarkably closed-mouthed about it all these years, whatever it was. He'd known the twins encountered the duke at social events and never hinted they were to avoid him.

Had something occurred of late to change that?

But what?

A growing suspicion niggled, and though she couldn't put her finger on just what made her uneasy, Gabriella was convinced Grandpapa kept something significant from her, Grandmama, and Ophelia.

"Just like an arrogant Pennington, passing judgment on others." Grandpapa's mouth twisted into a contemptuous sneer. "Always thinking you're superior to everyone else, whilst forgetting the plank in your own eyes."

"At least we're honest and forthright in our business and *other* dealings." Gone was the tender duke who'd cradled her in his preposterously strong arms as they sat atop his horse. This man glaring daggers at her feeble grandfather she could very well believe would put them from their home without a qualm.

"Just exactly what are you implying, Pennington?" Grandpapa asked slowly, his rancor palpable in the set of his shoulders and the muscle flexing in his jaw. He raised his crop threateningly, and for a blink, Gabriella feared he meant to strike Pennington.

She rushed to intervene. Striking a peer, let alone a duke, would have harsh consequences. "Grandpapa, after the axel broke, ruffians came along. They stole the team and the mazurine velvet cloak I commissioned for Ophelia's birthday present." His tobacco too, but she'd spare him that triviality. "They also stomped upon Grandmama's medicines and destroyed our new chemises."

"Why?" Sorrow and disbelief riddled the clipped word. "I've made no enemies."

Save the Penningtons, it would seem. Neither had he made friends, and that knowledge saddened her.

The night had grown brisk, and a frigid shudder stole down her spine. Shivering, she rubbed her arms in a vain attempt to warm herself. "I don't know why," she admitted in a hushed tone.

He swung an accusing gaze at the duke. "I'll be bound it was no mere coincidence. No, by God, this smacks of Pennington deviousness."

"Grandpapa!" Pennington might mean to reclaim his familial home, but until today, there'd not been a single instance of nefarious behavior. Nothing suspicious directed at the Breckensoles. "If the duke hadn't come upon Jackson and me and lent us his assistance, we'd both be stranded right now."

Well, she wouldn't have been, because she'd have walked home.

Her defense of the duke earned her a furious glare from her grandfather and an enigmatic half-smile from the man himself. Unexpected pleasure burgeoned behind her ribs. The duke was pleased she'd defended him. How absurd, and how unlike her. Still, she wasn't so churlish as to refuse to give credit where it was due. They did owe him a debt of gratitude.

"I'll ride to Colechester to fetch the doctor," Pennington offered after handing Gabriella into the carriage.

His touch burned through her gloves, and continued to heat her palm after she'd claimed a spot on the seat.

Pale and drawn, his injured leg thrust out before him, Jackson rested his head upon the squab.

Grandpapa gave the duke a dark scowl. "I already told you, we don't need help from the likes of you."

Pennington closed the door and dipped his head. He'd unfastened his coat and lost his hat. A shock of raven hair hung boyishly over his brow. She'd never seen him other than immaculately groomed and found his partial dishabille rather appealing. It made him less intimidating. More her equal. Which, of course, he was not.

There was a lot about the Duke of Pennington she found appealing— or had found appealing before she discovered the fine trappings and impeccable manners hid a completely different man. An unethical sod bent on her family's destruction. That knowledge filled her with an aching sadness, caused by more than disappointment.

There was no denying the secret thrill that had zipped from her hips to shoulders as his solid muscled thighs bunched against her bum or the welcoming hard-planed wall of his chest she'd sagged into as she rode before him. What woman wouldn't find such blatant maleness tempting?

Dangerous musings I'd best put an end to at once.

Any benevolent thoughts toward the Duke of Pennington were misplaced. He meant to put them out of their home. *Don't forget that,* no matter how solicitous and pleasant he might be at this moment.

Besides, something dark, intense, and secret simmered between him and her grandfather. And it was powerful and eerie enough to make her nape tingle. It also stirred her curiosity, and she meant to find out what it was. Instinct told her it had something to do with the duke's plan to claim Hartfordshire Court.

With a concerned glance toward Jackson, Gabriella said, "Grandpapa, please be reasonable. We do need Pennington's help. None of us is capable of driving into town tonight, and if Jackson's leg is truly broken, he cannot wait until tomorrow to have it set." She scooted to the edge of the seat mindful of her grandfather's mulish silence. "Your Grace, we'd be most grateful for your assistance."

"Always a pleasure, Miss Breckensole." From his genial low-timbred tone, she could almost believe he meant it.

One hand on the vehicle's side, she said softly, "Thank you...for everything."

Giving his head the merest inclination, his mouth slid upward a jot, but it was a far cry from a sincere smile. "You never answered my question," he murmured for her ears alone, giving the tips of her fingers a little squeeze.

What have I done to offend you?

His probing, confused gaze made the inquiry again, and if she didn't know better, if the shadows weren't playing with her senses, she might've detected the merest thread of hurt. Surely, he didn't expect her to answer now? Especially here? Particularly when Grandpapa looked as if he'd like to take the crop to him, duke or not?

Her movement barely discernable, she shifted her head and eyes to indicate she wouldn't answer. She hadn't a doubt he'd ask her again, and she was sorely tempted to tell him the truth of it just to see what he'd say.

Would he lie, deny it, or make an excuse? Or would he own his words and explain himself? She so wanted it to be the latter, no matter how irrational. Disgust at her traitorous inclinations brought her up short, retangling the confused knot in her empty belly.

Maxwell, the frustratingly attractive and enigmatic Duke of Pennington was the enemy. Was *her* enemy. She'd be an utter fool to believe any of the smooth words he put forth. Wasn't that what the serpent in the Garden of Eden had done? Used his wiles to trick and deceive Eve?

But... would a man bent on causing harm to her family have been so helpful? Or, what if his assistance had all been a guise to win them over? To put her off the scent? Her musings circled around and around like a dog chasing its tail.

Bah. She was too tired, cold, and hungry to cobble more than two coherent thoughts together. Besides, Pennington wasn't aware she was onto his game. That gave her an advantage, albeit only a slight one, but one she meant full well to use.

With another polite angling of his dark head and a ghost of a bow, the duke presented his back, and a moment later, leapt into the saddle and rode away.

As improbable, illogical, and yes, utterly ridiculous as it was, an odd bereftness encompassed Gabriella. *Fool. Ninny. Goose cap.* She loathed the man. Despised him for what he intended to do to Grandpapa. To all of the Breckensoles.

But she'd spent time in his arms, and it hadn't been awful at all. In fact, if she were completely honest with herself—and she always strived to be so—the experience had been wickedly wonderful, and she'd enjoyed it. Enjoyed it far too much. Enjoyed it so much, she wouldn't mind experiencing more of that particular wickedness.

Another wave of self-loathing battered her. How could she even entertain such treacherous thoughts?

6

After a sleepless night of tossing, turning, and the erotic reliving of Gabriella's lush bum pressed to his loins, Max arose with a cockstand to rival Eros's and Pothos's. Deciding an early morning ride before breaking his fast would clear his head and hopefully reduce his state of arousal, he wasted no time in dressing, quite putting Filby out that he'd dared to do so without the valet's assistance.

Thirty minutes later, he slowed Balor, and patting the horse's withers, breathed in the fresh, crisp air. Song birds trilled cheerfully, and a slight breeze rustled the leaves and sent the tall grass to dancing. This was his preferred time of day, when everything was fresh and new, before his responsibilities and duties consumed his hours and thoughts.

As he had last night and continued to do today, he pondered Gabriella's reaction to him. If he didn't know better, he'd suspect she was as attracted to him as he was to her and fought the magnetism just as vehemently. He dared to consider what there could have been between them if the ugly truth of her grandfather's blackmail hadn't caused a permanent wedge.

He turned the stallion toward a favorite copse of oaks growing along the river where he often saw deer early in the morning. There the embankment narrowed to a few feet. As he approached, he canted his head. Someone was singing. More accurately, a female with a lovely alto voice sang *Lavender's Blue*.

He grinned at his good fortune.

Gabriella.

There she sat on the opposite side of the waterway, beyond where the fencing began. Bright as sunshine in a lovely yellow morning gown, her hair tied back with a jonquil ribbon and her straw bonnet beside her. She rested a sketch pad on her knees as she trilled away.

"You must love me diddle diddle,

'Cause I love you..."

She was the most relaxed and unselfconscious he'd ever seen her. And utterly enchanting. With a cluck of his tongue, he urged Balor faster, and the steed soared over the river, landing on the other side.

Unaware of him as yet, with adorable flourish, she swept her pencil across the paper, and neck bent, continued to sing beneath her breath. *"Diddle, diddle."*

He'd like to diddle diddle something. Someone.

"Good morning, Gabriella."

She started, dropped her pencil, and jerked her gaze upward, her mouth forming a delightful little "O" of surprise as she glanced past him. "I didn't hear you approach."

The river and the breeze rustling through the trees could be blamed for that.

He slid to the ground then looped Balor's reins over the pummel. The horse wouldn't wander far. Without waiting for an invitation, Max sank beside her and retrieved her pencil.

"May I see?" He indicated the sketch pad as he handed the pencil to her.

With a little shrug, she passed it over. She'd drawn her grandfather's cattle milling about the meadow, including three newborn calves resting beneath the trees. A robin red breast stood atop a fence post, its head raised in song.

"You have talent," he said returning the pad to her. He wasn't surprised. "You've a lovely singing voice too."

She angled her head at his compliment. "I find drawing relaxes me and is a welcome distraction from things weighing on my mind."

"Like the exchange between your grandfather and me last night?" He gathered her hand in his, fully expecting her to yank it away and renounce him for a bounder and an opportunistic rake.

Instead, she stared at their entwined fingers, hers charcoal-stained. "Yes, that and other things." She slanted her head, contemplatively. "Do you ever wonder what life would have been like if you'd been born a different person?"

Such a serious conversation for so early in the morning. She'd probably fretted all night as well.

"I do on occasion. I'd have much more freedom. There are obligations required of a duke that I don't always relish." Like restoring stolen lands to the duchy and ruining pretty young women's lives in the process. He released her hand before removing his hat and setting it beside his thigh then leaned back on one elbow.

She turned that expressive hazel gaze on him, searching his face. Wistfulness and yearning shone there, and he recognized a kindred spirit. He'd sensed that about her from their initial meeting. Neither would hesitate to do anything for their family. The difference was, his family was dead, whilst her grandparents and her sister lived.

"Honestly, I've never considered there are aspects to being a duke that are difficult or that you disliked." She skewed her mouth in the manner he'd come to recognize meant she was in deep thought. "I've always only thought of the privileges and opportunities your position brings." Gabriella took up her pencil again, but didn't put it to the paper. She seemed lost in ruminations once more.

Today, there was a melancholy air about her, and he yearned to take her in his arms and promise everything would be all right. But he couldn't, because he was going to make her life hell, and part of him wished he'd never found that damned journal.

"I wish that I had been born someone else at times." She pushed a stray tendril of almond-brown hair off her face, leaving a charcoal smudge on her cheek. "Not because I've been unhappy, though I do wish my parents had lived and I'd have known them. But because I'd like to have traveled and seen something of the world. Instead, I expect I'll take care of my grandparents until they pass, and then…?"

"And then?" he probed when she didn't finish.

She hitched a dainty shoulder again, indicating she didn't know what the future would bring.

It was on the tip of his tongue to ask her if she'd never thought of marrying. He checked the question. It wouldn't matter, for he knew her future even if she did not as yet.

"How fares Jackson and your grandmother?" He curled his hand into the grass to keep from grasping her silken locks teasing the mound of her derriere.

"Grandmama is determined to leave her bed today." She frowned at her drawing as she added a bit of shadowing. "And Jackson is resting as well as can be expected. He's in a lot of pain, poor man."

"I arranged to have your grandfather's coach repaired at my expense." Max hadn't intended to mention that. He'd wanted to surprise her. She'd blamed herself for the mishap, though in all honesty, the advanced age of the conveyance was to blame.

One hand half-raised to the wisp of hair flitting about her ear, she glanced at him in open-mouthed astonishment. "Why? He was utterly hateful to you last night. I still burn from mortification at his behavior. I cannot understand it."

"I did it for you, *chérie.*"

Gabriella laid her drawing materials aside then adjusted her position so that she faced him. "Why? You've no reason I can think of to be kind and generous, and to take such actions on my behalf."

So like her. Direct and to the point. Max would seldom have to wonder what went on in her head. She wasn't exactly reticent about telling him, even when it wasn't what he wanted to hear.

I also must ask you, once again, to direct your attentions elsewhere. I am not now, nor will I ever be, receptive to them.

Her words from yesterday hurt, and they ought not to.

He turned her hand over and drew his finger across her palm. "Because I want to be your friend. Possibly, something more."

She stared at him for the longest stretch. It dragged on and on, emotions flitting across her face in rapid succession. At last, she turned her pink mouth down, sighed, and withdrew her hand. "That's not possible, and I think you must know it."

Gabriella averted her gaze, afraid Maxwell would see the tears pooling in her eyes. She preferred it when he was his usual abominable cocky self, not this tender man. It made her wish for things that could never be.

He rubbed his thumb over her cheek, and she raised her wary gaze to collide with his. "You had a bit of charcoal, just there."

The queerest longing to turn her face into his hand assailed her. Why did he have this power over her? Her head told her he was dangerous. No good. A man not to be trusted. She *knew* that to be true of him as well.

Nevertheless, her fickle heart had taken to him months ago. Gabriella couldn't pinpoint the exact moment she suspected she was more than smitten with his charm and undeniably striking looks. With his smile, his droll wit, and the way his eyes lit up when he was with his friends.

Yes, she did wish she'd been born a different person and that he had been too. Then maybe there would've been a chance for them. As things were now…

"*Chérie.* You're crying."

His awed whisper tumbled her back to the present, but before she could swipe away the evidence of her upset, he sat up and gathered her into his arms. "What has you distraught?" He murmured into her hair while stroking her back. "Tell me. Mayhap I can help."

No, you cannot.

She should pull away. Slap his face. However, the plain truth was, she didn't want to. Being held in his arms felt the most natural thing in the world, and she'd dreamed of it so often before she'd overheard him that day last December.

He tilted her chin up. "Gabby?" His gaze sank to her mouth, and she was lost.

Leaning in, she grasped his lapel and lifted her mouth in silent invitation. With a strangled groan, he crushed his lips to hers. Lights and flashes exploded behind her eyes, as he nibbled and explored the recesses of her mouth. She looped her arms around his neck, desperate to draw him nearer.

To have this moment, no matter how wrong or how much she'd regret it later.

She breathed Max in, memorizing his scent, the shape of his mouth, the taste of him, the feel of his sculpted form beneath her palms.

He splayed a hand on the small of her back and framed her face with the other. "You are so beautiful." He nuzzled her neck, and she allowed her head to fall back to give him greater access. He skimmed her ribs, his fingers mere inches from her breasts. "Let me call on you, Gabby, and speak to your grandfather about paying my addresses. We could be so good together."

Those words doused her passion as surely as if he'd tossed her into the river sweeping past them a few feet from away. What game did he play?

Jerking away, she pressed her fingers to her throbbing mouth and shook her head so hard her hair ribbon came loose. What was she doing? Had she lost her mind? God, how could she kiss him when she knew what he intended. What kind of a wanton was she? Equally mortified and furious that he'd so easily duped her, she swiftly gathered her drawing materials.

A perplexed frown furrowed his brow. "Gabby...? What's wrong?"

She plopped her bonnet upon her head and scrambled to her feet, standing unsteadily. Shaking, angry at herself for being weak and stupid, and at him for kissing so wonderfully that she'd forgotten who he was, she jutted her chin out.

"I've tried delicacy due to your station being so much more elevated than mine, but at every turn, you continue to press your suit and now have dared to go beyond the mark and kiss me."

"Hold on there." He held up a hand, his tone and expression guarded. "You offered your mouth, and you wanted that kiss as much as I did. Don't you dare deny it."

Scorching heat swept from her breasts to her forehead. "Yes. Yes, I did. My curiosity overcame my common sense, but this was a huge mistake and shan't happen again."

"Are you suggesting you only kissed me out of virginal curiosity?" Curse his noble eyebrow flying high up his forehead in disbelief.

"Of course. What other reason could there be?" *Indeed, Gabriella Fern Miriam Breckensole. What possible reason?*

He rose, all lean, sinewy muscle and animal-like grace. "You tell me, *chérie.*" His voice as smooth as silk held a dangerous note, and a tremor rattled through her.

"Oh, you are insufferable! Simply impossible. A puffed-up, arrogant toad." She stamped a foot, wishing she had the nerve to kick him in the shin.

He folded his arms and smirked. "Indeed."

"Leave me alone, Your Grace. I mean it."

His smile grew wider and impossibly smugger, and he dared to shake his midnight head.

Itching to lay a palm across his angular face, she presented her back. "I shall give you the Cut Direct. I swear I shall." Though it likely meant goading a bear. Tears made dual tracks down her face as she all but ran from him.

"*Je suis désolé, chérie,* but it will make no difference."

7

Four days later, at precisely three of the clock, Gabriella climbed the impressive steps to Ridgewood Court, the Sutcliffes' ducal country house. The afternoon proved one of the lovelier this spring: the temperature pleasant, the sky crystal clear, and the gentlest breeze teasing the new foliage, budding flowers, and the wisps of hair framing her face.

Today, as they did every third Thursday of the month, she and her sister as well as several other of the local gentry not yet in London for the onset of the Season, met for tea and an afternoon of cards. If the weather permitted, guests might take to the lawns for strolls, shuttlecock, or lawn bowling.

Gabriella had deliberately stayed close to home these past days. No trips to Colechester, no evening engagements, and no much-coveted excursions about the countryside either. She'd take no chances of running into the Duke of Pennington. No chances of foolishly indulging in more exquisite kisses that left her senses reeling, and her common sense and indignation fizzled to pathetic embers. She must keep her umbrage fully ablaze to battle her ever-growing attraction to the man.

There was still the musical gathering at the Twisteltons' to sort out. She and Ophelia had already said they were attending, and Nicolette would be disappointed if they cried off now. Gabriella had no idea what excuse she could give Ophelia or their grandparents either. Nevertheless, she had severe second—make that third—thoughts about the wisdom of going since *he* would be there.

Especially given the delivery of two stunning cloaks yesterday: one mazurine blue velvet and labeled "Ophelia" and an emerald green one, with Gabriella's name pinned to the collar. No card accompanied the garments, which caused both grandparents' graying eyebrows to skip about on their wrinkled foreheads.

The conversation replayed in her head, word for word.

"It would seem you girls have an admirer." Grandmama had brushed her fingertips over the fine cloth before slicing them a considering glance. "Do you have any notion who it might be?"

"I haven't a clue, but the cloaks are magnificent. I suppose we must return them," Ophelia had murmured, clearly not liking the idea at all. She brushed her cheek against the fabric, sighing. "Is this similar to the one you ordered for me, Gabby?"

Grandpapa had let that tidbit slip during his rant about the stolen horses, damaged coach, and Pennington's unmitigated gall. Gabriella hadn't intended to mention it and distress her sister.

"Very much so," she had admitted. "But how can we return them, when we don't know who sent them? I suppose we could ask the local seamstresses, but that might prove awkward. Besides, there's no guarantee they were fashioned in Colechester."

Gabriella had a very good idea who was behind the gifts—a very good idea indeed— but she'd bite her tongue in half before voicing her suspicions. She didn't relish another scene with her grandfather and truly feared he'd do something awful, such as torch the gorgeous mantles, if he thought the duke was the benefactor. "I suppose we'll have to donate them."

She hated acknowledging how much that saddened her. Both were utterly exquisite, and she was womanly enough to appreciate the fine workmanship. How the duke had managed to commission them in such a short time bespoke his power and influence. Likely, the seamstress had a much heavier purse for her efforts as well.

Grandpapa poked his head above the week-old newssheet. He'd never pay for a current copy but gladly accepted the papers sent their way from the Sutcliffes and Sheffields. "Could they be a surprise birthday gift from

57

your cousin Everleigh, and the note somehow became lost? It is your first and twentieth birthdays in two days, and certainly the occasion warrants something remarkable."

Ophelia perked up and grabbed Gabriella's hand. "I vow, that must be it! We can ask her at tea tomorrow." At once a frown marred her pretty face. "Though I don't suppose we ought to wear them to tea until we know for certain."

"I must agree, my dear," Grandmama gently said. "I expect your grandfather has the right of it, however."

And so here they were for their monthly tea, Ophelia convinced Everleigh was behind the luxurious gift and Gabriella equally certain the duke was. She'd mentioned the mazurine cloak the day of the coach accident, and she didn't believe in coincidences. If she weren't so blasted annoyed with him, she'd have been touched by the thoughtful gesture. He knew it too, drat the charming rake.

Two reasons had compelled her to accompany Ophelia today. First, the duke had never put in an appearance in all the months Everleigh had hosted the monthly tea, and secondly, the only way to know for certain who sent the mantles was to ask her cousin.

As they reached the top riser, a shiny black coach bearing a ducal crest rocked to a stop.

Gabriella turned in expectation. Everleigh poked her head out and waved gaily. "Hello, darlings!"

Such a change had come over her since marrying the Duke of Sheffield. She positively radiated happiness these days. Gabriella eyed her cousin's belly. Was she *enceinte*? Hmm, that might explain the glow.

Everleigh's step-niece, Rayne Wellbrook followed her descent, and then another young woman Gabriella wasn't acquainted with stepped onto the courtyard.

Once inside and having been divested of their outerwear, Everleigh smiled and drew the petite, strawberry-blonde forward. "Gabriella and Ophelia, may I introduce Miss Sophronie Slater from the Americas? Her father is one of Sheffield's business partners. "Ronie, these are my cousins, Ophelia and Gabriella Breckensole."

Miss Slater offered a shallow curtsy and a bright smile, revealing not quite perfectly straight teeth. Her eyes glinted with excitement. "Everleigh speaks of you often. It's a pleasure to meet you. My, you are indistinguishable from each other. Did you ever play pranks and switch places?"

Everleigh laughed, whilst shaking a finger at them. "Yes, they did."

Chatting, the five women made their way to the drawing room. At once, Gabriella sensed this was no typical Thursday tea. Far more guests milled about than usually did, and there were several she didn't recognize. She sent Ophelia, a what-is-going-on? look, and her sister lifted her shoulder an inch.

Theadosia spied them and broke into a wide smile. She hurried their way, hands outstretched, the small mound of her belly preceding her.

Gabriella surveyed the room again, and her stomach pitched. *Ballocks and bunions.*

He was here.

There, by the window, too deucedly attractive for her peace of mind. His heated, predatory gaze met hers, and he inclined his sable head. She nearly turned on her heels and headed straight for the carriage. She'd promised to cut him, but Ophelia had already ventured farther into the room with Rayne and Miss Slater.

Gabriella edged near Thea and whispered in her ear. "Why are there so many in attendance today?

Theadosia pressed a hand to her throat and chuckled low. "Well, several of my regulars brought guests. It's a good thing I planned for yard games."

Thirty of the most uncomfortable minutes Gabriella had ever endured passed before she could bear it no longer and begged to be excused to use the necessary. Anything to put distance between herself and Maxwell. Besides, Theadosia and Sutcliffe were about to usher their guests outdoors.

Maxwell hadn't approached her, so perhaps he'd taken her warning to heart. Yet, she knew full well, as did he, she would not cut him here. Not with her sister present. Ophelia would never live down the disgrace. And then she'd have to explain her actions, for neither Theadosia or Everleigh would let such ill-behavior go any more than Nicolette would.

As she made her way to the room set aside for the ladies' personal needs, she frowned. Where was Nicolette?

After splashing a bit of water on her cheeks, then pinching them to bring a spot of color to her pale face, she stared at her reflection. Though it was two seasons old, her light blue gown complemented her coloring. It did nothing for the haunted look in her eyes, however. She feared the truth of Maxwell's plans must come out sooner than she'd wanted, and then where would she and the rest of her family be?

She closed her eyes and drew in a slow, deliberate breath. *Stop hiding from him. You're made of sterner stuff.* Nonetheless, she chose a meandering route to the lawns where the others had retreated and instead of joining them, took a seat in a sheltered arbor off the terrace.

From there, laughter and calls of encouragement and the occasional muffled curse carried to her on the breeze. What a fine bumblebroth this was. She, the keeper of a dastardly secret and much too interested in the man who could very well ruin her family.

"I wondered where you'd sneaked off to." Without an invitation, Maxwell settled his large frame beside her. What had been a comfortable nook at once became too confined and cramped. His scent filled the small area, and despite her determination not to respond to him, her nostrils quivered and anticipation made her stomach flip-flop.

Gabriella forced herself to inhale and count to ten to compose a civil retort.

"I didn't sneak, and you should not be here." She refused to look at him, for if she did, she would be lost. "And neither should you have sent the cloaks. Grandpapa is convinced Everleigh commissioned them for my sister's and my birthday presents, but I know it was you."

Maxwell neither admitted nor denied the accusation. Leaning back, he stretched his impossibly long, black-clad legs before him. He sighed and eyes closed, rested his head against the back of the arbor. "Thank you for not cutting me."

Sincere or mocking?

Examining him surreptitiously from beneath her half-lowered eyelids, Gabriella tightened her mouth. His thick lashes fanning his chiseled cheekbones couldn't hide the lines of fatigue at the corners of his eyes or the shadows beneath them. She'd like to think the past few days had robbed him of as much sleep as they had her. That he also struggled with his conscience as well as his attraction to her.

"You look tired, Your Grace," she murmured before she could stop herself then silently berated the impulse. He might mistake it for caring or concern.

But she *did* care and that frustrated her to no end. She shouldn't. Not about him.

He cracked his blue eye open, and gave her a long, undiscernible look. Was that regret and tenderness there or was the filtered light playing tricks? *Or*...was she manufacturing what she hoped to see?

"I've had much on my mind," he finally said, opening both eyes.

She made a noncommittal noise then tipped her mouth up at Jessica Brentwood's cry of delight. "I've bested you, Bainbridge," Jessica laughed. "Now you owe me an ice at Gunter's."

"Gabriella?"

The peaceful afternoon had lulled her into a drowsy state. Nights of little sleep might be blamed as well. She hid a yawn behind her hand, knowing she ought to join the others, but unable to muster the energy or the desire to do so. "Hmm?"

"You've never explained why you disdain my company." His usual arrogance was absent. "I can only assume I've offended you in some way, and for that I apologize."

She sighed, wishing she dared tell him all, but afraid to reveal what she knew. Hence, she decided on a different tact. "I see no point in encouraging your interest when we both know nothing can come of it. You're a duke, and I am a dowerless country miss. There can never be more between us. You are expected to make a brilliant match, and in truth, I am not certain I'll ever marry."

"I cannot countenance such a thing," he said quite forcibly. "You are young and beautiful. Surely you want a home and children."

The truth of her circumstances couldn't be denied though her heart ached to think of it. To never know a man's touch or to carry a child. A flicker of resentment fired in her veins too. She wasn't nobility, but a gentle-born woman had fewer prospects than the poorest peasant's daughter who might marry for love.

Maxwell covered her folded hands with his, his palm heavy and somehow reassuring. "I don't particularly care about station or dowries." *He is a rarity, then.* "Nor about political connections or expanding my sphere of influence."

Gabriella quirked a skeptical brow and laughed. "I cannot believe that." Not when he was determined to regain Hartfordshire Court at all costs. She twisted to face him. "What do you want from me?" A shocking epiphany danced through her mind, and she narrowed her eyes. "Since a respectable union is beyond our scope, I can only assume you've another, less chivalrous proposition."

It was his turn to look startled, and by Jove, not just a little guilty too. It was in the way he veered his gaze aside for an instant and the distinct rosy hue tinting his sharp cheeks.

By God. She'd made the estimable Duke of Pennington blush.

The air left her lungs in a rush as profound disappointment flooded her. Why she should be surprised he wanted her for his mistress, given what she knew him capable of, she couldn't fathom. But if he'd skewered her with a dagger, her pain would've been less. She tilted her chin up refusing to give her disappointment any power. "I admit, I'd foolishly thought you above such machinations."

She tried to pull her hands away, but he firmed his grip. "You have it wrong." He lifted a hand to his mouth and kissed the back of it, then turned it over to kiss the pulse beating a frantic tattoo at her wrist. "I swear, I would never dishonor you in such a way." Maxwell drew her into his embrace, his gaze locked upon hers. His voice, low and raspy as if intense emotion constricted his throat, he murmured, "You intrigue me as no other ever has."

In less than a blink, his mouth was upon hers, devouring her lips, demanding a response.

Gabriella couldn't deny him, and with a husky moan, twined her arms around his neck and gave in to her hunger.

This was madness. Sweet, wanton, wonderful madness. Her desire for this man would consume her, but in this exquisite sliver of time, she didn't care. Maxwell was here, and she was here, and there was no snuffing the inferno. His kisses went on and on, his tongue dueling with hers, their breath mingling as she lost all sense of anything but him.

A shriek of laughter only a few feet away pierced the heady passion, and this time, Maxwell, drew back, a lopsided smile slashing his mouth. "Forgive me. I lose my self-control the moment I touch you." He traced a finger down her cheek.

She was both delighted and terrified at his admission. Swallowing, her lips throbbing from the sensual onslaught, desire and perhaps something more wrestled with her sense of justice. She couldn't have it both ways. She didn't dare give into whatever this unnamed thing was between them. It would destroy her when—*if*—he claimed Hartfordshire Court.

Male voices echoed on the terrace, and he stood, straightening his waistcoat. "I shouldn't be found here. You would be compromised. But know this, *chérie*, I do not easily give up."

He must be made to do so. But how when every part of her longed to yield to him?

8

The next evening, one shoulder propped against the doorframe to the Twistletons' crowded music room, Max raised his champagne flute to his lips, savoring the quality spirit. From across the span, the Duke and Duchess of Dandridge nodded cheerful greetings as they settled onto the blue-tufted chair cushions. Sutcliffe and Sheffield, along with their magnificent duchesses, had claimed seats for tonight's soiree in the last row of neatly lined chairs.

Swathed in silks and satins, their jewels glittering in the glow of dozens of candles, the ladies resembled brightly-plumaged birds next to the gentlemen's more sedately-hued suits. Only in the human species did the female outshine the male.

Well, most males. The image of a dandified fellow Max had encountered a fortnight ago, attired in pink and canary yellow, intruded upon his musings.

Several other members of *Bon Chance*: The Sinful Lords Secret Society were present as well: Westfall, Bainbridge, and Asherford, dukes one and all, though the organization wasn't limited to dukes, hence the name sinful lords. The group was much more of a brotherhood than a club, a brothel, or gaming hell for debauched aristocrats. It was a place to escape the pressures and responsibilities of having been born a noble. A place where they could just be men. Equals.

A footman placed a violin atop the pianoforte as another arranged a harp just so. Normally, Max eschewed this particular sort of gathering. For a damned good reason too. One never knew what degree of skill those imposed upon to entertain the assembly might claim.

A person with a strong musical inclination himself, he could scarcely sit through the travesties that far too often took to the stage. Usually prompted by a parent oblivious to their progenies' complete and absolute ineptitude.

In London one might fare better, but in the country? No, he'd likely have to sit on his hands to keep from slapping them to his ears. But then how could he cover his mouth to stifle his groans?

Damn him for a fool for accepting tonight.

Forcing an expression other than abject boredom whilst trying to ignore what often amounted to noises similar to mating cats wasn't something he had quite mastered. Nor would he ever. However, he had it on good authority—those very same dukes now murmuring intimately in their wives' ears and from Miss Twistleton herself—that certain twins would indeed be present. He'd had his doubts, and it pleased him no end that after yesterday, Gabriella hadn't forsworn the gathering.

Never had a woman and her mouth held such allure. Or made him incapable of resisting the temptation of being in her presence. Toward that end, he donned his evening finery. Even taking particular care with his appearance and choosing a paisley waistcoat, because the fabric's colors reminded him of her fascinating eyes.

If Max had been prudent, he'd have secured a seat in the back row too. Much easier to make a subtle escape should Gabriella not attend after all. But then, he'd have endured his valet's disapproval over his choice of waistcoat for no good reason.

He finished the superb wine and after combing the room in search of a certain spitfire with dark honey-tinted hair and ever-changing eye color, placed his glass atop the tray carried by a passing hunter green-and-black liveried footman. When offered another flute, he gave a decisive nod. Although truth to tell, it would take three or four *or eight* more to make him less inclined to grimace or yawn during the tedious recitals he anticipated.

A derisive grin quirking his mouth, Ansley, Earl of Scarborough lifted his glass in a silent salute from where he'd positioned himself beside a tall plant. Another member of *Bon Chance*. Unfortunate for Scarborough that he'd chosen this weekend to visit his boyhood home. Since inheriting the earldom from his uncle two years ago, he'd done an admirable job of avoiding social gatherings, and his biting cynicism when forced to appear had earned him the unflattering moniker, the Earl of Sarcasm.

Max returned the gesture, recognizing a kindred soul. Obligation and duty made men do all manner of things they'd prefer not to. Sometimes things which teetered on the precipice of decency and muted their self-respect. Whereas Max more easily controlled his responses to unwanted social interactions, the tic twitching near Scarborough's left eye gave his unease away.

Scarborough's stunning sister, Nicolette Twistleton glided near her brother. She stretched up on her toes, tilted her raven curls toward his dark head, and whispered something in his ear. With a casual shrug, he downed the last of his champagne. Appearing very much like he wished he might indulge in something far stronger, he allowed her to tow him to a front row chair. *Poor, miserable bastard.*

Few people knew Max played the violin, or no doubt, he'd have been imposed upon to entertain this evening as well. He intended to keep that knowledge a secret. He played on a regular basis, but never for others. Not since he'd been fourteen years of age, and he'd eagerly set bow to string for his father whom he hadn't seen in six months. As he was wont to do, the seventh Duke of Pennington had ridiculed rather than praised him before dismissing Max with the aloofness he might've directed toward a tax collector.

Or a clap-ridden whore.

Another casual swallow and with an equally deceptive indifferent scan of the room, Max pulled his mouth taut. A glance to the mantel clock revealed five minutes past eight; the time this grand misadventure was scheduled to have begun. He'd wasted his damned evening, it seemed, for a predictably unpredictable woman. Was there ever a more frustratingly enticing vixen?

Did he dare escape now?

No sense dithering any more of the evening away when his time was better spent perfecting the details of the plan he intended to put into effect soon. Mayhap as shortly as tomorrow, if Gabriella didn't come tonight. And it certainly seemed she wouldn't.

After Max's encounter with her cantankerous grandfather a week ago, his man of business had paid a call at Chartworth Hall. Struthers brought information quite welcome to Max, but assuredly wouldn't be to that bastard Breckensole. And Gabriella, an unwitting pawn, was paramount to his success.

Actually, she was essential to his preferred plan. The one which showed a degree of mercy and which helped temper his fury with no small amount of sympathy for hers, her twin's, and Mrs. Breckensole's plight. His alternative strategy wasn't as compassionate, and he'd rather not resort to those extremes but would if all else failed.

If *she* failed to cooperate.

He dragged his gaze over the rows of chairs. Thirty in all. It was to be an intimate affair tonight then. At least, according to any society matron worth her salt's standard. He snorted, drawing a curious look from Jessica Brentwood, the Duchess of Sutcliffe's younger sister.

The single woman he'd hope to see, had counted on seeing, had yet to arrive. Another inspection of the clock revealed nearly half past the hour. Much too late to be considered fashionable. She wasn't coming after all.

Certainly, it wasn't disappointment pinging round and round in his chest much like pebbles shaken in a jar. No, by God. It was annoyance at his own stupidity for having accepted an invitation he oughtn't to have done. And for getting his hopes up after the amazing interlude in the arbor.

And damn his eyes, he couldn't very well leave before the first person performed and still remain in his influential hostess's good graces. Invitations must keep coming, and he must know which functions Gabriella would also attend.

When another discreet inspection of the assembled guests failed to locate the attractive female he sought, he brushed his fingers along his jaw. Sutcliffe's gaze met his, and Max raised a questioning eyebrow. *Where is she?*

Sutcliffe hitched a shoulder before bending his ear to his wife once more. He was of no help whatsoever, besotted fool.

Had Mrs. Breckensole's health taken a turn for the worse again, keeping her granddaughters at home? Max had spoken with Dr. Spratt two days ago, and the capable physician had assured him that Mrs. Breckensole recovered nicely.

Why he should be so anxious for Gabriella's presence, he refused to examine. He would have Hartfordshire Court, one way or another. Her cooperation simply lessened the hardship for her sister and grandmother. He didn't give a tinker's damn about *lessening* Breckensole's shock.

It hadn't escaped Max that Gabriella had avoided answering his question the other night. It also hadn't escaped him that she'd been appalled at her grandfather's frothing antagonism. Her reaction only confirmed what he'd suspected all along. None of the Breckensole women had any notion what Harold Breckensole had done. What the scapegrace continued to do.

An unfamiliar sensation constricted Max's chest and burned the back of his throat. If he were a better man, a kinder more forgiving man, he'd let the issue of Hartfordshire Court's ownership go. After all, the Breckensoles had resided there for decades. Surely the comfortable house was the only home Gabriella and her sister could remember.

Didn't she—they—deserve clemency? Their grandfather's sins weren't theirs. They shouldn't have to suffer because of his reprehensible decisions.

Max's eyes drifted shut for a blink, and the gaunt, haunted features of his opium-addicted grandfather burst into his mind. An image straight from the bowels of hell. No, dammit. Breckensole had done that to Grandfather. He may not have tipped the laudanum-laced whisky into a glass every day, but he'd stolen the one thing that meant the most to the old man.

Grandmother.

And the repercussions had been far reaching. Grandfather had become a man incapable of loving, or perhaps afraid to show affection to his only child. It had also made him powerless to resist the alcohol and opium that numbed his senses and blotted unbearable memories from his mind. As a result of his lack of love and approval by his sire, Max's father's soul had warped and twisted as well, and Max had been the recipient of *his* cruelty.

But what of Mrs. Breckensole? What of the twins? That common sense voice prodded his conscience for at least the hundredth time. Until he wanted to shout every foul oath he knew, and the incessant nagging still didn't stop. *They are innocent in this. Must they suffer in order for me to dole out vengeance? Especially as the offense wasn't against me?*

He quaffed back the rest of his champagne and soundly quashed his ruminations. Sometimes, when righting wrongs, other blameless parties had to suffer. That was just the way of it. Lest he forget, he reminded himself severely, Grandmother and the babe she'd carried had been innocents too.

"What has you looking so Friday-faced, Pennington? Downright glum, I might add."

Max slid Crispin, Duke of Bainbridge a quizzical glance then looked pointedly at the punch cup he held—no doubt liberally dosed with brandy or whisky from the flask always in Bainbridge's pocket.

"I never look Friday-faced, Bainbridge. I'm simply hoping tonight's entertainment proves more enjoyable than the last musical I attended." That had proved so dreadful, he'd abstained for five years. When he closed his eyes, he could still hear Amelia Johnson's off-key—*very, very off-key*—trilling and see her bursting into tears and fleeing the room when an insensitive, foxed-to-his-fleshy-gills clod pate tottered inside, snickered loudly, and asked where he might view the atrociously singing parrots.

"Of course you don't," Bainbridge put forth drolly. "So that downturned mouth and your gaze straying to the entrance every few seconds, not to mention the two glasses of champagne you've consumed already, means you're a cheerful chap?" he quipped as he slapped Max's shoulder.

"Stubble it, Bainbridge. You are no keener on these sorts of husband-hunting assemblies than I am. In fact, I'm surprised to see so many of our set here. I'd have thought they'd all be in London by now preparing for the Season." However, since Max had determined who his duchess would be, albeit for all of the wrong reasons, he needn't concern himself with the marriage-minded mamas here or in Town.

Bainbridge drew his sober attention from his study of the lovely Jessica Brentwood and offered another wry smile. "No small amount of truth there. But one has to have something to do on these tediously endless days until Parliament is in session and the Season officially begins. I'm not given to stalking and fishing, and even I grow a trifle bored with my horse breeding venture. I dare say, once the mare is impregnated, it's just a matter of waiting, is it not?"

"You're babbling, Bainbridge."

"Not a bit of it. If you're looking for the Breckensoles, I have it on good authority that they'll be arriving with Rayne Wellbrook and Justina Farthington. Miss Farthington's dragon of an aunt, Emily Grenville will likely play chaperone to the foursome for the evening." Bainbridge cocked his head, running a long finger the length of his champagne glass. "You do know Breckensole's coach was wrecked and villains stole his team. And Gabriella was only spared because she most prudently hid in the woods?"

Max closed his eyes until they were mere slits. Since when did Bainbridge address Gabriella by her first name? Christ on the Sabbath. Did *he* have a *tendre* for her?

What a distasteful notion. That one of the gentlemen he called friends might have a romantic interest in her galled. Except the way Bainbridge's regard kept straying to the fair Jessica Brentwood suggested his interest lay in another direction.

Good.

Max couldn't very well play his hand just yet and announce he intended to leg shackle himself to Gabriella. Thank God he found her attractive—*too deucedly luscious*—and keen of intellect. But even if she'd resembled a goose's hind end, had the protruding teeth of a buck-toothed hare, and possessed the acumen of a turnip, it would've changed nothing.

Well, the begetting an heir might have proven more of challenge had that been the case. Even dosed with spirits and in a pitch-black bedchamber, one needed a strong constitution to even consider that tedious task if the female weren't desirable. He needn't worry on that account, by God.

No, bedding Gabriella Breckensole wouldn't be a chore he forced himself to perform for the duchy's sake. He'd enjoy it as a man very much drawn to her softly rounded curves would. As a man who'd wanted her almost from the first minute he'd met her. Contemplating her warming his bed, desire tingled through his veins, a mellow, burgeoning warmth.

His body responded predictably, most inconveniently—damned his erotic musings. With deliberate intent, he turned his thoughts to her despicable grandsire and succeeded in curbing his arousal quite handily.

Gabriella wouldn't like what Max was about. In fact, he could all but guarantee her outrage, but wed him she would. And be glad for the opportunity when he explained the alternative.

"Pennington? Did you hear me? Wreck? Villains? Woods?" From the sardonic smirk twisting Bainbridge's mouth, he well knew Max had.

"Yes, I'm aware," Max admitted, giving him a moody smile. "I'm the one who saw her home. Rescued her driver too."

Except for the slightest lifting of one eyebrow, Bainbridge did a remarkable job of keeping his surprise contained.

A commotion at the door announced the onset of more guests.

"The Breckensole twins have arrived at last," Bainbridge offered needlessly.

The five late-comers burst in amid apologies, laughs, and heartfelt greetings.

At once, Gabriella's inquisitive gaze met Max's, almost as if she'd searched for him upon entering as he had for her this half hour past. He lifted his glass and brows simultaneously in a silent salute.

Resplendent in a chaste white gown adorned with cherry-colored ribbons and an embroidered overskirt, she outshone every other woman present. The candlelight caught the whispers of golden-bronze threading her hair and made her skin gleam with a pearly effervescence. Her berry red lips parted slightly in the tiniest of hesitant smiles, tipping those rosebud lips upward, before she drew her regard away. Nevertheless, wariness and distrust yet tinged her thick-lashed eyes when she regarded him.

Disappointment stabbed, chinking at his pride. For God's sake. What had he expected? That she'd suddenly welcome his company after months of avoiding him?

Yes, dammit. That's precisely what he'd expected.

At the very least a slight warming after he'd rescued her and helped her injured coachman. Most assuredly after he'd inconvenienced himself and ridden to Colechester to fetch the doctor. He'd gone so far as to make sure Mrs. Breckensole's every medical need was met at his expense.

Not that the Breckensoles were aware of that last bit. He wouldn't put it past Breckensole to refuse out of pride and spite. Max felt obligated to pay the fees after a lengthy, enlightening chat with Mr. Armstrong Edgeman, the brother of this evening's hostess, had revealed Breckensole's finances were in dun territory.

But mainly, he'd anticipated a favorable response because of the stirring kisses he'd shared with Gabriella.

Oh, she'd done the pretty in her feminine and flowing handwriting. She'd sent 'round a politely worded note thanking him for his assistance. It hadn't escaped him that she made the gesture and not her grandfather. Her perfectly worded missive held no hint of the sensual vixen he'd kissed more than once.

Her twin, also wearing a frothy white gown, only Miss Ophelia's bore lavender-toned accents, immediately swept to Miss Twistleton's side.

"May I have your attention, please?" Beaming, Mary Twistleton stood at the front of the room and clapped her hands twice drawing everyone's attention. "Please do have a seat. Now that everyone is here, we may begin the evening's entertainment. I'm sure you will be well-pleased." She swept a gloved hand toward the Breckensoles. "Ophelia and Gabriella have kindly agreed to lead off with a rendition of *Sonata for Violin and Piano in B Minor* by Johann Sebastian Bach."

Ah, they were part of the evening's entertainment. No wonder the party hadn't begun on time. Heaven forbid the order of performances be changed to accommodate late arrivals. Max took in Scarborough's stiff

72

mien and realization struck. For his sake, his mother couldn't adjust the agenda. To do so would completely disconcert the earl, a man who held to rigid routines and schedules. Sympathy again washed him for the other man's plight.

"My son, the Earl of Scarborough and my daughter Nicolette will follow with Mozart's *Sonata in C.*" Her proud, but fond gaze rested on her children for an instant before she flicked her elderly father a rather strict warning glance and then motioned expectantly to the guests still standing. Her brother, the banker, was noticeably absent. "Plenty of seats remain. Please find one."

Not exactly plenty.

Max waited as the others obediently filed to their places. All except the Breckensole twins. After bussing their hostess's cheek and exchanging swift hugs with her, they made their way to the pianoforte.

Other than their attire, the women appeared identical, and it never ceased to flummox him that while he appreciated Ophelia's loveliness, he'd never felt the slightest jot of attraction to her. Her sister on the other hand, had him in a constant state of arousal. That truth irritated as much as confounded.

He didn't hail from a family given to emotion or impulse, although he'd always had a devil of a time reining in his sense of humor. Nonetheless, he didn't like or appreciate his unfettered responses to Gabriella. They fogged his mind, muddled his intentions, and that he could not permit.

Ophelia settled gracefully onto the bench before the grand instrument, and his jaw loosened the slightest in astonishment when Gabriella collected the violin from atop the polished mahogany.

She played the violin? A pleased smile ticked his mouth upward. By Jove. They had something in common after all. Ridiculous that he should be so delighted at something so inconsequential. At once he desired to play Bach's *Concerto for Two Violins* with her. Perchance after they were wed...

Eyes narrowed slightly, he took note of the remaining seats. Another small, satisfied grin curving his mouth at his good fortune, he made his way to three unoccupied chairs in the front row. One was undoubtedly intended for their bubbly hostess. The others…

Without a pang of compunction, he claimed the pair for himself and Gabriella.

Her eyes rounded the merest bit as she shifted her gaze between him, the empty seat to his right, and the only two other unoccupied chairs in the room. Her mouth, a sweet, prim line of reproach, she looked pointedly to *those* vacant chairs.

Her expressive gaze fairly screamed, "*Move!*"

Not on his life. He gave a slight shake of his head.

Her eyelids lowered the merest bit, and her acute gaze promised vengeance and a proper dressing down. A perverse thrill scuttled up his spine. Oh, Miss Gabriella Breckensole was a worthy opponent, to be sure.

He cocked an eyebrow, crossed one leg over the other, and tipped his mouth upward in a silent challenge. *Do your worst, love.*

Fairly bristling with indignation, her eyes grew dark and smoky. Just as swiftly, her features softened into a benign mien, but she couldn't quite subdue the sparks spewing from her gaze. She'd happily plant him a facer, he hadn't a doubt.

Something—surely not guilt or remorse or a misplaced sense of integrity—scuffed hard and abrasive against his need for revenge. A lesser man might've quelled under her blistering stare. Beneath the knowledge that he was a manipulative blackguard. Yet he didn't move.

It wouldn't do to switch places now, in any event. After all, the presentation was about to begin, and indisposing the other guests and further delaying the performances would be most inconsiderate of him. Or so he assured himself.

Bastard, his conscience railed. *Knave. Cretin.* Jaw taut, he stifled his recriminations then dispassionately lifted a shoulder as if to say, "*It's too late now, chérie.*"

Up went Gabriella's chin; a sure sign he'd further aroused her ire. But unless she wanted to crawl across the laps of the other guests and claim the lone chair in the middle of the third row, she'd have to join him in the front. Well, she might take the chair beside Jessica Brentwood, but he'd vow Miss Brentwood had saved it particularly for Ophelia. Everyone knew they shared a special friendship.

Ophelia played a few opening chords, hauling his wayward musings back to the present, and the audience settled into a polite—perhaps the tiniest bit strained—silence.

Slightly angling away from the rows of guests, Gabriella lifted the violin to her chin. For several unexpectedly pleasant minutes, only the sound of the sisters' expert playing filled the room, and he found himself lost in Bach's hauntingly beautiful tune.

Gabriella played with grace and passion. Eyes closed, her lashes trembling every now and again as she swayed in time, emotions flitted across the smooth planes of her alabaster face.

That the twins practiced together often was apparent and that they'd had superb instructors, equally so. Their grandfather permitting the sisters this luxury astonished him. More than a little, truth be told. It seemed when it came to his granddaughters, Breckensole wasn't a complete and utter arse. The old sod reserved that characteristic for nearly everyone else.

Max found himself humming along, his fingers itching to play his violin. He didn't close his eyes, for he couldn't bear to tear his gaze from Gabriella.

The last note faded away, and after a brief, rather stunned silence, the audience interrupted into enthusiastic applause and calls of approval. Pink tinging their cheeks, the sisters dipped curtsies and after Gabriella set aside her violin, they made their way to the seats.

"Ophelia." Miss Brentwood patted the chair beside her. "Sit here. I saved it especially for you."

Just as Max had suspected.

With a questioning glance to her twin, Ophelia paused, obviously worried about deserting her sister. She had no choice. No other two seats were available together. He'd seen to that; God rot his black soul.

An affectionate smile bending her mouth, Gabriella nodded whilst giving her twin a little shove in the back. "Go along."

Fingering her fan, she faced him. She could either sit beside him or disrupt the third row. With a resigned sigh, only decipherable if one studied her closely, she claimed the chair to his right and promptly flicked her painted, lace-edge fan open. And snapped it shut. Open. Shut. Open. Shut. *You are cruel.*

He almost laughed aloud at her silent, terse message. Instead, tenser than he ought to be, he watched to see if she'd draw the frilly accessory through her hands. That meant *I hate you.*

Staring straight ahead, she didn't move except for the rhythmic rising and falling of her chest, the slow blinking of her expressive eyes, and the *tap-tap, tap-tap of* her slippered toes. Nonetheless, he felt the vexation radiating from her. A doubt didn't exist she'd love to have snubbed him once more. Instead, she'd sunk onto the blue-cushioned seat with the aplomb of a queen and disregarded him as if he were a lowly boot-shine boy.

Her decision revealed an aspect of her character he'd already suspected she possessed and which played perfectly into what he intended to do to regain Hartfordshire Court. Miss Gabriella Breckensole would suffer rather than cause others discomfort or inconvenience. That he would exploit the goodness in her for his own mean ends said much about him for all of his professions that he was a gentleman.

"Well done, Miss Breckensole," Charles Edgeman, Mrs. Twistleton's aged father, a retired banker, whispered loudly on her other side. More than a little deaf, Edgeman was wont to bellow when he believed himself inconspicuous. "I quite enjoyed your performance. One of the best I've heard, I do believe."

Once more, color climbed the slopes of her ivory cheeks, but Gabriella demurred with a kind smile and bowed head. "You are most kind, Mr. Edgeman."

"I quite agree," Max murmured. "Is there anything you don't do well?"

"Hold my tongue when you are about," she snapped, a false smile painted upon her lips.

Which only made him want to kiss the soft pillows until a seductress's smile bent her mouth. Her fresh fragrance tickled his nose, and he inhaled deeply. Yes, definitely a hint of lemon, lavender, and jasmine. An interesting, heady, and unexpected *mélange*. Much like her.

Scarborough, looking crosser than a scorpion caught by the tail, and his vivacious sister perched side-by-side on the bench. Miss Twistleton whispered something to her brother, and his features softened a trifle. He even deemed to twist his mouth into a half-smile.

Max hadn't any sisters. Not a brother either. He'd often wondered what it would've been like to have another child to keep him company. Maybe he wouldn't be turning into a cold, unfeeling bastard, not so different from his father, after all.

"Happy birthday, Miss Breckensole," he murmured softly. "Did you and your sister get your gifts?"

She gave him a reproachful glance, marked uncertainty shadowing her expression. "Fishing for praise? I already told you that we did, and I thank you. But surely you know full well it's improper, and we cannot keep them.

"Ah, yes, in the arbor. I forgot." He hitched a shoulder. "No one but you and I know where they came from."

"The seamstress knows," she all but hissed beneath her breath.

"Ah, but she's in London, and doesn't know who they were for."

"You are impossible," she muttered with a little shake of her head, causing her earrings to bob.

"So you've remarked before." From the side of his mouth he whispered, "I didn't know you played the violin."

"I should think there are a great many things you do not know about me, Your Grace," came her equally hushed but acerbic retort. She tilted nearer a fraction. "Cats make me sneeze. I abhor fish of any sort, most especially shellfish, and I don't take milk with my tea. I cannot resist maid of honor tarts, I enjoy long walks and sketching, and I have a distinct dislike for bullies and liars."

Touché, chérie.

"Now do be quiet, Duke. We're being most rude." A censuring sideways glance accompanied that pert comment.

He hid a grin. If any woman could bring him up to mark, if he cared

77

to be brought up to mark that was, it would've been Gabriella Breckensole. Appearances mattered to her. He'd already garnered that truth. Another factor in his favor.

Scarborough's and his sister's fingers whisked back and forth upon the keys, and under cover of the music Max murmured in Gabriella's shell-like ear, "I should like to call upon you tomorrow. To take you for a carriage outing."

So swiftly did she whip her neck to gawk at him, she nearly smacked his head.

Another delighted chuckle threatened to escape. Her strong reaction was sure to have drawn attention, and only sheer will prevented him from turning to see who'd noticed her shock. He didn't want the gossip starting just yet.

Her pretty, pink mouth parted in astonishment, she stared as if he'd sprouted several more noses or eyes or a pecan-sized boil on his chin. The colliding of their gazes proved astonishingly intense, and lingering far too long for propriety, had a surge of sensual awareness slamming into him.

Merde, but if she didn't put him off his stride like no other.

He did venture a swift, casual glance around. As he suspected, a few guests peered at them curiously. With an insouciance he was far from feeling, he affected a mien of ennui, and ever so slowly, focused his attention on the infuriated woman beside him.

The music grew to a frenzy, and she snapped her mouth shut even as green flecks sparked in her eyes once more. She faced forward.

"No."

That was it. No niceties to temper the rejection. No explanation. Just *no*, which revealed she'd erected her battalions once more.

He leaned nearer, staggered at the self-loathing spearing his gut at the moment. He really was a ruthless, bloody cad. "Yes. You will, my dear. Because I have the means to ruin your grandfather, and only you can decide which course I'll take. Utter annihilation or a mite more benevolent bend."

9

Pacing the length of the bridge for at least the seventh time, Gabriella checked her watch. She'd deliberately arrived fifteen minutes early in order to make sure the Duke of Pennington didn't do as he'd vowed last night and call upon her at Hartfordshire Court.

His arrival was sure to send Grandpapa into an apoplexy and Grandmama back to her sick bed. Ophelia, on the other hand, would be agog with curiosity and sure to ask a myriad of questions Gabriella either had no answers for or was unwilling to reveal.

How she despised lying to her grandparents and sister, but this was better. She could discover exactly what the duke schemed and determine what troubles he plotted, and how to best foil his ominous plans.

She swung around and marched back over the cobblestones, the clacking of her sensible half-boots a welcome distraction to the tumultuous thoughts roiling about in her head. Clutching her sketch-pad and pencil case she glowered at the undeserving ground.

Oh, how tempted she'd been to give him a proper set down and cut him as she'd threatened to do, but then thought better of it. It behooved her to stay in his good graces, even if his opinion meant less to her than the terrified mouse that had scrambled across the road a bit ago as she tramped down the drive

Just when she had thought—*hoped*—that perhaps there was a streak of decency in the Duke of Pennington, that she might be able to approach him, and perchance strike a bargain, he'd resorted to heavy-handed tactics once more. Weighty and bitter disappointment fueled her anger. He'd left her with no choice but to agree to see him today. She'd much rather have told him to go bugger the devil.

Stupid. Stupid. Stupid.

The very first thing she'd done upon entering the Twistletons' was to search him out. As if seeing him in person would erase the hours he'd consumed her thoughts. And not just because of his vile intentions.

No, other things kept sifting into her mind: their meeting in the arbor. His strong hands encircling her waist. The almost sensual brush of his thighs cradling her bum as she rode before him. His warm breath caressing her ear as he whispered to her. And his crisp, alluring manly scent which she could still smell if she closed her eyes. And hardest to erase from her memory, his wonderfully, delicious mouth upon hers.

Her lids drifted downward, and with a little start, she popped them wide open again.

She most certainly wasn't indulging in daydreams about the insufferable man or how magnificent he smelled. Or the queer way her body responded to him. Indeed, she was not. She forbade it. The foolish optimism she'd allowed after their meeting in the arbor had evaporated, leaving her disillusioned and all the more distrustful.

Face lifted to the sun's soothing rays, she wrestled her ire and attraction under control. At least the weather had cooperated, and for that small reprieve she was grateful. When she'd declared she was off for a lengthy stroll on this fine spring morning, her sketchpad in hand, no one had quirked so much as an eyebrow. She took frequent walks, often drawing birds and other wildlife she happened upon.

Today, she daren't ask Ophelia to come along as a chaperone, else her sister be pulled into the dishonest charade as well. Besides, her twin had a headache and wanted to recover before having tea with Jessica Brentwood this afternoon. Gabriella had cried off joining them.

Head lowered she gave an unfortunate stone a vicious kick.

One hour.

That was precisely how long she would allow Pennington to explain himself before she demanded that he return her here. It had taken all of her self-restraint not to bolt from the Twistletons' last night. But that would've given rise to gossip, and intuition told her there was already going to be enough tongue wagging. Nearly everyone had seen her reaction, and several of her friends and her sister had questioned her about it when the performances ended and the guests were enjoying the tasty refreshments.

Gabriella had laughed off her response, claiming she'd been startled when the duke revealed he, too, played the violin. It pleased and annoyed her that they had that in common. A smug smile arced her mouth. She'd made sure that tidbit made the rounds. He'd not get off lounging like a great, spoiled cat in the audience next time.

Still, she'd been obligated to sit beside him for the next interminable hour, her mind a cacophony of raucous thoughts and worry and what very well might've been despair. If anyone had asked her impression of a single performance, she couldn't have answered truthfully. Thank God, no one had. Only, she'd bet her best gown, because her startling reactions to Pennington had piqued far more interest than anything she might have had to say about the recital.

Ophelia, on the other hand, had noticed. From the tiny vee pulling her fine eyebrows together, she didn't believe Gabriella's tarradiddle. She'd never been particularly astute at fibbing. Her eyes usually gave her away, as she hadn't mastered the ability to look directly into someone's face and lie through her teeth. Pennington suffered no such qualm, she'd be bound.

But was she so very different? After all, she'd been lying to him for months now, and yet she didn't believe the flaw was a permanent black spot upon her character.

Closing her eyes, she drew in a long, slow breath, counting to ten then reversed the procedure and breathed out slowly, counting to ten again. She repeated this process three times, and on each inhalation and exhalation firmly instructed herself to remain calm and in control. To employ wisdom. To use her wit and intellect. She would—*oh, God, I must*—find a way out of this conundrum.

How, she couldn't conceive.

A trio of ducks emerged from under the bridge, joining another half dozen or so farther along the embankment. Any other day, she would've been eager to sketch them. The crunching of wheels upon gravel alerted her to a vehicle. A smart gig approached from the direction of Chartworth Hall, and even with the sun reflecting off the shiny ebony lacquer, her heart sank impossibly further. The Duke of Pennington tooled the vehicle himself.

Of course he did

Hmm. Eyes narrowed, she tapped her toe. Had the duke anticipated she'd come by herself? He must have, because the gig only accommodated two occupants. She nearly swore aloud, realizing he'd outfoxed her. *Confound it.* She thought *she'd* outwitted him by meeting him on the bridge. She had the most childish urge to stick her tongue out and stomp her foot.

She'd anticipated a coachman or an outrider to observe at least a degree of propriety.

There was nothing for it, however. Pennington would have his say. She'd have hers. And perhaps, just perhaps, an amiable solution might be reached. Truth to tell, she hadn't much hope of that. But it was worth a try, at least. She *must* try. If she didn't punch him in his noble, perfectly straight aristocratic nose first.

Wise to control her fuming temper then, but how he infuriated her. He maneuvered to force her to sit beside him last night and then oh, so smoothly announced that if she refused to accompany him today, he'd proceed with ruining Grandpapa.

That he could turn so cold and mercenary after the kisses they shared, bewildered and wounded her. As he drew the magnificent cream-colored, black-maned mare to a stop, Gabriella didn't even try to conceal her scowl. If she weren't so irritated with the duke, she would've taken a moment to pet the gorgeous creature.

"Good morning, Gabriella." His simple greeting contained warmth, a hint of wariness, and perchance even a tinge of regret.

Giving her his tummy-fluttering smile that no doubt worked to woo other ladies of his acquaintance, he doffed his top hat. After he placed it back upon his midnight hair, he jumped to the ground with agile ease.

Adorned in dove gray trousers, his muscular thighs flexed with the motion. His navy coat strained tight across ridiculously wide shoulders, and she cursed herself for noticing.

Under the brim of his hat, his eyes almost looked the same color. Did their different shades ever bother him? Why did she care? She didn't, of course.

"I must return home within the hour, Your Grace, else my grandparents will become suspicious or worried. I told them I was going for a walk and to sketch." For emphasis, she wobbled her pad and pencils as she eyed the gig knowing full well she wouldn't be able to climb aboard without his assistance.

Gabriella didn't want him to touch her again. Her mind and body reacted in all kinds of silly girlish, foolish ways when he did. She must keep her faculties about her today, for she had but one chance to deter him from whatever he planned to do.

He swept a gloved hand toward the conveyance. "Shall we, then?"

No, we should not.

With a nod, just this side of petulant, she approached the vehicle. He took her pad and pencils and placed them on the seat. With the effortlessness of a man accustomed to physical exertion, he grasped her waist and easily lifted her into the gig.

Determinedly ignoring her frolicking stomach, she gathered her drawing supplies and claimed a spot. She scooted as far away from him as the bench allowed—a whole three inches. Knowing him, he'd probably chosen this conveyance precisely because the seat was so narrow.

The vehicle tipped as he sprang aboard, and after he collected the reins, he gave them a gentle shake and clucked his tongue. "Walk on, Aphrodite."

With a swish of her majestic ebony tail, the mare ambled forward.

He *would* have a mare named after the goddess of fertility. And love. And passion.

Do shut up!

Rather than proceeding toward Colechester, the duke steered the horse into a semi-circle, and headed back toward Chartworth Hall.

Gabriella glanced behind them before facing forward and knitting her brow. She fiddled with the edge of her sketch pad. "Why are we traveling this way? There's more to see in the other direction."

Pennington slid her a sideways look, an undefined smile kicking his mouth up on one side. "Because there's a secluded grove on my estate away from the main house where I am assured we'll have privacy, and no one will overhear us. You know the one. It's across from where I met you the other day."

She wasn't sure whether to be more shocked at his suggestion, infuriated by his brazenness, or worried for her virtue. She chose the latter. Giving a sharp shake of her head, her bonnet's pink ribbons flying around her chin, she drew herself up. "I've already risked my reputation by being alone with you. I shan't accompany you to some clandestine location where any number of things might happen."

The thick arcs of his lashes masking his half-closed eyes, he remained silent for a long, uncomfortable slice of a moment before nodding. "I take your point, Gabriella, but we can hardly have this conversation in the middle of the lane. And I *am* considering your reputation." He had the nerve to flash that cocky smile and wink.

She almost growled in annoyance.

"Besides, lest you forget, we've been alone several times, including the other night. I do believe your sitting before me on the saddle was much more scandalous than this sedate ride or our interlude in the arbor."

Tapping her toes in irritation, a frustrated growl did throttle up her throat, but she firmly squelched it. *Stay calm. Do not let him upset you. This isn't just about you. Think of your family.* Nevertheless, Gabriella struggled for cool composure, only achieving a semblance of poise after inhaling and exhaling to a count of ten.

"Your Grace, I remind you once more." *Gads, but the man could be obtuse.* "I haven't given you leave to use my Christian name. And as for this conversation, does it matter where we have it?" She flung a hand in the air. "You know as well as I that few people travel this track. Furthermore, if you were indeed concerned about my repute, why ever did you kiss me before or arrive in this?" She spread both hands to indicate the conveyance they sat in. On the other hand, a coach might've had a driver, but they'd have been enclosed inside, out of everyone's sight.

Perhaps... Perhaps this was the wiser choice, after all. How that truth vexed her that he'd likely considered that aspect when she had not.

Rather than answer, Pennington continued along the road, little puffs of dust rising with each step the mare took. *By Jupiter.* Did he intend to ignore her?

Anxiety knotted her shoulders and stomach, and she pressed a hand to her middle. Mayhap she should have broken her fast with something more substantial than tea. She wasn't afraid exactly. Not of him, or what he might do to her. He'd had the chance to ravish her on more than one occasion, and except for his scalding kisses and that ear nuzzling business, he hadn't pressed unwanted attentions upon her. Even those didn't count, since she'd enjoyed them.

No, what assailed her now was fear of the unknown. She *knew* he wanted Hartfordshire Court. She also appreciated he wasn't above using any means to obtain the estate. What she didn't know, was what role did she play in his plans? Why did he continue to woo her?

She alternated tapping her feet as the wheels' crunching and soft *clop-clop* of Aphrodite's hooves accented the strained silence between them. A goshawk cried overhead, and a grayish-brown hare, one ear raised in caution, paused in its watchful journey across the grassy meadow. The hawk screamed again, and the hare darted beneath a nearby bush.

Gabriella well knew how the poor creature felt. This weighty silence and anticipating whatever Pennington wanted to say plucked at her tattered nerves like an out of tune violin.

An unladylike snort nearly escaped her at the bad comparison.

"There's a place just a little bit further along where we can stop near the river," Pennington finally said. "It's visible from the road but will allow us a degree of privacy."

Twisting on the seat, she faced him. "I don't understand why you don't just tell me what is on your mind. Last night, you threatened to ruin my grandfather, and I know you're plotting to take Hartfordshire Court from him. I overheard you at the Sutcliffes' house party."

There. Let him make of that what he would. She'd been burning to confront him with the truth for days now. He'd find she was no reticent miss, willing to sit by and watch him destroy her family. She'd not make this easy on him.

A vaguely nonplused look skittered across his face, and she swore red tinged his angular cheeks. "*That's* why your behavior toward me changed," he murmured. Something akin to pain or regret seeped into his tone and glinted in his eyes.

How dare *he* seem hurt? *He* was the one scheming to destroy her family. To take their home. So firmly did she grip her pencil case, her knuckles turned white. Only counting to ten kept her from releasing the full fury of her tongue upon him.

His chest expanded with a deeply drawn breath as he steered the mare off the road and down the mildly sloping meadow to the river. He better not suggest this was difficult for him too. By Jove, she *would* plant him a facer if he even hinted at such a preposterous thing.

Gabriella remained obstinately silent. She'd not absolve him nor would she continue to entreat him to explain himself. A harpy, she was not.

Once the duke had brought the gig to a stop, he cleared his throat, and after removing his hat and gloves and propping them atop one thigh, scraped his long fingers through those dark sable strands. They glinted the merest bit coppery in the sunlight. "I truly regret you overheard that exchange, Gabriella. And even more so, I apologize for the angst you must've endured these past months." Genuine contrition deepened his voice to a mellow purr, and instead of going all prickly as she ought to, Gabriella cursed herself for softening toward him.

Dangerous. Very, very dangerous.

And yet, she had no idea how to respond. She'd expected vehement denials or excuses, not what seemed very much a heartfelt apology. Certainly not that he cared about her feelings or that he felt remorse she'd been worried frantic.

So, she chose boldness and to go on the offensive as the wisest tactic. "Why are you determined to wrest our home from us? What does my accompanying you today have to do with your ruining my grandfather? And pray tell, how could you possibly conceive that I would aid you in any way, knowing what I do?"

He relaxed against the seat and holding his hat and gloves in place, propped one booted foot on the edge of the gig then braced a forearm across his bent knee.

She scowled, steering her avid attention from the interesting bulge at his loins, made prominent by his casual repose. He certainly appeared well-endowed. Mortification consumed her at her wanton thoughts. Why must he appear so dratted manly, so deuced attractive even in this situation?

Maxwell's signet ring glinted in the sunlight as he rubbed his fingertips together. Surely he wasn't anxious as well? He was a duke. *A duke!* A man accustomed to power and privilege. All he had to do was snap his manicured fingers and just about anything he desired was his. The ludicrous concept that *he* was uncertain, bewildered her. She knew him capable of tenderness and kindness. She'd witnessed it and had personally experienced his gentleness.

He stopped fidgeting and laid his hand flat on that absurdly well-formed knee. "I have evidence—indisputable evidence, mind you—that your grandfather cheated my grandfather. Then he blackmailed my grandfather into selling him Hartfordshire Court, which had been my grandmother's familial home for generations."

She choked on a gasp, her gaze flying to his face. "No. That's utterly absurd. Simply not possible." Her sketchpad and pencils slid to the floor as she clasped a hand to her throat. "I don't believe you." Gabriella slowly shook her head.

Don't or cannot? Or...shan't?

An excruciatingly minute inched by before he hitched a shoulder, his gaze trained somewhere beyond the frothing river. "Whether you believe me or not, it is the truth. I have irrefutable proof. As a result of your grandfather's shady dealings, my heartbroken and pregnant grandmother died."

No. No. He fabricated that codswallop. Grandpapa wouldn't. But—

She shook her head again, as much in denial of his words as her unbidden, perfidious thoughts.

"A shattered man, incapable of loving anyone afterward—including my father—my grandfather turned to strong drink and laudanum to numb his pain." A steely harshness rendered his tone clipped and cool. "He grew ever more bitter, unforgiving, and cruel, eventually taking his own life. As often happens when subjected to neglect and unkindness, my father was also given to drink and abuse."

Had Maxwell been mistreated by his father? Is that what he was saying? Did he realize his actions were not so very different than his sire's and grandsire's? A soft cry escaped her. "I…"

"Please, hear me out." His jaw tense, the duke held up a palm. A faint scar marred the flesh from forefinger to thumb.

Unprepared for the sympathy engulfing her, Gabriella swallowed and folded her hands in her lap. She clenched her fingers so tightly, the tips tingled.

He lied. That was all there was to it. He couldn't be telling the truth. He'd concocted this fanciful tale to steal Hartfordshire Court. Naturally, a wealthy duke's word would be believed over a humble land owner.

Her gentle Grandpapa was not capable of this sort of subterfuge. This evilness. This vileness. He simply wasn't.

Was he?

Tears stung her eyes, and she allowed the lids to drift shut as she battled to subdue her shock and grief. She would not give the duke the satisfaction of seeing her defeated and weeping.

"I only learned of this…your grandfather's part, last December," he continued softly. Again, a hint of regret or compassion made his voice rough. "Since then, I've been determined to return Hartfordshire Court to its rightful owners. Although my grandfather signed the deed of sale, the property was never legally transferred." He scrubbed a hand over his jaw. "The duchy has continued to pay the land and window taxes. I've spoken to my steward about that oversight, and he said the previous steward had always paid them, so he assumed he should continue to as well."

"It's not true," Gabriella breathed, barely recognizing her own raggedy, fragile voice. She swallowed again. "It cannot possibly be true." She sounded like a well-trained parrot. But, a person didn't live with someone for fifteen years and not know their character. Grandpapa was not a charlatan.

She wasn't ready to admit defeat yet. What proof could Maxwell have?

"Yes, Gabriella, it is. I swear, every word."

Such gentleness, and yes, even sympathy tempered his words, that tears welled again. Far easier for her to bear if he'd been all haughty, cold, accusing arrogance. *Oh God.* She held herself tightly, rocking forward and back. She didn't want to believe a single word, but it explained so much over the years.

Why her grandfather rarely left Hartfordshire Court. Why he hadn't any friends to speak of. Why Grandpapa held such animosity toward Maxwell.

"What...?" Bile, bitter and hot burned her throat. To have to even ask meant he knew she had doubts. She swallowed and forced the words out. "What proof have you?"

Maxwell took her hand, the action natural and comforting. A loyal granddaughter would've jerked free, railed at him, and rained curses down upon his handsome head. Yet she didn't.

Never before had she felt so fragile, that she might shatter with her next breath. Her whole world crumbled around her, and she was powerless to stop the destruction. To prevent the inevitable devastation this would wreak upon the people she most loved. Gabriella refused to berate herself for her momentary weakness. She was strong, but anyone who'd been dealt such a blow would need time to recover.

"I found my grandfather's journal in a hidden desk drawer. An entry revealed there'd been a card game with marked cards." The duke spoke slowly, his voice neutral, much like a barrister presenting a case before judges. "The entry also included the names of two other men involved. Herman Wakefield died a number of years ago, but my man of business was able to locate Wilson, Baronet Garrison. I've personally spoken with him, and he's provided a sworn statement. As young bucks up from university, a trifle disguised and short on funds, they agreed to vow my grandfather marked the cards in exchange for a few pounds apiece."

Gabriella pinched her lips together. "How do you know this Garrison person is telling the truth, Maxwell?" It occurred to her she'd slipped into using his given name with unnerving ease.

Even if he was lying, why would his grandfather have made such an entry if it weren't true? By their very nature, that was what journals were. A place to share all the secrets one couldn't reveal to the world.

Only the merest movement of his eyes indicated he'd heard her use of his given name. "What reason would he have to do so after all of these years?" He still held her hand. "No, Garrison's sickly and not long for this world. He said he wanted to right a wrong, and swears he had no idea your grandfather later blackmailed my grandfather and obtained Hartfordshire Court as a result."

She pulled her hand free, needing to cover her face and hide the stubborn tears seeping from her eyes. This couldn't be happening. It was impossible. Her grandfather couldn't be that kind of a scoundrel. A cheat. For if he was, then everything she'd known for the past fifteen years was a lie, and the Penningtons were indeed entitled to Hartfordshire Court.

Gabriella had never considered Maxwell might have a legitimate reason for his actions. She'd behaved abominably toward him, and he'd always remained a gentleman. Profound remorse and chagrin turned her cheeks hot.

Did Grandmama know of her husband's duplicity? Is that why she seldom ventured from Hartfordshire either? Had their dishonesty made them prisoners in the very house they'd stolen?

Listen to yourself. Have you so little faith in the people who've cared for you for over fifteen years? Can you so easily put aside your trust? Surely there's a logical explanation.

Lifting her face, she stared at the wildly rushing river. She appreciated how that tumultuous water felt. Tumbling over itself, bashed against the banks and the stones. Having no control over where it went, pushed and pulled along pell-mell.

A silent sigh whispered past her lips just as a crisp, white handkerchief appeared in her line of vision. "Here, *chèrie.*"

"I'm sure you understand that I should like to see the journal and Garrison's statement," she said softly. Guilt riddled her at even speaking the words.

"That can be arranged." No victory or triumph colored his voice. "I plan on presenting them to your grandfather in any event."

After drying her face, she folded his handkerchief and clutching it in one hand, studied her lap. "Why did you tell me this? I'm quite certain there's nothing I can do to prevent you from continuing along the path you've already started." A path he had a right to pursue if what he said was true. She raised her gaze and canted her head, straining to read his indecipherable features. "You spoke of ruin last night."

After wedging his hat and gloves between his thigh and the carriage side, he cupped her cheek. Rather than pulling away as she ought to do, as a woman presented with devastating information about the man who'd raised her was obliged to do, she closed her eyes instead.

And then she was in Maxwell's strong arms, his warm, firm lips kissing her forehead, her eyes, her nose and finally, settling wondrously upon her mouth and tasting of coffee.

The world went silent. Utterly and completely. For certain the river still tumbled along, birds sang in the treetops, and the wind brushed her fingers through the verdant leaves and branches, but Gabriella heard them not. A coach and four might have passed on the road or thunder pealed through the heavens and she'd have heard neither.

And how did she respond to the passionate play upon her lips, the miserable, traitorous wretch that she was?

She looped her arms around his sturdy neck and kissed him back. Kissed him like a drowning woman gasping for air. Kissed him, as if this was the very last day she had to live, and everything she'd kept hidden, had denied even to herself, she could at last reveal, because nothing mattered anymore. And if in the midst of this horror, this nightmare, the imploding of her life, she could seize one tiny particle of happiness then by God, she'd do so.

I deserve it.

Even if Maxwell was the man about to wreak hell itself on her family and destroy everything Ophelia and Gabriella had ever known?

That sobering thought finally brought her to her senses, plunging her back to the awful present, and she jerked away, regret replacing her passion. "Your Grace…"

His breathing raspy, as if he struggled every bit as much as she to bring herself under control, he swiped the tears from her cheeks with his thumbs. Tears she wasn't even aware leaked from her eyes once more.

"Since I aim to marry you, *chérie*, you might as well continue to address me as Maxwell."

10

Whatever reaction Max had expected Gabriella to have, this wasn't it. She laughed. Not a dainty feminine tinkle, but a full on bent over at the waist, gasping for breath, belly laugh. His lips quirked of their own accord at her jubilant chuckles. He'd never seen her unfettered mirth and it was glorious. The reason for it, not as much.

Her focus snapped upward, her eyes going wide as she slapped a hand over her mouth. Her shoulders continued to shake, and the moisture pooling in her eyes now the color of turbulent clouds, was humor-induced. Beneath the straw bonnet shading her face, her beautiful gaze rounded impossibly more with realization.

"You're not serious?" Sobering, she knuckled away the moisture at the corner of her eyes. She leaned away, working her attention over him twice. "Stars above. You *are*. Are you utterly mad?"

Yes, he probably was.

Rather put a man off having his proposal laughed at, but then again, he hadn't exactly proposed in the most romantic way. Nothing about this was meant to be romantic. In fact, he wouldn't call it a marriage proposal at all, but rather bartering terms. She didn't know that yet, however.

Nonetheless, he knew her well enough to realize she wouldn't be pleased at what he said next. Would that he could go back six months, when he first recognized his feelings for Gabriella were more than admiration and attraction. Before he found his grandfather's diary, and Max started them upon this irreversible course.

While he had no doubt she would eventually agree to become his duchess, might even enjoy the physical aspect of their joining, he never believed she'd come to hold him in any regard. Especially after she learned of his terms.

What did that matter?

Most peers married for convenience. For power, position, coin. In this, he wasn't so very different, except that he meant to reclaim that which had been stolen from his family.

Damn his eyes, but a part of him wished it wasn't the reason.

She sat silent, her head slightly angled and her keen gaze still roving his face. Her attention lingered on his lips before flitting away. Was she remembering what had transpired between them but a few minutes ago?

Gabriella was attracted to him. The smoldering kisses they'd shared left no doubt.

He didn't dare ask for more. Didn't deserve more.

He'd chosen this path, perhaps not knowing all the consequences, but fully aware of what he must do. For justice, for righteousness and fairness. To avenge his grandmother, grandfather, and the child—the aunt or uncle he'd never known. And perhaps, part of this was revenge for himself as well.

His grandfather's inability to show kindness or love to his son had made Bronson a victim as well. And Bronson, a stranger to affection, had never learned how to love anyone, let alone his only child. Max had never experienced the love of a parent. Or a grandparent's. Or a sister's or brother's.

For all of his many friends at *Bon Chance*, some he considered as close as brothers and for whom he'd willingly die, no one in the entirety of his life, had ever said they loved *him*. He'd never heard the words, "I love you," directed to him.

He gave a little shake of his head, dispelling his self-pitying musings. This wasn't about him. *Isn't it?*

Perchance, he wasn't so very different than his sire or grandsire, after all. He hadn't expected his duchess would love him any more than he'd ever anticipated being struck by Cupid's arrow. *Ah, but Grandfather had*

94

loved Grandmother. And look where that landed him? Too late for sentiment now, in any event. The die was cast, and there was naught to do but for Max to collect his winnings, no matter how acrimoniously acquired. *What's done is done.*

What an absurd time for Shakespeare to intrude upon his thoughts.

Gabriella had at last brought her chuckling under control, and as she continued to do at every turn, she surprised him once more. Rather than resort to histrionics or become a watering pot, she squared her shoulders and jutted that pert chin upward. "Your Grace—"

"Maxwell or Max, which is what I prefer. Unless you wish to address me as Pennington," he corrected quietly. "But even after seven years, whenever I hear the title, I still expect to glance over my shoulder and see my grandfather standing there."

Her eyebrows shied high on her smooth forehead. In that, she must've decided to concede. To mollify him or simply because it was easier?

"Maxwell, you may have the means to reclaim Hartfordshire Court, and though I'm loath to admit it, I do suspect what you're telling me is, at least, partially true. Nonetheless, I'm certain you can appreciate how devastating this news is. However, and regardless of the outcome, no way exists which will compel me to marry you." She skewed her mouth and crinkled her nose in the adorable way she did when confused or vexed. At least her toes weren't pattering away. *Yet.* "Besides, I fail to understand how one has anything whatsoever to do with the other."

Leaning back, he threaded his fingers together behind his head. This was where she would kick up a dust. Where he could expect recriminations, accusations, and protestations. No displays of emotions would make a jot of difference.

The sun's warmth felt glorious, and despite the impossibility of the situation, he relaxed, almost sliding into a drowsy doze. He hadn't slept last night. Truth be told, he hadn't slept much since deciding on this course of action. Because, despite being an utter arse for what he was about to do, he meant to proceed. His conscience and self-recriminations be damned.

"Maxwell, I need to return ho—that is to Hartfordshire Court." As she spoke, a bold bird landed atop Aphrodite's back and cocking its head, stared at them with curious little ebony eyes. A small smile quirked Gabriella's mouth as she whispered, "Hello there."

The bird took to wing as Max observed her through half-open eyes. "Already decided Hartfordshire isn't home any longer, have you?" He'd never been particularly fond of his childhood home, yet her distress was tangible and regret speared him.

A stricken expression chased her smile away, and angst whisked across her lovely face then was gone. He couldn't help but admire her ability to swiftly compose herself, and neither could he prevent the remorse gripping him that he'd caused her distress.

"Over an hour has passed, and they'll be expecting me," she quietly reminded him.

Gabriella Breckensole had pluck and resilience. She'd accepted the situation and attempted to make the best of it.

"I intend to speak to my grandfather about this matter as soon as I return home, Maxwell. I'm still not convinced your tale is true or accurate."

Her straightforwardness didn't surprise him. Did she truly believe Breckensole, who'd built his entire life on a series of lies, her life and Ophelia's as well, would tell the truth?

Straightening, Max dropped his foot to the coach floor. Hard. "I intend the same thing. But before we go, please listen to my proposal."

Her arched eyebrows crumpled together, and she brushed away an insect that had landed on her pale pink gown. "Is that a marriage proposal or another sort of proposal? For surely, you cannot believe I would marry you after this. Besides, I'm certain you wish a more noble duchess than the granddaughter of a clergyman's disgraced son."

That she could make a quip, given what she'd just learned, impressed him.

Max clenched his jaw and curled his toes in his too-damn tight boots, going over the speech he'd rehearsed so many times in his mind. Speaking the words aloud though, wasn't as easy as he'd anticipated. Saying them made everything all too real. Cruel and heartless.

"Gabriella." He chose to focus on the burbling water rather than her pale face with those too-big accusing eyes. "I intend to tell your grandfather that he, your grandmother, and your sister may continue to reside at Hartfordshire Court—"

"You would do that?" she gasped, clasping his forearm. "Even with what you know?" Wonder filled her voice.

"Don't become too excited or raise your hopes, *chérie*." He cut her a short glance.

She dropped her hand back into her lap, her mouth pursed and hazel gaze accusing.

He focused on a large boulder dividing the river. Far easier to do than witness her reaction. Her disappointment and disillusionment. Perhaps, even her hatred. *When did I become a coward too?*

At the moment, he didn't much like himself and doubted he'd ever do so again.

"I shall insist upon your grandfather offering Hartfordshire Court as your dowry. Through our children, the estate will revert to my family as it should." The idea of this woman carrying his child speared a burst of lust so strong, he had to swallow and shift his position before continuing. "Until such time she weds, Ophelia may either reside with your grandparents or live with us. I shall also permit your grandparents to remain at Hartfordshire until their deaths."

His man of business had done his research. Harold Breckensole had no legal heirs, save Gabriella and her twin. The estate would've passed to them had it been properly transferred.

Gabriella slumped into her seat, disbelief wreathing her face.

"By taking these measures, my family will regain Hartfordshire Court, but your grandparents, and thereby you, and your sister, will be spared the scandal that will ensue if I have to make your grandfather's cheating, blackmail, and tax fraud public. Furthermore, since the duchy has paid Hartfordshire's taxes all these years and the estate is still registered in my family's name, this is the wisest recourse." He pulled on his gloves, giving her time to digest what she'd just heard.

Putting two fingers to her temple, she rubbed them in a circular motion and began tapping her toes in that familiar cadence. "Can't you simply have a written agreement with my grandfather that upon his and my grandmother's deaths, the property reverts back to you? Or is that even necessary?" She scrunched her nose. "According to you, the deed was never transferred. Could we not just pay rents?"

Yes, he could permit Breckensole to remain and let Hartfordshire Court, but he doubted the man had the funds. The matter of the back taxes must be addressed as well. There was no way on God's green earth Breckensole hadn't known he wasn't paying his taxes. The blasted deed of sale was also an issue.

Max's solicitor had warned if they went to court over the matter, there was a small—very small—chance the document might be enforceable. As if things weren't complicated enough, even if it turned out Breckensole legally owned Hartfordshire Court despite the manner in which he'd gained the estate, he owed decades of taxes plus interest to the duchy.

Funds, Max knew full well, Breckensole didn't have and had absolutely no hope of acquiring. In essence, the taxes were a lien upon the estate. And what was more on point, he wasn't feeling at all charitable. He wanted Breckensole to suffer. Wanted him to suffer the way his grandfather and grandmother had suffered. The way his father had suffered.

The way *he* had suffered.

What he didn't want, damn his eyes, was for Gabriella to suffer too. The only way that wouldn't happen is if he was a bloody magnanimous saint and forgave the whole debacle. Resentment welled, and his gut cramped. That he couldn't do. Wouldn't do.

Breckensole didn't deserve the reprieve.

"Couldn't we, please?" she all but pleaded, placing her small hand on his forearm again.

Max understood what it took this regal woman to put aside her pride and utter those words. To beg. She didn't grovel for herself, but for her family, as he'd known she would. Her sacrifice heaped more coals upon his already guilty conscience.

He shook his head before donning his hat. "It's not possible. My desire is to avoid gossip and a scandal. There's been enough of that in recent years, tarnishing the dukedom."

Damn my duchy and my family's reputation. Some things, Gabriella and her wishes, are more important than my bloody good name and repute.

So expressive were her eyes, he could practically read her thoughts tripping about in her mind. "I've already had my solicitor draw up an agreement," he advised without looking in her direction again, for his resolve wavered. "I also have a special license. And as soon as the contract is signed between your grandfather and me, you and I shall be married. *If* that's the route you decide you want to take." Bringing his attention back to her, he ran his gaze over her face.

Ire flared in her bright eyes and color flushed her cheeks.

God, she was absolutely glorious when riled..

"This is more about revenge and retribution than it is about restoring Hartfordshire Court to your family." She jabbed a finger at his chest. "You've taken up someone else's offense as your own, and while part of me understands your anger, the solution you've arrived at is ludicrous."

"Gabby—"

Making a curt gesture with her hand, she scowled. "Have you truly convinced yourself that by forcing me to marry you, you're being benevolent? Everything you've suggested can be done without us resorting to nuptials. It seems you intend to be as cruel as your father and grandfather," she scoffed. "The apple doesn't fall far from the tree, does it?"

Her accusation stinging, he leveled her a thunderous scowl. Wasn't she taking up her grandfather's cause? But there was a tangible difference. She protected the living, whilst he wanted to exonerate the dead.

She gave a short, caustic, entirely humorless laugh, the harsh sound lancing his soul. "And to think, more fool me, at one time I believed myself enamored of you."

The fool doth think he is wise, but the wise man knows himself to be a fool.

More ill-timed Shakespearian wisdom?

The next thing he knew, he'd start recalling Bible verses, which would, in truth, not be so very astonishing as one of his overly zealous tutor, Mr. Fogart, had made Max write verses for the merest infraction. For instance, substituting molasses for ink or flavoring the lemonade with vinegar. He'd been made to write, "The student is not above the teacher" from Luke, no less than five hundred times for placing ants in the man's bed.

At one time, I believed myself enamored of you.

Of all the things she just said, the truth, she'd unhesitatingly hurled at him, that bit was what reverberated in his mind. It stirred what he heartily hoped was not doubt or misgivings at this late juncture.

Arms folded in a defensive posture, she tilted her head. The breeze caught the pink ribbons of her bonnet and sent them fluttering. "Tell me, Maxwell. Why me and not Ophelia?"

"I think, *chérie,* you already know the answer to that."

"Stop calling me that," she snapped, giving his shoulder a hard punch. "And I do *not* know the answer, else I wouldn't have asked. Please do enlighten me. I cannot wait to hear what rubbish you concoct." She really was a tart-mouthed minx. Most excellent. Such fortitude would be useful and sustain her going forward.

"There's been a powerful attraction between us since we first met, Gabriella. Tell me it doesn't call to you as it does me."

She snorted, loudly and indelicately. "Ballocks, you vain popinjay."

Max checked a delighted chuckle. She'd truly kick up a fuss if he dared laugh at her frustration.

"God knows, I've tried to fight it, resist the draw." He drummed long square-tipped fingers atop his thigh. "Especially when I learned of your grandfather's treachery." Shrugging again, he gathered the reins. "I know you won't believe this, and I don't expect you to, but I rather think we would march along well. I had intended to call upon your grandfather to ask if I might pay my addresses before this ugliness came to light."

Not that old Breckensole would've consented with the history Max now knew existed between the families.

For once at a loss for words, she simply stared. Inhaling a ragged breath, she touched the shoulder she'd just clobbered. A thrill bolted through him. Even now, when he was at his worst, when he'd delivered such ugly information to her, the merest touch sent his lust soaring.

"Maxwell, you don't have to do this. I'm sure we can come to another solution." Looking lost, she glanced around, blinking almost as if surprised to see where she was. "My family can... we can move. Go somewhere else."

No. I don't want you to leave.

He'd considered that option for all of one second before dismissing the idea. It wouldn't deliver the outcome he desired. "Where? And live on what? You have no source of income. Do you have relatives you might impose upon?"

"No."

The single syllable said much. The Breckensoles had nowhere to turn. No place to go. No one to take them in. He made an I-suspected-as-much-sound in the back of his throat.

"The way I see it, there are three options." He lifted his forefinger. "I take your grandfather to court for fraud, blackmail, and tax evasion. He'll spend the remainder of his life in prison, and you, your sister, and your ailing grandmother would be left to deal with the ensuing disgrace and would end up on the street."

She notched her chin upward, clearly not the least impressed with her first choice. "The other options?"

He held up a second finger. "Your grandfather agrees to destroy the deed of sale, pays monthly rents, and repays the taxes that the dukedom has paid on his behalf for decades. Mind you, we're talking thousands of pounds." He steeled his facial features and his emotions against her tiny, distressed gasp. "We both know he doesn't have those kinds of funds nor can he lay his hands on them."

No friends or family stood in the eaves ready to lend him a hand, a factor that played to Max's advantage.

He raised his ring finger. "Or three—"

"I marry you," she said very softly, her voice a mere whisper. "And my grandfather dowers me with Hartfordshire Court. Which, you must own, is just plain stupid since you claim the estate belongs to you anyway."

"It saves a great deal of complication and public scandal, which I'd prefer to avoid," he said. "I can only presume you would as well for yourself and your family's sake."

The silence lengthened, stretching out before them, tense and uncompromising. Finally, she released a wispy sigh. "You'll allow my family to live at Hartfordshire without paying rents? No taxes due? No possibility of eviction?" She flicked three of her fingers up.

Then a fourth levered upward

The little vixen. Had to outdo him, didn't she?

"And my grandfather continues grazing his cattle on the property without any fee or a partial commission to you when they are sold? And…"

Her thumb sprang up.

Five bloody conditions? Damn, but he'd underestimated her negotiating skills.

Her chin notched skyward another inch. "You'll also provide Ophelia a ten-thousand-pound dowry."

Astonishment jerked Max's head up, but after a moment of staring into her wounded gaze, nearly drowning in the fathomless depths, he gave a terse nod.

She'd added terms he hadn't considered and not a single request had been for herself.

Nonetheless, he had no qualms with her provisions. If it brought her peace of mind and helped her to feel like she had a measure of control, so be it.

"As you very well know, you could grant every one of those conditions now if you wished to. Not the dowry for Ophelia of course, but all of the rest." Though her face was alabaster pale, she met his gaze unflinchingly.

By God, she was brave. A remarkable woman, indeed.

"I could. But Harold Breckensole doesn't deserve that kind of grace or forgiveness. And knowing one of his beloved granddaughters had to sacrifice herself, because of his selfishness, will eat away at him for the rest of his days." He couldn't prevent the rancor edging each clipped word.

Just as losing Grandmother had gnawed at Grandfather.

"You are a cruel man, Maxwell." Something akin to profound disappointment along with resignation and no small amount of resentment shone in Gabriella's eyes. "You would do well to remember, that someday, you will stand before God, and you'll be judged as harshly as you have judged others. You'd best pray the day never comes that *you* need forgiveness."

Too late.

Max flexed his jaw. Yes, he was cruel. He'd learned about cruelty firsthand. As for the other? Well, wasn't it true that those who'd committed wrongs were usually the first to demand forgiveness and often quoted scripture to enhance their manipulation? He suspected though, he might very well end up as miserable as his sire and grandsire.

"Which is it to be, Gabriella?" Hands on the reins, he spared her a short glance from the side of his eye. "The choice is yours."

"No, it's not. It's never been mine." She gave a fragile, broken laugh. "I shall grow to hate you. You know that, don't you? Anything that may have turned into warmth or affection, any desire I may now have for you, bitterness and resentment will eventually corrode into loathing. If you insist upon this path, are you prepared for a life every bit as miserable as that of your father's and your grandfather's?"

"I know what I'm doing," he bit out, not at all pleased to have his thoughts read and vocalized.

She pressed on, relentless in *her* judgment. "You're making me pay the penalty for a crime that wasn't mine. My only sin is being Harold Breckensole's granddaughter. Something I have no control over whatsoever. You, however, do have a choice whether you choose to forgive or carry a grudge. I'm not saying you and yours weren't wronged, or that if my grandfather is guilty, there shouldn't be recompense, but this…"

"It is what a duke would do. What he does for his duchy and family," Max ground out.

She flicked a hand between them. "I vow you will come to regret it, and if this is what a duke would do, then I am very much glad I was born a commoner."

They'd reached the road, and the gig jostled her against him as the vehicle crested the low embankment. They rode in strained silence until the bridge came into view, and Max slowed Aphrodite once more. He turned to look straight into Gabriella's eyes, the anguish there, the accusation and condemnation, stabbing him to his core like a rusty two-sided sword.

Yet, it wasn't enough to put aside the vengeance that had burned inside him for months. How could he just let it go? Forgive the offense? The treachery? A better man might be able to, but then again, he'd never claimed to be a good man. Dutiful, loyal, well-mannered, the epitome of *haut ton* refinement, honest, and on occasion given to mirth and benevolence.

But never good.

"What's it to be then, Gabriella?" He used the same tone he used to soothe a skittish horse. "Which of the three do you choose, because as you said the sin is not yours? So you will make this decision. Not me. Not your grandfather or your grandmother or your sister. You."

Snorting, she shook her head, her disgust palpable. "As if any of them have appeal." Her eyes drifted closed for a moment, and she released a ragged sigh, her cheeks puffing out slightly with the exhalation. "You've given me no alternative, and you well know that. Since I must pick, as you knew I would, I select the third option."

Max gave a curt nod, at once exalting in the small victory and also grieving for the wound he'd inflicted on this gentlewoman. She wasn't deserving of this. She was a pawn and he'd used her unforgivably for vengeance. This doublemindedness would likely drive him mad. He hopped to the ground and allowed himself a moment to bring his chaotic thoughts under control before striding to her side and lifting his arms to help her down.

She stared at his hands, indecision whisking across her refined features. He had no doubt she wanted to tell him to go to the devil—was actually surprised she already hadn't.

Still, they would be man and wife. And damn it all, he'd treat her with the dignity and respect a duchess deserved, because that's what a duke did, as he'd told her. A duke took care of his dukedom. His family. Of the people entrusted to his care. Of his lands, village, tenants, and servants, and God knew the Pennington Duchy had long, *long* been neglected.

Dukes don't destroy young women's hopes and futures.

At last, she permitted him to assist her from the conveyance. Head held high, and shoulders squared, she met his gaze directly. "I'll explain to my family what has occurred. You may come for dinner at seven."

He lifted his hat and canted his head in a brief bow. "I shall be there."

"But know this, Your Grace."

He didn't miss the deliberate cool politeness she'd reverted to.

"I shall never come to your bed willingly. *Never.* You'll have to force me each and every time we copulate if you want your heirs." A miserable smile pulled her soft mouth upward. "I wonder, in a decade or two, if you'll still think your revenge was worth it."

Hell, he was beginning to doubt it even now. Though he knew it was her anger speaking, he could no more violate his sweet Gabriella than pluck the sun from the sky or dam the ocean. Seduction, though… Her kisses told him, she desired him too. "Gabriella?" He touched her cheek, but she flinched away, her expression hard and gaze frosty.

"I'll not succumb to your seductive wiles anymore, Duke."

She meant it. The magical kisses they'd shared would be the only affection he'd ever receive from her. From anyone. She spun on her heel and took several strides before swinging back to face him, utter devastation ravaging her lovely features.

"I could have loved you, Maxwell," she said on a sob before running down the drive.

Tears pricked his eyes.

I could have loved you too, my darling Gabby.

11

One glimpse of Gabriella's face when she returned from her outing with the Duke of Pennington, and Ophelia dragged her to her bedchamber. With a swift glance up and down the corridor, she closed the door then spun to face her twin, demanding an explanation.

"Gabby, whatever has happened? You were gone for nearly two hours, and you appear as if... Well... I'm not certain exactly what you look like except there is a haunted glint in your eyes that frightens me." Three neat lines appeared on her forehead, and she wrinkled her nose, staring pointedly at Gabriella's empty hands. "And where are your sketch pad and pencils?"

"Botheration." Gabriella groaned as she untied her bonnet wishing she might speak the foul oath on the tip of her tongue. "I left them in the duke's gig."

Ophelia stopped fussing with the fringe of the pillow she'd picked up and went poker stiff. "Perhaps you should explain from the beginning, because I believe I just heard you say, your drawing supplies were in the duke's gig. I presume you refer to the Duke of Pennington?"

Something in Gabriella's expression must've given her away for Ophelia tossed aside the pillow and said, "Yes, just as I presumed. But you told me you were going for a walk and to sketch, and you do not, in general, dissemble."

"I lied." No sense in prevaricating about it. She had, and from her sister's astonished expression, she'd deduced more was afoot. No one could ever mistake Ophelia for a bacon brain. "But I assure you, dearest, I had an exceptionally good reason for doing so."

Trying to save her family from utter ruin and a madman's vengeance. She'd failed. No, not entirely, she hadn't. She'd protected her family, but at a cost most dear.

Gabriella dumped the bonnet on her dressing table, avoiding glancing in the mirror as she reached to unfasten her spencer. "How is your headache? Aren't you to leave for Jessica's soon?"

"My headache is gone, but dear Jessica has a megrim now," Ophelia said. "A note came while you were out. We've rescheduled for next week." Impatience fairly radiating off her, and arms akimbo, Ophelia drummed her fingertips on her hips. "What's this explanation for lying, for I've never known you to flat out fib before?"

More of the duke's unsavory influence.

Gabriella was aware turmoil roiled in her eyes and also that her lips might be the merest bit rosy from that extraordinary kiss. Hopefully, her sister would credit her countenance to the blustery weather.

After removing her spencer and gloves, she sank onto the mattress, completely drained. Not surprising since her life had just been toppled teapot handle over spout. Once she'd reconciled herself to what she must do, a peculiar sort of peace had enveloped her. Rather, a numbness that enabled her to function in a sort of hazy, incredulous cloud.

As succinctly as possible, she shared the dismal tale, somewhat amazed at her ability to do so without collapsing into a weeping blob of hysteria. She judiciously omitted the part about the scintillating kisses. Of everything that had occurred, this last kiss made the least sense. How could she have responded so wantonly? How could she have permitted a knave of his caliber such liberties?

Not fair, her conscience scolded. She couldn't place all the blame for that intimate interlude on his shoulders. Not when their previous kisses had made her eager—hungry—for his embrace. She'd enjoyed the experience far too much, and as furious as she presently was with him, feared her declaration about sharing a bed might've been incensed bluster. She'd all but melted into his arms with little provocation.

True, but that was before he'd shown his hand, and she'd seen what an immoral lout he truly was. She mightn't have any control over these circumstances, but she could withhold her affection and passion. "So, you see, Fee Fee, there's naught else to be done but for me to wed the duke."

Her twin's jaw dropped open, and her hazel eyes so like Gabriella's rounded in incredulity before the irises almost disappeared as she narrowed her eyes into wrathful slits.

"Oh, my God. Oh, my *God!* The churl. The fiend. The…the…reprehensible, scapegracing bastard." Ophelia's voice jumped an octave on the last word, and she, too, plopped unceremoniously onto the bed. "Gabby, you cannot—*simply cannot!*—marry Pennington under these wretched circumstances. Why, it amounts to nothing short of extortion."

It did indeed. And in Gabriella's mind, that made Maxwell no better than Grandpapa. Worse, for she held no affection for the duke. *Keep telling yourself that and perchance you'll come to believe it.* Teeth clamped until they ached, she squashed the intrusive thought. She wasn't one to mistake feminine lust and curiosity for something more meaningful.

She grabbed another floral pillow and plunking the soft square on her lap, plucked at the silky gold fringe. "There isn't any alternative. If Grandpapa is guilty, and I fear he very well might be, I cannot allow him to go to prison for the rest of his life. He's old and frail and would die within months.

"Nor would I ever consider permitting you and Grandmama to be put out of your home. I suppose we ought to appreciate the duke allowing me any choice at all. He might've booted us to the curb and seized all without consideration."

All outraged sisterly protector, Ophelia snuffled loudly and scrubbed at her damp cheeks. "And here I believed Pennington a decent, chivalrous sort. I even suspected you held a *tendre* for him. I would never have believed him capable of such vileness. Oh, my darling sister, I cannot bear it. I simply cannot comprehend that you would even consider making such a sacrifice." She punched her pillow. "God rot the blackguard. If I were a man, I'd call him out."

Now there was a lovely thought. A duel at dawn. Fisticuffs at four? Swords at six? Sabers at seven? Gabriella snorted at her own absurdity.

What would the pompous, self-righteous Duke of Pennington do if she challenged him to an affair of honor? Had such a thing ever been done? A woman demanding satisfaction? Not with a man, though there were a few isolated instances of women dueling other women.

He wouldn't accept of course. A duke most certainly wouldn't concede to duel with a woman. And most definitely not a lady very nearly his affianced. Oh, what a succulent treat that would be for the gossip rags. What that wouldn't do to his efforts to keep everything hush-hush.

Mayhap she'd pen a letter or two *or ten* to the most notorious of the tattle magazines.

No, she wouldn't. Because it wasn't only his name and reputation that would be dragged through the filth. She stopped fiddling with the fringe and shot a frantic glance to her bedchamber door.

Dear God, Grandpapa wouldn't do something so rash as to demand satisfaction, would he? Did he even own a blunderbuss or a blade of any sort except for kitchen and garden utensils?

Flopping onto her back, she stared at the familiar, pleated fern-green canopy. "The duke is coming to dinner at seven tonight. I must talk to our grandparents beforehand. It will be horridly awkward when he arrives." She turned her head, reaching for her sister's hand. "He wants us wed straightaway, as if he almost fears Grandpapa will contrive a way to save Hartfordshire Court. Though, I confess, if all that Pennington said is true, I cannot conceive it."

"Neither can I," Ophelia whispered, her voice breaking. "This is awful beyond belief."

Biting her lower lip, Gabriella closed her eyes for a blink. "Maxwell is ruthless and unforgiving, Fee Fee. He cannot be reasoned with. God knows I tried. I really, truly tried."

And he was absolutely undeterred in his quest for retribution.

"No. It's unthinkable. You cannot bind yourself to such a monster." Ophelia thumped the mattress with her fist. "Grandpapa shan't permit it. You'll see. There must be an alternative."

"I'm of age now," Gabriella reminded her quietly. "The decision is mine to make."

Her twin shook her head vehemently. Several pins came loose, and tendrils of hair tumbled to her shoulders. She put a shaky palm to her forehead. "I fear what the shock will do to our grandparents."

Gabriella's exact concern.

Swallowing, she dipped her chin in a nod. "I've the same worry, and that's why my mind is made up. Trust me when I tell you, Pennington has thought of everything. He provided me with three options, and I've selected the least dire. This way, I am assured you and our grandparents won't suffer from his wrath. You'll still have a home, and the duke is willing to cancel the tax debt grandpapa owes the duchy. In truth," she gave a raspy, unhappy chuckle, "I suppose there is a degree of benevolence in this particular solution."

She doubted the verity of the words even as she murmured them.

Ophelia snorted and launched the pillow across the room. "Ballocks. He's a selfish blackguard for reclaiming Hartfordshire Court and entrapping you. I'll bet my best bonnet, you're what he's been after all along."

Even if nothing was further from the truth, Gabriella adored her sister for the suggestion.

"The knave knew you were beyond him," Ophelia insisted, torturing the poor coverlet with her nails. "That he was undeserving of someone as wonderful as you, so he resorted to nefarious means to claim your hand."

Genuine amusement caused Gabriella's burst of laughter. "Oh, Fee Fee, come now. The duke can have his pick of any number of women. A penniless commoner most assuredly does not top his list of eligible ladies. Rest assured, I never set my cap for him, and there's no danger of a broken heart."

He'd already shattered the organ to fragments. She doubted she'd be capable of feeling anything romantic for a very long time.

If ever again.

"Hmph." Arms crossed, Ophelia glared moodily at the canopy. "Our maternal great-grandfather was an Italian count. That ought to amount to something. And I don't believe you when you say, you've no interest in Pennington. I'm your twin, remember. I *know* you. You did entertain warm feelings for him."

"I'll warrant, I found him charming when we returned from finishing school." Intriguing and exciting too. "I was also struck by his good looks and humor, and prior to learning he intended to take Hartfordshire Court from us, I may have engaged in silly schoolgirl notions. But that's all they were. In any event, I have since discovered that a handsome face can hide a blackguard's heart."

As she spoke the words, Gabriella knew them to be false. But if the untruth eased Ophelia's worry a jot, she'd keep vowing to feeling nothing for Maxwell but enmity.

I could have loved you. Those words replayed in her mind, a relentless mantra of what would never be. She could have loved him. Might've been well on the way to doing so. But not now. She wouldn't permit the tender emotion to grow and bloom. Not when he forced her into a union.

He'd have his duchess, all right. A frigid, hardhearted harridan of his creation brought about by the reprisal he demanded. She'd make sure he was as miserable as she, and there'd be no more willing kisses or anything else. Perchance, she'd stipulate they didn't reside in the same house.

Mouth pursed, she blew out a wobbly sigh before sitting up. Not only would she hate Maxwell, in time, she feared she'd come to despise herself too. For it wasn't her nature to be vindictive and unforgiving.

She peered over her shoulder at her twin.

Ophelia sat up, but her face remained twisted in indignation as she worried her lower lip.

"Will you come with me to talk to Grandmama and Grandpapa? I don't think I can approach them with these ugly allegations alone." Cowardliness was foreign to Gabriella. Nonetheless, assertions such as these…Well, they weren't easy accusations to make. "I feel an absolute traitor," she confided. "I know beyond a doubt, it will break their hearts, and neither is as strong as they once were."

At once, Ophelia pulled her into a fierce embrace. "Of course, dearest. Of course I shall. You may think there's no other recourse but for you to marry Pennington, but I'm not ready to quit the field quite yet. Perhaps Grandpapa has an explanation or a remedy. Mayhap there's a way out of this conundrum that you haven't thought of."

"Such as?" There was no way out.

Waggling her winged eyebrows, Ophelia gave a wicked wink. "What about poison in his wine? Loosening his saddle's girth? A fall down the stairs?"

"Shall I bring the shovel, or will you?" Permitting a rueful smile, Gabriella gathered her scattered thoughts and emotions. "Let me freshen up, and we'll go below. Pray to God the shock doesn't overwhelm our grandparents."

12

Fifteen minutes later, Gabriella had settled comfortably in the parlor, her favorite room at Hartfordshire Court. The sun shone through a beveled-leaded glass window, adorning the chamber in a myriad of miniature rainbows. A hearty fire snapped and popped in the hearth framed by a carved mahogany mantel. The outdated furnishings, intended for comfort rather than to impress, gave the chamber a welcoming ambiance.

As she curled her legs beneath her in her usual corner of the blue and gold-striped brocade sofa opposite the fireplace, she examined the room with a fresh eye.

She'd read dozens, probably hundreds, of books in this very spot. Birthdays and Christmastide had been celebrated here as well. She still remembered being a frightened five-year-old and her grandmother's soft arms embracing her as she whispered soothing, reassuring words in her ear despite her own grief at having lost her son and daughter-in-law so tragically.

Now Gabriella's newfound knowledge tainted the comforting room. Had the house been furnished when Grandpapa acquired the estate? If not, where had the funds to purchase the furnishings and everything else in the house come from? What about the monies to send her and Ophelia to school? To buy their clothing? Did the sale of the cattle truly provide enough capital to live on?

Were there more dark secrets yet to be revealed?

So much doubt plagued her when once there'd been absolute trust. She wanted to shout at the unfairness, but histrionics and emotional outbursts served no purpose. She'd seen the unyielding granite hardness of Maxwell's jaw. Recognized the flinty ruthlessness in his steely gaze. He was a man bent on vengeance.

Come hell or highwater.

That was what he'd vowed months ago, and he'd kept his word.

True, it was beyond her comprehension to understand the kind of hatred and animosity that motivated a man to go to the extremes for revenge that he had. But she had been raised in a loving home with caring grandparents, whereas he'd never known kindness or affection. While it was true her grandfather was reluctant to part with his coin, she and her sister had never lacked for essentials, including love.

Sorrow pinched her heart, and she blinked away the sting of hot tears. Had this life been based on a lie? Was all of this, she glanced around the cozy room once more, a lie too?

Despite the robust fire, a shiver skittered down her spine. Just how soon did Maxwell expect the wedding ceremony to take place? Three months ago, she would've been over the moon to think she'd gained the attention of a much-sought after gentleman. A man who'd captivated her since their first meeting.

He'd been right about their mutual attraction, though she'd chew shoe leather rather than confess such idiocy to him. There had been something sparking and sizzling between them before he trampled it unmercifully on this path of retribution.

Bearing a tea tray, Ophelia entered, followed by their grandmother, looking much recovered from her bout of ill-health. Her silver-threaded hair twisted into a tidy knot at the back of her head, Grandmama wore her gray gown trimmed in burgundy braid today.

Once Ophelia placed the tray on the low tea table, she promptly set about pouring the fragrant brew. Ah, new tea leaves, and even two kinds of biscuits. A rare treat indeed.

Gabriella caught her sister's eye and sent her an appreciative smile.

A moment later, Grandpapa shuffled into the parlor. Purplish half-moon shadows darkened the skin below his eyes and weariness etched his beloved face, deepening the many craggy creases. Almost three and seventy, he'd aged much this past year. He'd lost weight too.

Did the secrets and guilt he bore haunt him? Rob him of sleep and peace and his appetite? Well, at least he'd be able to rest easier now, once the truth was aired. Secrets ate away at a person. Gabriella would've preferred to have this ugliness kept hidden, despite the cathartic effect of confessing.

"What's this?" He motioned toward the tea service, in the tiniest hint of disapproval at the extravagance. "New tea leaves and *two* types biscuits," his taut eyebrows said.

"Shush, Harold," Grandmother admonished gently. "We didn't have a birthday celebration for the girls. I think they're deserving of an extra dainty."

He harrumphed but helped himself to a ginger biscuit. "You asked to speak to your grandmother and me, Gabriella?" Wearing the same faded walnut-brown suit he'd donned for years, he assumed his usual place in the parlor, the wingback chair angled slightly away from the fireplace and which afforded him the window light as well.

With an unexpectedly grateful smile, he accepted the cup Ophelia handed him. Once Grandmama had her tea and a Shrewsbury biscuit in hand, her sister picked a seat on the sofa beside Gabriella.

His bald pate shining from the fire's and the sunlight's reflection, Grandpapa quirked a wiry gray eyebrow. "Well, what has you both looking like you have a case of the blue devils? Did a beau fail to pay you proper attention last evening?" He straightened, his faded gaze flicking between the twins. "I say, did something untoward occur at the music party last evening?"

Gabriella hid a wince. He couldn't know.

Before she could answer, he turned his faded gaze on Grandmama. "We'd best send a chaperone along from now on, Irene." *Who? The maid of all work?* "We wouldn't want the chinwags targeting our girls."

Our girls. Yes, she and her sister had been their girls for these past fifteen years, and Gabriella hadn't a doubt what she was about to say

115

would crush her grandparents. Either because they revealed the truth, or because she mistrusted them enough to put forth the harsh questions.

Summoning her resolve, she wrapped both hands around the teacup, savoring the warmth. She hadn't realized how chilled she'd become. Could it be that bitterness had already begun to turn her heart cold? Could resentment truly do so that swiftly? A shiver tip-toed across her shoulders at the wretched thought.

God, what a miserable future she faced.

Yes, but my family will be secure.

With a boldness that astounded her, she lifted her head and peered squarely into her grandfather's eyes. "Grandpapa, the Duke of Pennington claims he has evidence that you cheated his grandfather at cards and blackmailed the sixth duke into selling you Hartfordshire Court." She rushed on before he could interrupt. "Pennington will join us for dinner at seven of the clock tonight. He's demanding you settle Hartfordshire on me as a dowry and that I marry him to keep the scandal quiet."

The shattering of china wrenched a gasp from Ophelia. "Grandmama!"

Gabriella's attention flew to her grandmother. Pale as death, Grandmama held a quaking hand over her mouth as she stared aghast at her husband of almost five-and-forty years.

"I told you it was too great a risk, Harold," she whispered hoarsely. "I *told* you."

His jaw stiff and eyebrows forming a harsh vee, Grandpapa set his teacup down. It rattled and clanked, sloshing tea over the rim into the saucer. Shoulders slumped, chin tucked to his chest, he covered his eyes with one gnarled hand.

It's true.

God above, was *everything* Maxwell claimed true?

By the reaction of her beloved grandparents, a great deal of what she'd suggested must be. Hands shaking, she set her teacup down too. More from a need to do something, she rose and after tossing a serviette upon the puddle of tea, gathered the broken china and set the pieces atop the table.

She mopped up the tea as best she could, the whole while a righteous anger she didn't know she could feel toward her grandparents burgeoned in her middle. The emotion welled ever higher and higher until she climbed to her feet and whispered accusingly, "How could you have done something so despicable? Didn't you consider the long-term consequences?"

Tears sliding down her papery cheeks, Grandmama shook her head and fumbled for the handkerchief in her sleeve. "He did it for me. Everything was for me."

Struggling for control, Gabriella slowly sank upon the sofa's arm. "Grandpapa cheated at cards and blackmailed the sixth Duke of Pennington for you? I do not understand—"

"May he burn in hell," Grandpapa snarled. "I'd cheat him again, and I'd blackmail him again too. I'd do it over and over and over a thousand times for what that devil put Irene through." He pointed a shaking finger at his wife. "She was the duchess's companion, and that spawn of Satan forced himself upon her."

Gabriella felt every bit of color leave her face as a peculiar iciness and a wave of light-headedness engulfed her. She exchanged a horrified glance with her twin, and could see her own shock reflected in her sister's eyes. "Are you saying...?" Oh God, Gabriella could barely form the foul words. "That he took *liberties* with Grandmama, and that's why you cheated at cards and blackmailed him?"

"That's precisely what I'm saying." Bitterness dripping from each word, he slouched in his chair, looking old and defeated and feeble beyond description. "A peer always escapes justice for his crimes. Nevertheless, by God, I made certain that Benedict, the inglorious sixth Duke of Pennington paid a price."

"But," she blurted, scarcely able to comprehend what she'd heard. "He was married. In fact, that's one of the reasons the current duke is so angry. He claims his grandfather resorted to drink and laudanum after his wife died. He blames you for her death and that of their unborn child as well. Possibly the spare heir."

"Horseshit!" Grandpapa banged both fist upon the chair's arms, then slammed them down again. "That's utter horse. Shit."

117

The women gasped in unison. Grandpapa didn't curse in the presence of ladies.

"Pennington had a penchant for opium and drink long before I took advantage of his vices," he practically growled. "His poor wife died of a broken heart, because the bastard swived anything in skirts. Whether the woman was willing or not."

"Harold," Grandmama cautioned, her face and posture radiating her unease. "The girls…"

"Nay, I'll not temper my speech. Neither of the twins is a wilting flower." Grandpapa jabbed his thumb toward his wife. "Your grandmother wasn't the first, or the last woman he forced himself on. I've no doubt he raped the duchess too."

Surely Maxwell had no knowledge of this…ghastliness. Fighting the nausea swirling in her belly, Gabriella pressed her fingers between her eyes. "But the duke found his grandfather's journal. It speaks of two other men involved in the card game and how upset the duchess was when her familial home was lost."

Grandpapa sat back and folded his hands over his stomach. He nodded gravely but without a hint of remorse. "'Tis true Hartfordshire was the duchess's ancestral home. I have no compunction about admitting I wanted to inflict as much misery on Pennington as he'd caused your grandmother and me. I do regret the duchess's sorrow. She was a kind woman deserving of some happiness."

"Indeed, she was," Grandmama's soft voice intruded, her eyes slightly unfocused as she gazed blindly out the window to the charming, sundrenched flower garden. These memories obviously distressed her greatly. "You see, my darling girls, Harold and I were betrothed. And after Pennington…" She dragged in a juddery breath. "Well, after he defiled me," she dabbed at her eyes again, "I found myself with child."

"Dear God," Ophelia cried, hurrying to crouch before her grandmother's knees. "How awful it must've been for you all these years as that family is our nearest neighbors."

"Yes, indeed," Grandmama acknowledged. "Which is why we've stayed so close to home. After a few years of doing so, it became more comfortable than going out." She closed her eyes and rested her head against the back of her chair. "I knew it was wrong to allow your grandfather to seek vengeance on my behalf. But how I hated Pennington. *I* craved revenge."

Her eyelashes trembled before her eyelids swept open, and what Gabriella saw there scoured her soul. The deadness in her cherished grandmother's eyes nearly drew a sob from her.

"I was glad to do it, Irene. To teach him and those other toffs a lesson," Grandpapa said. "He deserved everything that happened to him. And more for all of the lives he callously ruined, just because he could."

Perhaps so, but did the rest of the sixth duke's family have to suffer the consequences too? Couldn't Grandpapa see that now she and her sister and even Grandmama were going to reap the cost, much as the duchess, Maxwell's father, and even Maxwell himself had?

Or did vengeance blind one to all else, make a person disregard everything, so keen was the drive to retaliate? That Maxwell and Grandpapa were capable of such behavior grieved her spirit. In the wake of the visceral emotions, the air had become thick and cloying, the simple, involuntary act of drawing air into her constricted lungs, a monumental task.

"He laughed," Grandmama murmured, her voice cracking with strain. "After he had his way, and I lay there weeping, he laughed as he tied his robe. I'd told him I was betrothed. Begged him not to..."

Her throat worked convulsively, and Grandpapa swore foully again.

"Irene, you don't have to do this," he said with tender solicitude.

"Yes, Harold, I do. The girls need to know the whole of it, most especially before Pennington arrives with his demands. I'd hoped he'd be a better man than his father and grandfather." She shook her head again. "But it seems the fruit doesn't fall far from the tree, does it?"

Precisely what Gabriella had said.

Grandmama gave her a sympathetic glance, and though Gabriella was quite certain she didn't want to know the whole of it, she must.

Her expression grave, but admirably valiant, her grandmother went on. "When I threatened to report the duke to the authorities, he laughed again, vowing no one would believe me. That if I dared to be so foolish as to attempt to blacken his name, he'd destroy Harold too. Neither of us would ever work in England again." She jutted her chin up in defiance, a gesture so like Gabriella, she couldn't help but see a degree of her own obstinance in her grandmother's posture.

And she admired the stubborn resilience and show of strength.

"So yes, Gabriella and Ophelia, we plotted and schemed so that when the opportunity arose, we could put the screws to that despicable sod." That last bit deflated her grandmother, for she too slumped into her chair. "But after all these years, the wretch has finally come back to haunt us, as he swore he would."

Another horrific thought intruded upon Gabriella's already muddled mind. "Oh, my God. If the old duke impregnated you, that means Pennington is my, my...what? Second, third cousin once removed?"

She'd never been able to keep distant relations straight, but while others might think it perfectly acceptable, the very idea of marrying a cousin appalled her. That alone ought to be sufficient to dissuade Maxwell.

"No, you're not." Grandpapa's harsh voice broke through the anxious silence. "Irene miscarried that child. It nearly killed her, and it took over five years for her to conceive your father."

Grandmama reached for her husband's boney, age-spotted hand, and he promptly clasped her fingers. "After Henry was born," she said, "We came to realize we couldn't permit our hatred to taint our son. After all, we had Hartfordshire Court, and we determined then to put the ugliness behind us. Not to forgive, because I'm not certain either of us was capable of it, but to forge a new, happier future for ourselves."

This changed everything. Maxwell must be made aware. He must capitulate when these sordid facts were made known to him, surely. Except... "But what about the taxes, Grandpapa? The duke said you haven't paid the taxes these many years. The duchy has continued to pay them."

"As it well should. That was part of the terms of the agreement. I possessed the estate, and the duchy would continue to pay the taxes. I knew bloody well I could never afford to maintain Hartfordshire and pay the taxes too." He thumped his chair arm again. Poor tormented piece of furniture. "I have the documentation to prove what I say is true. I even made old Pennington put up the blunt for the starter herd of cattle."

Grandpapa had truly manipulated the duke. Gabriella wasn't sure whether she was appalled or grudgingly proud.

A rather wicked chuckle rattled his frail chest. "By God, how he swore at me. Called every curse known to God down upon me, and a few I'd never heard before. And yet, so desperate was he for an heir at his age, he acquiesced to my every demand."

Instinctively, Gabriella knew Maxwell would never be manipulated like that, but he also wouldn't defile women. *He'd force you to marry him and your grandfather to relinquish Hartfordshire Court.* Ironic how her grandfather and Maxwell both used the excuse they were righting a wrong. "But the ownership of Hartfordshire was never transferred or recorded at the register's office. How can that be?" she asked.

"I'll wager the nasty old duke bribed someone. A clerk or some official to *forget* to make the change," Ophelia put in.

Grandpapa nodded slowly. "Sounds like something that hell's spawn would do. I'd have had no reason to check the recording after my initial visit, and I was assured everything was in order. It's most unfortunate the current duke happened upon the journal and this sordidness came to light."

"The tax issue would've eventually alerted the duke." Honestly, it was surprising Maxwell hadn't discovered that piece of the puzzle before this. Gabriella shook her head. "What a positively monstrous mess. A monstrous, monstrous tangle. I fear we may have to hire a solicitor." She searched her grandfather's lined faced. "I don't suppose there are funds for that?"

He shifted uncomfortably, his focus sinking to his lap. "I cannot even replace the coach and team at this juncture," he mumbled, his papery cheeks flushed with humiliation.

"I thought not," she acknowledged with a resigned nod. "That makes me think. I forgot to tell you the duke arranged for the repair of the coach, and he also sent word to the auction houses to be on the alert for the team."

Her grandfather's regard sliced to Grandmother. "That was decent of him, but also beyond the mark." He opened his mouth as if to declare something else, but the quelling glance his wife leveled him, silenced whatever he was about to say.

How could they possibly hope to fight a wealthy duke in court?

"I cannot see that it would do any good, even if we could afford a solicitor," Ophelia ventured. "Grandpapa is correct. In circumstances like this, aristocrats always win. Justice is only for the rich and powerful."

What about the court of public opinion? The elitist circles Maxwell traveled in? What would the *haut ton* make of these juicy tidbits? Could Gabriella spin the facts and make the Dukes of Penningtons the villains and the Breckensoles the victims?

Probably, but the disgrace would ruin her family. What was more, *le beau monde*, didn't give a fig about commoners being rode roughshod over by some pompous duke. Peers were exonerated of crimes all the time with no more than a bored blink from their aristocratic compatriots.

"But if the duke *thinks* we'll make a public scandal of it, a reeking royal stink, that may well do the trick," Ophelia offered hopefully.

Gabriella could well imagine how her twin would affect that. Hadn't she suggested poisoning the duke in jest?

Maxwell had been most adamant he wanted to avoid any *on dit*. But such a scandal would reveal Grandmama's humiliation and likely settle Ophelia and Gabriella firmly on the shelf.

Besides, this was becoming a vicious cycle of extortion and retribution, and it didn't sit well with her. When would it end? She'd like to believe she and her family were above such ugliness. Maxwell too. In truth she objected more to the means by which she would be compelled to marry him than any personal objection to him.

"There is a way…" Grandmama hesitated, her mouth pressed into a tight line. "I possess something that may well do the trick."

A sick feeling cramped Gabriella's stomach, and she closed her eyes for a blink.

"What's this?" Grandpapa asked, wrinkling his forehead and probing her with his gaze. "You've kept a secret from me, Irene?"

"I have. Because the duchess was a sweet, gentle woman, forced into a marriage with a man old enough to be her grandfather. I always pitied her." She dropped her focus to her hands where she tormented the poor handkerchief. "The sixth duke," she continued softly, "beat and violated the poor woman. I cannot tell you how many times I cared for a split lip and helped her to dress to cover the bruises he inflicted upon her. The brute carried on with whores in the chamber adjoining hers. Even made her watch sometimes."

Gabriella put her palms to her churning stomach and swallowed, so sickened, she truly feared she'd cast up her accounts. Maxwell's grandfather had truly been evil, but to blackmail him in turn? It wasn't right.

"That's why she loved Hartfordshire Court so much." As Grandmama relived the events that had transpired so many years ago, her gaze went vacant again. "It was where she escaped from him and his string of strumpets. When she learned he attacked me, she'd had enough. She planned to leave him."

Grandpapa and Ophelia regarded her with expectation, and Gabriella wished herself anywhere else. As furious as she was with Maxwell, she didn't want to be a part of any scheme that inflicted harm upon him.

"You see, the duchess despised her husband, and she had a lover. I helped her arrange meetings with him." A defiant glint entered Grandmama's eyes. "I don't regret it. That poor woman deserved some small measure of happiness. I swore I'd never breathe a word, but her lover was the seventh duke's father."

13

Max turned on his heel, a cheroot gripped between his thumb and forefinger, and circled the flagstone terrace at the rear of Chartworth Hall once more. In the hours since he'd watched Gabriella—proud and magnificent as any Amazonian warrior—run away from him, taking his heart and his self-respect with her, he'd been deep in soul-searching contemplation.

Not a particularly religious man, he'd nonetheless sent several prayers skyward asking for guidance. For the ability to forgive. To know what course to take.

What had seemed just and fair a few months ago, even a few days ago, had faded into ambiguity with the knowledge he'd wounded her. Unforgivably.

You've taken up someone else's offense as your own.

I shall grow to hate you.

I could have loved you, Maxwell.

He took a long draw of the cheroot, then with a grimace tossed it to the pavers, crushing it rather viciously beneath his boot heel. He'd all but given up smoking straight out of university. He rarely indulged anymore, but this hellish day had sent him in search of a smoke, only to have him realize after two brief puffs he really couldn't abide the smell and taste. Another example of the many idiotic things men did just because someone, somewhere, at some time, thought it a splendid idea.

A bloody, disgusting idea.

Scraping a hand through his hair, not caring the least the disheveled strands would likely send his valet, Filby, into an apoplexy, Max brought his gaze up to survey the manicured lawns. Topiary hedges enclosed immaculately groomed gardens. Blossoms had begun to form on the early blooming flowers and trees, and soon their fragrance would perfume the air.

He rarely stayed at Chartworth, the memories of a lonely childhood, austere and frightened servants, a mean-spirited and perpetually soused grandfather, and a neglectful father were enough to keep him away. He'd often considered letting the estate, so he'd not be obligated to oversee it any longer.

Thank God he'd been sent to boarding school before his eighth birthday. It—and the life-long friends he'd made there, had been his saving grace. Visits home had been infrequent, dreaded, and in later years avoided. But Max had often enjoyed school breaks with other young scamps, mainly because his sire, quite frankly, didn't give a damn where he spent the holidays or summers.

He rested a hip on the elaborate balustrade while squinting into the cloudless azure sky. An unusually brilliant day for early spring in the English countryside. Beyond the hedgerow, a classic white marble garden arbor's domed roof peeked above the lavender, purple and cream lilacs and the crimson, fuchsia, and white camellias planted by his mother.

Another severely unhappy duchess.

Had any Duchess of Pennington ever been happy and content? Truly, wholly happy? Had a duke ever been? Not even he, renowned for his droll humor and teasing witticisms?

Gabriella deserved happiness.

Who was he to rob her of any chance of it?

A selfish, bastard. That was who. He'd known that all along, so why did he suddenly care?

A pair of accusing hazel eyes framed by lush lashes, momentarily blinded him.

It all came down to Gabriella Breckensole. She'd handily taken his well-thought out plans, and pitched them arse over noggin. What's more, he didn't mind nearly as much as he ought.

A slight smile quirked his mouth, and a peculiar urge to run and conceal himself in the arbor as he had as a youth gripped him. Within the stately columns, elaborate marble benches had provided the perfect backdrop for an errant boy to read his favorite books, pretend he slayed dragons and other mythical creatures, or simply hide from his latest starchy tutor or sot of a father when he'd been in his cups.

Which was most of the time.

Max's focus gravitated over the greens. He owned this. These thousands of acres. As had his father before him and his grandfather before him, and the previous generations of Pennington dukes too. Money and position and power accompanied the title, as did expectations and obligations. Max claimed all of this as his, and yet, he begrudged a simple man a few acres and the house it stood upon.

No, it is the means by which Breckensole acquired the estate I object to.

Over the decades, had his forebearers committed equally unjust crimes? One ancestor—his two times great-grandfather?—married five, increasingly younger heiresses with the sole purpose of expanding his holdings. It was rumored that not all of his duchesses had met with natural deaths.

Max roved his gaze over his lands again. Everything within his sight bespoke wealth and quality. Yet, never had Chartworth Hall felt less like a home. Never had the opulent halls and rooms rung more emptily. Never, *ever,* had he felt this lonely and hollow aching for what he'd unlikely ever have. Love. The love of a woman like Gabriella.

Who did he think he fooled? Certainly not himself. Not a woman *like* her. Her. Gabriella Fern Miriam Breckensole. He yearned for her love. Freely and willingly and wholeheartedly given.

His attention shifted to the east, toward Hartfordshire Court. He'd dine there in less than two hours. Afterward, he'd present Breckensole with the evidence that ensured the older man's ruination and thereby, guaranteed his cooperation. Only then would he explain his terms. Conditions which, he hadn't a doubt for a moment, she'd already informed her grandfather of.

126

The old curmudgeon would agree; after a bit of posturing and grumbling for his pride's sake.

Victory was within Max's grasp. He'd all but won. So why didn't exultation thrum through his veins? Instead, his mouth tasted acrid and bitter, and a peculiar sense of having failed in some vital way beat relentlessly against his self-respect.

Men at some time are masters of their fates.

Another damnable quote from Shakespeare. Of all the incongruous thoughts to invade his musings. For God's sake. He didn't even particularly like Shakespeare and for certain hadn't made an effort to memorize the bard's poems. He'd found the plays and sonnets tedious at best and when compelled to watch a theatrical performance of one or the other, often could barely keep his eyes open or suppress his bored yawns.

Men at some time are masters of their fates.

Was he? Could he be? Must he follow the less than praiseworthy footsteps of his ancestors? Did what had come before truly have to mold him into a callous, cold-hearted blackguard no better than the previous dukes of Pennington?

Or…could he be the one who initiated change?

If he forgave Breckensole his offense and debt, the duchy wouldn't suffer one way or the other from his decision. The dukedom, unlike many others, had plodded along quite nicely these past decades, despite the despicable dukes born into its prestigious lineage.

But the Breckensoles would suffer tremendously if he persisted. Wasn't that what he'd wanted?

Not anymore. Gabriella's happiness mattered more than all else.

More than Father? Grandfather? Revenge?

He chuckled, lifting his face to the sky. Yes. Hell, yes! A thousand times more.

She was all that was good and decent and wonderful. Her radiant smile lit the room and shadows descended, cloying and heavy, upon his soul when she departed his presence. Could this, whatever this unfamiliar feeling heating his blood and causing his heart to beat an uneven cadence, be love? Could he, the offspring of generations of unfeeling bastards, actually be capable of love?

As Max strode indoors and climbed the risers to his rooms, his internal battle raged on.

Forgive and forget?

Punish and demand restitution?

Could he forsake the duty to his family for something as wholly selfish as love for a woman who could scarcely stand to look upon his face?

Ah, but Gabriella had kissed him. More than once. Willingly and passionately, so she must've felt something toward him, if only desire. She wasn't a flirt nor fast, and she'd succumbed with a fervor that had startled but pleased him.

He needn't peer into a looking glass to know a satisfied grin curved his mouth.

Pausing along the second-floor gallery, he swept his gaze over the very first duke of Pennington's portrait. Complete with a neat black beard, a high-necked doublet under a dark blue and gold brocade overgown, and accented by a gaudily jeweled collar—*a truly heinous thing, actually*—his forefather stared back at him with haughty arrogance.

Prideful lot were the Dukes of Pennington. God only knew how many bastards these dukes had sired over the generations. As was typical of all the Dukes of Pennington, the first duke wore a solemn expression.

Mayhap they all had bad teeth? He ran his tongue over his own teeth, all straight except for one slightly crooked lower tooth. He faithfully cleansed them twice daily.

Hands clasped behind him, he slowly meandered the length of the carpeted corridor, his head slanted in concentration. He studied the serious faces of his ancestors, none particularly handsome, save his sire. His father bore classical striking features: a straight blade of a nose, a high forehead, sculpted cheeks and jaw, and dark hair that women seemed to find deucedly attractive.

Max didn't include himself in that category.

His face was far too angular, his nose slightly too large with a distinct hump, and his different colored eyes had always vexed him. Not that he minded them all that much when he glanced into the cheval glass, but others seemed to find them wholly unnerving or intriguing, depending upon who the observer might happen to be.

Gabriella, he realized with a small start, had never made him self-conscious about the abnormality. Many were the times she'd looked deeply into his eyes, and not once had there been even the merest flicker in hers. But then, that was so like her. To accept people as they were, without judgment or prejudice. To see the good in them.

He suspected he could've had a gross facial disfigurement, and she'd have treated him with courtesy and kindness, nary a flinch marring her comportment.

When he at last stood before his grandfather's and father's portraits, he straightened, and with a critical eye, narrowed his gaze. They bore little resemblance to one another, except in attitude, behavior, and speech. Actually, that wasn't quite true either.

At one time, his father had wanted to pursue a military career. The navy to be precise. Max had learned of that desire during one of his father's intoxicated rants. Naturally, as the only heir, he was forbidden any such thing. He'd also been forbidden to wed the woman he loved. She'd been far beneath his station.

Max had concluded as a young lad that his father was a weak man, compelled to become something he didn't have the character or fortitude for.

He glanced back down the row of austere ancestors in their gilded frames.

By damn.

When he sat for his portrait, he was going to grin as wide as a cat in the cream, even if it meant he appeared half mad. He wouldn't pose as a somber-faced wretch looking as if death or the pox or the plague was about to descend upon him.

Except…He unclasped his hands and leaned forward. One arm bent across his waist, the elbow of the other resting upon his forearm, he cradled his chin between his finger. Except, if he continued along this course, determined to destroy Breckensole, would he have reason to smile ever again?

His vivacious Gabriella would be destroyed in the process. In that moment, the pain in his heart crested, writhing with such severity, he gasped and clutched both hands to his chest.

He couldn't do it. Couldn't exact his revenge. Not out of any misplaced mercy or grace directed toward Breckensole. Gabriella, his sweet, unpredictable, vexing Gabriella had stopped him as surely as if a royal decree had been issued.

Max loved her, and love forgave a multitude of sins. None of the other signified. It was as if he was able to finally see clearly. What mattered most was that he not destroy that incredible, remarkable, beyond comparison woman.

Pennington duty and honor could burn in the seventh layer of hell's flames, which he strongly suspected, a few of these very same ancestors might very well be doing at this moment.

He, by God above, would not further blacken the dukedom with misplaced revenge.

Gabriella had reason to hate him. He'd given her every reason to. But he would not force her into a union she didn't want. That much he could do.

At once, as if heavy, binding chains had been removed, a weight lifted from him. Melted off like a candle held to a fire. He laughed out loud, causing a passing chambermaid to give him a queer look and scuttle past him a mite faster.

He wasn't sure what he'd do about the tax situation, but Breckensole could keep Hartfordshire Court and Max would never make a claim against the estate again. He'd inform the Breckensoles of his decision at dinner. Then tomorrow, he'd be straight for London. For staying in the vicinity, with Gabriella so close but utterly and forever unattainable was unbearable. Even for a hard-hearted Duke of Pennington.

14

At precisely seven of the clock, a leather portfolio and Gabriella's sketchpad and pencils neatly tucked beneath his left arm, Max rapped upon Hartfordshire's stout door. Dead silence met his knock, and after a couple of minutes, he pounded the door a jot harder.

He'd never been inside Hartfordshire Court and had no idea if the house's layout prevented the servants from hearing a knock upon the entrance. Another extended moment passed before the door finally swung open.

A plump, slightly breathless maid holding a candlestick bobbed a curtsy. "Your Grace." She swept her arm to the side, indicating he should enter. After setting the taper down, she managed a timid smile and accepted his hat and gloves.

"Thank you," he intoned, more formally than he'd intended. To his ears he sounded like a bloody, pompous windbag. Not the impression he wanted to make at all. He tried again, this time offering a cordial smile. "That's very kind of you."

Her unplucked eyebrows skittered upward, and she gawked at him as if he were dicked in the nob before finally murmuring, "Not at all, Your Grace."

It wasn't bloody kind of her. It was her job, as they both knew full well.

"Yes. Well…" He cleared his throat, turning his head and listening for voices. "I appreciate it nonetheless."

Now she did gape at him as if he were stark-raving mad. Dukes didn't go about complimenting servants for mundane tasks.

For God's sake, man. Shut up. You're babbling like a tabby.

"Miss Breckensole's drawing supplies." He passed them over as well. He retained the portfolio, and though the maid eyed it curiously, didn't offer to take the case.

Were the servants aware of what tonight's visit was truly about? Entirely possible in a household of this size.

After a long blink, she placed his possessions and the sketchpad and pencils upon a marble-topped hall tree stand and collected the candlestick. "The family awaits you in the drawing room. This way, if you please."

And even if he didn't.

So Breckensole didn't even permit candles lit in the entry. More evidence of his miserliness. Still, it wasn't Max's business whether the pinch-penny lit one or a hundred candles for his guests.

Uncharacteristic nerves pattered along his spine as he followed the maid's brisk pace.

Likely, she was needed in the kitchen to finish the meal's preparation. He hadn't been surprised the Breckensoles didn't retain a butler. His man of business had reported they kept a small staff of four: A cook, this maid of all work, the injured groomsman, Jackson, and the stable lad who'd led Balor to the small stables positioned to the back and left of the main house.

The single candle threw weird, tremulous shadows along the sparsely furnished corridor. Dark wainscoting—walnut?— covered the lower third of the passageway, and faded floral wallpaper, the upper two thirds. A lone painting of a Dutch landscape interrupted the monotony.

At the drawing room door, the maid paused after sending him an uncertain glance. She knocked lightly, then leaned in and pressed the handle. "His Grace, the Duke of Pennington."

Dead silence met her announcement as four wary gazes took him in: Breckensole's blazed with hatred, his wife's blatant distrust, Miss Ophelia's accusation, and Gabriella's brimming with sadness.

I could have loved you.

"Adel," Mrs. Breckensole said. "Please light the hall sconces."

"Yes, Mrs. Breckensole." The maid dipped her chin and after another swift glance about the tension-filled room, made her escape. No doubt the kitchen gossip would include the family's less than warm welcome.

Gabriella, wearing an extremely becoming pale pink gown trimmed in ivory lace, her hair piled atop her head with jaunty curls framing her face, and pearl earbobs dangling from her dainty ears had never appeared more lovely. Slightly pale, but supremely composed, Gabriella being Gabriella, broke the awkward silence.

She sunk into a graceful curtsy which Max acknowledged with a bow. "Your Grace, I believe you are already acquainted with my grandfather, Harold Breckensole."

Not exactly acquainted. There'd never been a formal introduction in all the years their properties had paralleled each other. They'd seen the other in the distance, of course, but the first unfortunate meeting had occurred the other night. Nevertheless, determined to be at his most charming for her sake, he angled his head. "Sir."

He received a stony glower in greeting.

Splendid. Things were off to a romping, jolly good start.

Gabriella's mouth flattened minutely, and he could've sworn she sent her grandfather a reproachful glance. *Easier to catch flies with honey and all that*, her silent message implied.

She was all the sweetness Max needed to persuade him to do almost anything.

"Please permit me to introduce my grandmother. Your Grace, Irene Breckensole. Grandmama, Maxwell, Duke of Pennington." Simple and direct without embellishment or pretense.

He bent into a formal bow, and Mrs. Breckensole deemed to lower her chin a fraction. Something in the handsome woman's frosty gaze sent prickles of unease up and down his spine.

Neither Mr. or Mrs. Breckensole had bothered to rise as he was accustomed to, and he wasn't certain whether he was more amused that his title didn't impress them in the least or miffed at their insolence. Then again, Mrs. Breckensole was still recovering from her bout of ill health.

Her husband, on the other hand, was just being an ornery ass. In a word, himself.

Max angled toward Miss Ophelia and bowed again. "Miss Ophelia."

"Duke." Her curtsy was so shallow as to be just this side of rude.

What had he expected? That they'd be giddy he'd deemed to call upon them?

Another stilted silence filled the room—evidently the fire the only thing capable of moving or showing any degree of cheer. Hell, Breckensole had yet to speak a word, although had his glare been a weapon, Max would've been eviscerated upon entrance.

Gabriella tapped her toes, back and forth, back and forth. Was she even aware she had that nervous quirk? When she caught sight of his slight grin and his pointed stare at her slippers, she stopped at once. Rather than off-putting or annoying, he found the trait endearing.

Wasn't he a completely besotted bumble-brain? And it was quite the most puzzling, incredible thing.

Still, his reason for being here wasn't pleasant. He breathed out a silent sigh. There was no point in waiting until after dinner and extending everyone's discomfort to say what he'd come to say. Lacing his fingers together behind his back, he splayed his legs. "I think it best for all if I speak directly."

Breckensole snorted, and Miss Ophelia placed a hand on her grandmother's shoulder in a reassuring fashion.

"Wouldn't you prefer to wait until after we've dined?" The look Gabriella leveled him suggested she thought whatever he had to say might put them off their food.

Or maybe they plan on poisoning me and thereby eliminating their problem altogether. Max wasn't serious, of course. She would never countenance such malevolent behavior.

Breckensole, on the other hand, certainly appeared up to the task. Max eyed the man's fingers, looking for a poison ring. The safe at Chartworth Hall contained one, and he'd always wondered which duke it had belonged to and if he'd ever used if for nefarious means.

Harnessing his wayward thoughts, he procured his diplomat's smile, and Gabriella's eyes rounded then shrank into contemplative slits. "I've had all afternoon to *reconsider*"—he made certain to emphasize the word— "the circumstances, and I've concluded—"

Harold Breckensole made a hostile, animalistic sound deep in his throat. With some effort, he stood and stabbed a wobbly finger at him. "We know precisely what *your* ignoble intentions are, you blackguard. But before you proceed with your demands, you had best read this." He produced a wrinkled, yellowed rectangle from within his outdated coat pocket; the fabric a peculiar faded brown much like weak tea.

A letter?

Holding the scrap of paper as if it were a rapier, a smug smile wreathed Breckensole's face.

"Grandpapa, I thought we agreed to wait until after we'd dined." Gabriella clasped her hands, tension making her fine cheekbones stand out. The smattering of light freckles on her nose contrasted starkly against her alabaster face.

"Why? Let's be done with this falderol and the false niceties. We can all appreciate this is not a social call, no matter how politely masked." Breckensole waved the foolscap, and it crackled in protest. "Then I can send this bounder on his way, eat my dinner, and actually enjoy my meal."

When Max made no effort to cross the room to accept whatever the correspondence was, she glided forward, the epitome of womanly grace. She'd have made a magnificent duchess, and his heart panged again that it would never be so. He'd had but one chance for this woman's love, and in his mistaken quest for honor, he'd callously dashed it to ribbons.

She accepted the paper from her grandfather. Edging that obstinate little chin up, she crossed to where Max stood, her skirts swishing around her ankles. Ankles which he knew to be dainty and well-formed. Lips slightly pursed, which only served to remind him he'd tasted their deliciousness but a few hours ago, she held the letter before her.

"I do believe it would be beneficial for you to read this before you proceed." Over her shoulder, she spared her grandmother a short, pointed glance before addressing him again. "I only learned of this particular after I returned home today, else I would've apprised you of its existence."

Gratitude for her loyalty, no matter how misplaced, bloomed behind his ribs. She tried indirectly to warn him, and that could only mean the contents were rather damning. From Breckensole's gloating smirk, rather somewhat more than damning, Max would vow.

Something close to compassion tinged her self-assurance, but she met his gaze straight on. Fearless, was his Gabriella. He'd never known a time it wasn't so.

"What is it?" He skeptically eyed the note clasped between her fingers. No name or address appeared on its aged face, and mustiness wafted upward from the crumpled missive.

"It's a letter, Your Grace," Mrs. Breckensole put in, her tone clipped and guarded. "Written by your grandmother when she was the duchess."

He jerked his head up from inspecting the paper. First, he searched her gratified countenance before gravitating his focus to Breckensole's smug expression that all but screeched, *"I've-got-you-by-the-ballocks-now."* Prickles of unease zipped along Max's spine for the third time in less than a half hour, and goose pimples raised from wrist to shoulder. He laid his portfolio on a nearby chair then studiously brushed a piece of lint from his sleeve.

He wasn't going to like this.

After a side-eyed glance at Gabriella and her twin, he flexed his jaw.

No, he wasn't going to like this in the least. He still intended to relinquish all claim to Hartfordshire Court, so whatever the letter said was moot.

He hoped.

"Your Grace." Gabriella fluttered the missive toward him, and he reluctantly accepted it.

"Why would you be in possession of a letter from my grandmother, Mrs. Breckensole?" he asked.

"I was her companion before I married." Mrs. Breckensole patted Ophelia's hand still resting upon the elderly woman's shoulder. "She trusted me absolutely, because she knew I'd never betray her. I was to have delivered that letter, but a series of calamitous events prevented my doing so."

That sent his eyebrows crashing together. How had his man of business not uncovered that detail? That very vital detail, indeed? Even now, Mrs. Breckensole defended his grandmother, and that more than anything, convinced him she spoke the truth.

Spine rigid, jaw tight, and white-knuckled hands clasped before her, Miss Ophelia claimed a spot on the striped sofa. That she felt the need to sit disturbed him even more.

He turned the missive over, searching for a name or address or anything on the reverse side. *Nothing.* That suggested something clandestine. Warning bells began to toll, first a gentle chime, but gradually increasing into a discordant cacophony. "To whom did she entrust you to deliver the letter?"

Breckensole planted his palms on his thighs, leaned forward, and blurted, "Reverend Michael Shaw. Her lover, and your father's *true* sire."

Those last four words, ringing extraordinarily loudly in the similarly unnaturally still room, tilted Max's world on its axis. His hearing grew muffled, as if he'd submerged beneath the bathwater. He shook his head to dislodge the wool and hauled his focus to Gabriella, silently asking for confirmation that he'd heard correctly.

Even before pity softened her eyes and framed her mouth, he appreciated he had. Heard every damning word perfectly clearly.

Reverend Michael Shaw was killed in a duel. Margaret is dead. She was with child.

His grandfather's journal entries also confirmed the truth.

Compassion shone on Gabriella's face.

After all Max put her through and had threatened to do, she commiserated with him? It only reinforced her goodness, and the oddest urge to laugh engulfed him. Instead, he unfolded the worn, thickly creased paper, the rustling oddly ominous. Only the longcase clock in the corner's *tick-tocking* disturbed the dense quiet.

That and Breckensole's heavy breathing. The air whistled in and out of his nose in a fashion that made Max yearn to offer his handkerchief and demand the old man blow heartily. Or take a pair of embroidery scissors to his hair-clogged nostrils and groom a pathway the air might enter and exit through with a greater degree of ease.

Training his attention on the short missive, he recognized the penmanship as that which he'd seen inside the cover of numerous books within Chartworth's extensive library. His grandmother's delicate, rather flourishing hand.

The note was short. A mere two lines: A time and location for a clandestine meeting. Grandmother and this Michael Shaw had planned to run away together.

Max read it again. And again. And again.

Off guard, his lungs cramping as if he'd been kicked in the ribs by a team of draft horses, he meticulously refolded the note. Doing so gave him something to focus on besides the tumult careening about in his head and his inability to draw anything but little puffs of air into his lungs.

Grandmother had meant to leave his grandfather. Father wasn't Grandfather's progeny.

His head spun from trying to sift fact from fallacy, and again, an absurd urge to laugh assailed him. "But why is the letter still in your possession?" he at last managed to ask. No hint of the turmoil within reached his modulated voice.

"I never had a chance to deliver it. As I said, circumstances prevented my doing so." Sadness tempered Mrs. Breckensole's tone.

"Why not?" What other shocks awaited him?

She stared into space; sorrow etched upon her aged features. She'd cared for his grandmother. Truly cared for her. The knowledge startled and humbled him.

"Somehow your grandfather learned that they intended to run away, and he challenged the reverend to a duel." She shifted her gaze to him for a moment. "I doubt the man had ever touched a pistol, let alone fired one, and the duke likely knew it as well."

Max swallowed the bile burning his throat.

"It was to have been to first blood." Mrs. Breckensole shifted her focus away again. "But the reverend died instantly from a bullet to his heart. Sorrow drove the duchess slightly mad, and she attacked her husband. Tried to stab him with a letter opener."

"Holy God," Max whispered.

She jutted her chin upward, reminding him of Gabriella. "I witnessed the act myself and sorely wished she'd succeeded. The duke locked her in her chamber for a month, permitting no visitors, no bathwater, no fires or candles, and only gruel and stale bread for her to eat." Her voice grew raspy and her eyes watery. "Such cruelty to that gentle soul, and she was with child too."

God, his grandfather had been a tyrant. A fiend. Surely his soul had been blacker than the devil's himself.

It didn't escape Max that his grandfather's journal had made no mention of any of this. What else had he left out? Neither did it pass his notice that Mrs. Breckensole had been crafty enough to know that such a letter might be of worth at a later date. What other reason could there be for hiding it away for decades? He was about to ask that very question, when her next words tied his tongue.

"I've always suspected he pushed her down the stairs and to her death in one of his fits of rage. For that babe she carried wasn't his either." She looked straight at Max, her eyes slits of accusation and condemnation. "'Twas guilt and a raging fury that he was forced to claim another's seed as his heir that turned him into a drunkard and opium addict. Not devastation."

15

The emotions skating across Maxwell's face tore at Gabriella's composure. She'd wanted him to be taken down a notch, longed for him to understand how she felt, but this comeuppance brought her no joy. No sense of satisfaction. Because the plain, inarguable truth was, when he hurt, so did she.

A fierce, ache burned in the depths of her being. And that suggested she was beyond—way beyond, in fact—*I could have loved you Maxwell* and had come full circle to, *I do love you. So very much, that each beat of my heart is agony.*

Statue stiff, he clenched the paper. His eyelids drifted closed, the fringe of his lashes, thick and dark across his high cheekbones. He didn't argue, which suggested he believed the letter's legitimacy. The long ago, undelivered note to a lover now fisted in his grip might well be what it took for him to cry off. To change his mind about reclaiming Hartfordshire Court, marriage to her, and all the rest.

This was the miracle she'd prayed for. The means to save her home and her family. So why did tears blur her vision? Why did she want to wrap her arms around Maxwell and comfort him?

"Gabriella, take the letter before he destroys it," her grandfather ordered, a hint of panic in his tone as if the thought had just occurred to him.

"Grandfather, you're being churlish. The duke is too much of a gentleman to do any such thing." She astounded herself by defending

Maxwell. She meant what she'd said though, knowing it to be the truth.

"Here, Gabriella." Arm stiff, he extended the crumpled parchment.

Her grandfather released a derisive snort following Maxwell's declaration. "Ah, yes, because you're descended from such noble blood you wouldn't destroy evidence? Yet you intended to force us from our home and blackmail my granddaughter into wedding you. And you presume to use her given name without leave?"

A slight flush tinged Maxwell's cheeks. "I beg your pardon for overstepping, Miss Breckensole. I spoke without thinking."

She bit the inside of her cheek against the urge to tell him she didn't mind.

How she despised this—seeing him defeated—every bit as much as she'd hated the uncompromising position he'd placed her in this morning. Grandfather's reveling rankled, and once she'd accepted the fragile rectangle and placed it upon the table beside her grandmother, she peered out the window. Or else she might say something wholly disrespectful to the man who'd raised her and her sister.

Nightfall obscured the garden view, but the unending darkness was preferable to seeing the pain and dismay etched on Maxwell's face. To observing this normally unflappable, composed man with his dry wit and spirited ripostes reduced to whatever wretched state this was.

Besides, what he'd intended was a far cry from disregarding the rules of dueling and slaying his opponent or shoving an *enceinte* woman down a flight of stairs. Even after everything he'd said and done, when he'd been an unmitigated cad, she yearned to smooth the angst from his features.

He'd received a monumental blow.

Not as appalling as what Grandmama had endured. Gabriella hugged her arms around her shoulders against a sudden chill.

Legally, it was of no account whether Michael Shaw or the sixth duke had sired Maxwell's father. He'd been born in wedlock, and the duke had acknowledged him as his son. Under the eyes of the law, he'd been the legal heir.

She angled toward Maxwell. She would've spared him this had she been able to.

Beneath his neatly tied cravat, his Adam's apple moved up and down, as if he struggled to control is emotions. Was he terribly disappointed? Shocked? Furious?

His attention lit upon her and rested there, his expression revealing nothing of the turbulent emotions he must surely feel. His imperious gaze, the blue eye darkened to indigo and the other a deep forest green, regarded her keenly. As if he searched for something within her eyes. Within her.

What did he seek?

The love she'd hidden from him all these months? His trust? Forgiveness? They were his for the asking.

"If you try to either force my granddaughter into marriage or to take Hartfordshire Court from us, *Your Grace,*" Grandpapa spat with such contempt, Gabriella spun to stare at him, aghast, "I shall make that letter public. Along with other unsavory information we haven't yet discussed."

"Harold, no!" Grandmama gasped, clutching her neck and spearing him a stricken look. "You cannot."

"Grandpapa, your speech and attitude do our family a disservice." Gabriella could scarce believe her boldness, but he'd gone beyond the mark. "The duke has been the epitome of politesse, and we would all do well to model him. Disagreements can be solved without lowering ourselves to petty bickering."

Another round of tomb-like silence followed her scold.

Ophelia studiously examined the worn carpet, brushing at a stain with her slipper toe. Grandmama looked askance at her husband, and to Gabriella's astonishment, Grandpapa flushed, ran a finger around the edge of his neckcloth, and with the very merest downward flicker of his eyes, acquiesced.

The inner corners of Maxwell's eyebrows lashed together as he swung his attention between her and her grandparents.

Gabriella offered a small, encouraging smile.

"There's no need for further shocks or unpleasant disclosures, I assure you. I came tonight with the intention of informing you that I've changed my mind. I've concluded that no good can come of pursuing the course I had intended to embark upon." Formality weighted his speech, but a tinge of pain colored the jagged edges of his stilted words. Although he addressed everyone, his regard remained on her. "There are additional particulars that preclude me taking the action I'd originally contemplated."

Such as?

He couldn't possibly know about Grandmama's ordeal. He'd been so unrelenting only a few hours ago. What then, in the whole of England, had been compelling enough to change his mind since this morning?

She examined the planes of his beloved face and searched his eyes for any hint. She ought to be overjoyed. This was exactly the reprieve she'd hoped for. So why, fiend seize it, did tears burn behind her eyelids and her throat twinge? Her emotions had become as fickle as a spring breeze. "You've truly changed your mind?"

Maxwell's gaze caressed her, and he gave a scant nod.

"Yes. I've come to see the error of my ways, so to speak. I shall lay no claim to Hartfordshire Court." He motioned to the forgotten leather portfolio. "All of the necessary documentation is within. My man of business will ensure the deed is properly recorded as it should have been done decades ago. Only the issues of the taxes remain to be addressed."

"I have the original documents signed by your grandfather that ensure the duchy maintains the tax liability for as long as my wife and I live." Pleasantly civil, so much so that Gabriella nearly gaped, Grandpapa gestured toward the door. "They are in my study."

That took Maxwell aback, and he blinked. "Why would he...?" Lowering his head, he cupped his nape. At last he glanced up, the earlier tumult in his eyes replaced by calculated blandness. "I presume there are other unsavory factors that warranted such benevolence?"

"Indeed, there were, Your Grace," Grandmama stated with regal dignity, a glimmer of the striking woman she'd once been surfacing.

She and Maxwell exchanged an intense, speaking glance, and something flashed in his eyes. Again, he gave the slightest acknowledgement with a half-blink and the merest downward slant of his chin.

"I believe I begin to understand. I also truly, and sincerely, regret that I may have greatly wronged you." His gaze swept the room, lingering the longest on Gabriella. "I should've approached this matter as a gentleman rather than hurl accusations and contemplate retribution. I am not proud of my behavior and most humbly ask, that in time, perhaps you'll be able to forgive me."

She only just managed to keep her mouth from unhinging. She did, however, blink several times overcome by joy and relief.

Maxwell had apologized. Honestly. And he'd asked for forgiveness. Did dukes ever do such things? This one had, and another powerful wave of love for him throttled from her belly to her throat.

"Forgiveness?" Grandpapa suddenly laughed, slapping his knee in genuine glee. He laughed so fervently, he swiped at his eyes. "Oh, this is too perfect."

She exchanged a worried look with Ophelia. Had the strain been too much that he'd snapped and lost his faculties?

Shoulders shaking, he wrestled his mirth under control and managed between chuckles, "I've just realized his high-and-mightiness there is the grandson of a reverend. And you, Gabriella, are the granddaughter of a vicar. What a wicked sense of humor Providence has."

What a peculiar thing to say. She said as much. "Grandpapa, I hardly think such talk is appropriate or relevant."

"If I might have a look at the documentation you mentioned, Mr. Breckensole?" Posture rigid and jaw taut, Maxwell sliced an impatient glance to the door whilst flexing his fingers. Clearly, he couldn't wait to be on his way. "You may peruse mine as well."

For the first time since Maxwell had arrived, her grandfather deemed to behave like the gentleman she knew him capable of being. Likely because he had the upper hand and well knew it. "Certainly, Your Grace. Irene, please ask Cook to hold dinner until I'm finished."

"I shall do so at once." Grandmama rose, as did Ophelia. "Your Grace, you're certain you won't stay and dine with us?" She, too, must have decided a truce of some sort had been called between the Breckensoles and him.

He gave Gabriella an intense stare but declined with slight shifting of his gaze. "No, but I thank you."

"Perhaps another time?" My, wasn't her grandmother all solicitousness now? Keeping the dark secrets she and Grandpapa had harbored these many years no doubt had been a tremendous burden and to be free of them at last, quite liberating.

He shook his head. "I fear not. I'm for London first thing tomorrow and don't anticipate returning to Chartworth."

Ever? Or just not in the near future? Or distant future?

Once more his gaze found Gabriella's, and such regret shone in his eyes, she nearly gasped. *Don't go. We need to talk,* she wanted to cry. Naturally, she couldn't. What could she say with her grandparents and sister staring on, in any event?

I don't want you to leave? I want to explore what this thing is between us? Yes, you've been a knave, and I most probably ought to detest you, but my stupid, stupid, stupid heart insists on loving you instead.

I beg you. Do not leave me behind. Give me a chance to ask for your forgiveness, for I've wronged you as well.

No, she couldn't confess something so private in front of her family. But she most assuredly would find a way to speak with Maxwell before he left. And that would be no easy task. She jutted her chin out, only the tiniest bit, lest anyone notice the determined spark she was certain glinted in her eyes.

"Girls, come along." Grandmama extended her elbows, indicating each twin should take one. "Your grandfather and the duke have important matters to discuss."

How Gabriella wanted to object. She wracked her brain for a feasible excuse to stay. She might argue the women should be permitted to be a part of the discussion since Hartfordshire would pass to her and her sister one day. Wouldn't it? She had always presumed as much, but nothing of the kind had ever been suggested.

For certain she didn't want to toddle down that bumpy road with the duke listening.

What then?

Perchance...? She slid Ophelia a contemplative side-eyed look. Yes. It might work. If she was careful. She tapped her toe once, then promptly stopped. She'd give herself away if she weren't careful.

Maxwell bowed. "Ladies."

Even Grandmama deemed to sink into a curtsy.

"Your Grace," the women murmured in unison.

Another refrain pealed in Gabriella's head. *Don't go. Don't go. Please. Don't go.* Her feet carried her forward, despite her protesting mind, and she gained the corridor.

Adel had lit the sconces as directed. Well, two of them. It was unheard of for the Breckensole household to waste six candles in one evening to light the passageway, even for a duke. Halfway down the corridor, she slowed her steps, closed her eyes, and pressed her fingertips between her eyebrows.

"Grandmama?" She concentrated on sounding breathless and feeble.

"Yes, dear?" Her grandmother quizzically peered up. "Why, Gabriella, are you quite all right?"

She shook her head. "I don't believe I am. I'm not feeling at all well and urgently need to lie down."

Worry folding her features like a fan, Grandmama *tisked* and *tutted*.

"This has been too much of a strain for you. Thinking one moment to protect your family and enter into a horrid union, and then learning all of these sordid particulars no woman with delicate sensibilities ought ever to hear. I cannot say as I blame you." She patted Gabriella's cheek. "Go along. Change into your nightclothes, and I'll have a simple tray sent up later if you are feeling more yourself."

Gabriella caught Ophelia's eye. "Come with me," she mouthed above their grandmother's head.

An imperceptible flicker of Ophelia's lashes suggested she understood. "Grandmama, permit me to help Gabriella. I'll come down straightaway once she's settled."

A smile arced their grandmother's lined face. "I sometimes forget how close the two of you are. Go along, Ophelia. I suspect your grandfather will be several minutes more in any event. I don't know how I shall pacify Cook. She was quite put upon, having to prepare a meal worthy of a duke on such short notice, and when she learns he's not staying to dine, I truly fear she may give notice."

Gabriella bent and kissed her grandmother's cheek. "I'm sure you can console her adequately."

"Let us hope so, for as we all know, I am a dismal cook." She chuckled, in the best humor Gabriella had seen her in for some time.

She didn't exaggerate. Ophelia and Gabriella could do a kitchen justice if required to do so, but Grandmama's talents were with a needle or a hairbrush and hair pins, not a pot and spoon.

Once in her chamber, Gabriella made straight for her wardrobe. Before Ophelia had finished closing the door, she'd pulled out a simple gown and her half boots.

"What are you about?" Ophelia demanded, crossing her arms. "Hasn't there been enough chaos and calamity for one day?"

"I must speak with Maxwell before he leaves. I'll await him in the stables." Gabriella presented her back. "Now, do hurry and unfasten me. I'm counting on you to keep my confidence and to prevent Grandmama from checking upon me too." Impatient and fearing he'd leave before she caught him, she glanced over her shoulder.

Ophelia hadn't moved but regarded her with a rather too astute stare. A fine eyebrow crept upward and a hint of amusement played about her mouth. "Maxwell?"

Oh, piddle. His name had slipped out without Gabriella even noticing.

"Oh, Gabby. You *do* care for him." Suddenly, she grinned and rushed to Gabriella. "I knew it. Naturally, when he was being so very beastly and impossibly ducal, you couldn't agree to marry him. I confess, I do quite like him despite his being a Pennington," she declared as she swiftly unfastened the hooks holding Gabriella's gown shut. "And I think he's good for you."

Good for me?

Yes, he was.

In short order, Gabriella had changed and donned her simple woolen cloak. Holding hands, the sisters stepped into the empty passage. On tiptoes, Gabriella hurried to the landing, carefully leaning over to inspect the blessedly empty foyer below.

Ophelia winked, giving a cheeky grin. "I'll go first and signal when all is clear." She was enjoying this misadventure too much. "This is jolly good fun," she whispered, grabbing Gabriella's hand and giving her cold fingers a squeeze.

Gabriella hadn't thought to don her gloves. She'd been in too much of a hurry. There wasn't time to go back for them now, however. Maxwell might depart at any moment.

"Just don't do something foolish and impulsive such as elope with him." A tiny frown scrunched Ophelia's nose. "Grandmama and Grandpapa would never let me out of the house again. I'd die here, a prune of an old maid." She squeezed Gabriella's hand again. "Besides, I want to see you marry. Promise me, Gabby."

If Maxwell asked her to trot off to Scotland, Gabriella would. Indeed, she would.

"I don't think there's any chance of that, Fee," she murmured, wishing with all of her heart that there was.

Scandal be damned.

16

Five minutes later, Gabriella carefully slipped into the stables. Maxwell's horse poked his majestic head over the stall door, raising it up and down, almost in an equine bow. A long swoosh of breath blew past her lips.

Thanks be to God, he hadn't left yet,

A lone lantern hung on a peg, lighting the tidy barn. Grandpapa would have a tantrum if he knew. Wanton waste and all that. But Davy had likely thought, and rightly so, a duke worthy of a bit of light.

Of the stable hand, there was no sign. That was also a welcome blessing.

He'd probably fallen asleep in his quarters already. Up before dawn every day, he worked hard—too hard—and usually sought his bed after sundown. As the Breckensoles never had guests in the evening, Davy had probably assumed it quite gracious to provide a light before he found his mattress.

Tomorrow, Gabriella would speak to him about the danger of leaving a lantern unattended and about expectations for attending guests' horseflesh. The duke shouldn't have to see to saddling his mount. However, she wouldn't scold too severely since the young man's absence provided her with the perfect opportunity to speak with Maxwell alone.

She hadn't any idea what she would say. There'd been no time to rehearse. And yet here she stood, unwilling for them to part with so much unsaid between them.

The horse lifted his head again, his great brown eyes watching her.

She greeted the other two horses before making her way to his stall. "Hello, handsome boy. I never did thank you for the ride the other night. It was most gentlemanly of you to accommodate two riders."

At the mention of that sensual ride, any remaining denial ebbed, and her true feelings flooded upon her like a massive ocean wave. Overwhelming, powerful, and wholly inescapable.

Maxwell had been absolutely right.

Attraction *had* sparked between them from the onset. The magnetism had steadily grown into something more over these past months, strengthened upon every encounter, and had culminated this last week. Had all of her attempts to ignore and slight him at every turn been more of an internal battle to fight her escalating fascination? Because, though her head said she should detest him for what she'd discovered, her heart had a mind of its own and frankly refused to cooperate.

Running a hand over Balor's neck, she murmured, "How can I tell Maxwell any of that? Hmm?"

"Tell me what?"

A hand to her throat, she whirled to face the entrance. "You startled me, Maxwell." It came out a strangled squeak, and she cursed inwardly for stating the obvious and for sounding like an oversized mouse.

Marked uncertainty shadowing his features, he lingered a foot inside the door. He'd donned neither his hat nor gloves, but held them in his left hand.

She permitted herself a leisurely perusal of this ebony-haired powerful lion of a man, from impressively wide shoulders, to a narrow waist, long well-muscled thighs, and calves ensconced in midnight Hessians. Her gaze made the return journey, every bit as enjoyable as the first, until her attention rested upon the molded planes of his dear face.

Perhaps, she also permitted her focus to hover on his lips as she recalled the kisses they'd shared. If she closed her eyes, she imagined she could feel his lips upon hers still.

Gabriella's heart gave a queer flutter. She loved him.

Had loved him since…Well, she didn't know exactly when he'd

entered her heart and set up house without so much as a by-your-leave. But he had entrenched himself there. Had taken over, and now Maxwell, the eighth Duke of Pennington, had absolute rule of the organ.

What's more, she didn't mind at all, and she wouldn't object in the least if he felt the same. But did a lady just come out with it? Ask a gentleman if he loved her too? If that was the reason he'd changed his mind about seizing Hartfordshire Court before learning of his grandmother's letter?

But what if he didn't love her? What if his only interests were Hartfordshire and lust for her body? Straightening her shoulders, she brought her chin up. She'd know the truth, at least. That was something. Everything.

A hint of vulnerability creased the corners of his eyes. "You shouldn't be out here, Gabriella."

Not chérie or minx or vixen?

She almost bit her lip and had actually lifted her right toe before she caught herself.

He shook his head and took a pace forward. "It's not—"

"Done?" she shrugged, and forming her mouth into a disinterested *moue,* brushed her hand down Balor's neck. "I know. But, you see, Maxwell, I wanted to speak with you before you left. I feared that after you departed for London on the morrow, it might be some time before you returned. *If,* you returned at all." Nothing too terribly subtle about that. Would he understand the meaning in her words she wanted him to?

"And that distresses you?" After setting his possessions on a low stool, he prowled nearer.

Swallowing, she managed a small nod. "Yes, I find that it does. Very much, in fact."

He was upon her now, and she pulled her gaze upward from his waistcoat, past his starched neckcloth and the ruby pin twinkling there, over the light stubble shadowing his strong chin, to his firm mouth then higher still until she met his gaze.

The intensity of those hot eyes sent a sensual shiver jolting to her knees, which had inconveniently decided to take this moment to become the consistency of strawberry flummery.

"Why, may I ask?" His regard sank to her mouth.

Was he also remembering their passionate embraces?

"I find the idea of you leaving for a lengthy stretch quite distresses me." Good Lord, could she sound anymore prim or tight-laced?

He brushed her cheek with his finger, then her jaw, then the seam of her lips. "Why?"

She tingled all over, and he appeared as cool as the proverbial cucumber. *Blast the man.* He wasn't making this easy.

Shouldn't a gentleman, a duke for goodness sake, do the gallant thing and declare himself first? But what if he believed the gentlemanly thing was to let her make the choice, because before, he hadn't given her an option?

Gabriella grasped his lapels, running her fingertips along the fine fabric. "I shall miss you beyond measure. Quite unbearably, truth to tell. And I don't wish to be miserable every day, wondering when you will return. *If* you will return." He started to open his mouth, but she quickly put a finger to his lips. "Don't you dare ask me why again," she ordered, low and husky.

At that, he cocked an eyebrow, maddeningly wicked and self-assured, and had the gall to nip her finger before capturing it in his palm and whispering, "Why?" his voice deep and gravelly and seductive.

Standing on her toes, she cupped his nape. "Because, you obnoxious, irritating man, I love you."

The very instant that I saw you, did my heart fly to your service.

What an appropriate time to remember a line from Shakespeare.

With a rough groan, Maxwell swept her into his arms, capturing her mouth in a scorching kiss that promptly sent every coherent thought in her brain straight out of her mind. He gripped her bottom, pushing his rigid length into her belly, and devoured her mouth.

Time stood perfectly still as they explored the other's mouth between whispers of adoration and heartfelt apologies. A hunger and yearning swirled within her, increasing in intensity, until she made little mewling sounds against his lips.

"Maxwell, please," she pleaded, for what she didn't know.

A horse snorted in what very much sounded like an equestrian chuckle, and Maxwell finally lifted his head.

She cried out in protest, trying to claim his lips once more.

His features strained and eyes hooded, he shook his head. He rested his forehead against hers. "No, *mon amour*. I'm almost beyond restraint, and I refuse to tup the future Duchess of Pennington in a pile of straw."

She didn't think the idea so very awful. In fact... "Perhaps not the first time, but mayhap *some* time?" she asked coyly.

He growled low in his throat and nipped her neck. "Vixen. Siren. Temptress. Minx." Smoothing errant strands of hair from her cheek, his gaze so tender, she wanted to weep, he asked hesitantly, "Do you truly love me?" Awe, wonder, and disbelief blended together to make the question harsh and raspy.

"I do, Maxwell." She put a palm to his cheek. "I truly do. I've loved you for so long, but I was so hurt and angry, I refused to see it. Stubbornly refused to acknowledge what I knew to be true."

Something wondrous lit in his eyes, and he pressed a reverent kiss to her forehead then encircled her with his arms.

"And you'll marry me? Because you want to?" He spoke against her hair, his lips a warm caress. "I cannot imagine ever loving another woman as I do you. And if you should refuse me, I'll understand. I shall, truly, because I doubt your grandparents will ever agree to the match. They might even cut you off and forbid you to see me." His embraced tightened. "But I shall never wed, then. I'll carry you in my heart until I draw my last breath, Gabriella, my love."

"I'll gladly marry you." She smiled up into his face, caressing his bristly jaw. "Without regret, whether or not my grandparents' consent. Although, I suspect they'll be amendable as long as they know I wed you of my own free will. I love you, dear man."

Emotion choked his ragged voice, and he swallowed audibly, pressing his cheek into her hair. "No one... No one has ever said they loved me before."

A broken cry escaped her, and tears leaked from her eyes. "Oh, my darling. I shall tell you every day upon awakening, every night upon going to sleep in your arms, and a thousand times in between. I love you. I love you. I love you."

He tilted her chin upward until their eyes met. "Forgive me, Gabriella. I was an utter fool. The things your grandfather revealed to me tonight..." He closed his eyes. "Well, let's just say I'm profoundly glad the sixth Duke of Pennington's blood *does not* flow through my veins."

"I regret you had to learn that ugliness," she whispered.

"I'm not," he said quite fiercely. "It's a relief. I've often thought my father and I were somehow different than the previous dukes. Now I know why."

"It's all so sad, really."

"How long must I wait to make you my wife?" Maxwell smiled into her eyes, and she wanted to weep from joy. To shout her jubilation. To take him to her bed right then and there.

Head angled, she tipped her mouth upward. "I believe you mentioned a special license?"

"I did, indeed, *cherie*."

"Then I choose tomorrow, by the river where you first kissed me." She clasped his hand, bringing to her heart. "Shall we tell the others our good news?"

"I'll need a fortifying kiss before I interrupt your grandfather's dinner," Maxwell claimed, mischief and desire playing across his mouth. "The man fairly terrifies me."

Gabriella was happy to oblige for several long and most delicious minutes.

Epilogue

London, England
Late April, 1810

Lilting music filled his ears as Max guided his wife of just over a month around the sanded parquet floor of Mathias, Duke of Westfall's ballroom. Invitations had awaited them upon their arrival in London, and a steady stream continued to pour into the Mayfair manor every day. News of his nuptials had traveled throughout London's elite circles with prodigious speed.

Upon his first foray to *Bon Chance*, after being heartily congratulated, the dukes of Asherford, Westfall, Bainbridge, and San Sebastian had taken him aside for a finger's worth of brandy. Unwed themselves, each had teased him unmercifully about having been snared by the parson's mousetrap.

"Yes, and now that I'm off the Marriage Mart, my friends, there's one less peer for those title-hungry huntresses' to snare. You'd best be on your guard, lest you find yourselves saying, 'I do.'"

They'd cursed him for the worst sort of friend for even suggesting such a wretched thing. But like Max, each knew full well he was expected to marry and produce an heir, no matter how reluctant they were to enter the blissful state of matrimony.

A primal smile bent Max's mouth. Those gents could mock all they wanted, but he had no complaints whatsoever. His wonderful, unpredictable Gabriella was every bit as capricious inside as outside the bedchamber. That promised tumble in the hay had proven quite invigorating. As had the delightful joining in the library yesterday and the exhilarating tussle in the carriage the day before. Each and every one initiated by his seductress of a wife.

Yes, indeed, God had smiled upon him the day he'd met this enticing armful he now called wife. "Enjoying yourself, Duchess?" He adored calling her that and seeing the pink bloom in her cheeks.

"You well know I am." She discreetly craned her elegant neck. "So are Ophelia and Jessica Brentwood." She slid her eyes sideways, and he followed her glance.

Ophelia danced with a dashing ship's captain, and the Duke of Kincade, only arrived from the Highlands last week, skillfully swept Jessica amongst the other dancers.

"And Rayne Wellbrook and Sophronie Slater too." Gabriella tipped her head toward the young women. "Though, honestly, they look slightly more terrified than excited."

"The Season can be a bit daunting for those unaccustomed to it." He would've eschewed most of the invitations they'd received, but as Gabriella had never had a Come Out or a Season, he felt compelled to allow her to attend whatever routs, soirees, balls, and other assemblies she desired.

The set ended, and she excused herself to use the lady's retiring room. Halfway across the floor, Nicolette Twistleton, Miss Ophelia, and Everleigh, Duchess of Sheffield joined her. Their gay laughter rang out as they made for the ballroom's exit.

"You look exceptionally pleased with yourself. Not at all like the sour-faced chap at the Twistleton's musical a few weeks ago."

He tore his gaze from his wife long enough to nod a greeting at Bainbridge. "I'm happier than I deserve."

Unusually reflective, Bainbridge leaned against the column conveniently situated between them. "I wonder if I'll be as fortunate as you, Dandridge, Sutcliffe, and Sheffield. Somehow, I think not. Particularly since you were privileged to pick your duchesses, and mine was chosen for me many years ago. And as my dear mama reminds me on a daily basis, Lady Lilith Brighton is now eight-and-ten. Everyone expects me to set a wedding date."

Sutcliffe approached, champagne in hand. "What's this? Bainbridge, are you contemplating marriage as well?"

"Not by choice, by God," Bainbridge vowed. "Not yet, in any event."

"I've been in search of you all evening," Sutcliffe said. "Westfall wants a word. Something about a horse he wants to acquire."

With a weighty sigh, Bainbridge straightened. "Yes, I think I've located the stud he's been seeking. Oh, and Pennington, so far, I've not been able to find the matched grays you asked me to watch for. I'll let you know if I hear anything."

Max had been trying to find Breckensole's stolen horses for the better part of a month without luck. They'd show up eventually though. A fine pair like that would draw attention and when they did, he intended to recover the team. Not out of any great love for Breckensole. Although, he'd been admirably civilized since Gabriella announced she would marry Max with or without her grandparents' blessing.

Personally, he believed Breckensole had agreed to the quiet ceremony the next day because he truly loved his granddaughter and was absolved from having to part with coin for a formal wedding. That, and if the old curmudgeon cut her off, not so much as a farthing would make its way from Max's purse to Breckensole's.

Though it was boorish of him, Max had no interest in standing up with another lady for a set or two, and instead went in search of the card room. At least that's what he told himself as he wended a path to the exit Gabriella had disappeared through several minutes before.

Once he'd ascended the magnificent curved staircase, he turned right. If memory served, Westfall's private salon and the retiring rooms were along this wing. He contemplated Bainbridge's dilemma as he marched along. Poor sot. An arranged marriage with a child, practically.

Praise God Max had been spared that horror.

A white-gloved feminine hand shot out and grabbed his arm as he passed the salon. "Maxwell," Gabriella whispered, hauling him into the room. "You must see this."

Had she been snooping again? In his four weeks of marriage, he'd learned his darling wife had a curious streak. About more than sexual acts.

She swiftly closed the door and with an impish wink, guided him to the fireplace. Flames burned low in the grate, and a turned down lamp sat upon a side table.

"What exactly is it I'm supposed to be looking at, *chérie*?"

She captured her lower lip between her teeth and pointed to the fur rug before the hearth. "It's fur," she needlessly announced as she removed her gloves.

"Yes?" Max crooked an eyebrow, glancing between her and the thick sable fur. He grinned as comprehension dawned. "Why, Duchess, are you suggesting an erotic assignation on a fur rug during a ball?"

What a wonderfully naughty minx.

"What if I am?" She tilted her chin up.

Chuckling, he locked the door then gathered her into his arms. "I can deny you nothing," he murmured, lowering her to the lush pelt. He leaned over her, brushing a kiss across her rosy lips as he raised her skirts. "You do realize we shall be hopelessly rumpled and wrinkled afterward. Everyone will guess what we've been about."

"We're newly wed." She rolled a shoulder, giving him a sultry look that singed his hair and hardened his groin. "Besides, I don't care if you don't."

She should, and so should he. But damn, he didn't. She reached between them, unfastened his falls, and encircled his sex with her warm hand.

Max groaned, burying his face in her shoulder. "I love you, Gabriella. You are my very life."

"Make love to me, Maxwell," she whispered against his throat before kissing his jaw. "I want to feel you inside me. I want you to give me a child."

And of course he did. In that precise order.

Wooed by a Wicked Duke

1

London, England
Late April 1810

With a nervous glance over her shoulder to assure no one had observed her ill-advised flight from the Duke of Westfall's ballroom, Miss Jessica Brentwood hoisted the skirts of her white silk gown and dashed through the open French windows. She'd steal a few minutes of much-needed respite and return before anyone noted her absence.

At least she hoped to do so. After all, this was London and a *haut ton* event. Dozens of busybodies' tongues wagged and ears flapped, either spreading *on dit* or eagerly listening for a succulent tidbit to pass along to their cronies.

Some claimed wealth and power the ruin of human decency. Jessica, however, believed the tongue far more destructive.

As she slipped onto the terrace, the brisk night air hit her with the force of a wet towel thrown in her face. The temperature was such a drastic contrast to the over-heated ballroom, and she gasped in surprise. A shiver skittered across her almost-bare shoulders and slithered down her spine as she swept a wary glance about the deserted verandah and lawns.

Good. No one she must avoid or offer explanations to about her hasty departure from the festivities. No one to raise a haughty eyebrow in askance. No one *else* to judge her.

Constantly surrounded by people since she'd come to Town, she simply needed a few moments alone to compose herself. Unlike the practiced and polished members of the *le beau monde*, Jessica hadn't acquired the ability to disguise her feelings and reactions behind a mask of disdainful politesse. She doubted she ever would, and she couldn't claim remorse for the deficit.

Her dratted expressive eyes gave away her every thought. She might as well blab them aloud, so transparent was she. Or so her sister, now the Duchess of Sutcliffe, claimed. In point of fact, Jessica wasn't altogether positive she'd be better off if she'd been able to master such a facade anyway. Plainly put, she wasn't deceptive by nature.

Her gloved hands wrapped about her shoulders to help ward off the sharp chill, she hurried forward rather than return to the crowded ballroom, with its abundance of sweaty bodies, cloying perfumes, and stifling atmosphere.

Stealing a few calming minutes outdoors, gathering her equanimity, and reining in her seething temper wouldn't result in a chill or ague. Possessed of a robust constitution, she rarely suffered from illness.

Wrestling her anger into submission might take more than a few minutes, truth to tell. Much more, such restrained fury simmered behind her ribs. No, she mightn't be dishonest by nature, but she did have a temper when incited. And, by damn, she'd just been provoked mightily.

Guilt poked her for silently swearing. Her parents would be mortified. Jessica gave a mental shrug. Sometimes an expletive was required, if only in one's thoughts, and despite being swathed in virginal hues.

Even with the mansion's windows aglow, her pale gown—unfortunately similar in color and style to those worn by every other insipid debutant present tonight—stood out in stark reprieve against the night's crisp darkness.

An image of dressed-up dolls on display came to mind—ladies on the Marriage Mart. Paraded before potential husbands, the misses' qualifications—or lack thereof, in her case—were easily attainable with a murmured request in the right ear.

She'd have preferred a rich emerald or royal purple gown, but young women were expected to appear pure and untouched in their shades of whites and ivories. Innocent. Unspoiled. Untouched. *Bah. What poppyswallop and baldercock.*

Or was it poppydash and balderswallop?

Jessica shrugged. What difference did it make? What *did* matter—a great deal, truth be told—was that she mustn't do anything untoward to draw the acrid eye of an Almack's peeress or other noble.

Such as slap the faces of tart-mouthed, mean-spirited chits. No matter that they heartily deserved a harsh, public reprimand.

To do so would've brought immense satisfaction. Oh, indeed, it would've done. She tightly pursed her lips. Alas, immense censure, too. Disapproval, she could ill afford, more's the pity. Not that she'd give a hen's tail feather about what anyone thought about her.

Well, she might care a *little*, but not enough to change who she was. Such artifice sickened her. A grimace pulled her mouth downward.

Still, Jessica had promised to *try* to conform. She wanted to embody the epitome of decorum. To display pretty manners and modesty. Truly, she did.

Liar!

Fine...not truly. But she did strive to—to the degree she wouldn't knowingly disgrace herself or her family—and she still might also enjoy a lovely time. For London did offer ever so many entertainments and distractions. One Season ought to see her curiosity satisfied. Then back to the country for her, where she could be herself again. Where she wouldn't have to worry about every word or action.

Briskly rubbing her arms, Jessica wet her lower lip. As nippy as the outdoors was, she'd welcome a glass of lemonade or ratafia. She'd become quite parched while dancing in the ballroom's sweltering heat.

Her partners thus far had been amicable, the dancing passably good. She wasn't a nymph on her feet, so she didn't hold her partner to a higher standard than herself.

In fact, unable to locate her sister, brother-in-law, or a friend to accompany her, she'd decided—perhaps unwisely, she grudgingly admitted to herself—to make her way to the refreshment tables in search of a much-needed glass of...anything.

That was another silly rule. Why a young woman couldn't traverse a room milling with people without a chaperone did not make sense.

A most unpleasant encounter with a trio of claws-bared females had detoured her from her goal, and now her thirst remained unquenched. Three smugly satisfied female faces paraded before her mind. God save the poor chaps who ended up married to those mean-spirited shrews.

Prior to that, she'd genuinely been having a grand time, her youthful bashfulness no longer a constant, exasperating presence. Why, her dance card bore the names of several gentlemen—including no fewer than three dukes. And although undoubtedly not the belle of the ball, she couldn't complain that her first official foray into Polite Society was a dismal failure.

She permitted the tiniest little proud smile to arc her mouth. It seems she truly had outgrown her shyness. Not that she'd ever be outgoing or seek attention. A diamond of the first water she was not, nor did she have any desire to be. Not that she was a dowd, by any means.

Though appropriately white, her gown, with its delicately embroidered overskirt and seed pearls, was a confection straight from a fairytale, as was her sapphire parure and her intricately styled hair.

Theadosia, her dearest sister, vowed the sapphires exactly matched Jessica's eyes. Not exactly. Her eyes were green-blue. Nonetheless, she quite felt like a princess, silly as that might seem.

As a little girl, she'd always pretended she was a princess. Only, as an innocent child, she'd believed a charming prince would fall madly in love with her. Never mind she was a humble vicar's dowerless, youngest daughter.

Not dowerless any longer.

She shoved the intrusive thought aside and resumed her fanciful reverie. Dowerless worked better for her daydream, and fairytales weren't based in reality, after all. It was much more romantic to wed for love than to be bartered off for a substantial marriage settlement, a title, or a parcel of land.

Her handsome and oh-so-entrancing prince would place her before him on his magnificent white steed—for fairytale princes must always ride white steeds—and they'd gallop away into the burnished sunset to live happily, passionately ever after. Because, quite naturally, happily-ever-afters required passion.

A wry smile tilted the edges of her mouth.

Twaddle, rubbish, stuff and nonsense. The whole of it.

Jessica had been all of ten when she first realized marriage was often something far different than happily-ever-afters. Nevertheless, good fortune did fall upon a lucky few, like her older sister, Theadosia, and her adoring husband, Victor.

They boasted friendships with several prominent peers and could be credited with her pleasant reception and acceptance into *le bon ton* so far. Almost everyone she'd met had been agreeable, if a trifle stuffy, formal, and exuding self-import.

But the upper ten thousand held pompous, elevated opinions of themselves and believed everyone else ought to as well. They also hid their true characters behind facades. At least, that was her perception of them thus far. Most were harmless, but a few—like the viper-tongued Medusas she'd just overheard—were the embodiment of cruelty and spite.

Vicious gossips.

She couldn't abide tattlemongers in any form. People who had nothing better to do than spread rumors as casually as buttering warm toast. Or who were such miserable wretches they sought to make themselves feel better by disparaging others. The worst of the chinwag lot, however, were those that contrived *on dit* simply because they enjoyed the trouble their tarradiddles wrought.

Such were despicable, contemptible dolts, and she had no patience for them or their nastiness. Nor did she have any desire to be their target, which meant she'd need to return to the ballroom before her next dance.

Pulling her eyebrows together, she studied the elaborate fan-shaped dance card.

If she recalled correctly, this set remained unclaimed. She'd be remiss to leave a partner searching for her. Such inconsideration wouldn't do. Not when she must remain above reproach. Already, dishonor hovered about her family like a soiled gray mantle.

Initially, she'd been eager to leave Colechester behind, mistakenly believing the mortifying shame and humiliation of Papa's disgrace would lessen with a bit of distance between her and the parish he'd stolen from. How wrong she'd been.

It was almost as if *le beau monde* was waiting, watching, expecting her family to misstep, and if they inadvertently did, those lofty denizens would pounce like a panther on a defenseless gazelle.

After perusing the dance card in the filtered light, Jessica relaxed a fraction.

Yes, she was free for the next thirty minutes. However, the dance afterward was promised to Crispin Rolston, the enigmatic Duke of Bainbridge. The arresting nobleman had positively flummoxed her by explicitly requesting that particular waltz.

She scrunched her forehead further, uncertain why a degree of unease coiled in her belly, making her shudder in apprehension.

Bainbridge was a pleasant enough chap. Quite dashing, actually, if she were wholly honest. *Oh, very well.* Extremely dashing. From the moment she'd laid eyes upon him, she thought so. She'd encountered him several times in the past year, and he'd grown impossibly more stunning upon each occurrence.

Why had God deemed the male of the species should be the more attractive? It was most unfair. As a young girl of perhaps eleven or twelve, she'd voiced that thought to her mother. Mama had laughed and said that was often true of birds but not necessarily of humans and other animals.

The Duke of Bainbridge made her sweet, pious mother into a liar.

His rakish smile could melt a glacier. And those eyes. *Lord, those magnificent eyes.* Quicksilver gray, they shone with a seductive gleam that had stolen her breath more than once.

Not, by Jove, that she'd ever admit such a thing. Vicar's daughters didn't entertain such notions. *Seductive gleam? Stolen breath?* She shook her head in self-reproach but allowed her mind to wander a bit longer.

Bainbridge's wavy, dark-blond hair—a lovely shade similar to sugared pecans—had a tendency to fall over his noble brow, enhancing his devil-may-care roguishness. His sculpted cheeks, angular jaw and chin, striking, almost severe eyebrows—several shades darker than his hair—and the sharp blade of his nose all added to his masculine appeal.

He was tall, of course, but not overly so. She didn't have to crane her neck to meet his startling eyes. And he had nice hands: clean nails, square tips, a light smattering of honey-colored hair across the knuckles.

Couldn't he have one flaw? Crooked teeth? Long nostril hair? Bad breath? A squeaky voice?

Honestly, she was hard put to find a single fault in his appearance. Neither, evidently, could the dozens of other simpering, ogling women continually surrounding him. To Jessica's credit, she didn't blink like a fly had landed in her eye, turn lobster red, or trip over her tongue in his presence. He was, after all, just a flesh-and-blood man.

Yes, but such a scrumptiously attractive one.

If she could've scolded her subconscious for stating the obvious, she would've done so.

But it was his voice, such a deep, resonant timbre, she found nearly irresistible. Jessica could listen to him speak for hours. Did he sing? She thought he might with that voice—as rich as melted chocolate. She'd never sat close enough to hear him when the hymns were sung the few times he'd attended Sunday services.

Placing her palms flat on the balustrade, she breathed out an exaggerated sigh. Crispin, Duke of Bainbridge, in all his sleek, male glory, was precisely the stuff of which fairytale heroes were made.

No. He isn't!

She narrowed her gaze at his name, scrawled across her dance card in penmanship as indolent as the scoundrel himself. Bainbridge was exactly the type of wicked libertine and philanderer Papa had always warned his daughters against.

Handsome. Wealthy. Confident. Privileged. Charming.

Rakehell. Roué. A man about town. Heartbreaker. Scoundrel.

Papa's list of unfavorable characteristics went on considerably longer. Pages longer. And yet, her own father, a clergyman, couldn't cast stones. Not with the burden of his own sins made so very public. In truth, the duke was the more honest of the men. He didn't hide his flaws behind piety.

Bainbridge was an aristocrat who drew women of every station and status to him like plump, fragrant summer blossoms enticed, clumsy, nectar-drunk bees. If his allure weren't so awfully pathetic to witness, she might find female reactions to him amusing.

Elderly dames batted their stubby eyelashes while thrusting out their saggy bosoms, hoping for a kind word or one of his devastating smiles. Married women and widows curved their painted mouths upward seductively and slid him inviting glances.

Precisely what those invitations entailed, Jessica refused to ponder, lest her cheeks heat with blistering color. Blushing debutantes and calf-eyed wallflowers observed his every move with something akin to hunger—or huntresses stalking their unsuspecting prey.

Albeit, he couldn't precisely be stalked when he knew full well—exploited, even—the enticing effects he had on women.

Extraordinarily, as much as she could appreciate his attractive outward trappings—she did have perfectly good vision, after all—Jessica had never been physically attracted to him.

Except for the difficulty in breathing on occasion. And my irregular pulse that one time.

She pressed her lips tight. *Fine. Thrice.*

And then there was the time your tummy went all wobbly, her annoying conscience gleefully reminded her.

Bah! She'd made it a point never to let her guard down around Bainbridge. To do so was utter idiocy. He was a seducer of innocents. A hedonist. A man with a new mistress or lover every month.

Or so she'd heard whispered. Not always in shocked disapproval, either. No, often there'd been yearning, possibly even a morsel of admiration, in those covert discussions.

While Jessica might have a tendency toward shyness and was by no measure a woman of the world, she assuredly was not an empty-minded fool, either.

She wasn't worried about standing up with him, however. On the once beautifully chalked dance floor, in full view of all, he'd be required to act the gentleman. Point of fact, she'd never known him to do otherwise with her, despite his reputation as a debauchee.

A particular friend of her brother-in-law, Bainbridge wasn't bacon-brained enough to attempt anything untoward and risk Victor's wrath. In any event, he'd never shown the least interest in her.

Of course, Jessica had spoken to the duke previously, just the two of them. Several times, in truth. Had, in fact, bested him at a game of Pall Mall a few weeks ago. Why come to think of it, he still owed her an ice from Gunter's as her prize.

Oh, he'd better not think to renege, the cad.

She meant to collect on that ice. Or a sorbet. *Mmm.* She shut her eyes for a blink, imaging the deliciousness melting on her tongue. Sorbets were even more scrumptious than ices, particularly the lemon-flavored frozen treat.

She adored almost anything flavored with lemon. Lemon curd, lemon drops, and lemonade amongst her other favorites.

Upon reflection, she concluded Bainbridge had probably only signed his name to her dance card as a favor to Victor. But of course. That made the most sense. She suspected as much of a few of the other gentlemen who'd also requested dances.

Not that she minded.

Far better to be partnered out of obligation than to lurk with the sad-eyed wallflowers gazing wistfully, sometimes sullenly and enviously, at the other misses enjoying themselves. In truth, she'd expected to be amongst the wallflower ranks, but she should've known Theadosia and Victor would assure she was not.

They, and the Duchess of Pennington—the sister of her bosom friend, Ophelia Breckensole—would never permit her to pine away as an onlooker at the ball. Ophelia's twin, Gabriella, the new Duchess of Pennington, no doubt played a not-so-subtle part in encouraging gentleman to seek a dance with Jessica as well.

She didn't mind their interference since affection motivated them. They were dears, one and all. Ophelia would be wondering where she'd disappeared to, though. Jessica shouldn't linger too much longer.

As she made her way to a secluded corner and leaned against a balustrade overlooking a quaint, walled garden alit with lanterns, beyond which lay what must be a hothouse, she pressed her mouth into a prim line and permitted her shoulders to slump. Slivers of iridescent moonlight bathed the garden and a figure-eight-shaped pond in a shimmering, silvery glow. The picturesque scene almost appeared fairylike.

Snorting, she shook her head and rolled her eyes heavenward. There she went again with her fairytales. She was much too old to harbor such nonsensical fancies.

A toad's throaty croak echoed from the vicinity of the foliage edging one side of the pond. Its raspy calls reminded her of the humble parsonage in Colechester where she'd spent her girlhood. A wave of homesickness and an intense longing to see her parents engulfed her.

It would be at least a year, likely two or three, before she saw them again. At times, she felt such a burden to Victor and Theadosia. She'd been foisted upon them as newlyweds. They never complained, but Jessica felt she was an imposition.

A shiver scuttled up her spine, and she renewed rubbing her arms.

How very different her life had been less than a year ago.

Before scandal had sent her disgraced father to an Australian penal colony to minister to criminals. How stupid and naïve she'd been to believe the *on dit* wouldn't follow the Brentwoods from Colechester to London.

A well-respected solicitor, her brother, James, didn't give a fig what Society thought. Her eldest sister, Althea, had eloped several years ago and was happy as a grig with her husband and children. And, of course, Theadosia had made a love match with Victor, the Duke of Sutcliffe.

No one looked askance at the Sutcliffes and didn't reap the consequences.

Jessica, alone, had the most to lose from the ugly murmurings—namely, a respectable match. But she wasn't altogether keen on landing a husband, unless she loved him. Her mother's and sisters' marriages had given her high expectations. Perhaps, unrealistic expectations. *Fairytale* expectations.

But why shouldn't she desire love? Wait for love?

Without love, how did one forgive? Find contentment and happiness?

Bear the heartaches and difficulties life served up more often than not? With a loving spouse, someone to support and encourage, a man she could trust her deepest secrets and innermost desires to, she could be more than satisfied.

Even when Mama had railed at Papa because of the shame he'd brought upon the family, she'd never stopped loving him. She'd willingly accompanied him to Australia, leaving her grown children behind. Leaving Jessica with Theadosia. Because a single woman, even accompanied by her mother and vicar father, had no place amongst hardened convicts.

With deliberate intent, she inhaled a deep, cleansing breath of chilly air. As she exhaled, she released her concerns. It was too early in the Season to be mooning about such piffle.

If she didn't meet a man who looked at her the way Victor regarded Theadosia, or the Duke of Pennington gazed at Gabriella, the world wouldn't tilt on its axis, nor would the sun fail to rise.

At almost twenty, she wasn't quite on the shelf or in her dotage. There was yet time. Not all would agree with her assessment. *Breeding years and all that claptwaddle.*

Inhaling the cleansing air again—it was most invigorating—she deliberately tried to turn her thoughts to more pleasant musings. A Come Out and a Season had never crossed her mind, even after Theadosia married Victor. He'd generously dowered her, too.

Now, here she was. In London. At a posh ball. With a new wardrobe, a sizable settlement, and about to launch into her first Season. Not the merest bit terrified.

Really?

Fine, perhaps a trifle nervous.

The breeze toyed tauntingly with the curls on either side of her face.

Uh-hum, mocked that perturbing voice that never permitted her to lie to herself.

Very well. She was entirely out of her element but determined to do her best. For Theadosia's benefit. And Victor's. And, yes, even for James's sake, too.

Damned, dashed nuisance to have such a rational conscience.

She *had* been having an enjoyable time earlier. Much better than she'd anticipated, until she'd overheard that trio of sharp-clawed she-cats gossiping about her and Theadosia. Or, more on point, about Papa's public dishonor.

Positive they'd seen her approaching the refreshment tables, in *sotto voce* voices, they'd tittered and feigned shock about his embezzlement of church funds and the subsequent gambling away of said monies. Of nearly finding himself defrocked. Of Theadosia almost being forced into marriage with a horrid reprobate.

Fresh humiliation stabbed Jessica, and she swallowed. Or tried to. Her throat truly was dry.

She'd make sure to drink a glass of lemonade before her waltz with the duke, else she'd not be able to converse without croaking worse than the amorous amphibian in the garden.

"There you are."

2

Jessica glanced toward the speaker. A pretty, dark-haired, plump young woman approached, carrying two glasses in her fine-boned hands. Lemonade or ratafia?

Searching behind her for a chaperone and finding none, Jessica offered a genial smile. It seemed she wasn't the only one to brave a bit of censure by venturing outdoors alone. "I'm sorry, but I don't believe we've been introduced."

The girl—for she couldn't be much more than seventeen or eighteen—shook her head, causing her pearl-and-emerald earrings to bob. A mischievous glint in her eyes—were they brown?—she made an exaggerated pretense of inspecting the area. "We haven't. But I shan't tell if you don't."

Jessica liked her instantly. "I'm Jessica Brentwood."

Blast. Another faux pas. Introducing oneself wasn't *de rigueur*. She was supposed to find someone who knew the other woman and ask them to do the honors—a silly waste of time.

"I'm Lilith Brighton," the girl said, offering one of the glasses.

Jessica wasn't familiar with the name, but that wasn't a surprise. As this was her first week in London, she knew few people. A quick inspection of the cloudy liquid, and she dubbed it lemonade.

"I saw you earlier," Miss Brighton said. Then her forehead puckered, and she turned her mouth down. "And, I fear, I couldn't help but overhear what those malicious twits said about your father. I suspected you'd intended to relieve your thirst, so after I gave them a piece of my mind, I set out in search of you. Please believe me when I tell you not everyone is as shallow or judgmental as they are."

Gratitude suffused Jessica that this stranger would champion her and had even realized she'd been thirsty and come looking for her with lemonade, too.

She racked her memory.

Had Miss Brighton been nearby when she'd gone in search of a beverage? Mayhap. After hearing the unkind conversation, Jessica had been quite upset. Miss Brighton might've been standing within an arm's reach, dressed as an Amazonian warrior, and Jessica wouldn't have noticed.

Her only thought had been to put as much distance as possible between herself and the vile gossipmongers before she said or did something that would add more fodder to the inferno that was her family's reputation.

Despite her determination, otherwise, Jessica had a bit of a quick temper when provoked. But only when provoked. Tonight, she most assuredly had been.

"Have you seen the darling puppies yet?" Miss Brighton cheerily asked, trailing her attention around the terrace and gardens before bringing that inquisitive gaze back to her.

Jessica adored animals, as anyone who knew her at all could attest. Particularly baby animals. "Puppies?"

She took a long, grateful sip of the lemonade. Gracious, it was tart, but also very welcome to her dry mouth and throat. Not everyone liked the citrusy drink as sweet as she preferred. In fact, Mama had claimed plain lemon water a curative, though they seldom had the funds to spend on the fruit.

Grinning, Miss Brighton nodded eagerly, her attention once more sweeping the area.

Was she afraid of being caught outdoors?

Perhaps she wasn't as bold as Jessica had first thought, which made her efforts to find her all that much more generous. However, as they were in each other's company now, no one could proclaim them improper.

"Oh, yes. The Duke of Westfall's grandmother's Pomeranian had three precious puppies a fortnight ago. They're absolutely *adorable*." She scrunched her nose and drew out the word. "She so dotes on the dog. Treats her like a pampered child. My parents have said that I might have one if—"

A shadow passed over her round face but quickly disappeared, replaced by her bubbly countenance once more.

Two gentlemen tripped down the steps to the garden below, and a moment later, one lit a cheroot. He angled in the terrace's direction briefly before they wandered away along one of the serpentine pathways, their footsteps crunching on the gravel. At the far end of the porch, three couples made a slow turn, the ladies briskly waving their fans before their faces to create a breeze.

The ballroom must've become more unbearably warm, for more attendees had braved the less-than-hospitable outdoors. Their numbers would likely increase as the evening wore on.

However, it had grown impossibly cooler in the past five minutes, and Jessica had become quite chilled. She should probably go back inside before she was missed and before she became any colder.

After draining her glass, she set the etched crystal on the balustrade, her thirst not quite quenched. A drink of water wouldn't go amiss, but she'd yet to sample water in London as fresh as that in Colechester.

Miss Brighton placed her half-full cup beside Jessica's.

"Come, I'll show you. They're in the conservatory." She sliced Jessica another friendly grin. "Well, it's too small to be a real conservatory. But there are several lush plants, a fountain in the center, and a pair of settees and few chairs scattered about. It's quite charming."

Jessica hesitated. She'd been absent for several minutes already.

She spared a glance toward the house. Through the windows and open doors, she made out the shapes of a few dancers and the black-clad shoulder of one violinist. She'd be wise to seek the retiring room, too, to make sure the slight breeze hadn't loosened any of her hair from its pins.

Ruffled hair might give the wrong impression.

Ophelia and Theadosia might very well be looking for her by now. Jessica had been outside for several minutes already.

But she adored animals, and a chance to see puppies greatly tempted. She missed her chickens—the *girls,* as she called them. Silly to have pet chickens, but she'd had chickens since she was eight years old.

The Season would be over soon enough, and then she could return to Colechester and her pets. Well, to Ridgefield Court. That's where she lived now, in a house grander than this one.

Though not yet eleven of the clock, she smothered a yawn. Theadosia said the ball might very well last until early morning. Accustomed to country hours, Jessica already felt the initial hindrance of fatigue. In truth, she preferred staying up late at night and sleeping in to mid-morning, but that lifestyle didn't suit in the country.

"How long will it take? Jessica asked. "My next dance is promised."

"Not more than five or ten minutes, I shouldn't think." Miss Brighton pointed to the building beyond the gardens. "It's just there. I'd love for you to help me pick which puppy I ought to choose. They are all so sweet. It's impossible to decide."

How could she refuse? "All right," Jessica conceded, with another swift glance to the humming ballroom. "I can spare five minutes, I suppose."

Miss Brighton's effervescent demeanor was a welcome change, and Jessica could use another friend. Especially one who wasn't afraid to take on vipers in her defense. "I wonder if I might convince my brother-in-law to permit me a puppy, as well?"

She'd adore a dog of her own. Her hens were sweet, but one couldn't very well cuddle a chicken in bed, nor have it sleep on her lap. And, *dear heavens*, she couldn't imagine trying to housetrain the girls.

"Oh, wouldn't that be splendid? We could walk them in Hyde Park or Green Park together." Miss Brighton fairly simmered with enthusiasm.

Her enthusiasm seemed a trifle overdone, but perhaps that was her nature. Jessica and Theadosia had never been what one would call high-spirited, and Miss Brighton was the epitome of exuberance and impetuousness.

It only took a couple of minutes to reach the hothouse. After a bit of fumbling with and grumbling at the uncooperative latch, Miss Brighton managed to open the door. She and Jessica slipped inside the considerably warmer building. Only a faint coolness tainted the air.

A single glowing lamp reposed upon a table between two mint-green divans situated in an L-shape. Arranged in clusters on the far side sat several healthy potted trees and plants. Between them, a trio of beautifully painted screens depicting exotic landscapes added vibrant color.

"I didn't think the latch was going to give, and I feared we wouldn't be able to see the little darlings," Miss Brighton said with a short, tense laugh. She pointed to a shadowy corner behind one screen. "They're over there."

The mother hadn't even barked upon their entrance. Either she was calm-natured, or she was asleep. "I'm surprised they aren't kept in the house, given, as you say, the dowager duchess is so fond of her pet."

Miss Brighton's sunny smile faltered, and she shifted her gaze to the side before lifting a shoulder. She plucked at the dance card dangling from her wrist. "Ah, well...ah, they usually are. But I suppose...ah, with the commotion of the ball..."

Jessica would've removed them to a quiet bedchamber rather than the conservatory. The puppies might become chilled out here. Then again, there was no accounting for the eccentricities of the nobility.

She stepped forward then stumbled as severe dizziness overcame her.

Good Lord. I feel so peculiar. She held perfectly still, willing the unsteadiness to leave.

Pressing a palm to her forehead, she closed her eyes, trying to regain her equilibrium. The tilting increased to a frenzy, and her thoughts became muddled.

Why was she here again?

Oh, yes. To see puppies.

Why had it become so difficult to concentrate? She blinked several times, attempting to clear her vision and focus her thoughts.

"Miss Brentwood?" Miss Brighton's voice, hollow and distant, permeated the dense fog enshrouding her mind. "Are you quite well? You look about to swoon."

"No, I don't believe I am. I feel most irregular." Jessica swayed. "So dizzy." Her head felt thick and wooly. Her limbs weighty and cumbersome. Her thoughts sluggish and incoherent. "I...cannot...think..."

Speaking was becoming difficult, her words hard to form and thick upon her swollen tongue.

Was this the vapors?

But she'd never swooned in her life.

What had triggered an episode now?

"Permit me to assist you to the divan." All solicitousness and concern, Miss Brighton snaked an arm about Jessica's waist. "It's just here. A few more steps. Be careful."

Jessica forced her leaden legs to shuffle forward as Miss Brighton unerringly guided her to the seat.

"Here we are. You may sit now. Slowly." She gently urged Jessica down, her voice seemingly reaching through a long tunnel. "Sit back. There you are."

Releasing a grateful sigh, Jessica sank onto the welcoming cushions and promptly shut her eyes. The mad swirling didn't stop. In fact, the frenzy spiraling increased. Spinning and whirling, a muddled tornado of confusion and light-headedness.

"Shall I go for help?" The divan dipped as Miss Brighton sat beside her and took her hand. "Miss Brentwood? Can you hear me?"

It was simply too much effort to answer. Too dashed difficult to open her eyes. Her head spun round and round and round. Sounds and sensations faded and receded. Diminished, waning farther and farther away. She floated, spiraling into vast darkness.

What is happening?

That was her last coherent thought before blackness claimed her.

3

Crispin tossed back his last swallow of champagne and returned the nod Mathias, Duke of Westfall, sent him from farther along this side of the ballroom. Earlier, they'd discussed horseflesh—a stud Westfall wanted, to be precise. Depositing the empty flute on the tray a passing black-and-crimson-liveried footman carried, he casually surveyed the milling crowd, seeking Jessica Brentwood.

He'd dared to claim a waltz with her, although his common sense rebuffed him for the foolish impulse. Sutcliffe had asked him to dance with his sister-in-law, and Crispin was only too willing to honor his friend's request. Never mind that notion had been at the forefront of his mind since he'd ascended the steps to the house.

Laughing, Nicolette Twistleton and Ophelia Breckensole, along with Rayne Wellbrook and Justina Farthington, hurried from the ballroom. Ladies never seemed to be able to seek the retiring room unless they did so *en masse*.

It made him grateful to have been born a male.

Across the way, near an elaborate column, the Dukes of Pennington, Kincade, and Asherford engaged in earnest conversation. Victor, the Duke of Sutcliffe, danced with his duchess, as did the Dukes of Dandridge and Sheffield. Each was nauseatingly content in their wedded state, and he couldn't help but envy them.

If compelled down the marital path forced upon him at present, Crispin would leave his duchess at his remotest estate while taking himself off to India. Or China. Or the Americas, regularly. He and Lilith Brighton were as compatible as oil and water, and he'd be damned if he'd impose his presence on her or hers upon him.

Even his closest friends didn't know of his less-than-gallant intentions. He rather suspected they'd point out how unbecoming cowardice was, as well as abandoning one's spouse. Except, he wouldn't precisely be abandoning Lilith. She'd want for nothing, and he would have to return to England annually, at the minimum, to inspect his properties.

Chagrin chafed him, and he glared at the chalked floor. It wasn't her fault that he felt nothing for her and never would. His heart was too full of another.

Earlier in the day, he'd learned the Sutcliffe household was to attend the Westfalls' ball this evening, and he'd immediately altered his plans so he might see Jessica. It wasn't the first time he'd done so, which made him a complete assling. But as long as no one else suspected his *tendre*, he'd continue to do so.

Miss Jessica Brentwood was an enchantress and had consumed his musings for months. He'd secretly admired her from afar for as long. Nonetheless, he'd been diligent not to make overtures or give anyone cause for gossip or speculation.

After all, he was betrothed.

Not, *by God*, of his own free will.

And that frustration chafed raw and sharp. Gnawed at his peace and kept his mind in a constant turmoil. He did not desire the union with Lilith Brighton. Never had. Never would. How was he to escape the cursed match?

No, the real difficulty was dissolving the contract without ruining lives.

What about my life?

Somehow, he must make it so. He'd oppose the forced marriage until he'd exhausted every avenue.

The settlement had been drawn up when he was but a lad of twelve. At the time, he'd had no idea what his father had rushed him into signing.

He'd wanted the deed done so he might return to the stables and to his best friend—a sweet-natured gelding named Ross.

His father had ordered him to put his name to the official-looking document, and so he had. One did not argue with the intimidating, formidable previous Duke of Bainbridge. Most especially not skinny, pimply-faced heirs whose fathers only deigned to criticize and find fault with everything they did.

Since coming into his title seven years ago, at the age of twenty, Crispin had consulted his solicitor in multiple instances regarding the intricacies of flouting the agreement. Unfortunately, the consequences would be most unpleasant, particularly if both parties were not amenable to the dissolution. The drafters of the contract had been cunning and wily. *Damn their eyes.*

It wasn't their lives being manipulated.

Personally, he didn't mind scandals too terribly much—if a scandal meant avoiding a union he deplored. Decades with a woman not of his choosing was, in essence, a lifetime prison sentence for a crime he hadn't committed.

Crispin glanced around the milling crowd, wishing he dared take a hefty swallow from the flask in his pocket. Ruminations of his impending marriage always made him want to get foxed.

Several years ago, his mother had married a widower with two grown sons and after the death of her husband, lived contentedly as the Dowager Baroness Waverly. Nevertheless, destroying Albertina's and Lettice's prospects wouldn't make him a hero in her—or his cosseted and indulged sisters'—eyes.

Right now, he didn't much care what they thought of him, truth be told.

While their dowries were sufficient to attract numerous suitors, they had, regrettably, taken after Waverly in form, intelligence, and disposition. Though he loved his sisters and wished them the best, given they were turnip-shaped, scatter-brained, and given to fits of temper and histrionics, neither would readily find herself a husband.

Perhaps they'd mature, adopt more biddable temperaments, before their Come Outs. At fourteen and fifteen, that wasn't entirely impossible. And neither was Prinny losing two stone and putting aside his mistresses. Just improbable as hell.

An eruption of high-pitched giggles behind him dragged him back to the present.

Crispin scrutinized the guests again before returning to the matter plaguing him. The ever-present burr in his bum, which permitted him no relaxation.

When the betrothal contract had been drafted fifteen years ago, the duchy was nearly destitute. Since he'd come into the title, he'd made several lucrative investments, and now the dukedom sailed along quite smoothly. He couldn't afford to be unwise, but if he stayed the course, his heir wouldn't bear the same financial trials that had burdened him upon inheriting the dukedom.

Money wasn't the only issue, however. Years before, Crispin had repaid the funds advanced to the duchy. Well, he'd had his solicitor deposit the funds in Hammon Brighton's account.

What was trickier to negotiate was the property Father had acquired in the agreement. Property upon which sat the house he had commissioned and which Mother and his sisters now resided.

Not only was it forfeit if Crispin broke the agreement, but Brighton was also guaranteed two other unentailed estates, including Pickford Hill Park, where Crispin conducted his horse-breeding ventures. The reverse was true if Lilith Brighton, his intended, refused the match. All the properties remained Crispin's holdings.

By damn, Brighton would *not* put his grubby paws on Pickford Hill Park.

However, Crispin still hadn't contrived a suitable solution to the betrothal.

Lilith had recently celebrated her eighteenth birthday. The agreed-upon age when he and she would exchange vows. Since that auspicious day had come and gone, his mother and Lilith's father nagged worse than fishwives for Crispin to set a wedding date. Soon. Before Season's end, by God. He could feel the noose tightening more and more with each passing day.

"Ballocks," he swore beneath his breath.

He didn't fool himself that his mother's concern was for him. She'd never been an affectionate woman. Her union with Father had been arranged, and there'd been no love between them. She fretted that his pampered sisters would have to leave their preferred home. And Albertina and Lettice *always* demanded and usually had their way.

Which, until now, had suited him fine. As long as they didn't take up residence at Pickford Hill Park, he didn't give a dozen damns where they lived. Pray God, he wouldn't be required to assist with their Come Outs.

A shudder rippled across his shoulders at the horrifying notion. God save him from such cruel punishment.

Bored, Crispin took in the revelers again.

Where the blazes was Miss Brentwood?

His affianced was also in attendance tonight. Strangely, the moment she'd spied him, she'd flown from the ballroom, apparently no more thrilled to see him than he'd been to see her. He felt neither offended nor pleased at the knowledge. In truth, Lilith Brighton stirred no emotion, or anything else, in him. His intended was little more than a cossetted child.

Crispin hadn't bothered to determine if she'd returned to the ballroom yet.

He had no intention of asking her to dance. He didn't want to encourage Lilith. Young women too easily fell in and out of infatuation. Far better for all if she remained leery of him as he pondered a means of dissolving their marriage contract.

Sighing, he scrubbed a hand over his chin. Physical fatigue didn't cause his weariness, but rather mental exhaustion. If only there were an honorable way to put an end to their betrothment. Mayhap he could persuade Lilith to terminate it or, together, come to an amicable settlement for dissolution.

Not bloody likely.

Weren't all marriage-minded misses eager to become a duchess? Shallow ones such as Lilith most assuredly were. Except her behavior tonight said otherwise.

It mattered naught. Her social-climbing father, Hammon Brighton, would never consent. He'd purchased their daughter a title, and now Crispin and Miss Lilith Brighton must somehow forge a future together that neither had chosen.

He'd spoken to her father, and the blackguard had made it most clear; his daughter *would* become a duchess. More specifically, the Duchess of Bainbridge. Or there would be hell to pay.

Nevertheless, Crispin wasn't leg-shackled yet, and he'd damn well enjoy his dance with Jessica Brentwood.

"Bainbridge?" Ronald, Viscount Brookmoore, approached, yanking him once more from his unpleasant musings. His aristocratic features tense, Brookmoore glanced around before lowering his voice. "Might I impose upon you to assist me with my brother? Inconspicuously?"

A sot and a rakehell of the worst order, Randolph Radcliff was notorious for becoming embroiled in one disgraceful conundrum after another.

Crispin cocked an eyebrow. "What's he up to now?"

"He's foxed to his gills." Brookmoore made a sound of disgust. "Drank nearly a half bottle of Scotch before we left home, and God only knows how much he's consumed since."

And Brookmoore asked *him* to help? Why not one of his usual cronies?

The viscount must've anticipated the question. "I require a man of some…ah…discretion to assist in bundling my brother into our carriage. It's parked outside the alley, by the garden. For my family's sake, I'd rather not ask the footmen to help. You know how servants gossip." He gave a rueful twist of his lips and shook his head. "Mother hasn't recovered entirely from the last debacle."

Was that the one where Radcliffe had been caught with the maid in the linen closet, her skirts over her head? Or the episode with the new-to-London widow whose very-much-alive husband had returned home at the most inopportune moment? *Egads.* Radcliffe made him grateful he only had stout sisters with difficult temperaments to deal with.

"I'd be most appreciative," Brookmoore murmured, brushing a hand over his weak chin while surreptitiously examining the company. "You don't gossip as many do, and I know I can rely upon your circumspection."

With a sharp nod, Crispin angled toward the doors leading onto the terrace. As the Duke of Westfall was a good friend, he was well-acquainted with the grounds. A gate exited directly to the mew's alley from the garden. Quite convenient for furtively removing foxed dandies from the premises.

Aiding Brookmoore also provided him an opportunity to take a nip from the flask in his pocket. He required something stiffer than lukewarm champagne or weak punch suitable for tipsy tabbies. His discussion earlier in the evening with the blissfully happy, newlywed Pennington hadn't improved his sour mood either.

Four of his closest friends—Dandridge, Sutcliffe, Sheffield, and now Pennington—had managed to marry for love. They'd found women that complimented them and made them into better men. No wonder he felt disgruntled at the woman foisted upon him.

Miss Brighton was attractive enough, he supposed. Quite pretty actually, if a man preferred empty-headed, dark-haired, brown-eyed fashionable dolls. However, the few occasions they'd spoken—when he'd been trapped with no ready escape—she'd babbled inanely about lace and buttons and rose water. Kittens. Tea. Oh, and Lady Wimpleton's *divine* tea cakes.

There'd also been envious tripe about somebody's betrothal. Even a gloating whisper regarding the scandalous crimson gown somebody-or-other had worn to...*something*.

A ball? Rout? Theater? *Funeral?*

By that time, Crispin had so detached himself from the conversation, preferring to have his eyes gouged out with a salt spoon rather than attend to her nattering, he wouldn't have recalled if she'd declared Almack's patronesses had paraded through Hyde Park, wearing nothing but peacock feathers in their hair and bells on their toes.

"I'm afraid my brother has become the bane of our dear mother's existence," Brookmoore was mumbling when Crispin stopped his ruminations and, once more, focused on the viscount.

"You really ought to do something about his drinking, Brookmoore. Cut off his allowance, if you must. Have him banned from his clubs." Disgust riddled him. When deep in his cups, Radcliff became boisterous and obnoxious. No woman was safe from his groping hands. "If he keeps on this dubious track, he'll have a pickled liver by the time he's thirty."

A hand on his pocket, prepared to withdraw his flask, Crispin paused. He'd be obligated to offer Brookmoore a swig. Best wait until he'd seen the viscount and his errant brother on their way.

Heaving a gusty sigh, Brookmoore fell into step beside him. "You're right, of course. I'm considering sending him to the Continent. At least, there, his antics wouldn't constantly embarrass the family."

Crispin gave a noncommittal grunt. That might be worse. Brookmoore would have no control over his brother, and God only knew what the pup would embroil himself in. Besides, Brookmoore's behavior wasn't exactly above reproach.

In truth, Crispin had only agreed to aid him to prevent anything untoward happening at Westfalls' ball.

A minute later, they trotted down the terrace steps, their heels softly clacking on the stones. Sure enough, the polished ebony top of a coach glinted above the garden wall directly beside the gate.

Several other guests' equipages also lined the alley.

Raising his face to inhale the reviving air, he eyed the cloud-scattered, inky sky. Moonbeams sliced through branches laden with plump buds. Spring hovered, ready to burst forth in a week or two. "Let's be about it, then. I have a waltz I don't wish to miss."

Slicing him a wolfish glance, Brookmoore scratched his temple. "A little dallying before committing yourself to the parson's mousetrap, eh? I take it you don't intend to keep yourself only to your Miss Brighton, despite her sizable dowry? A veritable fortune, I hear. If I were you, I'd not want to anger her dear papa. He might tighten the purse strings."

186

Was that a note of criticism in his voice? *Him?* A known rakehell? Talk about the proverbial pot calling the kettle black.

Brookmoore made Prinny look like a monk. How many mistresses had he gone through this past year alone? *Seven? Eight?* The poor woman who found herself Viscountess Brookmoore had better have a physician examine her for the clap. Monthly.

Brookmoore wasn't at all particular in the feminine company he kept.

Tightening his jaw to quash his instinctive terse retort, Crispin glanced overhead again. "I'm sure you're aware the match was arranged when I was a mere lad." He needn't explain his personal business, though the underlying details weren't a secret. "I'm unconvinced it's the best course for me to continue to pursue."

A guarded expression descended onto Brookmoore's features, appearing almost sinister in the half-light, with the tree branches casting weird shadows over them. "But how do you intend to avoid...?"

Fishing, was he?

"That, I don't know, as of yet." A sardonic chuckle escaped Crispin. "I'd rather there wasn't a scandal. It would be much better for all, including Miss Brighton. I wish no disgrace or discomfort upon her. She's a pawn as much as I."

Hands linked behind his back, Brookmoore merely grunted.

They'd reached the conservatory, and he opened the door, permitting Crispin to enter first.

He stopped short.

Pale and nervously wringing her hands and biting her lower lip, Miss Brighton stood beside the fountain. Something akin to relief flitted over her face upon spying them.

Why, in blazes, was she here?

He fired an accusing glare toward Brookmoore.

"What's this? Miss Brighton, why—?" He started forward, but a woman lying prostrate on a divan snared his attention. He blinked once, not believing his eyes. "*Miss Brentwood?*"

His brows lashed together in alarm. *What the devil?* His nape hair stood straight up as alarm bells pealed loudly in his head. Why was Jessica here, incapacitated, and Radcliffe—the bounder—obviously was not?

Brookmoore had lied. Fabricated the whole bloody story.

But, *God's teeth*, why?

Something was too deuced smoky by far.

"Where's your brother, Brookmoore?" Crispin snapped, shooting the disconcertingly silent man a half accusing, half questioning glance as he strode to Jessica.

What drivel would he concoct?

He knelt beside the divan. "Miss Brentwood?" He gave her shoulder a gentle shake, but she didn't stir. Didn't so much as twitch. What the hell went on?

How long had she been in the hothouse? If she didn't return to the ball soon, she faced inevitable ruination. He raked an accusatory gaze over Miss Brighton, who'd skirted the divan to stand before the door. No, to stand beside Brookmoore.

She was Crispin's affianced, yet he felt more concern and regard for the insensate woman on the divan than he did for her. "What's wrong with her?" he demanded, stonily. His taut gut told him Miss Brighten knew full well what ailed Jessica.

When she didn't answer but flicked her anxious gaze to Brookmoore, Crispin firmed his lips together. Did affection soften the worried lines about her mouth?

Ah, so that was which way the wind blew. Ire replaced his satisfaction with the discovery. Those two fiends were behind this…whatever the bloody nuisance this was.

By God, he'd get to the bottom, but first, he must ascertain what was wrong with Jessica. His betrothed and Brookmoore had a great deal of explaining to do.

He touched Jessica's forehead with the back of his hand, relieved when he detected no fever. Her chest rose and fell, her breathing even and unlabored. She appeared peaceful and deeply asleep. She hadn't responded to their talk nor when he touched her.

Drugged. Jessica acted drugged.

Hell's bells! He jerked his head up, prepared to give Brookmoore and Miss Brighton a tongue lashing requiring a fortnight's recovery. "Precisely what—"

Excruciating pain lanced the base of Crispin's skull. He toppled forward, collapsing atop Jessica's bountiful chest.

A woman gasped, the sound muffled and appalled. "Ronny! You might've killed him."

His vision grew narrower and narrower until the last vestige of light disappeared.

4

Crispin groaned, his skull threatening to crack with the harsh, guttural sound. He touched his fingertips to the bridge of his nose, applying pressure to ease the hammering in his head.

What the hell had happened?

He'd recalled bending over Jessica, and then—

Goddammit. Brookmoore had walloped the back of his head.

The whole thing had been a calculated ploy. But why?

Was Jessica part of the scheme, or was she a victim, too?

He dropped his hand to his naked chest. *Naked?* Why was he naked?

Fingers splayed, he waited for his mind to catch up to the undeniable evidence beneath his palm. It took another second for him to comprehend he was completely unclothed. Nude as the day he'd been born.

Shit. Shit. Shit.

And what was more—*God dammit!*—he wasn't alone on the divan. His breath hissed out from between his teeth, and every muscle in his torso tensed.

Could things possibly become any worse?

A lush feminine body curled into his, a slim thigh thrown across his legs and a slender arm across his bare chest. The tantalizing scents of cloves and vanilla surrounded him as he slowly turned his head, dreading yet knowing, he'd find Jessica Brentwood in his arms. Also deliciously naked as a robin, her honey-blonde hair splayed over her shoulders and back.

He might've been knocked senseless and still struggled to cobble a coherent thought together, but he was aware enough to appreciate the exquisiteness of the form tucked so intimately next to his. Like a contented kitten.

She made a soft noise and shivered, burrowing deeper into his side, and despite his head threatening to split at the slightest movement, desire sluiced through him. She was even more incredibly beautiful than he'd imagined. And he *had* imagined her naked—many, *many* times.

He supposed that made him a bounder and a reprobate. *God rot me.* But, despite what others believed, it wasn't something he did with all women. Just this special, unique creature.

Jessica's unbound golden hair fell over her creamy shoulders, and her bountiful breasts pressed enticingly against his chest, her delectably plump buttocks sloping downward to long, lithe legs.

To anyone coming upon them, it would appear they recovered from a rousing round of satiating love play. Damn his eyes. He would kill Brookmoore—*slowly*—for looking upon Jessica and touching her.

He squinted through half-closed lids, the pounding in his head preventing him from opening his eyes wide. When he'd entered the hothouse, a single lamp had burned on the table. Now, however, three more glowed brightly. Someone had gone to a great deal of trouble to make it appear as if he and Jessica had just coupled. To compromise and entrap them.

Lilith.

The devious, little bitch.

Rage such as he'd never known pummeled behind his ribs and boiled his blood. If it weren't for his cracking headache and the woman nestled beside him, he'd have been up, dressed, and in furious pursuit. No doubt, Lilith and Brookmoore had counted on his being incapacitated for some time. They'd ensured it by bashing him on the head.

That bastard Brookmoore and his witch of a betrothed would feel the full effect of his wrath. He was typically much better at reading people and cursed himself for being ten times a fool for being so damn gullible.

Concern for Jessica had dulled his instincts.

His question as to whether she was as bitterly opposed to the match between them as Crispin, had been answered. Once she'd turned eighteen and knew a wedding date was forthcoming, Lilith had determined to take matters into her own hands.

Why hadn't she approached her father? Mayhap she had.

Brighton wouldn't have given ten tinkers' damns about her feelings. He'd already proved that. So, Lilith had used other nefarious means to achieve her end. It seems his betrothed—*former* betrothed, after this unforgivable stunt—was a cunning, plotting witch.

As awful as the situation was at present, at least he'd learned the truth about her.

But why in the hell had Brookmoore schemed to help her? Unless…

Ah. Of course.

He wanted Lilith for himself. Wanted her fortune-of-a-marriage-settlement.

Did they think Crispin wouldn't bring charges against them? If Brookmoore had gambled he wouldn't drag him before the House of Lords, he'd gambled wrong. Or had Brookmoore and Lilith truly intended to kill him? Crispin intended to find out, by God.

He would obliterate him for disrobing Jessica, looking upon her naked form, and touching her. Fury throttled up his throat, and he gritted his teeth. He damn well might challenge Brookmoore to an affair of honor.

However, despite Jessica being a victim too, she was thoroughly and undeniably compromised. Even if whatever had caused her insensate condition was proven, the facts were the facts.

They were naked. Together.

It didn't matter that nothing had occurred between them. That he was injured, and she was unconscious. Or that he wasn't in any condition to rouse her, let alone see them both into their clothing.

Shutting his eyes, he battled the waves of nausea assailing him. He swallowed, willing the contents of his stomach to stay where they were. Vomiting on Jessica wouldn't endear him to her.

Brookmoore may very well have concussed him. Gingerly, Crispin touched the back of his head, unsurprised when his fingertips came away sticky with blood. The blow that damned wretch dealt him had left a gash in his skull.

He wiped his fingers on the back of the divan then grimaced at the bloody smears. Westfall's mother would not be pleased.

Had Lilith and Brookmoore contrived this debacle to place the blame on Crispin by causing the scandal of the year? He'd wager on it. Had Brookmoore already bedded Lilith?

Probably.

Which meant, if Crispin's hunch proved right—and by God and all of the saints, he was positive it would—someone would burst through the door any moment. And most conveniently find him and Jessica *dishabille*.

Perhaps he should feign unconsciousness again to lend credence to the truth that they'd been set up. He skimmed his gaze over her creamy skin, and his instinct to protect her won over. No others would have an opportunity to leer at her when she was defenseless. She'd be utterly humiliated.

She would be, in any event. There was no help for it.

"Jessica. Jessica." Gently but firmly shaking her shoulders, he whispered in her ear, "You must wake up, sweetheart."

God help them. She didn't revive except to sigh and press her lush curves closer, reinforcing his suspicion she'd been drugged.

How much time had passed? *Minutes? Hours?*

God damn Lilith and Brookmoore to the lowest layer of hell. May they burn for eternity.

How could they involve Jessica? An innocent. She'd done nothing to either of them to warrant this type of hostile treatment.

She'd be utterly compromised. Destroyed. Shunned through no fault of her own.

Brookmoore or Lilith had probably heard the ugly tattle about Jessica's father and decided she was expendable. A woman with a slightly-tainted reputation by association. They'd targeted the weak, and that only made Crispin all the more determined to seek revenge on Jessica's behalf.

Murderous fury burgeoned within him, wave after wave of ire so blistering that if Brookmoore had been present, he'd have run him through on the spot.

Through slitted eyelids, Crispin located their clothing, scattered haphazardly beside the settee. Lilith and Brookmoore had been in an all-fired hurry to disrobe them, the fiends. The garments were tossed about as if he and Jessica had been frantic to couple.

Her gown was within reach, and stretching out an arm, he managed to seize the fine silk as voices rang outside. With a jerk that threatened to separate his head from his shoulders, he yanked the gown over them, concealing their nudity a fraction before the door flung open and several laughing guests paraded in.

A chorus of stunned gasps and exclamations echoed throughout the hothouse as they came up short, bumping into one another.

"I say," Radcliffe boomed with mock astonishment. "It's Bainbridge and the Brentwood chit."

"Good Lord," his female companion tittered. "And they're *naked.*"

5

Jessica groaned and rolled over, pressing a hand to her throbbing head. The last thing she remembered was feeling wretched in the Westfalls' hothouse. She swallowed, her mouth dry as ash and tasting of soiled linen. And mayhap feathers. No, a dirty feather duster.

Why had she been in the conservatory, again?

The details flitted around the periphery of her memory, almost within her grasp then darting away each time she nearly had them in her grip.

Puppies.

Yes, she'd gone to see puppies with Lilith Brighton. But she'd become dizzy and fainted. For the first time in her life, and for no apparent reason, she'd swooned. It was all so peculiar.

Opening her eyes, she peered at the familiar emerald canopy above her.

Puzzling her brow and crimping her mouth, she rifled through her inadequate recollections of last night. How in heaven's name had she come to be in her bed and not recall the journey home from the Westfalls'?

Turning onto her side, her mind still in a thick-as-cold-porridge muddle, she examined the draperies. Bright, golden light filtered between the small crack. Morning, then. She'd been unconscious all night.

Suspicion niggled. A simple bout of the vapors didn't cause one to remain incapacitated for hours. Jessica became more confused with each passing moment. *What*, precisely, had happened last night?

Struggling to a sitting position, she groaned again at the fierce ache encompassing her skull like an unyielding vise. Once propped against her pillows, she cradled her head in her hands. This aftermath was most definitely something more than a simple swoon.

Tap. Tap. Tap.

Faint, almost tentative knocking preceded Theadosia gliding into the bedchamber, followed by a maid with a breakfast tray.

"You're awake, at last. I'm so very relieved." At once, Theadosia sat beside her on the mattress and took Jessica's hands in hers. "Even though the doctor assured me you—"

"Doctor?" Jessica cut a bewildered glance at Sally, in the process of setting out breakfast and pouring a cup of tea. The servant's ears practically flapped as she listened, though her bland expression never changed.

"That will be all, Sally." Theadosia rose, and head tilted regally, waited expectantly for the maid to depart.

Ah, so Theadosia wanted privacy before she filled Jessica in on what had happened last evening. A bit curious, but not alarming.

Sally bobbed a shallow curtsy. "Yes, Your Grace." She left the chamber, closing the door with a soft *thud* behind her, but not before cutting Jessica another curiosity-filled glance.

Theadosia took her place at the table, fiddling with the tea service. She added milk and a lump of sugar to Jessica's cup and, after stirring the tea, brought her the fragrant brew.

India tea was her favorite, and this morning more than usual, she welcomed the soothing beverage. She took a sip, relishing the sweet warmth trickling down her throat. A fortifying cup of tea did much to set the world to rights.

If Theadosia didn't look like she was about to cast up her accounts, Jessica wouldn't be troubled. Her sister was with child, after all, so perhaps her wan expression was due to morning sickness.

"Are you feeling unwell? I thought your morning malaise had passed."

"What?" Her sister stared at her in bafflement before her expression cleared. "Oh, no. Not at all. I feel perfectly well," she assured her. "That is, I'm not ill in the stomach."

"Then why the Friday-face?" Jessica took another sip. She felt much improved already. "And what's this about a doctor? I but fainted." That might not be entirely true. Mayhap she had a debilitating ailment, and that's why Theadosia acted so oddly. "Did Miss Brighton send for help? Well, naturally, she must've, else I'd still be in the conservatory."

When her sister didn't respond to her attempt at lightness, Jessica placed her cup upon her night table and canted her head.

Something *was* the matter.

Her chest expanded with a deep breath. Well, if there were something mortally wrong with her, she'd just as soon know. "What, precisely, did the doctor say, Theadosia?"

Cancer? Consumption? Some other nameless disease?

Apprehension sang through her veins, but she corralled her cavorting thoughts and presented a false mien of composure. Whatever Theadosia had to say that was so godawful, Jessica would face it courageously.

Her sister stood beside the bed, her upper teeth resting on her lower lip, her face pinched in consternation. "The doctor examined you last night, after the, ah, *incident,* and assured me once the sleeping draught wore off, you'd be fine."

Crumpling her brows in confusion, Jessica tried to make sense of her sister's words.

Sleeping draught? Incident? "I didn't take a sleeping draught." She shook her head and immediately regretted doing so when a pang speared her forehead. *Lord above.* "Why in the world would I need a sleeping draught at a ball? And what incident occurred?"

"My dear, you didn't knowingly drink the draught." Sighing deeply, Theadosia sank onto the mattress. "Did you accept a beverage from anyone?"

Miss Brighton's sunny countenance immediately sprang to mind, and she gave a cautious nod. "A glass of lemonade from—"

"Miss Brighton," her sister finished, staring past Jessica and gazing blankly out the window on the chamber's far side. Tension and, perhaps, regret radiated off her, and after a long, resigned sigh, she said, "Yes, I know. Or at least, I suspected that was the case."

Then, why had she asked? This conversation was most peculiar.

"The Duke of Bainbridge suggested as much," Theadosia admitted, in a strangely distracted tone.

Now Jessica crinkled *her* nose. "The Duke of Bainbridge?"

How was he involved? What in the world had happened after she'd swooned? Had she hit her head? Was that why it ached as ferociously as if a hammer pounded an anvil inside her skull?

"Theadosia?" She touched her sister's cold hand. "You'll have to begin at the beginning, for I am hopelessly lost. What has Bainbridge to do with this? And what makes you think Miss Brighton would dose my lemonade? She was quite kind to me after..."

Jessica didn't finish. Theadosia needn't know about the viperish trio.

Come to think of it, though, the lemonade had been exceedingly tart. But her thirst had been such that she'd disregarded the flavor. A low gasp escaped past her parted lips. "The lemonade *did* taste rather peculiar."

The uncertainty gripping her rapidly transformed into alarm at the devastation shining in Theadosia's eyes, at whatever unpleasantness her sister seemed unable to voice. It couldn't be all that dreadful. Could it?

Using two fingers, Jessica rubbed slow circles over her temples. Why would Miss Brighton drug her? It made no sense whatsoever.

"What...?" Dropping her hands to her lap, she swallowed past the lump of trepidation lodged in her throat. "What has happened?" She pressed her sister's fingers. "Tell me, Thea. I shall have to know eventually."

Her sister closed her eyes for a long blink, and when she opened them, moisture glimmered there. "Darling, you and the Duke of Bainbridge have been the unfortunate victims of an atrocious, simply malicious scheme."

"A scheme? Perpetuated by Miss Brighton?" Had she unknowingly offended the girl somehow? Unlikely, since Jessica was new to London and, until last night, had never laid eyes on the dark-haired vixen.

"Yes, and Lord Brookmoore. We believe they eloped last night, for no one has seen them since they disappeared from the ball. It was some time before anyone noticed their absences. To throw the scent off their disgraceful intentions, the despicable rotters, they arranged for you and the duke to be found in a very indecent situation."

Jessica absently scratched her jaw, still uncertain why her sister was in such a dither. It wasn't like Theadosia in the least. "So...they created a scene to draw attention away from their clandestine disappearance?" Rather extreme and not just a little addled. "Why did they choose the duke and me?"

Pausing, Theadosia distractedly straightened her lace cuff. Instead of answering Jessica's question, she said, "You do know Miss Brighton and Bainbridge are—were—betrothed, don't you? Arrangements were made when they were children. She was an infant, I believe."

Atrocious practice, that. Marriages of convenience and arranged marriages between adults were awful enough.

"No, I wasn't aware." Something akin to envy speared Jessica, but before she could examine the irregular emotion further, she forced herself to focus on the matter at hand. "But, be that as it may, the duke wasn't in the hothouse."

Had the whole lemonade episode been a farce, as well? Jessica suspected she already knew that ugly truth. Miss Brighton had probably been in cahoots with the other girls who'd been so unkind. She'd been play-acting. That was why her high-spirits had seemed somewhat affected.

"He *was* there. He arrived after you succumbed to the sleeping draught. We've puzzled the pieces together as best we can." Theadosia shifted, pulling one leg higher on the mattress, her lavender skirts rippling with the movement and thrusting her rounded belly forward. "After drugging you, Miss Brighton somehow lured you to the conservatory."

"She said there were puppies there, and she was to have one. I thought perhaps I might have one as well." *The devious, lying chit.* Just wait until she had Miss Brighton alone. Her ears would ring for a month. Jessica might even slap her pretty face.

Hard.

"Ah." Understanding dawned in her sister's compassionate, brown-

199

eyed gaze. "We did wonder since you have a level head on your shoulders, and we couldn't imagine you would rashly go off with her."

Why shouldn't she have trusted Miss Brighton? After all, she wasn't a thief or a woman of ill repute. Nothing of the sort. She'd been cheerful and friendly. A consummate actress.

"What happened after I lost consciousness?" It was worrisome that she had no recollection of anything between plopping onto the divan and waking up in her bed a few minutes ago.

Theadosia touched a finger to her chin, her eyes narrowed in concentration. "It's a bit garbled, but we've gleaned the duke was lured to the hothouse as well. Under the pretense of assisting Lord Brookmoore with his drunken brother. Radcliffe wasn't there, of course."

This entire scenario was as calamitous as a Drury Lane tragedy. Jessica would laugh if it weren't so disturbing. It didn't say much about her or Bainbridge that they were so gullible, either.

"His grace found you drugged on the divan and at once surmised foul play was afoot when he couldn't rouse you," Theadosia said, her manner hesitant and subdued. "Someone struck him in the back of the head with a brass candlestick, and when he awoke—"

6

"**M**y God!" Jessica stiffened, anger rippling over her. "He might've been killed!"

Lips parted and rapidly blinking as if to stave off tears, Theadosia seemed unable to go on.

Jessica was afraid to ask how Crispin fared. What wasn't her sister telling her?

She scooted higher against the pillows, her stomach pitching worse than a skiff in a tropical hurricane. "Is Cris—that is, is the duke all right?"

Theadosia slowly nodded, though none of the tension left her face. "He will be. He required several stitches and suffered a concussion. The physician has ordered bed rest for a week. We've no doubt he speaks the truth about what he remembers."

Quite right. What man whacks himself on the back of the head so he can be found with a woman, even if he is a rake?

"I was drugged, and he was clobbered. Why? None of this makes any sense, and it certainly paints Miss Brighton and Lord Brookmoore as villains of the worst caliber." If Lilith were a man, she'd call her out, the wretch. How dare they conspire to ruin her and Crispin?

"They are, indeed." Theadosia nodded vehemently. "We're convinced—Victor, Bainbridge, and I—they acted so that Miss Brighton and Lord Brookmoore might elope. You and the duke were to be a distraction."

"There are easier ways to break a betrothal." Jessica released a contemptuous snort, her opinion of the bubbly Miss Brighton having descended to somewhere below a maggot in chicken manure. "I have decided I do not like Miss Brighton or Viscount Brookmoore in the least."

"Neither do I." The faintest smile curved Theadosia's lips, though no humor lit her eyes. "They are utterly despicable, and their part in this debacle will not go unpunished. *However...*" Her tone changed, and she cinched her mouth tight.

Another wave of alarm engulfed Jessica, and she flashed cold. "What aren't you telling me?"

"Oh, darling." Droplets slipped from the corners of Theadosia's eyes. "Those monsters undressed you and Bainbridge and placed you in a *suggestive* position atop the divan. A half dozen guests found you together."

Undressed? Suggestive? Found by guests?

Oh God. Oh God, oh God!

Time stretched out, lengthening impossibly with disbelief and denial as Jessica sought to comprehend what her sister had said, the absolutely desolating consequences of what she'd disclosed.

Only the bedside clock's ticking punctuated the solemn silence.

"Thea, you're saying we were found *naked?* Together?" *Damn them.*

Humiliation blazed fiery heat up her cheeks.

Could a person perish from mortification?

No, but they could certainly want to.

Theadosia nodded, looking utterly miserable.

"And others *saw* us?" Jessica whispered, hands pressed to her flaming face.

No. No. No.

Her tummy toppled so violently that she feared she'd be sick all over her counterpane.

How could Lord Brookmoore and Miss Brighton have been so calculatingly malicious? Vile? Evil?

Scorching tears borne of chagrin, rage, and frustration sprang to her eyes. She'd do a great deal more than slap Lilith Brighton and the Lord Brookmoore when next she looked upon their despicable persons.

"Bainbridge managed to reach your gown and cover the essential parts of you both before the other guests barged in. Even injured and bleeding—barely conscious, the witnesses claim— he valiantly tried to protect you," her sister said, her voice tremulous with suppressed emotion.

Crispin had tried to preserve her modesty.

A little flicker of something undefinable fluttered behind Jessica's ribs. Perchance he wasn't the knave she'd believed him to be.

More likely, he didn't want a crowd viewing his man bits.

A flush swept her to think she'd been in his arms, naked, and assuredly, he'd seen her...*bits*. Felt her body, too. *God save me.* Jessica made a strangled sound, deep in her throat, which very much tried to become a moan. She'd never be able to look him in the face again. Never.

Theadosia withdrew a handkerchief from her bodice and patted her damp face. "Randolph Radcliffe was amongst the guests to discover you and the duke. We've no doubt he conspired with his dastardly brother. Though, as expected, he pleads absolute ignorance."

Devil take him. And the bubbly, black-hearted Miss Brighton, too.

Her sister's expression became steel-hard, and a flintiness entered her usually warm, chocolaty gaze. "Victor assures me he has the means to extract the truth from Radcliffe."

"God forgive me, but I sincerely hope it involves a degree of torture." Jessica emphasized her words with a vicious thwack to a pillow, which had the unfortunate fate of being nearby. "Tar and feathers or thumb screws, at the very least, the bloody bastard."

A raspy laugh escaped Theadosia, and she didn't even chide Jessica about her foul language. "No, nothing so medieval, more's the pity. Victor is buying all of his vowels and ensuring no one extends him credit. He'll be in no position to deny Victor anything."

Jessica fisted her hands in the sheets, her breath coming in shallow rasps. "What's to be done? I'm ruined," she whispered, bile's acrid burn stinging her throat.

Ruined? No, it was much worse than that. Despite her innocence, she'd be branded a whore. She'd have to leave London straightaway. Today, perhaps. And now, because of those selfish blighters, she'd probably never marry. What man would take a woman to wife who was found naked in public in another man's arms?

A scourge of stinging tears flooded her eyes again, and she shoved a fist to her mouth to stifle the cry of denial, throttling up her throat.

"The scandal will destroy you and Victor, too," she choked out.

"Victor and I are not concerned about any of that. We'll survive this storm, perhaps a little weather-beaten but not destroyed." Theadosia tenderly smoothed the hair away from Jessica's face, her closed-lip smile apologetic. "You and Bainbridge will wed. There's nothing else for it, my dear." Laced with sympathy and compassion, her sister's voice also held uncompromising authority.

Wed Crispin? A rake and a roué?

A man who could no more be faithful to one woman than fruit trees could retain their foliage in wintertime or snow could fall upward? *No.* There must be another solution. There *must* be. Marriage to him would guarantee a broken heart and a lifetime of unhappiness.

"I don't want to marry him, Theadosia. I scarcely know the duke." She heard the pleading in her voice but didn't care. She couldn't wed a virtual stranger. "I'm confident Bainbridge doesn't want this either."

For all she knew, he lamented his broken betrothal with Miss Brighton. Or, if he didn't, he'd not be eager to enter into a marriage of convenience when he'd just escaped an arranged marriage.

Jessica was no fool. She knew how womanizers of his ilk behaved: They married, beget an heir or two on their wives, then bustled their inconvenient spouses off to the country so the rogue could carry on, unhindered, with his string of mistresses and lovers.

"I'm truly sorry, but you must, Jessica. It's the only way to preserve his name and your reputation."

Rakehells don't have any honor.

"The nuptials were Bainbridge's suggestion," Theadosia went on, either unmindful of Jessica's mutinous scowl or choosing to ignore it. Likely the latter. "He is an honorable man and, from what Victor has told me, kind, too." She touched two fingertips to the bridge of her nose as if her head also pained her. "James intends to procure a special license on your behalf today, should it be required. I prefer the banns be put up, but that might not be possible."

Both notions rather galled.

Heavens, why not just hie off to Gretna Green? Do things up brown? Why, the only tidbit that might make this *on dit* juicier was if she were already increasing. *Oh God.* She could taste the bitterness of fresh bile in her mouth. People would likely believe she was pregnant, too.

Their brother, James, was a highly sought-after solicitor and, of late, a successful investor. A keener, more intelligent mind, Jessica had never encountered. Perhaps he might have an alternative solution.

Say, an extended holiday to France or Italy? For a decade. No, better make that two decades. Wouldn't do to rush home before *le beau monde's* exasperatingly long memory had faded.

"Victor, as well as the Dukes of Dandridge, Sheffield, and Pennington, are already spreading their own tattle," Theadosia revealed. "It's a rather good tale we concocted last night while you slept."

Jessica slanted an eyebrow up, skeptically. "Just what is this *tale*?"

Appearing a mite chagrined, her sister pressed her lips tight. She clasped and unclasped her hands before releasing a long sigh, her shoulders slumping.

"We're saying that Bainbridge recently became aware of Miss Brighton's affair with Brookmoore. He formally intended to break their betrothal on the grounds of infidelity. We're also spreading it about that the duke once confessed to Victor that, if he were a free man, he'd ask for your hand," she said, her voice slightly raspy. "We'll let people think they're clever and put two and two together."

Jessica shook her head and made a harsh movement in the air with her hands. "And you think anyone with a brain larger than a grape is going to believe that twaddledash?" She was forever mixing up her expressions, but right now, she didn't give a fig.

She fisted her hands, curled her toes, and clamped her teeth until they were in danger of cracking, so overwhelming was her fury.

Jessica resisted the impulse to thump the undeserving pillow again. But something—no, somebody—needed to be throttled. Make that two somebodies. "I wouldn't believe that fustian rubbish if I heard it. It sounds exactly like what it is. A monumental tarradiddle, confabulated to detract gossip. It won't work."

"The *haut ton* may not believe it, but given the rank of the peers insisting it's the truth, they won't dare imply otherwise." A note of satisfaction threaded Theadosia's voice. Apparently, she was learning just how advantageous it was to be a duchess.

It seemed everything had been decided while Jessica slept. Her life and future had been mapped out without a word of input or consent from her. A twinge of anger sliced through her.

Yet, in her core, she grudgingly acknowledged her sister spoke the truth. Her only hope of salvaging anything from this scandal was a prompt marriage. And marrying a duke, particularly the duke in question, was even better.

Miss Brighton and Brookmoore deserved one another. *God rot the wretches. May they be miserable every day of the rest of their despicable lives.*

"Brookmoore had better watch himself if he ever dares to return to London. James or Victor might very well call him out." After tucking her handkerchief back into her bosom, Theadosia rose. She ran her palms over her tummy, a gentle smile framing her mouth.

She'd make an exceptional mother.

"If Bainbridge doesn't first," Jessica muttered sourly, convinced Crispin wouldn't turn a blind eye to the destruction of his honor and good name. Or for being compelled into the marriage trap.

Except James, Victor, or Crispin shouldn't have to jeopardize their lives on a field of honor with a soulless scoundrel such as Brookmoore.

"Come, my dear." Theadosia held out her hand. "Let's see you dressed to call upon your soon-to-be betrothed. I think you should wear something colorful. That new ice-blue gown and spencer will do. They fairly shout nobility to anyone who might see you. And we want to ensure the gossips don't find you lacking in any way."

Dear Theadosia. Surely she knew they would, in any event. Jessica would be dissected from toe to top. Every glance, every word, judged.

"But the duke is confined to his bed." If she met with Crispin today, this horror would become a reality. "I believe it would be wiser to wait until he's recovered."

That would give her time to contrive another solution.

"He's able to converse just fine, and he insisted your betrothal be made public today. We can't very well do that unless he asks you, now, can we?" Theadosia's false smile slipped a trifle.

Feeling mutinous and altogether cross, Jessica tossed the bedcovers back, snapping, "Don't be so very sure I'll agree to this farce."

7

Stifling a foul oath, Crispin sat perfectly still as his valet, Marsters, finished fussing over his hair, mindful not to bump the fresh bandage encircling his head.

"I don't think it's necessary to brush the top, Marsters, when this confines the rest of my hair." He waved two fingers at the linen strips. "I'll look ridiculous, despite your diligent efforts."

The valet spared him a brief look, his brows quirked in a mixture of annoyance and amusement. Though a foot shorter and at least two stones lighter, Marsters inevitably made him feel like a recalcitrant schoolboy.

"You're meeting with your betrothed, Your Grace," he explained with the patience one would address a gravely ill or mentally deficit individual.

Not betrothed *yet*. But before the day was out, Jessica Brentwood would be the future Duchess of Bainbridge. Pleasurable warmth swirled outward from Crispin's middle until it engulfed him like a cocoon.

"I cannot," Marsters went on, "in good conscience, permit you to leave this room unless you are at your very best."

Yes, someone might judge Marsters's skills deficient if Crispin's neckcloth wasn't tied just so. Or if a single speck of lint were spotted upon his fine-cloth burgundy coat. And heaven forbid if a smudge marred his footwear.

The stars might drop from the sky.

He gave one last flourishing swipe of the brush then stood back, inspecting Crispin from his head to his just-polished-to-a-high-gleam Hessians. With a satisfied nod, he declared, "You'll do."

"You're quite certain?" Crispin quipped, unable to keep the drollness from his tone.

Head cocked, Marsters *tutted* to himself. He stepped forward and flicked a minuscule speck of something invisible from Crispin's shoulder.

Thank God he'd spotted that; the world might've ended, had he not.

Why, Miss Jessica Brentwood might've torn from the room, yanking at her hair and screaming at the top of her lungs if she'd spied the speck.

Crispin would've shaken his head in amusement, just to fluster Marsters, but his skull still ached bloody awful. After all, it had been less than four and twenty hours since he'd been knocked from behind hard enough to require twelve stitches. An egg-sized lump protruded beneath the bandages.

It was almost enough to make him wonder if Brookmoore hadn't been intent on killing him, rather than rendering him incapacitated. Did the sod seriously think he could avoid repercussions for his actions? It made more sense to believe Brookmoore had taken leave of his faculties.

Or, perhaps, he was desperate. Desperate men did all manner of stupid things.

Nevertheless, Crispin would be damned if he'd propose to Jessica from his bed, like an invalid. Bad enough, he didn't have a ring for her. That could be remedied in short order, however.

Since he didn't know her gemstone preference, mayhap they'd make an outing of it. He'd determined to give her something unique. Something no one else had ever worn. A ring that would make her eyes sparkle with appreciation.

Naturally, there were dozens and dozens of majestic gems, parures, and other blinding and glittering baubles in the family safe. But Jessica warranted a betrothal ring that commemorated their union. He couldn't help but wonder how she'd reacted to the news of their disgrace and forthcoming nuptials. Crispin would do all within his power to ease her discomfit and any concerns.

Toward that end, he would meet his future duchess in the drawing room. Despite Marsters's fierce scowl and downturned mouth; his housekeeper, Mrs. Peedell's, *tsking* and issuing vexed and dire warnings that he would kill himself; and his majordomo, Barlow's, elevated nose and loud sniffs of disapproval, he'd left his bed two hours ago.

There'd be no chastisements to his domestics for overstepping, for their actions were born out of affection and loyalty. In truth, he counted himself lucky to have them.

The long soak in the tub had helped a degree, as had the medicinal tea laced with herbs that Mrs. Peedell had threatened to pour down his throat while Marsters and Barlow held him unless he drank the bitter concoction. He'd far have preferred Scotch or cognac, but he'd been forbidden spirits until his concussion healed.

That was bloody inhumane torture.

All the while he readied himself for his meeting with Jessica, rage—acrid and lethal—simmered behind his ribs. A steady, bubbling fury.

No one, by God, *no one* conspired against him in the manner Brookmoore and Lilith had and didn't dearly pay for their perfidy. That he was forced to ask for Jessica's hand in marriage only magnified the insult.

Now, she'd never believe he'd yearned to marry her, to make her his. Before this debacle, he'd not been able to declare himself or ask permission to court her. Being betrothed did rather curb wooing another woman, even if the duke possessed a wicked reputation.

A reputation he'd methodically and diligently cultivated, hoping to dissuade the Brightons. A reputation built on falsehoods and fabrications. And although his carefully constructed facade had failed to convince the Brightons to void the betrothal contract, Society had been all too eager to accept the charade as absolute truth.

Nevertheless, he couldn't deny the prospect of marrying Jessica excited him.

What infuriated Crispin, and what he'd never be able to convince others of, was that she'd have been his choice had he been given one. He'd have courted her, wooed her, hoping that, in time, she'd come to care for him.

Nevertheless, due to the duplicity of others, the decision of whether to wed or not had been ripped from them.

A slightly evil grin tipped his mouth on one side.

How was Hammon Brighton dealing with his darling daughter's treachery?

Wouldn't Crispin like to be a fly in the room when Brighton learned of her duplicity. Her ruination, for she was every bit as disgraced as Jessica, if not more. And when her part in the fiasco wrought upon him and Jessica became known, not a door would remain open to her or her parents, no matter how deep and heavy their purses.

Only an absolute idiot bashed dukes over the head, stripped them naked, and arranged them for discovery with an equally nude, drugged female and hoped to escape unscathed. Hoped to escape his wrath.

Never having struck him as a female with particularly sharp intellect, Lilith probably hadn't even considered the ramifications for herself. He'd be bound, her only consideration had been how to discredit Crispin in order not to wed him. That she'd also injured an innocent, someone incapable of the degree of deceit and callousness she had shown, made her contemptible and unworthy of mercy.

He scratched his nose, considering the steps he'd take to assure appropriate justice was meted out.

It would be hers and Brookmoore's word against his and Jessica's, though. That might prove a trifle tricky, particularly since Radcliffe could be counted on to substantiate any tale his foul brother concocted.

If only there'd been a witness to Jessica entering the hothouse with Lilith. Better yet, someone who'd seen Brookmoore and Lilith undress him and Jessica, or him being struck upon the head. That was about as likely as snow in August.

Pink snow.

Hammon Brighton, the mule-headed mushroom, had refused for years to release Crispin from the contract. But now, Lilith had assured his freedom.

A half-snort, half-chuckle escaped him, causing Marsters to give him a dubious look before turning his attention back to the task at hand.

Perchance Crispin ought to thank Lilith for helping him snare the one woman he'd dreamed of making his own; rub a little salt in the wound, as it were. His grin grew wider at the thought. No court would uphold the betrothal contract now —neither a court of law nor the court of public opinion.

What was a little humiliation and discomfort to be rid of the chit once and for all? Well, a jot more than a little, but he was thick-skinned. But was Jessica? He'd found women tended to be much more sensitive about matters of this nature.

Victor had already bought up Radcliff's vowels on Crispin's behalf, but he wasn't done with Brookmoore and his brother. Not by half, by God. They'd only begun to feel the power of his wrath. By the time he'd finished with them, they'd never show their faces in London again. Maybe not even England.

Slowly rising, for sudden movement sent his head and his stomach swirling, he stood and waited for the room to stop wobbling. He shouldn't be up and about yet. He blamed his deuced pride. One did not propose while flat upon one's back in bed. Truth be told, he shouldn't have to propose under these circumstances at all, but little good it would do to voice that fact.

Lines of concern stamped Marsters's face, but he wisely kept his apprehension to himself. "I'll just walk with you, Your Grace."

In other words, *I'll make sure you don't fall flat on your face and ruin my efforts to see you presented in the first stare of fashion.*

Crispin wouldn't dismiss his offer.

He might very well need an arm to lean on if his head didn't stop spinning. In truth, he also might cast up his accounts. Jaw clenched against the pain stabbing his brain, he managed to make the drawing room without disgracing himself. And with seven minutes to spare before the clock struck four, he sank onto the brocade sofa before the comfortably snapping fire.

He'd opted against meeting Jessica in his study. The atmosphere would be too formal and intimidating. Most likely, she was already apprehensive and embarrassed. As much as possible, he'd ease her discomfort. The truth was, the whole situation was deucedly awkward.

Last night, barely able to string one thought after another, he'd demanded the flustered women, who'd intruded upon him and Jessica in the conservatory, remain to lend the merest thread of respectability while he'd sent the gawping men for help. Namely, to locate Jessica's family and Westfall, as well as Dandridge, Sheffield, and Pennington and their duchesses.

Once her sister and his friends had arrived, he'd sent the first intruders on their way, in no uncertain terms. Sheffield stood guard outside the door, deterring additional inquisitive guests who'd made their way from the main house when word of the debacle had broken.

At that thought, he pressed his mouth into a harsh line. That had to have been something to witness. He could only imagine the *sotto voce* whispers, sly smiles, and waggling eyebrows.

Bainbridge and Jessica Brentwood are tangled together, naked as cherubs, in the hothouse.

The young duchesses, amid appalled whispers, had bundled the still-unconscious Jessica into her clothes as best they could, while the men gently assisted Crispin, peppering him with questions he could scarcely answer, half-unconscious himself.

Someone had sent for a physician, and Pennington and Sutcliffe had accompanied him home. Once the physician had examined Crispin and he'd explained Brookmoore's and Miss Brighton's part in the scheme,. Made more so by Mrs. Peedell, Marsters, or Barlow waking him every hour to ensure he hadn't cocked up his toes.

Not before vowing he'd wed Jessica at the earliest opportunity, however. Even in his befuddled state, he recognized that was their only recourse.

There was no help for it, as he'd told Sutcliffe, who whole-heartedly agreed with no small amount of relief as well.

Barlow rapped lightly before striding into the drawing room. "The Duke and Duchess of Sutcliffe and Miss Jessica Brentwood have arrived."

"Please show them in, and ask Mrs. Peedell for tea and refreshments." Careful not to jostle his head, Crispin shoved to his feet. A gentleman would never remain seated when a duchess entered the room. The stilted movement nearly caused his eyes to cross in pain, but teeth clamped tight, he'd donned a benign mask.

"At once, Your Grace." Head lowered, Barlow backed out, the epitome of a deferential servant. For the moment, at least.

Uncharacteristic and unexpected nerves rioted around in Crispin's gut. As thankful as he was to no longer be betrothed to Lilith, he'd not thought he'd ever be in a position of asking a woman to marry him to avoid a scandal.

Avoid a scandal?

Too bloody late for that.

But, as an influential duke, he could provide Jessica with a position of power. Duchesses were forgiven much. Not that the troublesome circumstances surrounding their discovery in the conservatory wouldn't keep viperish tongues wagging for a few weeks. Even when the truth came out—for he'd see it did—the havoc had been wrought.

And it was damning.

The *haut ton* was more willing to turn a blind eye to a duke's or duchess's imprudence than to those of lower ranks. He held no qualms about exploiting his position if it ensured buffering Jessica against maliciousness.

A few deep, steadying breaths later, in which the turmoil in his head abated a degree, Barlow ushered the Sutcliffes and Jessica inside the drawing room.

Crispin succeeded in remaining upright without gritting his teeth or feeling faint. "Thank you for coming." He spoke directly to Jessica.

She wore a stunning, pale-blue day gown, the shade a perfect enhancement for her fair hair and vibrant eyes. Slight plum-tinted shadows ringed those pretty eyes today, and her features appeared more pronounced in her oval face. To the unpracticed eye, she exuded poise, but the angle of her jaw, the slope of her shoulders, and her stiff spine bespoke untold tension.

"I hope you are recovering well, Your Grace." Her voice had always fascinated him. Low and lilting, it held none of the arrogant coolness so many women of station affected.

After meeting his gaze and offering a cordial, if somewhat hesitant smile, her attention shifted to inspecting the room. Or, at least, she made a pretense of doing so.

He imagined, given what she no doubt knew about how they'd been found last night, she wrestled with a great deal of chagrin. He caught her regarding him from the corner of her eye.

Inquisitiveness and speculation shone there.

"How are you feeling, Bainbridge?" Sutcliffe asked as they shook hands. "I didn't expect to see you up yet. Didn't the doctor restrict you to bed for a week?" He chuckled and brushed a finger across an eyebrow. "Though, if it were me, I'd likely be out of bed against the physician's orders too."

"Indeed, you would." The duchess came forward and offered Crispin her hand. "Thank you, Your Grace. I cannot express how indebted I am to you for what you did for my sister last evening. I'll be forever obligated to you."

Crispin counted himself extremely fortunate that not a single one of his friends or their wives had doubted his tale. Though the evidence indicated he and Jessica had been the victims of foul play, there were still those with suspicious minds who suggested he was somehow at fault.

His friends were not amongst them.

As for being at fault... He berated himself a hundred times over for not at once suspecting Brookmoore was up to mischief when they'd entered the conservatory and he'd seen Jessica. He'd never been a particular friend of Brookmoore, but he'd never have suspected the churl would act so dishonorably, either. The truth was, seeing her lying there had so alarmed him, he'd cast aside his usual caution.

Still, the Duchess of Sutcliffe wouldn't be so appreciative if she knew he'd looked his fill at Jessica's lush curves. But then, he'd had little recourse, positioned as they were, both incapable of rising without assistance.

Something that felt very much like a flush warmed his face. "I shan't lie and deny my head hurts like the devil himself is kicking the inside of my skull, and the stitches are tender. But the physician assures me I'll recover, in due time."

Jessica cut him an assessing glance, her gaze probing. Her concern seemed genuine. "I hope you do so swiftly."

Her contralto voice wrapped around him like warm silk and took root in his heart. Only this woman had ever affected him thus.

"Please, won't you have a seat and make yourselves comfortable?" Crispin gestured toward the sofa as he claimed an armchair. The women sank gracefully onto the broad, ivory- and mint-hued cushions, and Sutcliffe took possession of the other plush armchair.

Jessica met his eyes, hers uncertain and apologetic beneath fine, winged eyebrows. As she removed her gloves, she delicately cleared her throat. "Before anyone says anything, I have something I wish to say."

8

Going on the offensive, was she? Crispin rather liked Jessica's gumption. She'd never been retiring or simpering. She'd just been…Jessica. Sweet and kind and wholly desirable.

She gently laid the gloves on the sofa's arm. The Brentwoods had been quite impoverished, and although Sutcliffe had provided her with a new wardrobe, Crispin liked that she continued to take care of her possessions, lest they become ruined.

Surprise registering on their faces, her sister and brother-in-law exchanged befuddled glances before turning their attention to her.

"What is it, dearest?" the duchess asked. The sisters were extremely close.

Jessica had gone to live with the Sutcliffes after her parents sailed to Australia under a shroud of disgrace. That was all she needed. More ignominy after her father's dishonesty had tainted the family name.

Drawing in a breath deep enough to expand her chest, she clasped her hands and tilted her dainty-but-determined, slightly impertinent chin. "I know why we've come here today. I want to make it known that such a gesture is not necessary. I shan't accept, in any event."

"Pardon?" Her sister sent a panicked glance to her husband.

Jessica's chin inched up a trifle more, and she met Crispin's gaze straight on. She was a plucky thing, by Jove.

"But, Jessica, we spoke of this." The duchess's concern for her sister was tangible. He'd seen her alarm last night. He saw the tears she'd shed upon spying her younger sister. Witnessed the sharp snap of anger jerking her eyebrows together and straightening her spine when she realized the May game that had been played upon Jessica.

She only wanted what was best for her sister and, like Crispin, acknowledged the most prudent of actions was a swift exchanging of vows.

Sutcliffe leaned forward, compassion etched upon his usually sardonic features. "Why don't we discuss the situation first, and then you can make a decision?"

He glanced at Crispin for confirmation, and he gave a slight nod, cognizant any abrupt movement might send his head bouncing across the floor as violently as a nut shaken in a tin. His soon-to-be bride might not appreciate the scene.

Barlow entered with the tea service. "Will there be anything else, Your Grace?"

"No. Thank you. Please close the door."

He appreciated the servants would likely listen at the keyhole, and he hadn't a doubt news of last night's debacle had already swept through the house, from the attic to the kitchen. In all likelihood, they also knew why Jessica was here and had already begun to assess their new mistress.

"May I impose upon you to pour, Miss Brentwood?" She might as well begin her role as his duchess.

A startled look whisked across her refined features before she schooled her emotions and dipped her chin in acquiescence. "Of course."

As always, her voice washed over him, at once soothing and arousing. He didn't let his imagination trot down the latter, more sensual path, or he'd be sporting a cockstand. That, he didn't want to have to explain to his future brother-in-law.

With the inherent grace he so admired about Jessica, she completed the task, and after everyone held a cup of tea and had selected an assortment of sandwiches and dainties, he cleared his throat. "Thank you for coming today. I shan't dally or mince words."

He slid Jessica a glance, but her focus remained fixed on her shoes.

Or the carpet. Or perhaps it was the absolutely riveting turn of the table's leg.

"You needn't ask for my hand in marriage, Your Grace," she quietly said, without a hint of regret or subterfuge as she brought her gaze up to meet his.

Again, she reminded him of a marine-eyed kitten.

"It's noble of you if that's your intent," she conceded. "But I find, in truth, I have neither the temperament nor the inclination to become a duchess."

The room grew unnaturally silent, the Duchess of Sutcliffe casting her husband a panicked look, her teacup poised in midair. The exuberantly crackling fire and the clock's steady ticking filled the awkward space.

Turned down before he'd even proposed. This didn't bode well. Jessica must be convinced to change her mind, must see that marriage to him was the only solution.

Sutcliffe cleared his throat. "See here, Jessica. I'm your guardian in your father's absence, and I don't believe there's any other recourse. If there were, I'd not have brought you here today."

Well, thank you very much. Crispin speared Sutcliffe a dark glower.

Once she'd set her teacup aside, the duchess touched her sister's arm, concern shadowing her pretty face. "What's really going on, my dear? There's more to this than simple reluctance to wed a man you don't know well. I explained this morning how unfortunate the circumstances are. We"—she swept her hand in an arc to include Crispin and her husband—"fear for your future."

"Might I have a few moments alone with Miss Brentwood?" Crispin asked, his focus never straying from her.

The duchess darted him an astonished look before her features settled into a contemplative mien. She sent her husband a speaking glance. One that demanded he'd bloody well better acquiesce, and he nodded.

"It's rather unorthodox, but yes. I suppose you might," he slowly agreed, uncrossing his legs.

Jessica snorted indelicately, shaking her head as if they were silly children. "I cannot imagine a few moments alone would be any more objectionable than a half dozen people coming upon us lying naked and entwined together."

Clearing his throat, Sutcliffe shifted uncomfortably, and his wife blushed as she pressed a palm to the juncture of her collarbone.

Why did adults act all discomfited and constrained whenever anyone mentioned the words *naked* or *nude*?

At once, Crispin's mind flashed back to last night. Of Jessica's pearly-white, satiny body melded to his. Of her scintillating cloves and vanilla scent. It took every ounce of his will not to drop his attention to her breasts. He could still envision them in his mind: plump, creamy mounds with perfect rosebud-pink nipples.

Sutcliffe would run him through if he had any notion the dangerous path Crispin's thoughts had jogged down.

Despite her advancing pregnancy, the duchess angled agilely to her feet. At once, the men stood, and Crispin's head spun dizzily from rising too swiftly. "I should very much enjoy a stroll through your gardens, Bainbridge." She gave her husband a blinding smile. "Darling, shall we?" She took his arm for, *of course,* he didn't dare say otherwise.

"I know the way," Sutcliff allowed. "I'll permit you ten minutes."

"That's all I require," Crispin assured him.

The room remained unnaturally still after their departure. Jessica poured herself more tea and then, teapot in hand, inquired, "Do you care for any more, Your Grace?"

"No, and please call me Crispin. Or Cris. And I shall address you as Jessica. Unless you have another preference?"

A golden eyebrow flexed at his suggestion, but she didn't argue. "No. Unlike Theadosia, my name was never shortened. I cannot abide being called Jess or Jessie. What is it you wished to discuss with me that you couldn't say in front of my sister and Victor?"

She blew lightly on her hot tea, drawing his attention to her cupid's bow mouth. A shade between pink and cherry, her kissable lips all but begged for him to sample their sweetness.

Condemning propriety to a fusty corner, he took her sister's place beside her. If she hadn't been clutching the teacup like a miniature shield, he'd have taken her hand in his.

"Jessica, I believe you feel I've been pressed into asking for your hand against my will. That the circumstances of last night have necessitated it, and that is the only reason why I would marry you."

Both eyebrows shied up her forehead before she wrinkled her small nose.

"You shan't convince me otherwise, Your Grace. And I shan't marry a man for no other reason than he is obligated by duty and honor to offer for me because of the nefarious actions of others." She shifted her focus away, staring at the fire, unhappiness and melancholy shadowing her lovely face.

Ah, she was more overwrought than she'd let on. How could she not be?

That her concern was for him, and not herself, caused an indecipherable twinge behind his breastbone. For the truth of it was, he could choose to walk away and maintain his social standing.

Oh, there'd be chatter, of course. But a wealthy duke would never be permanently shunned, and women would still vie to become the next Duchess of Bainbridge.

She, on the other hand, had no future. Not a respectable one, if she didn't accept Crispin's offer. He'd replace her despondency with laughter and gaiety if she'd only permit him. They could be happy together.

"As silly as it may seem to you, my sister, and brother-in-law, I'd rather suffer the snubbing and disgrace than enter into a compulsory union. The shame will fade eventually, replaced by other titillating *on dit*. But a marriage…" She shook her head, golden ribbons from the window's light shimmering in her blonde hair.

He reached to touch a flaxen curl but drew his hand back. Too bold, too soon. But, someday, he'd run his hands through those sunny curls, bury his face in their silkiness, and inhale Jessica's heady fragrance.

"Marriage is for a lifetime," she said. "And I cannot imagine a more dissatisfying scenario than to enter into what could very well be an incompatible union."

Making a sympathetic noise, he took the cup from her and set it aside. He did claim her hand then, running his thumb across the palm. "And what if I told you that I've held you in high esteem for quite some time? That only my betrothal to Miss Brighton kept me from proclaiming myself and asking for permission to pay my addresses?"

It was God's honest truth. And damn it all, if it didn't feel blessedly wonderful to declare himself finally.

Her luscious mouth went slack for a second, and she blinked her big blue-green eyes twice, appearing adorably birdlike in her astonishment. Her gaze plumbed Crispin's, solemn and penetrating, as if she sought something within the depths of his eyes.

An assurance? Affirmation that he spoke the truth?

Aye. That and perhaps more. Mayhap a desire, a hope that he felt something for her? He'd been her secret admirer for some time.

He'd confounded her. It rather stung his pride that she should be so shocked.

"In no way did you ever hint of such interest, in word or deed," she said, narrowing her eyes slightly, the silver flecks glinting with suspicion. "How am I to believe you now?"

He sensed her hesitation, her uncertainty. That it would make a difference to her if he wed her because he wanted to instead of out of obligation.

"I am a gentleman, Kitten. I could not speak of my interest while betrothed to another. I vow others have noted my attentiveness to you." He recalled the Duke of Pennington teasing him about his hang-dog expression as Crispin surreptitiously observed Jessica. "They've seen me covertly watching you."

Devil it. The confession made Crispin sound like a stalker.

"Watching me?" A scowl tweaked her eyebrows and framed her mouth. "Who saw you?"

Such distrust and suspicion.

If Jessica noticed the term of endearment, she'd chosen to ignore it. He hadn't meant to let it slip.

"Pennington. Sutcliffe. And others." He might as well admit it. There was no longer a reason to hide his fascination for her. He pressed her fingertips, wishing he might lift the slender fingers to his mouth. "I've attempted to have my betrothal contract canceled for some time. If you think about it, I often arranged to be present where you were. House parties, and the like."

He *had*, more fool him.

"Did you?" Her nose angled slightly higher. "I hadn't noticed."

Was that the truth, or was the vixen toying with him? He detected no subterfuge, but her comment was slightly too flippant.

"You do owe me an ice from Gunter's," she reminded. "Which I shall have before Season's end, mind you."

"Name the date, and it shall be done." He breathed a silent sigh of relief that she'd changed the subject.

Jessica pursed her pretty mouth before blurting, "Your betrothal didn't prevent you from numerous dalliances."

Good God. She wanted to discuss his lovers? *Past* lovers.

That, he would not do, out of respect for the few women who'd graced his bed and from a desire to protect her from what surely could only be painful and embarrassing disclosures.

Her color high and nostrils slightly flared, she challenged him in that direct way he so admired.

"I heard of your exploits before I came to London, Your Grace. I'm not a woman who could look the other way." Sadness and resignation settled on her features. "You're not the sort to keep yourself only to your wife."

I could be. For Jessica, he had no doubt he could.

It did, however, rather rankle to be dismissed so readily. To be found wanting in her eyes.

She bent her pink mouth into an unrepentant smile, her eyes flashing with turquoise sparks. Lifting a graceful shoulder, she flippantly waved her hand. "I'm old-fashioned that way. Vicar's daughter, and all that. I'd expect fidelity, and I doubt you're capable of faithfulness."

Crispin wasn't sure whether to laugh or be offended. Life with her would certainly be an adventure.

Releasing Jessica's hand, he considered how to reply. She deserved transparency and honesty. He unthinkingly cupped the back of his head as he did when in thought, and a sharp breath hissed from between his clenched teeth.

Christ on the cross! He almost swore aloud. He'd forgotten about the bloody wound. He squeezed his eyes shut, clamped his teeth tighter, and held his breath, waiting for the stab of pain to pass.

As it eased, he opened his eyes.

"Crispin?" Sincere worry tinged her voice. "Are you quite all right?" At once, her features pleated into concern, and she laid a dainty hand atop his forearm. Her fingers were slender, but not overly long, the nails short and oval-shaped.

"Should I send for someone?" she asked, her fingers still resting on his forearm, further disrupting his equilibrium. Her innocent touch sent his libido racing. "Do you require pain medicines? Or should you lie down?" She made as if to rise, but he stayed her with a palm over her hand.

"No, I'm fine, Jessica. Truly." He wasn't, but they must work out the issue of their nuptials. He could rest later.

"I don't suppose you'd believe me if I told you the bulk of what you've heard was a ruse, fabricated to encourage Brighton to break the betrothal contract?" He leaned back, welcoming the sofa's support. He bussed his hand over his jaw. "I'd hoped if I were a bad enough scapegrace, he'd refuse to bind his only daughter to me."

Jessica's delicate eyebrows shied high onto her alabaster forehead. Her expression fairly shouted liar. Prevaricator. Charlatan.

When he laid it out like that, his plan sounded damned absurd, even to him.

No man with Brighton's social aspirations would object to something so trivial as a sordid reputation. *Or by-blows and mistresses.* In short, Crispin might've been a diseased debauchee, and Brighton would still insist the marriage take place.

"That was rather extreme, wasn't it?" Jessica toyed with her earring, considering him the whole while.

She appeared neither shocked or judgmental. No, if anything, he'd say she was mystified.

"You burden yourself with a much-tainted repute to escape marriage, Crispin? Such an albatross, obviously, would be problematic to overcome."

"Not marriage," he denied with the merest shake of his head.

"No?" Her probing gaze said she didn't believe him.

"I have no dislike of the institution itself. What I object to, most strongly, is matrimony to a woman I was pledged to as a child, to whom I have no warm regard whatsoever." He played his fingers upon his knee, realizing just how little he felt for Miss Brighton except scathing anger. "Besides, I was determined to see the engagement ended without a scandal," he admitted, crossing his ankles.

Her wry smile, hilarity in her aquamarine eyes, and the mocking angle of her winged, golden eyebrows spoke volumes. "Yes, well, that certainly worked out well, didn't it?"

She jested. *Minx.*

When was the last time he'd enjoyed a conversation this much? Even if the circumstances were, to say the least, trying as hell.

Two could play at teasing, though why they were verbally parrying when they should be discussing the terms of their marriage, he couldn't quite define. He'd thought to take control of the situation, and Jessica had neatly turned the tables on him. Crispin would have to remember that in the future.

Despite having been outmaneuvered last night by Miss Brighton, Jessica was not easily manipulated. He rather liked that. Liked that she knew her own mind. Appreciated that she wasn't weepy and hysterical at her plight.

He angled his own eyebrows in feigned reproach. "Have *you* ever seen me with a woman on my arm? Has a particular lady's name *ever* been linked with mine?"

Crispin had been most diligent that neither of those occur.

His rake's reputation was built on inference and insinuation. Whispers and conjectures. Implication and allusion. It had been remarkably easy to create something out of nothing. There were always those at the ready to embellish a whisper. Add intimations and innuendos.

She slanted her head in an endearing fashion, indecision and doubt darkening her eyes to almost indigo. "Not a respectable woman, no. But there are, ah…" She blushed furiously but plowed onward, the brave

225

darling. "There are *establishments* men might frequent. Women whose favors might be purchased."

Her cheeks glowed pink with chagrin.

Jesus and all the saints. How did a vicar's daughter know about bordellos and courtesans? He frequented neither, restricting his ventures to White's, Boodle's, and *Bon Chance*, none of which were gaming hells or brothels.

"Jessica, how can I convince you my exploits have been greatly exaggerated?" *Devil and damn.* His ploy to appear a philandering rakehell might very well make him irredeemable in her estimation.

And, unfortunately, it didn't matter what she thought of him. Though, of course, he'd much prefer she didn't dislike or disdain him, as he'd be her husband for many years, the good Lord willing.

For wed him, she must. In short order, too. She'd be the target of every whoremongering churl in England if she didn't. Each thinking to sample charms they believed her eager to share. And some wouldn't wait for her permission; they'd force themselves upon her at the first opportunity.

Crispin would spare her that foul knowledge, if possible. No woman should ever know her good name had been reduced to such despicable depths.

She'd be dismayed to know there were already bets on the books at White's for who'd have her in his bed next. Marsters had shared that particularly unsavory tidbit with his usual stoic drollness while shaving Crispin. The valet had heard it from the underfootman, who'd heard it from his cousin, a waiter at White's.

Not even a full day had passed, and wagers were flying.

His stomach churned, and his head ached bloody awful, making him question the wisdom of leaving his sickbed. Pride, in his case, might literally go before a fall.

Plucking at her serviette, Jessica wrinkled her forehead. As if realizing she tortured the unfortunate cloth, she folded the square and set it aside.

He could practically hear the whirring of her brain as she considered what he'd said.

"Papa always said actions speak louder than words." She sighed and brushed a hand over the silky fabric of her skirt. A small sardonic smile skewed her soft mouth, and she slid him a glance from beneath her golden-tipped lashes. "This is a fine pickle, isn't it?"

"It is, indeed." It could be a most delicious pickle if she'd but agree to be his duchess.

She turned toward him then, her mouth quirked in the winsome way it did when she was contemplative. "Do you think Miss Brighton and Lord Brookmoore have married? Theadosia said everyone believes they've eloped, after…uhm, what they did to us."

Crispin gave a casual shrug. He didn't give a snap about either of them except that they be held accountable for their actions. "I cannot say, but that seems to have been their plan. No one knows for certain, of course."

Sutcliffe had sent a rider after them to report on their intentions, but to Crispin's knowledge, the man hadn't returned yet. Brookmoore and Miss Brighton might've evaded the man, too. Brookmoore was cunning. A scurrilous lout. He'd likely been bedding Miss Brighton for some time. He *was* precisely the sort to steal a maiden's virtue. She could count herself fortunate he'd been gentlemanly enough to wed her.

He'd left bastards in the wombs of many a woman. A responsible fellow made sure not to impregnate his partners. Brookmoore, by no stretch of the imagination, fit that category.

Crispin speared a glance at the spotless tall windows illuminating one side of the drawing room. The day had darkened somewhat, and a breeze ruffled the meticulously groomed shrubberies. Sutcliffe was most probably on his way back with his wife.

"Your sister and brother-in-law will return soon, Jessica. They'll expect you to have accepted my proposal."

She cradled her chin between her forefinger and thumb, head tilted to the side as she observed him. A spark of mischief gleamed in her eyes. Even now, she remained light-hearted and impish, when both of their futures hung in the balance.

"Ah, but then you haven't proposed, Your Grace, have you?"

9

Why in heaven's name had Jessica jested about Crispin's proposal? The words had poured from her mouth of their own dashed accord. She'd meant what she said about not accepting his offer, however. Meant she'd somehow shoulder the cuts and snubs. Endure the doors slammed in her face. Bear the whispers and snide comments. Learn to accept the isolation and boredom ostracism brought.

It did bring her a smaller degree of satisfaction that Miss Brighton—possibly Viscountess Brookmoore, by now—would also bear a degree of rejection. Not, naturally, to the extent Jessica would. A vicar's daughter did not measure up to a viscountess—even a devious, deplorable, conniving one.

No wonder Crispin had no desire to wed the girl.

When he'd admitted he'd been trying to break his betrothal contract for some time, a little bell had pealed. She wasn't precisely certain what kind of signal it was—a warning or one to grab her attention?

Why would a man who'd been intent on avoiding marriage with one woman readily agree to wed another, especially one tarnished by scandal? Even if he was the other party contributing to her disgrace.

A man of Crispin's caliber, a philanderer, wouldn't jump straight from the pot directly into the fire. He'd celebrate his escape from the parson's mousetrap, wouldn't he? Sow more wild oats? Enjoy his narrow escape?

Nonetheless, his tone held a degree of sincerity Jessica couldn't readily dismiss. It shone in his compelling, smoky eyes, which drew her to him on a level she didn't understand but yearned to explore.

Even his scent—sandalwood, shaving lather, and starched linen—and the permeating heat of his body, mere inches from hers, beckoned. Enticed. Seduced.

And though she was inexperienced in such things, she believed he felt it, too. His focus kept dipping to her mouth, and several times, it appeared as if he would touch her then thought better of it.

Was she so gullible, so desirous of his attention, that she wished it so? Was she simply another female with whom to satiate his lust? That unsolicited thought made her ridiculously despondent.

She'd hoped he was as attracted to her as she was to him. Not wishing to be another notch upon his bedpost, metaphorically speaking, she'd fought that fascination for months, truth to tell. Some might argue she was easily deceived.

Miss Brighton was the perfect example of that.

No, by juniper. Jessica pulled her lips tight. She wouldn't blame herself for that treachery. There'd been no reason to mistrust the innocent-faced girl. It just went to show that first impressions could be most deceiving. She'd always looked for the good in people and wasn't adept at reading body language or eyes.

"Well, then, I'd best go about it properly, hadn't I?" Crispin slid to the floor before her knees, abruptly dragging her back to the present.

She drew in a sharp breath, afraid he'd cause himself further injury. "You don't have to do that, for pity's sake." She speared the bandage circling his head a hard look. "Please do rise. I shall not be responsible for further injury to your person."

He was in pain. A lot of pain.

Fine white lines bracketed his mouth, and discomfort cinched the corners of his arresting, silvery eyes. But it was the dullness in their depths that revealed how much he suffered from his concussion.

He truly ought to be abed. Jessica would feel wretched if he didn't recuperate quickly because of some inane moral code that said he must propose upon one knee.

"I was but jesting, Crispin. I've already told you my decision." When had she started addressing him by his given name? It had seemed so natural; she'd slipped into doing so without thought.

He gave her one of his bone-melting smiles, and she was thankful her bum was planted firmly on a cushion, for her knees surely would've gone weak. Her ridiculous heart pattered unevenly, and something akin to giddy anticipation made her hot then cold in turn.

Bah, what a ninny.

Rakehells did this. Made each woman feel like she, alone, was precious and cherished. That they had no eyes for another. How Jessica wanted that to be true. She'd agree to marry him in a trice if it were.

On one knee, he took her hands in his. She couldn't help but notice the way the fabric stretched tautly over his indecently muscled thigh. He was a deuced fine specimen of manhood.

Good Lord. What would Papa say if he knew I curse in my head? Sometimes aloud, too.

She trailed her gaze over Crispin. His undeniable physical attributes had never been a cause for argument. In that, he was nearly incomparable. It was his character that lacked polish and morality.

He cradled her fingers in his warm palms, the gesture at once tender and enticing. "Jessica, I would be incredibly honored if you'd consent to become my wife."

"*Incredibly,* Your Grace? Isn't that doing it up a bit brown?" She spread her fingers, not at all surprised when he linked his with hers. "I'm not exactly a brilliant catch."

Not a blueblood, but a woman with a reputation besmirched beyond repair.

His hawkish eyebrows swooped together. "You're supposed to either accept or decline, Kitten, not critique the proposal. And I shall decide if you are a brilliant catch. And you most assuredly are."

"Oh, do pardon me. I'm just finding it somewhat difficult to take this quite as serious as I should, I suppose. Which, come to think of it, is rather peculiar, given the situation is most dreadful."

At his loud snort and wry look, laughter bubbled up her throat.

His eyebrows grew impossibly tauter.

"Not that your proposing is dreadful, I don't mean." She extracted her fingers—it was impossible to think straight with his thumb caressing her—and folded her hands atop her ice-blue gown. "Though I suppose it is, in a way, since it's not a proposal born of love. But I referred to last night's incident." She drew in a long breath and, eyes closed, slowly released it until her lungs were empty.

"Forgive me, Crispin. I'm babbling. I do so when I'm nervous."

She used to become tongue-tied and couldn't speak at all.

Which was worse?

"And I make you nervous?" His voice came out a silky purr, and her tummy turned over.

He knew he did. *Wretched man.*

She was no match for him when he decided to be charming and seductive. Was any woman?

"How can you not, Your Grace?"

Jessica shut her eyes for a blink but promptly envisioned them sprawled together, bare limbs entwined upon the divan. No one had explained precisely what that had entailed, and her imagination produced a most naughty image.

She popped her eyes back open and said in a rush, "I keep recalling we were found naked together. You, however, were awake, and I was not." She gave him a sideways glance. "I suppose you, um…saw me?"

Good God Almighty.

Jessica hadn't meant to blurt any of that. Yes, the question had been on the tip of her tongue since arriving, but she wrongly believed she'd tamed the dratted urge. She should only feel mortification and distress, not this unrelenting curiosity.

Had Crispin liked what he'd seen? Why should she care?

The darkening of his eyes to onyx and the dilating of his pupils revealed the astounding truth. His lazy gaze slipped to her bosom before gravitating upward to meet her eyes.

It felt as if he could see through her garments to the pale flesh below. As if he'd caressed that tender skin. She should be outraged and offended, but those most assuredly were not the feelings firing through her, causing weird tremors in unmentionable places.

And then he answered, leaning near, his breath feathering her cheek. A gentleman wouldn't have done so. "Indeed." Rich. Husky. Wicked. And tempting as sin.

She'd need to pray an extra hour tonight that God might forgive her for the lustful thoughts and feelings.

His lips moved near her ear. "From what I observed through my blurry vision, Jessica, you were *exquisite*."

Her breath caught and held.

Exquisite. Crispin finds me exquisite.

He's a rogue. Her sensible, moral, vicar's daughter self reprimanded.

All *roués* whisper such lovely nonsense. *Don't they?*

And now she'd gone and done the most humiliating of things: reminded him of their nudity. Of the reason she was here, and why he now suffered a fractured skull. Of the impossible situation they found themselves amidst.

"Incomparable," he purred silkily. Sincerely. Honestly. And the merest bit raspy.

"Oh." That was all she could achieve. One unimaginative syllable.

Oh, I'm delighted you liked what you saw? *Oh*, I should be swooning from mortification, but I'm not. *Oh,* precisely, what *did* you see? How long did you stare?

Had he *touched* her?

Would he now?

Because Jessica very much wanted Crispin to. To kiss her. To wrap those strapping, powerful arms about her, and let her decide if the rumors about him lived up to the reputation. God, she certainly hoped they did.

Wicked. Wicked. *Wicked.*

A weak, mortified moan did escape her then.

A rough sound rumbling deep in his throat, Crispin wrapped a hand around the back of her head and pulled her to him. His mouth descended, fastening on her lips in a wit-scattering, pulse-stuttering kiss. She went perfectly still for a few heartbeats before the tender pressure had her opening to his probing.

"So sweet," he murmured. "I knew you'd taste of raspberries and honey."

He had? He'd wondered how her mouth tasted?

She parted her lips, and he slipped his tongue inside, brushing it across her teeth, then finding hers and parring seductively. Tantalizingly. Skillfully. God help her; she nearly incinerated on the spot.

He tasted of tea and mint.

Sensation flitted across her every nerve. *Closer. Yes, closer.* She must move closer to Crispin. She scooted to the end of the sofa and placed her hands flat, fingers spread, on his wonderfully sinewy, broad shoulders.

His muscles bunched and flexed beneath her palms, all rounded hardness and exciting virile maleness.

The kiss went on and on *and on*. Each moment more delicious and wondrous than the last. Each more sizzling. Satisfying yet oddly unfulfilling.

The passion dragged her under, encompassing, chasing away any thoughts of resisting or remorse. She *wanted* this. Had wanted it for so very, very long. Only she hadn't known it until his mouth took hers.

Her body felt hot and hungry in a way she couldn't understand, let alone explain.

"Ahem." A slightly amused, somewhat censorious male cleared his throat and had her issuing a startled squeak and leaping backward as if singed.

Jessica *had* been seared. Branded. Burned by a desire so scorching, she'd nearly become a conflagration. No one had ever said passion could be like that.

"I do hope that means you've accepted Bainbridge's marriage proposal, Jessica," Victor said, not quite able to snuff the gleam of warning in the stern gaze he leveled on Crispin. "Else, I'll be compelled to demand satisfaction with pistols at dawn. It would be most unfair, given his current ill health."

"Don't be absurd, Victor," Theadosia interjected, swatting his arm, not quite playfully. "You're no more challenging Bainbridge to a duel than I am. Do you forget you are to be a father in a short time? I am not raising this child without its father." Though she bantered, there was a steely edge to her words. "It's only natural for a betrothed couple to share a kiss."

Jessica's sister had no intention of permitting her husband to risk his life over something as foolish as a kiss. But neither did she intend to ignore what the kiss implied.

Jessica and Crispin would wed.

Cheeks burning at being caught in another compromising situation, though this one was far less scandalous and of her own making, she summoned her composure, and Crispin stood, quite nimbly for a man battling acute pain.

Flicking those long fingers of his at her, his gold signet ring with its knight's helmet and trio of battle axes glinted on his little finger with the casual movement. "I haven't received an answer yet."

At the dark look Victor stabbed him, Jessica quickly stood as well and shook out her skirts. "Yes. Yes, I agree to the union."

A trio of eyes swept to her. Relief and a degree of surprise in her sister's and Victor's gazes. A sensual, seductive promise simmering in Crispin's.

Another wave of awareness flooded her, heat swelling from her waist, over her bosoms, up her neck, and clear to her hairline. She swiftly averted her gaze, lest he see the answering spark that surely must shine in her own eyes.

She wasn't exactly sure at which point she'd made the decision. Before or after that breath-taking kiss? *Lord, but the man knew how to kiss.* Her mouth still throbbed from the delicious onslaught, and she was sure her lips were red and swollen.

"But," Jessica forced her attention back to them, disregarding the flush skittering over her when Crispin's hooded gaze settled upon her. "I want to wait until Crispin's concussion has fully healed. The gossip will be dreadful enough without rumors that he wasn't in his right mind when he proposed and we wed." She sliced him a glance. "I know you'd prefer we marry straightaway, but I must insist on the reading of the banns for three weeks. And no public announcement of the forthcoming nuptials until then."

"You have a valid point." Victor slowly nodded. "I hadn't considered that."

Crispin looked none too pleased, but after pulling on his ear, he also nodded. "I'll wait for three weeks. Not a day more. I fear we cannot delay longer than that."

They couldn't afford to wait *that* long. But three weeks gave her a little more time to become acquainted with him. To change her mind if she decided she couldn't go through with it.

Jessica gathered her gloves. "I would ask one thing of you, Your Grace."

10

"Crispin," he corrected. "We are affianced, after all." Taking Jessica's small hand in his much larger one, Crispin smiled that dashing smile that made her thoughts scatter like snowflakes in a blizzard. "I shall endeavor to make it come to pass, my dear."

My dear? Was he laying it on thick for Theadosia's and Victor's sakes? No need. Those two were prudent if naught else. They knew full well this was a marriage of convenience. Actually, more of a marriage of inconvenience, but a necessity, nevertheless.

"I want my pet chickens moved to your country estate."

She drew on a glove, refusing to be embarrassed at her attachment to her chickens. She'd very much like to ask for a puppy or two, a kitten or three, a horse of her own, and a donkey. Maybe even a pig and a sheep. Geese. Ducks. Goats. Best not to push her luck so soon, however.

Crispin might well change his mind when he realized his duchess intended to assemble a menagerie. Not exotic animals. No, they should remain free. But an assortment of domesticated ones would be lovely.

Theadosia giggled and covered her mouth with her hand.

Looking nonplussed, Victor drolly muttered, "Thank God. I should warn you, Bainbridge. She puts crocheted jumpers on the things."

At Crispin's incredulous look, Jessica squared her shoulders. "They become chilled, particularly when molting. I've had Lady Featherston, Countess Chirpsalot, Baroness Beaksworth, Princess Poultry, and Queen Cluckingham since they hatched. They think me their mother."

"They do," Theadosia said between laughs. "They follow Jessica everywhere. And the minute those hens hear her voice, they come running, squawking away. It's something to behold when they're wearing their jumpers."

Crispin pressed his lips to the knuckles of her bare hand. "By all means. Bring the brood. Shall I have a special coop built for them? Do they prefer one story or two? Perhaps cozy, satin-lined nesting boxes? China dishes from whence to eat?" He chuckled, his eyes alight with mirth.

"Make fun all you like, but they love me, and I love them." Yes, it was odd. But she adored animals. Chickens were the singular pets Papa allowed her, and only because they produced eggs.

"You may have as many chickens or other fowl as you like, Jessica." Crispin turned to Victor. "We are in agreement, then? The ceremony will be in three weeks? The Monday after the last reading of the banns?"

Victor looked to Jessica for affirmation, and she dipped her chin. "*If* the doctor agrees you're well enough."

What was the recovery period for a concussion?

Barlow cleared his throat as he stepped into the drawing room, holding a salver with a card atop it. "I beg your pardon, Your Grace. Mr. Hammon Brighton insists that he must speak with you at once. I told him you were otherwise engaged, but he was most insistent."

He turned to Victor. "This also arrived for you, Your Grace."

If the servant found anything unusual about delivering correspondence to someone other than his employer, he in no way revealed his astonishment.

Barlow passed a letter to Victor, who promptly broke the seal and read the contents. His mouth pulled into a grim line before he refolded the missive and tucked it into his pocket.

How peculiar. Why would Victor have post delivered here?

Before she could ask, a rotund man wearing a garish, bright-blue jacket and orange-and-yellow striped waistcoat shoved past the butler. Face flushed and his sparse red hair standing on end as if he'd repeatedly plowed his hands through its scraggly lengths, Mr. Brighton drew up short upon spying Jessica, her sister, and Victor.

Eyes narrowed to hostile slits, he stomped toward Jessica, pointing accusingly. "*You!*"

At his visceral animosity, she shrank back, thankful for Crispin's arm protectively snaking around her waist.

"I know who *you* are," Brighton snarled, revealing slightly uneven, yellowed teeth. "You're the strumpet everyone's been talking about. The lightskirt bent on stealing my daughter's betrothed."

"I beg your pardon?" Jessica bristled, curling her fingers, ready to scratch his eyes out for calling her a whore. "How dare you?"

"Stay calm, Kitten." Crispin spread his fingers at her waist and gave a little pulse of pressure while whispering in her ear. He leveled Brighton a frosty glare. "You overstep, Brighton."

Such icy contempt weighted each word that Jessica shuddered. Crispin wasn't a man to cross, and she was grateful they were not on opposing sides.

Theadosia's glare eviscerated the man, and she swept her furious gaze about the room as if looking for something with which she might skewer him. "You are beyond the pale, sir."

"I shan't have it. Do you hear me?" So angry his ears glowed red, Brighton spun to face Crispin. "This is just another stunt to try to avoid marrying my daughter. It won't work either, *Your Grace.*"

Why would any father who claimed any affection for his daughter insist she wed a man she obviously loathed?

Smirking, Brighton shook his head, causing the sparse hairs atop to sway like giant orangey feelers. *Is orangey a word?* "I'll see you in court if you try to break the betrothal contract. And I'll not hesitate to drag this shameless harlot's name through the shite."

"Sir! You forget yourself." Theadosia raked her gaze over him in much the same way one would scrape manure from one's shoe.

"Every gossip rag and newssheet will be eager to print the tales I feed them about her," Brighton crowed, confident he had the upper hand.

Did he?

Much like raptors, gossips hovered about, ready to swoop in and attack anything weaker than themselves. And blackguards such as

238

Brighton possessed no integrity. A tiny frisson of fright tip-toed across her shoulders, and she wrapped her hands about her waist in a protective gesture.

"Not if they want to remain in business, they won't." Crispin drawled with commendable calm but wintery finality.

Brighton leaned in, going toe to toe with him. "Watch me. I already have men willing to swear they've bedded the tart."

Bloody cur! Jessica made a choking sound as she clamped her teeth against several other unsavory oaths throttling up her throat. Shaken by the rage thrumming through her, she dug her fingernails into her palms.

"No doubt paid handsomely by you to say so," Crispin bit out, each word razor sharp.

"Prove it," Brighton sneered, folding his arms, his features smug. He bloody well thought he had them, the cur.

Theadosia gasped. Her appalled attention swung to Jessica then bounced right back to Brighton. "You're a monster."

"My God," Jessica whispered, slanting into Crispin. As if things weren't already abysmal, this villain was prepared to lie to blacken her name further.

"Now, see here." Victor took up a position beside Crispin, his features taut with indignation. "You've gone beyond the mark, besmirching Miss Brentwood's good name when it was *your* daughter who drugged her. And her lover who bashed Bainbridge on his head."

Lover? Just how had Victor come by that morsel?

"Lies. All lies, I tell you—every foul, libelous word. Lilith told me *everything,* not more than an hour ago," Brighton spluttered, shifting his muddy-brown glare between the three of them.

"Lilith?" A chill of trepidation slithered down Jessica's spine. "But...she eloped with Lord Brookmoore last night." She cast Crispin a questioning glance. Hadn't they eloped? Had someone twisted the facts there, too? Or carelessly failed to learn the truth?

"She did no such thing." Brighton drew a handkerchief from his pocket and mopped his damp forehead. "More of your slanderous lies, wench."

Crispin went rigid, yet he kept his arm about her. It was an anchor, holding her steady in this emotional tempest. "Yes, she did. But Brookmoore threw her over, didn't he? Did he learn she wouldn't inherit a dime if she wed without your consent?"

Brighton blanched but still puffed out his chest. He looked like an oversized, brightly-plumed pigeon. "Are you casting slurs on my daughter's good name, Bainbridge?"

"No, but *I* am, Brighton." Victor raked a fuming glance over the sweaty little man, and his upper lip hitched in contempt. "I have it from a knowledgeable source your daughter did, in fact, enter a coach with Brookmoore. That said, coach had valises stashed inside, and that it did, indeed, make straight for the Scottish border." He patted his coat pocket where the letter lay.

Ah, so that was what that was all about.

"They stopped at the Cat and Crock Lodging House *overnight*," Victor went on. "They shared a chamber and were overheard quarreling in the common room the next morning."

Jessica couldn't help but admire the speed at which her brother-in-law had seen Brookmoore and Miss Brighton pursued. Nor fail to appreciate his defense of her. Or Crispin's, either.

Victor cut Crispin a steady gaze and gave a sharp nod before pointing a scathing scowl at Brighton. "Your daughter did indeed reveal to Brookmoore that she'd be cut off without a cent for eloping. Poor chit fancies herself in love with the bugger."

If Miss Brighton hadn't been so conniving and devious, Jessica might've felt a twinge of pity for her.

"I'm sure Brookmoore vowed everlasting love," Victor drawled, sarcastically. "Until he realized he'd be saddled with a wife but without a marriage settlement. He, being the gallant gentleman that he is, acquired a mount and deserted her, leaving your daughter to return to London on her own. Which, I presume, she promptly did and fed you the cock-and-bull story she contrived along the way."

"That romance didn't last long," Theadosia remarked dryly, with perhaps the merest hint of gratification in her tone.

Brighton directed his scornful stare at Crispin's arm around Jessica's waist. "I don't care how many *loose* women you entertain before or after your marriage to my daughter. But marry her, *you* will."

"I think not," Crispin denied, a wry smile quirking his mouth as his welcoming heat burned into Jessica's side. The pleasant aromas of sandalwood, soap, and starch floated past her nostrils.

"Your daughter dissolved our betrothal when she arranged to have Miss Brentwood and me incapacitated and then absconded with Brookmoore." He crooked a superior eyebrow over merciless slate-dark eyes, his disdain palpable. "Do you comprehend the seriousness of the charges they face for attacking a duke?"

Brighton's fleshy, bewhiskered jowls worked as he clenched and unclenched his hands.

Scorn and anger emphasizing his angular, clean-shaven features, Crispin leaned over, intimidating the shorter man, who had the good sense to step back a pace. "I confess to being most grateful to Miss Brighton." He skewed his mouth sideways.

Casting him an astonished glance, Jessica tried to discern if he was serious. How could he possibly be grateful to the chit?

Bold as brass and in front of all, he gave her a devilish wink, and her tummy turned over in giddy excitement.

Gathering her hand in his, he brought it close to his chest, the gesture almost reverent. "Now, I am free to marry a woman of my choosing. Miss Brentwood has granted me the highest honor possible and agreed to become my wife. You, Brighton, can deal with your wayward daughter any way you see fit. But know this: If you do anything to disparage my future duchess, I. *Shall.* Destroy. You."

Moisture beading his forehead and upper lip, Brighton blanched, swallowing audibly while tearing at his neckcloth.

Crispin jerked his chin toward the door. "Now, leave my house, and never darken my doorstep again."

"I shall see you in court, then." Brighton stomped to the doorway. He looked over his shoulder, spearing Jessica with a loathing-filled glare before swinging his wrathful focus to Crispin. "Lilith carries your child."

11

Jessica stared blankly at the page of the novel in her lap, a new Gothic romance Nicolette Twistleton had sent over the morning after the *incident*. Far better to be busy and concentrating on something—*anything*—but the debacle on everyone's lips. Or Mr. Brighton's last vile, world-tilting accusation.

Was Lilith Brighton truly with child? Was the babe Crispin's?

Her stomach sank and clenched as it always did when she entertained the possibility. It left a hollow, sick feeling in her belly. She didn't want to believe the ugly accusation. Found it almost impossible to accept.

But his reputation.

Crispin had vowed his romantic escapades were exaggerated. Claimed he'd created a false persona with the intent of off-putting his betrothed. Twisting her mouth to the side, she furrowed her forehead into a scowl, directed at the unread words on the page.

Jessica wanted to believe him. Needed to believe him. *Had* believed him. For if the claim was valid, what was she to do?

Her tummy pitched sickeningly again.

In truth, Crispin and Lilith assuredly wouldn't have been the first couple to have anticipated their vows and consummated the union prematurely. Still torturing the edges of the poor book, she worried her lower lip.

Yet that didn't make sense.

Why would Miss Brighton have Crispin knocked over the head, then?

Why arrange for Jessica to be caught and disgraced with him? Why elope with the viscount? It was much more likely Lord Brookmoore had impregnated the daft chit then, as Victor suggested, abandoned her.

Afterward, the wily wench had thought to entrap Crispin. Oh, how Jessica longed for five minutes with the devious snake. She'd give Lilith Brighton a tongue lashing she'd not soon forget.

Bah! How many times had those same musings circled each other in her brain, like a dog chasing its tail? Why, she'd almost made herself dizzy. And that was why she did her utmost to keep her mind occupied. Yet, she hadn't advanced beyond the first chapter since the day Crispin had proposed.

Pinching her mouth tighter, she uncrossed her legs, stretched out before her on the rather hard settee. She wiggled her toes to ease the slight cramping of her muscles from having remained in the same position for too long.

Crispin had attended the Christmastide house party hosted by her sister and brother-in-law. Jessica had seen him at several gatherings in the ensuing months since, including the musical at the Twistletons' and tea and garden party at Theadosia's, where he'd lost the match of Pall Mall to her.

Not privy to his comings and goings, she had no way of knowing if he'd ventured to London regularly. Town was but a four-hour journey on horseback. But to her knowledge—and Victor believed it true as well—Crispin had only just arrived in London with the rest of his cohorts in time for the start of Parliament.

As he was a close associate of Crispin's, Victor would know, wouldn't he?

She permitted a tiny smile of relief to curve her mouth and the tension knotting her shoulders and neck to relax a trifle. Victor was an excellent judge of character.

During the day, Jessica fared well enough. But at night, as she lay in her too-big bed when all was quiet except for the peculiar noises a sleeping house made, and she attempted to sleep, her mind replayed the dreadful scene in Crispin's drawing room.

With his incessant, unpleasant monologue, Mr. Brighton had been positively beastly, calling her a whore.

What was more, her deuced overly-creative imagination made a remarkable effort to fill in the lurid details she'd been oblivious to in her drug-induced slumber that night of the ball. Small mercy, that. She didn't want to know everything that had transpired. What she did know proved distressing enough.

How could Crispin stand to face the people who'd come upon them? Her instinct was to run and hide. His, she'd venture, was to confront and demand truth. Ducal airs, and all that.

What was it about aristocrats that made people bow and scrape before them? Those same sycophants wouldn't give her the time of day.

When that horrible night wasn't haunting her ruminations, or the humiliation of the snubs she'd already received from several denizens, genuine worry for Crispin smothered her.

Once Brighton had departed, he'd nearly collapsed. She'd vowed to herself, right then and there, she'd not discuss any of this ugliness until he was much improved. She'd keep her worries to herself.

He'd written daily, reporting on his tactics, when he should've been resting and concentrating on recovering. It could not be good for his health to deal with Brighton, the rumors, the authorities, and the rest of the odiousness that now enshrouded both of them.

That was how she thought of their situation. *Odious. Ugly. Vile. Loathsome.*

The situation continued to deteriorate, and honestly, she hated the helplessness she felt. Despised feeling powerless to rectify the wrong done to her and Crispin. She'd agreed to wed him because, if nothing else, she was pragmatic.

A woman in her precarious position had few—*very few*—respectable options. In truth, she didn't relish hieing off to some fusty corner of England or Scotland. To live in obscurity for the remainder of her days, kept company by a few cats and chickens. Maybe a goat and a donkey as well. And a darling puppy.

After all, it was her fondness for puppies that had landed her in this mess. She might as well benefit from it in some small measure. Plus, marriage to a man who could kiss her breathless and turn her bones to custard wouldn't be so awful. She'd secretly admired Crispin, never once considering she might catch his attention.

If his sizzling kisses were any indication, he wanted her just as madly, but his letters conveyed none of the passion he'd introduced Jessica to that day.

She hadn't known how to respond to his terse, fact-filled correspondences. It was as if he briefed a court on proceedings rather than penned missives to his betrothed. How odd to think of him as such. Except, he'd signed the letters, "Ever yours, affectionately," followed by a flourishing *C*.

Ever yours? Affectionately?

The kind of warm regard one held for a long-time acquaintance? Or the tender care or fondness reserved for a beloved sister? Possibly—that was what she fervently hoped—a stronger emotion?

The man was an enigma. A puzzle she couldn't quite piece together. These past months, she'd caught glimpses of who she believed Crispin was, and then he'd say or do something she hadn't expected, and the image she'd built of him in her mind had to be reconstructed all over again. He was far more complex than a simple rakehell. He hid a noble side, and she found herself admiring him more than she ought.

With a sigh, Jessica brought her gaze up to the window and idly fingered the page edges, the movement strangely soothing. An ebony-headed coal tit flitted from branch to branch in the dogwood tree outside the library window. Cocking its head, the little bird scampered along, dipping and bowing, singing all the while.

She adored birds, particularly songbirds. An abundance of coal tits populated Colechester, so she was quite familiar with the sweet, little things. Looking closer, she spied another coal tit bearing slightly more muted plumage.

Ah, he was showing off, the wee gallant gentleman.

Were they already mates? Or was he trying to win her favor?

Even as Jessica contemplated the thought, the female gave what could only be called a flirtatious dip of her beak and suggestive flick of her tail before flying off. At once, the male pursued her.

Oh, to be like those birds. How much simpler their mating habits were than humans.

Hushed feminine voices in the corridor announced she was about to be interrupted. Jessica hadn't even swung her feet to the floor when Ophelia Breckensole, Nicolette Twistleton, and Rayne Wellbrook sailed into the chamber. Each resembled a spring blossom in their colorful gowns.

"Ophelia? Nicolette? Rayne?" She shoved to her feet, delighted to see them and simultaneously concerned at the risk they'd taken. *Good Lord.* They'd be ruined if anyone knew they'd called upon her. She was soiled goods, and they chanced degradation by associating with her. "Surely, you know you shouldn't be here."

"Darling, we could stay away no longer." Ophelia enfolded her into her soft embrace, holding her in a fierce hug. She drew back, and after bussing Jessica's cheek, she examined her features. "I've been so very worried about you. How are you managing, dearest?"

Her hazel gaze overly bright, Ophelia blinked rapidly, valiantly fighting the moisture pooling in her eyes.

"Of course Jessica's beside herself, but she's still holding her head up, as she well should," Nicolette declared, swooping in for a hug and smelling of lilies, as usual. "Never you mind, Jessica." She gave Rayne and Ophelia a knowing look, her vivid, blue eyes conveying a silent message. "Your friends know the truth, and that's all that matters."

Not as reassuring as Nicolette, no doubt intended. Truth, Jessica had concluded during her short stint in London, seldom accounted for as much as titillating *on dit.*

Nicolette arced a long-fingered hand between herself and the other women. "Besides, our being here is part of a grand plan contrived by our ducal friends, their duchesses, and a few others who aren't to be trifled with. My mother, as well as my brother, also lend their support." She quirked her mouth into a wry smile. "Though as much as Ansley deigns society, that's not much help, I fear."

That was true. Ansley, Earl of Scarborough, was a unique man. Kind but subdued, and he tossed off nearly all social strictures in favor of his preferred interests and regimens.

Nicolette stepped aside so that Rayne could buss Jessica's cheek. More reserved than either Ophelia or Nicolette, she clasped Jessica's hands in her own. "Is it true? You're to wed Bainbridge?" A naughty grin tipped her mouth. "He is devilishly handsome."

How, precisely, had they learned that tidbit? Ah, part of the grand plan, no doubt.

"He's proposed, and I've accepted." No need for her to tell them neither of them had any choice in the matter. It was an unstated fact. No one with a lick of sense would attempt to spin a romantic slant on the situation.

Theadosia glided in and glanced around with satisfaction. "Excellent. I shall request tea. You girls are precisely what Jessica needs."

Her sister should chastise their friends for taking such a chance, but Jessica couldn't deny she was grateful they had. The fickle world of London Society seemed a trifle less daunting when surrounded by her dearest friends.

Subdued laughter and forced gaiety filled the next two hours. Everyone avoided mention of the puce hippopotamus in the room. Namely, the sordid events that had taken place at the ball. She could tell by their side-eyed glances they were dying to know the details but would bite off their tongues before asking.

Not ready to reveal all just yet—she mightn't ever be—Jessica studiously turned her attention away when she noticed their inquisitive gazes.

Finally, Nicolette peeked at the watch pinned to her spencer and released a loud, distinctly disgruntled sigh. "I'm loathe to be the one who puts an end to our lovely visit, but Mama wishes me to walk Belle in St James's Park with her this afternoon." She pulled a face. "Which means she's probably arranged for a gentleman or two or three to accidentally come upon us. Mayhap Belle will bark and growl and dispel any need for conversation."

The sweet-tempered pug was more likely to beg to be picked up and petted.

Nicolette still hadn't completely recovered from being jilted two years ago. She now viewed men as one would a pox sore or a carbuncle. Her mother, a consummate matchmaker, used ploy after ploy to introduce her most reluctant daughter to eligible gentleman.

And Nicolette, being Nicolette, rebuffed them all, refusing to take a chance on love again.

Another round of hugs commenced, with many murmured assurances that all would be well, when in fact, each woman knew that wasn't precisely true. Jessica had only ever wanted to marry for love. Now her wedding gown was a shroud of ruination, her bridesmaid, a tarnished reputation. At least the groom was pleasing.

She looped her arm through the bend in Ophelia's elbow as they walked to the entrance.

Ophelia slowed her steps until they trailed several paces behind Rayne and Nicolette. Her soulful hazel eyes searched Jessica's. "Tell me true, dearest. How are you really? I cannot think you are happy to marry a stranger, no matter how handsome he might be."

"Miss Brighton is with child." Why had Jessica blurted that out?

Ophelia's eyes went round as the moon. "Oh no," she whispered, her voice equal parts aghast and stunned. She darted a swift glance at the other women then turned her head side to side, before hauling Jessica into a secluded corner. "What will you do? Is it...? Is it Bainbridge's?"

Jessica filled her lungs.

Is it?

No. She felt confident it wasn't. She released the breath in a whoosh and shook her head. "I'm confident it's not. I cannot explain how I know, but there's a decency in Crispin, which he conceals behind wastrel and libertine ramparts and bastions. He's not the sort who'd father a child on a woman and leave her to deal with the situation."

If he were such a cad, he wouldn't have offered for her. He'd have left her to deal with her tarnished reputation alone.

Jessica brushed her hair away from her face. "He kissed me."

Her blasted tongue seemed to have acquired a mind of its own today. The good Lord only knew what else might come spilling forth.

Ophelia's jaw went slack, practically hitting her bosom. Then a wide, delighted smile spread across her face. "And you *liked* it." Her grin widened, and she gave a little, excited hop. "You did! Why, Jessica Miriam Emerald Brentwood, you liked it very much, indeed."

"I did." Oh, she had. Indeed, she had. She'd like to kiss Crispin again. And again. And again.

What would've happened if Victor hadn't interrupted? For certain, they'd not have ended up naked on the divan. Once in a lifetime was more than sufficient to be discovered as such.

Squinting, Ophelia glanced upward in concentration. "Forgive me for overstepping, but we *are* the dearest of friends, after all. I couldn't help but notice the way you've watched him these many months. And you admit you enjoyed his kiss. Aren't you a just little pleased about the match?"

More than a little pleased, and yet dismay also marred what should've been joyful anticipation.

"I am, but I wish the union weren't forced upon us." It didn't hurt to admit the truth to Ophelia. She'd guard the secret with her life. "It's not the ideal way to begin a marriage."

Jessica dropped her attention to her hands. Untold numbers of people before they had entered into arranged marriages and marriages of convenience and still had managed to carry on with their lives.

Yes, but many had also trudged along, wretched and bitterly unhappy.

"I'd hoped for a love match," she admitted, unable to keep the forlorn note from her voice.

"But..." Ophelia hesitated, her gaze keen and probing. "Oh. I see." She leaned near and drew Jessica into her arms. Offering the comfort only a dearest friend who knows one as well as one knows oneself can provide. The kind of friend who never judged but accepted and loved unconditionally. "You love him?"

Do I?

I do. I do. I truly do.

God, help me. That's what this…this turmoil is.

How could she not have been aware all these months?

This weighty, aching sensation wasn't at all how she'd anticipated love would feel. No rainbows and stars and gaiety. No dizzying sensations of floating. No sparkling eyes and incandescent smiles.

She'd expected a fluttering pulse whenever she'd seen Crispin. For warmth to spiral outward from her middle when he spoke to her. His presence to muddle her thoughts and despondency to cloak her whenever they were apart.

What she felt at present was excruciatingly magnificent. An agony of splendor. A mélange of hurt and joy so entangled it was impossible to distinguish the pleasure from the pain.

She loved Crispin. Adored him.

When had it happened? How had it sneaked up on Jessica, catching her unawares?

How could she not have recognized falling in love with the seductive scoundrel?

Oh, love—*the tricky devil*—had wooed her. Won her.

Steadily. Stealthily. Slyly.

She was in the thrall of the insidious emotion. Snared, well and good. Much like a drunkard's dependence on spirits. The process wasn't instant or overnight. Nay. The twin demons of time and exposure gradually worked their wiles until, one day, one realized they craved the substance—were miserable without it.

Or as in her case, only felt whole when she was with Crispin.

Stupid. Stupid. Stupid. How could Jessica have been so foolish?

Blinking away the moisture stinging her eyes, Jessica gave a shaky, self-deprecating smile. "Is it that obvious?"

Likely, her dratted calf-eyed glances had given her away, despite her valiant efforts to mask her sentiments.

"No, it's not, if that reassures you." Ophelia stepped back, still holding Jessica's forearms. Forehead furrowed, sympathy shone in her eyes. "You're not happy about it, though, are you?"

Happy? Hardly. It was one thing to give her body to him.

But her heart? Her soul?

Such vulnerability terrified Jessica. She might very well lose herself, her identity, her self-respect.

"He doesn't love me. Yes, he wants my body, but I'm not completely convinced a man such as he is capable of enduring fidelity, Ophelia, let alone love."

12

A week after Brighton's unpleasant visit, Crispin marched up the six well-scrubbed steps to the Sutcliffes' ostentatious residence, complete with double doors painted a vibrant ruby-red. He was expected for tea, a guise to see Jessica contrived by him and the Duke and Duchess of Sutcliffe.

The stubborn woman had not called upon him again, which both relieved and exasperated him. Her absence provided an undistracted opportunity for his head to heal while he put mechanisms in place to prove Lilith Brighton and her father the bold-faced liars they were. It also gave him time to discover what foul hole Brookmoore had scuttled into or what rock he'd crawled beneath as well as report his crimes to the authorities.

Why, only this morning, his detectives had reported seeing Brookmoore slithering into his rented rooms, looking much the worse for wear.

Jessica, the maddening, darling woman, hadn't responded to his daily notes, and that worried him no small amount. He feared Brighton's libelous declaration had put her off. Raised qualms and questions.

Today, Crispin meant to set her straight on the matter.

He would've done so the day he proposed, but he'd all but passed out after Brighton's thunderous departure from the drawing room. Weak as a kitten, Sutcliffe supporting him on one side and Barlow on the other, he'd barely been able to raise his head to beg her pardon. To assure her, all would be well. That Brighton was lying through his yellow teeth.

Crispin had never even danced with Lilith Brighton, let alone bedded the chit. The notion repulsed him, making him realize all the more he could never have wed her and fathered a child on her. The dukedom would've gone to a distant cousin perched somewhere in the extensive family tree.

Pale, her delicate features taut, Jessica had stared at him, her gaze searching. Probing. Seeking. Not accusing, however. Several other emotions had flitted across her face: worry, fear, uncertainty, concern, doubt. The last lingered, shadowing her gorgeous blue-green eyes, and it was that uncertainty that lanced him afresh every time he summoned her exquisite face.

She didn't trust him. Why should she?

Because of their kiss. It had been unlike anything he'd ever experienced.

Even after their soul-shattering kiss, she had misgivings. It was only natural, he reminded himself. She couldn't know what they'd shared had been beyond rare, the fusing of spirits. Immediate. Unbreakable. Profound.

Why, he'd have scoffed at such tripe if he hadn't experienced it firsthand.

Jessica Brentwood was his. *His.* And, by damn, he was hers, whether she knew it or not.

He must somehow convince her she could trust him. That they could build a future together. The beginning might be a mite precarious, but that was no fault of theirs.

Brighton, the feckless bounder, had successfully planted a seed of suspicion. It stung how easily she'd believed the rotter, but Crispin couldn't blame her. She didn't know him well. He'd honed a devilish reputation, one he'd asked her to believe wasn't true without giving her any foundation for doing so.

Despite his doctor's orders that he should rest for a few more days, he'd left his house yesterday. There'd been a constant stream of people in and out he'd summoned since Brighton's harshly slung accusation, but there were tasks Crispin must attend to himself.

Only a niggling ache now annoyed him where the blow had fallen. That, and the blasted stitches. They itched something awful.

Since Jessica's departure, he'd been restless and edgy, needing to see her. Needing to assure himself she was well. Almost as if he anticipated Brighton or Brookmoore would spring another foul surprise upon him.

Or upon Jessica. Perchance both of them again.

He couldn't help but feel she wasn't entirely safe and had conveyed his concern to Sutcliffe. Rather than disregard Crispin's worries, Sutcliffe agreed to take additional security measures at home and when they ventured out.

Never before had Crispin felt such an overpowering need to protect another. To ensure someone's safety and wellbeing. There were no lengths to which he wouldn't go to safeguard Jessica. To make her his duchess.

Only, according to Sutcliffe, she hadn't peeked her delicate nose outdoors since she'd left Crispin's house the day he'd proposed. Evidently, upon their departure, they'd gone home by way of St. James's Park, after the duchess had insisted the fresh air might do her younger sister good.

Well acquainted with the workings of London Society, Sutcliffe had believed they ought to go directly home, but his wife was not to be dissuaded. The weather had been pleasant, and her grace had erroneously believed a turn about the park might lighten her sister's somber mood and lift her low spirits.

Jessica, in particular, was fond of the numerous fuzzy, dappled, ducklings paddling near Duck Island or drowsily sunning themselves upon the shore.

Crispin would have to see to it that he acquired a few ducklings and goslings for her to raise. A puppy, too, since that was what had lured her to the hothouse.

Until recently, the Duchess of Sutcliffe had also lived her entire life in a warm and welcoming community. Her inexperience with the sharp-tongued, critical *haut ton* had, most unfortunately, made her sister an easy target.

The outing, which was to have been followed by ices at Gunter's, had proved a colossal mistake, according to Sutcliffe. They'd encountered several members of the upper ten thousand, and Jessica had been given the cut direct by more than one.

Ladies had pulled their skirts aside while making blistering comments accompanied by smoldering looks of contempt. And, as Crispin had feared, many of the men had lewdly sized her up like a new type of pastry they couldn't wait to sample.

Sutcliffe cursed himself for a thousand kinds of fool for not anticipating what would happen. He'd honestly hoped that if Jessica were in his company, no one would dare turn a gimlet eye upon her.

He'd been dead wrong.

Which raised more concerns. *Le Beau Monde* had passed judgment, and it would take more than a duke's championing her to restore things to rights. The unpleasant encounter had only confirmed Crispin's suspicions.

There was no more time to delay. Arrangements must be made for their immediate marriage. It was astounding what quick nuptials could remedy. Crispin had seen that miracle work more than once, by God.

One day ruined and, the next, married and welcomed back into the *haut ton's* capricious bosom. Such bloody damn hypocrites. How many of those self-righteous pricks were sneaking in and out of bedchambers themselves? Most, truth be known. Or if they weren't now, they had in their heydays.

The banns were supposed to have been read two days after his proposal. But someone—probably that bastard Brighton—had whispered in the bishop's ear. Likely after *donating* a considerable sum to the Church.

More blasted hypocrisy.

Crispin squinted slightly and pulled his earlobe. Didn't Brighton have another connection to the Church? He couldn't precisely recall the exact nature, however. It would come to him eventually.

In any event, the man of God had refused to read the banns until the matter of the broken betrothal was resolved. The issue *was* resolved. Brighton's daughter had colluded with Brookmoore to ruin Jessica and smack Crispin over the head, and now the girl's belly swelled with Brookmoore's seed.

The contract was null. Void. Invalid. And Lilith had provided the means for the dissolution. As spelled out in elaborate detail on page seven, paragraph three.

The resignation in Jessica's eyes upon hearing Brighton's contemptible lie had nearly fractured his heart. Lilith Brighton was not the first woman to falsely accuse a man of fathering her child. In Crispin's case, he could prove he hadn't. When he explained the truth of it to Jessica, he was confident he'd reassure her. He must. He'd not wed her having her believe another woman carried his issue.

If he did, she'd see him as the basest sort of bastard.

Yesterday, he'd met with his man-of-affairs, his solicitor, and the investigators hired to poke around a bit about Brookmoore's clandestine meetings with Miss Brighton. It hadn't taken much sleuthing by the detectives to confirm the chit was indeed breeding.

Truthfully, it was somewhat astonishing, and not a little disturbing, what tattle might be learned from the mouths of domestics. Once located, Brightons' laundress confessed with alacrity—incentivized by a heavy coin purse—it had been months since she'd laundered any menstrual cloths in the Brighton household. At least since December, which meant Lilith Brighton was four months gone into her pregnancy and would show very soon.

The current fashions helped hide her swelling belly, and that she was plump to start with also played to her advantage. No wonder she'd gone along with Brookmoore's scheme. Or had she concocted the plan and ensured the viscount's assistance with promises of a considerable dowry?

The blackguard's pockets were always to let, and he was in debt up to his inadequately starched neckcloth.

Was Brighton truly so stupid he couldn't add two and two—couldn't recall that Crispin had wintered at his country estate? His servants could attest to that. He'd also attended Sutcliffe's Christmastide house party and dozens more country assemblies over the past few months, including Twistleton's musical soiree in March.

He could produce dozens of witnesses to swear he'd not left the country or been seen in London. Unlike the majority of the upper ten thousand, the Brightons lived in London year-round. Brighton ought to have considered those details before slinging false accusations at him.

Unless the man knew and didn't bloody well care. That seemed more the gist of it. Why settle for a viscount, even if he had compromised Lilith?

Crispin had refused to be bullied into marrying the girl before, but now that she'd spread her legs for Brookmoore... He snorted, loudly and contemptuously. Satan would be making snow angels in hell before Lilith Brighton became his duchess.

He damn well wasn't marrying her and essentially proclaiming to all and sundry the child she carried was his. For God's sake, she might well bear a male child; no by-blow of Brookmoore's would inherit the Bainbridge dukedom.

It certainly did make one wonder if both Brookmoore and Lilith had taken leave of their senses. Their plot was doomed to failure from the beginning. They would've had to have killed him to prevent him from naming them as the guilty parties.

His wound took that moment to twinge. Mayhap killing him had been their intent. Had they succeeded, Jessica would've been left with no defense whatsoever.

A grimace twisted his mouth. Why hadn't he considered that before? Because no man liked to think his betrothed detested him so much, she'd conspire to see him dead.

Brighton wouldn't spread word of his daughter's delicate condition. Not if he wanted to maintain his position on Society's outer fringes. He'd not been so foolish as to have Lilith examined by a physician or midwife either. Crispin's detectives had explored those avenues thoroughly.

Nonetheless, except for bribing the bishop, Brighton had been eerily silent. It raised Crispin's hackles. He had no doubt the blighter was plotting. But what?

As he rapped upon the bright door, he looked up and down the street. Several people regarded him with avid curiosity. A few haughty matrons lifted their chins and turned their faces away, but the men smiled or winked. The double-standard galled. Women snubbed Jessica, and men admired Crispin's prowess, and yet they were each as much a victim as the other.

He meant to coax her out of her self-imposed isolation. A trip to Gunter's was in order for a long-overdue ice. The more they were seen together, the more credibility would be given to his break with Miss Brighton and his betrothal to Jessica.

Crispin had no druthers about revealing Lilith's little secret. In fact, he was prepared to make her condition very public if Brighton didn't cooperate. He'd wait until his investigators had gathered all of the relevant facts to make his case impenetrable. Blackmailing a peer wouldn't weigh in her or her father's favor.

Dandridge, Pennington, Westfall, Asherford, Sheffield, Waycross, and several other friends and members of *Bon Chance* had vowed their support. No one was fool enough to take on a dozen powerful dukes.

He rapped again, surprised the door hadn't opened at once.

Did Jessica ride?

He flicked a speck of dust off his lapel. He'd never observed her riding in Colechester, but then again, her family was as poor as proverbial church mice. He rather imagined she'd enjoy his stables at Pickford Hill Park. There was something satisfying when a foal was born. As if Crispin had contributed something pure and innocent and useful to this wretched world.

The door finally opened, and Sutcliffe's bland-faced butler ushered him inside. Ah, he'd forgotten Rumsfeld never rushed at anything. Steady as she goes and slow as a tortoise. Or a snail. Through molasses. In wintertime.

"Good day, Rumsfeld."

"Your Grace," Rumsfeld, intoned in his usual monotone. After accepting his hat, gloves, and cane, the butler laid them aside and closed the door. Each movement slow and methodical. He lifted a gloved hand, the gesture practiced and perfected to convey haughty deference. "This way, if you please," he droned, sounding rather like an oversized, lazy bumblebee.

Crispin quirked a cynical eyebrow. His butler was stodgy and stuffy, but Rumsfeld made him seem like a drunken court jester.

"I do know the way, Rumsfeld." He couldn't resist teasing.

"Indeed." Rumsfeld returned without breaking his measured stride or inflecting any emotion into his voice. Momentarily, they arrived at the salon. "His Grace, the Duke of Bainbridge," he proclaimed, in the same tones one would deliver a deadly diagnosis.

Before he finished announcing his arrival, Crispin sought Jessica. She sat beside her sister, her flaxen hair twisted into a loose chignon at the back of her head. A few brazen curls had escaped their confines and lay teasingly over her shell-like ears.

Today, she wore pink and white—fresh as a morning rosebud—and a matching ribbon graced the crown of her head and was tied at her shapely nape. Dark bluish-purple smudges shadowed her eyes, which, to his immense satisfaction, lit at the sight of him.

She'd never looked lovelier, and he wished he had the right to take her into his arms and kiss her until the worry left her precious features. Until she was relaxed and went all feminine softness against him. Until she believed there'd never be another woman for him.

Poised, a practiced, benign smile arching her kissable mouth, she met his regard. Hope and something undefinably warm shone in her aquamarine eyes.

Crispin's pulse kicked up a notch in anticipation. Perhaps he hadn't given her enough credit, and she hadn't believed Brighton's drivel after all.

He returned her smile, putting into it all he couldn't say aloud. Not here and now. Later, if he was permitted a few minutes alone with her.

James Brentwood stood at his entrance and bowed. "Bainbridge."

"Brentwood." What the devil was Jessica's brother doing here?

Brentwood resumed his seat, appearing anything but relaxed. Unusual for him. Even though he'd chosen law as his profession and possessed a brilliant mind, he tended to be good-natured, though never jovial.

Neither was he a rogue, who with his looks and flush pockets, he might've been. There'd been a woman, years ago, if Crispin recalled correctly. She'd jilted him for a duke.

He possessed the same blue-green eyes as Jessica, but whereas his sisters had light hair, his was a rich auburn.

Recently, Brentwood had dabbled in several lucrative, very successful investments. He had an uncanny nose for sniffing out unusual, profitable ventures, and Sutcliffe and Crispin had both engaged in fruitful business dealings with him.

Today, pensive and somber, he appeared ready to present a criminal defense case in court.

"Come, Your Grace." The duchess waved him toward an empty chair. "Have a seat. I believe you prefer your tea plain?"

"Yes, please, and do address me as Crispin or, if you must, Bainbridge. We are to be family, after all."

The smile affixed to her face never faltered, but he didn't miss the strained look that passed between Brentwood and Sutcliffe.

Jessica busied herself with stirring her tea—she took hers with milk and sugar—and then she set the spoon aside and took a sip before meeting his eyes again. "Your Grace—"

"Crispin," he corrected, refusing to fall back into starchy formality. The room fairly crackled with unspoken tension. He accepted his cup of tea and, as he raised it to his mouth, asked, "Why is everyone so Friday-faced?"

Scratching his nape, Sutcliffe grimaced. "We've run into a bit of a snag."

"I'm aware Brighton bribed the clergy at my parish, if that's what you refer to." Crispin relaxed into the chair, hooking one knee over the other. "I should've expected it. I always like to believe men of God are above such machinations, but they're only human, and at times temptation—"

At the crushed expression washing over Jessica's face, he could've bitten his tongue. *Blast and damn.*

The duchess saved him from his blunder. "It is disappointing." She referred to her father, he'd wager. "I suppose, just like everyone else, they justify their sins."

"As you know, I petitioned for a special license on your behalf, as you requested." Brentwood leaned forward and accepted tea from his sister, neatly changing the subject. "It was denied. I suspected when the archbishop took so long to approve the request, that would be the case."

"It seems Brighton's reach is farther than I anticipated." Irritation, sharp and swift washed over Crispin.

"His brother is a close confidant of the archbishop," Sutcliffe offered, crossing his legs.

Ah, there was that connection Crispin hadn't been able to identify earlier.

"So no special license and no reading of the banns in London." He angled toward Jessica. "I suppose that means we'll have to journey to Colechester and wed in your old parish by common license. I regret the inconvenience, but it cannot be helped."

He'd plant Brighton a facer if he were present, older man or not. How dare he manipulate him? He'd learn soon enough he'd taken on the wrong foe.

Would it be difficult for Jessica to marry in Colechester? The parish had been her father's before he was disgraced. Or would she welcome the opportunity? To be wed in familiar surroundings?

Her chest rose and fell with a long sigh. "James just came from there. The new vicar won't perform the ceremony, either. I had hoped to escape London—"

Bloody damn hell.

That left Scotland. And they all knew it.

Holding her gaze, he said, "It's to be Scotland, then."

13

Jessica forced what she hoped was a tranquil mien to her face and took another long sip of tea. Her life had tumbled teakettle over spout in a week. After her treatment in St. James's Park, she never wanted to set foot anywhere in London again. Never wanted to encounter the critical, mean-spirited denizens of High Society who'd taken it upon themselves to judge her.

In fact, the urge to pack her trunks and flee to Ridgewood Court, Victor's country estate, and never show her face in public again sounded quite lovely indeed. Then, that part of her which rebelled at unjustness reared up and refused to let her take such a cowardly route.

Jessica hadn't done anything wrong. She was the victim, dash it all.

Nonetheless, Hammon Brighton was a greater, more cunning adversary than Crispin or Victor had anticipated. With relative ease, he'd made it impossible for her and Crispin to wed in England. The man wasn't a peer of the realm, yet his powerful hand was far-reaching. Wealth and bribery trumped position and status in this case, it seemed.

Firming her mouth against the disgust riddling her, she stared into her teacup.

She didn't believe Crispin had fathered Miss Brighton's child. The girl had proven herself to be a liar and manipulator. Foolish and rash, she'd been seduced, no doubt. And then, when her lover had abandoned her, she wrongly believed she could falsely accuse Crispin to save her skin. She was beneath contempt.

Or perhaps Lilith Brighton wasn't behind the false claim. Mayhap her sire was.

A thought struck with the sharpness of a well-honed arrow. Perhaps she wasn't with child at all.

How awful to be the progeny of a man who'd force her to wed someone she didn't want to. Daughters were little more than pawns and possessions, and God help the women whose fathers used them as such.

Jessica cut a covert glance to Theadosia. She'd faced a similar unpleasant fate, and their father had been—*was*—a vicar. He should've been above such maneuverings. Thank God above, Victor had rescued her sister.

Who, pray tell, would rescue Jessica?

Did she want rescuing?

Through half-lowered lashes, she peeked at Crispin. He seemed surprisingly at ease. Confident and self-assured. And a softness, a gentleness, tempered his features.

It wasn't that Jessica objected to a match with him. She didn't. She'd have preferred a courtship, and a bit of wooing by the wicked duke—who wasn't so very wicked after all—wouldn't have gone amiss. Nonetheless, one persistent, aggravating thought continued to plague her; would he ever have considered her for his duchess if this situation hadn't forced them together?

Jessica wanted to believe Crispin would have done. He'd claimed a long-held attraction to her. But the truth of it was dukes didn't marry country nobodies or vicars' daughters. At least he'd receive her substantial dowry, thanks to Victor's generosity.

Dear Victor. He'd treated her as a beloved younger sister.

"I'd hoped elopement to Scotland wouldn't be necessary," Theadosia said quietly, a pinched look about her eyes as she sliced a distressed glance to Victor.

Jessica's heart twinged. So had she. She wouldn't pretend eloping to Gretna Green didn't distress her. It did, but what alternative was there? She could at least voice her objection.

"And what if *I* don't wish to elope to Scotland?" There she'd said it. "It makes me so angry those *people* are forcing our hand."

"We've exhausted the other possibilities, Jessica," Crispin said, not unkindly. His perceptive gaze narrowed the merest bit, shrewdness replacing his earlier ease. "Unless you've changed your mind."

Theadosia cut him an appalled look. "She cannot."

"And I did not," Jessica said with more heat than she'd intended. "I simply resent having no control in any of this." She waved her hand in a circle in the air. "You're making all of these plans, and not once have any of you consulted me. This is my life."

"At this juncture," her sister said cautiously, "Scotland appears the only viable option, Jessica. Naturally, we shall accompany you."

As if that made everything well and good.

Victor gave a sharp nod, although his stern expression didn't relax.

Did he worry the journey was too much for Theadosia's delicate condition? The babe wasn't due for another three months, and they needn't dash pell-mell to Scotland. A more sedate pace might be set, which would accommodate her health, yet the concern couldn't be overlooked or dismissed.

How could she contemplate all of this with such cool detachment? *How?* Because if she permitted the whorl of emotions and feelings bubbling ever higher behind her ribs to escape, she'd become a distraught, watering pot. And blubbering and weeping would serve no purpose—

would change nothing and only serve to make her appear weak.

"How soon should we depart?" Theadosia asked. "Should I order the staff to prepare our trunks? Or do we need to travel light? Perhaps just a valise with the barest essentials?"

James set his teacup down then ran a finger down the side of his nose. His features settled into his solicitor's expression.

Ah, he was about to present an argument.

"I'd recommend two coaches be prepared," he said. "Bainbridge's, containing decoys—Theadosia and Sutcliffe—which will set out first but ramble around the outskirts of London for a few hours. And another unmarked conveyance with myself, Bainbridge, and Jessica. We shall be accompanied by armed outriders that will join us once on the road north."

That pronouncement set Jessica back on her heels. Was there truly such a need for deception? Or armed outriders? She hadn't considered that.

She didn't like this turn of events in the least. "What if Brighton arranges to have their coach waylaid? I shan't have Theadosia or the baby discommoded or endangered."

"I agree with Brentwood. Two coaches are wise." Crispin leaned forward, catching Jessica's attention. Encouragement and kindness glinted in those pearl-gray eyes. A gleam of emotion decidedly more combustible glittered in those tantalizing depths, too. "If your sister's coach is stopped—and I suspect Brighton might be imprudent enough to attempt such an ill-conceived act—the men we'll hire to protect your sister and Sutcliffe will close in on them."

He looked at James and Victor for confirmation. They both nodded their assent.

"I'll be armed as well," Victor said, his features gone fierce.

Her sister looked rather ill, and Jessica couldn't blame her.

"This sounds much too dangerous to me," she objected. She'd never have believed it could be so challenging to wed. The danger, plotting, and subterfuge stripped their elopement of any hint of romance. "How do you intend to protect Theadosia and Victor if Brighton or his henchmen become aggressive?"

"They'll be detained," Crispin said, as if it were the simplest, most logical of things. "And Sutcliffe will decide what should be done with them for accosting a duke and his duchess. It won't go well for them if they are foolish enough to act so recklessly."

"And I," James announced, giving Crispin a hard stare before turning a tender gaze upon her, "shall act as chaperone and assure no one can contest the legitimacy of your vows. No blacksmith's anvil for these two." He levered two fingers between her and Crispin. "They'll have a proper church ceremony conducted by a man of God."

Theadosia's face fell. "But I wanted to be present at Jessica's wedding." She tossed her husband a helpless look. "Especially since our parents aren't here."

Jessica couldn't prevent the resentment billowing inside her toward the Brightons and Brookmoore. Their selfish actions had wreaked havoc on more lives than just hers and Crispin's. Not only was she being denied a proper wedding with her friends in attendance, her beloved sister wouldn't even be there to witness the ceremony.

Tears threatened, but she doggedly willed them to subside. None of them were choosing this path. Circumstances and evil people had forced this course upon them.

Don't forget it's a forced wedding, too.

Not precisely forced, but most certainly one of inconvenience.

James shook his head. "You'll need to pretend to be Jessica, Thea. You look enough alike that you can pull it off. I've thought about this the entire journey back from Colechester. Brighton has gone to great extremes to prevent our sister and Bainbridge from wedding. And we all know how essential it is that the ceremony takes place as soon as possible. Granted, his claim that his daughter is breeding complicates the matter, but that's Brighton's problem."

That was true enough. Did Brighton honestly think Crispin would marry his daughter now? The man was dicked in the nob if he did.

"He's mad enough to try something devious," Victor murmured as he settled on the settee beside his wife and took her hand, offering her comfort.

"The fruit didn't fall far from the tree in that family, did it?" Jessica quipped, amazed she could do so. "One bad apple and all that rot."

Four pairs of eyes swung to her, but it was Crispin's that held her gaze. A glint of humor sparked there. He'd understood the poor pun and her failed attempt at humor to lighten the mood.

Warmth burgeoned within her. He understood her as no one else ever had. It strengthened the connection she felt with him. Made her want to be alone with him to explore it further.

"Brentwood is right," he said, giving a considering nod. "I wouldn't put anything past Brighton."

Could this become any more ridiculous? Or scandalous? Or infuriating?

Jessica cleared her throat, heartily regretting ever coming to London.

She'd take the country's sedate pace and lack of intrigue any day. Give her chickens, a library, paints and a canvas, and a puppy, and she'd be content.

Poppydash and codscock.

"So, where does that leave us?" she asked.

"We must depart for Scotland as soon as possible. The extra men to protect the coaches can be arranged for today, and I'll alert the authorities to our suspicions." Crispin took her hand, giving the fingers a gentle squeeze. "I know marrying in Scotland isn't what you wanted."

Tenderness and understanding softened the corners of his eyes.

"It's not what you wanted, either." How awkward to have this discussion in front of others.

"Perhaps we should permit Bainbridge and Jessica a few moments of privacy?" Theadosia suggested, ever the considerate hostess and always able to discern Jessica's innermost thoughts.

Victor looked as though he was about to object, but after leveling Crispin a stern glance conceded. "Very well. We'll adjourn to my study to work out the details. Join us there when you are finished."

"I'll instruct our maids to pack." Theadosia arched a winged eyebrow. "I presume at some point *someone* will inform me when we are to depart?" she murmured dryly.

"Yes, my pet," Victor assured her, wrapping an arm about her thick waist.

James rose then, in an uncharacteristic public display of affection, bent and kissed the crown of Jessica's head. "All will be well, little sister."

Easy for him to say. It wasn't his life in turmoil.

With a wink and a fond smile, he followed their sister and brother-in-law from the room, leaving the door cracked behind him for propriety.

The room remained silent for several minutes after their departure.

"Are you having second thoughts, Jessica?" Crispin didn't accuse but seemed genuinely concerned.

Third and fourth thoughts, too. But it made no difference. How could it possibly feel worse to marry Crispin now that she knew she loved him? Shouldn't it make the decision easier?

If he felt the same for her, it would've done.

"No." Jessica met his gaze with courage and strength. As she'd determined earlier, he'd not find her a weak, feckless female. "And I do not believe you are the father of Miss Brighton's child." Straightforward and to the point. Instinct told her Crispin needed to know that truth.

"I am not," he said, vehemence ringing in his voice. "And, if necessary, I can prove I remained in residence at my estate except for your sister's Christmastide house party."

She'd hoped for as much. Had, in fact, had similar thoughts, but to hear him proclaim his proof of innocence brought a flood of relief. Mr. Brighton could blather his lies about town, but Crispin had evidence to the contrary.

"Crispin, might I ask you something personal?" She brushed a finger over her eyebrow, behind which a minor ache had begun to make itself known. Adjusting the pillow at her back, she relaxed against the settee. If she were here, Mama would frown at her poor posture.

Heavens. Poor posture was nothing considering what had transpired these past few days.

Surprise lifted his eyebrows, but he nodded, his expression grave. "Of course. I'd have honesty between us, always. I believe honesty and trust are more important than love for a healthy marriage. Love and passion ebb and flow, but a union built on a solid foundation of trust will never crumble."

When had he become so philosophical? And why did his words make her ridiculously emotional? A lump the size of the African continent formed in her throat, and moisture blurred her eyes for a second.

I shall not cry.

"What is it you wish to know?" Expectancy and kindness warmed his slate-gray eyes.

In for a penny, in for a pound. Jessica bolstered her courage.

"You claimed that if you'd not been betrothed to Miss Brighton, you'd have asked to pay your addresses to me. Forgive me, but I cannot help but believe you were being gallant, trying to alleviate the awkwardness of the moment." Noble and chivalrous. Putting her needs before his own. Attempting to make her feel somewhat less than an unwelcome, unworthy, and an unwanted burden. "What else were you to say, after all?"

"I'm furious. I shall resent you for all of the days of our lives. Marriage to you is not of my choosing, but my damnable honor requires me to offer for you?"

"You are a kind man. A generous man," she went on. *Two more reasons why I love you beyond everything.* "I've known that for several months." But she'd also known him to be a rake, so she'd disregarded his more exceptional qualities.

Wasn't that just like people—to focus on someone's faults rather than the myriad of other noteworthy qualities they might have?

His steady gaze never wavered from her, nor did he attempt to interrupt. Another thing she appreciated about him. He listened to her. Really listened.

"You said what needed to be said at that moment to protect my feelings. I'm grateful." Jessica offered a half-smile as she ran her fingers along the carved edge of the settee. "I truly am. But you must know by now, I'm no wilting flower. I shan't dissolve into tears or become faint from hearing the truth."

Blast. Babbling again.

"Jessica?" Did a note of humor resonate in his tone? Impatience mayhap? "What, precisely, are you trying to say?"

No more dillydallying or beating around the bush. Frankness and candidness. Yes, well, that was far easier to contemplate than actually to do. "I realize it's none of my—ah—*business,*" she said, struggling for the right words. "Except for that, we are betrothed—in a fashion."

"In a *fashion?*" Mockery toggled his hawkish eyebrows together, creating a deep groove above his nose.

She chose to ignore his sarcasm and went on as if he hadn't interjected. With a little wave of her hand, she said, "But if you hadn't been betrothed to Miss Brighton since you were a child, and if these difficult circumstances hadn't arisen, compelling you to offer for me, is there a woman you would've chosen to be your duchess of your own free will?"

His ducal duty required him to wed and sire an heir. Perchance he'd have waited a few more years to traipse down matrimony's convoluted path, after the dissolution of his betrothal with Miss Brighton, but he'd have done so eventually. Crispin wasn't the caliber of man to forsake his duty to the Bainbridge dukedom.

Perhaps a woman *had* captured his heart.

A powerful wave of unanticipated envy stabbed her.

His lady love would be exquisite, of course. Sweet tempered—the epitome of grace and refinement. And beautiful. How could she not be?

She'd sing like a songbird. Jessica did not have a voice, to her mother's chagrin.

No doubt Crispin's lady rode magnificently, too. Jessica had never sat a horse.

Cataloging his sweetheart's attributes while simultaneously listing her inadequacies made her rather ill. The tea threatened to curdle in her stomach, and despair lanced her heart.

If Crispin married her out of obligation, he'd never be able to make his true love his own, now that he was finally free of his commitment to Lilith Brighton. Life was most unfair. Or fate or providence or the divine powers. Whoever, or whatever, was responsible for this bumblebroth had no sense of justice.

But now he had an opportunity for true happiness.

She must forsake her own to allow him that chance. *I must, even if it shatters my heart.* Having never loved anyone except him, she couldn't imagine how distressing it would be to adore him as she did, and yet circumstances required her to wed another.

How awful. Frustrating and infuriating. *Heartbreaking.* God, how she wanted to curl into a ball of misery and wail her anguish. How could her heart keep beating? Her lungs continue to draw air?

He gazed at her for so long, his sultry gray eyes charcoal-dark and those sinfully thick eyelashes partially lowered, she feared she'd overstepped.

Jessica, you dim-witted dolt. Of course she'd overstepped. Waded in, chest high. Chin high. She might very well drown in her foolhardiness. On her attempt at thoughtfulness and consideration. Because, above all else, she wanted Crispin to be happy.

It shouldn't hurt so bloody awful to love someone.

And still, he remained unnervingly silent, his expression intense and reflective. The seconds expanded, and with every punctuating *tick-tock* of the clock, she increasingly wished she could retract the intrusive question.

She didn't want to know.

Yes, I do.

No, it would hurt far too much.

I must know. Hers and Crispin's futures depended upon it.

His subtle cologne wreaked havoc on her senses, and his enticing heat drew her to him. Even now, she felt herself leaning toward him, attracted as if he were a magnet. Why must he be so mysterious and sexy? She could scarcely cobble two thoughts together when he was this close.

At last, he spoke, guardedly, as if considering his words with great care. "There *is* someone. Has been for some time."

Jessica pointed her gaze to the floor for a second, lest he see the devastation in her eyes. Her blasted, so-easy-to-read eyes.

"A remarkable, intelligent, beautiful woman," he went on. "I would've made her mine in a heartbeat, had I been free to do so." His voice dropped to that husky tone that curled her toes and made her want to crawl atop him, nuzzle her nose in his corded neck, and run her fingers over the light stubble darkening his rugged jaw.

Such excruciating pain lanced her heart; he might've pierced her with a rusty, double-edged sword. Somehow, she husbanded her composure and kept from doubling over and clutching her chest. Jessica forced her focus upward to meet his gaze. She'd asked and had insisted upon honesty. Far better to have the truth out in the open.

"Does she know of your regard? Does she return it?" My, how composed she sounded, considering her impaled heart oozed blood. In truth, she was acting a rude snoop.

"I've never told her." The corners of his beautiful eyes softened, and a small smile arched his mouth. That splendid mouth that had plundered hers mere days ago. "I hope she feels the same about me, but she's never said so. There's not been an opportunity for us to declare ourselves."

The only thing standing between Crispin and this woman he loved was her. Well, the Brightons were a hindrance, but he had them well in hand. He had waited long enough to be happy.

"It saddens me that you have been stripped of a choice of spouse again, Crispin." She clenched her fingers and somehow marshaled the fortitude for what she needed to say, fully aware of the consequences. She would lose everything.

Everything.

Yes, but it would be worth it, for *he* would gain everything.

"I release you from your proposal. I'd rather you found joy with her."

14

Crispin's heart nearly exploded with love and admiration, and he struggled to check a burst of exuberant laughter.

"My foolish, adorable darling." He swept her onto his lap, grinning at her startled squeak of surprise. He kissed her forehead. "Darling, adorable fool." Pressing his lips to her left cheek, he murmured, "Sweetheart." And then he whisked his mouth over her neglected right cheek. "*You,* my sweet Jessica, are that woman."

Clutching his arms, she blinked up at him, her wonder-filled eyes the color of the sea after the sun had disappeared from the horizon. "I am?" Her words came out in a hushed whisper. "Truly?"

"Truly, my love." He brushed his mouth across her incredibly soft lips. "My only love. Ever."

Did she understand what he was saying?

That he loved her?

Had for so very long.

And now, at last, Crispin was free to tell her. To tell her everything he'd secreted in his heart, and, *by God,* as soon as the vows were exchanged, he'd show her with his mouth and hands and body.

He'd worship every velvety inch of her, and when he finished, she'd have no more doubts that she, alone, was the woman of his heart. Had always been and would always be.

"I wasn't simply being kind when I told you that I'd have courted you had I been free, Jessica." He traced a finger down her satin-soft cheek.

"From the first time I saw you, I knew you were special. But I could only admire you from afar. Wishing, always hoping but never expecting, that you might actually be mine someday."

Nestling closer, Jessica wrapped one arm around his waist. She looped the other behind his neck and rested her cheek against his chest. "I noticed you, too. But as I said before, your reputation put me off. I didn't want to be another silly, infatuated girl who'd succumbed to your charms."

"My charms, eh?" He waggled his eyebrows as he crooked his finger and nudged her chin upward.

She gave his hair a slight tug, which also caused her generous bum to press into his loins. God help him. "You know full well, Crispin Harlow Benjamin Rolston, Duke of Bainbridge, what powerful affect you have on women."

"Do I?" he replied in his most seductive voice. "Why don't you show me?"

Their lips nearly touched, and as he spoke, he lowered his head, until but a hair's breadth remained between them. Her vanilla-and-clove scent wafted around Crispin, warm and inviting. Sensual and sultry. Sweet and spicy, just like the incredible woman in his arms.

With a little sigh, Jessica angled her chin upward until their mouths met. This wasn't the scorching, passionate kiss of a couple of days ago. This was two souls coming together, revealing what they'd hidden from the world and each other for so long.

He loved her. Loved this golden-haired, marine-eyed marvel of a woman. He spanned his hands across her narrow waist, worshipping her as he'd yearned to do for so long.

Soft and sweet and perfect, her mouth moved beneath his.

His adoration tempered his passion as he tenderly, reverently explored the sweet hollows, allowing his hand to roam the contours and curves of her lush form. There wasn't anything he wouldn't do to keep her safe. To make her his.

Crispin lifted his head, taking in her heavy-lidded gaze and kiss-swollen, slightly red and damp lips. He stifled a groan and the urge to plunder her mouth once more. There'd be time for that later. After they left London behind.

The trip to Scotland might bloody well kill him.

Mayhap Brentwood could be persuaded to ride atop with the driver or, better yet, upon a mount. There was about as much chance of that happening as Brighton coming to his senses.

Eyes glistening with emotion, she pressed her palm to his jaw.

"I love you, Jessica," he said simply. "I love you. I love you. *I love you.*"

There wasn't any need to embellish the declaration with poetic phrases or nonsensical fluff. He loved her. *I love you, Jessica.* Those four words were more potent than anything else he could say. She'd made a home for herself in his mind, his heart, and his soul.

Her gold-tipped lashes trembled as a joyful smile wreathed her face. "I love you, too."

A hint of the shy young woman he'd first met all those months ago in Colechester peered back at him, but an intrepid woman's gaze held his. A strong, intelligent woman. A woman who knew her mind and who would make him the ideal partner.

He kissed her nose, running his hands down the fine pink silk covering her spine. "I suppose we ought to join the others and finalize the arrangements. I'd like to depart for Scotland before dawn tomorrow."

She gave a small, regretful nod. "I wish we could marry here with our friends and family in attendance, but I understand why we cannot." A frown marred her smooth forehead. "Do you think Mr. Brighton will continue to give us trouble afterward?"

"He may try, but there'd be no point." Crispin helped her off his lap then stood, a distinct bulge pressing at the falls of his pantaloons. "I've had my solicitor send him a firmly worded note explaining point-by-point what crimes his daughter committed. They are serious, and it could be argued that she was an accessory to attempted murder."

Jessica gasped and paled, one hand flying to press against the hollow of her throat. "Do you think Brookmoore intended to kill you?"

He lifted a shoulder. "I cannot say. But I am prepared to bring charges against him, and the evidence supports such a claim. Brighton will not want his daughter to go to prison or risk deportation or hanging." He pulled his waistcoat and jacket into place. "If he's wise, he'll remove her to the country or marry her off to some ancient decrepitude who won't mind she's breeding."

Crispin extended his hand, and Jessica placed hers in it. Helping her rise, he didn't release the fine-boned fingers. He brushed his thumb over her ring finger. "I have something for you, Kitten." He fished around in his coat pocket and withdrew a sapphire velvet box. After lifting the lid, he held it out for her to inspect the contents.

A soft sigh parted her lips. "Oh, Crispin."

Two white diamonds sandwiched a square-cut, bluish-green-hued emerald.

"Will you put it on, please?" She extended her hand.

Once he'd lifted the ring from its white satin nest, he slipped the band on her finger. He held her fingers firmly in his. "Jessica, darling, will you marry me? Because I love you, and you love me? And nothing else matters?" Unfamiliar moisture blurred his vision. How he loved her. "Whatever the future brings, we'll face it together," he said huskily.

Her lower lip trembled as if she struggled to contain her emotions, as well. "I shall, Crispin. Gladly and unreservedly."

The tread of swift footsteps reverberating in the hallway caused him to retreat a step, to put a respectable distance between them. Sutcliffe and his duchess swept into the drawing room, strain evident on their faces.

"Where's James?" Jessica looked past her sister to the empty doorway.

"A messenger came 'round. James had to leave at once, but he vowed he'd be back as soon as possible," the duchess said, appearing rather wan.

"There's a message for you as well, Bainbridge." Sutcliffe veered Jessica a guarded look. "From one of your investigators." He raised the sealed paper.

Until that moment, Crispin hadn't noticed the rectangle.

The duchess held out her hands as she crossed to her sister. "Come, my dear. Have a seat and permit the duke to read his message."

Jessica placed her hands in her sister's and allowed her to guide her to a bench before a bay window. The sky had cleared, and only a few slightly ash-tinged clouds marred the azure horizon. She shook her head when the duchess urged her to claim a seat. "I'd prefer to stand, please. But Thea, you should sit. You appear as if you might faint."

The duchess gave a weak laugh. "I *am* a little shaken," she said as she folded onto the tufted crimson cushion. "But I do not faint any more than you do."

There was always a first time. In her delicate condition, the duchess shouldn't be exposed to all of these disconcerting happenings. Except, if she were anything like her strong-willed sister, she'd not be toddled off to rest, content to let others handle any unpleasantness.

A slight grin tipped Crispin's mouth. Thank God for strong-minded women.

"I take it, you know the contents of Crispin's missive?" Jessica's dubious gaze examined the note.

"I have a fair notion." The glitter of Jessica's ring caught her eye, and she grasped her sister's hand. "Oh my. It's simply lovely, dear. Emeralds have always been your favorite. And the color is so unique." She held Jessica's hand up to the window's light. "The stone has a slight bluish tint."

"It does, and I adore the square cut." A soft smile played around Jessica's mouth. A pretty, sweet, pink mouth which he very much wanted to kiss again.

The duchess slid him an assessing look.

Turning the letter over, Crispin broke the seal with his thumb. "I take it whatever is in here is what has caused you to look so glum?"

With a cautious glance toward the women, Sutcliffe gave a stiff nod. "It's either excellent or terrible news, depending on your perspective."

"As serious as all that?" It must be. Sutcliffe was a virtually, unflappable pillar. The tight lines bracketing his mouth and the taut look about his eyes suggested the letter's contents were of great import and impact. Brow lifted questioningly, Crispin unfolded the sheet. Angling his back toward the women, he perused the contents. His gut knotted, and a low oath escaped him between tight lips. "Good God!"

He shot an astounded glance over his shoulder as he refolded the letter then tucked it inside his pocket.

Sutcliffe responded with another tight nod. "Thea knows. James's correspondence was similar. He went to assure no one altered the crime scene before the authorities arrived."

That explained the duchess's chalk-white face when she'd entered.

"Do you wish to tell Jessica, or would you prefer her sister or myself do so?" Sutcliffe asked beneath his breath.

"All that intense whispering is only making me more anxious," Jessica said starchily. "Since the three of you are aware, might not I also be apprised of whatever it is that has everyone looking so morose?"

Crispin didn't miss the hint of trepidation in her tone. He crossed to her and, after taking her hands in his, urged her to sit beside her sister. "We've just had word that Brookmoore was found murdered. Shot in the heart."

She blanched, her confused gaze racing from person to person. "Brighton?"

He shook his head. "No. Lilith killed him. She's…" He glanced to the duchess.

"She's taken leave of her senses, poor girl." Her grace patted her sister's knee. "It was all too much for her. When he discarded her, and her father still insisted she wed Bainbridge, she must've decided to seek Brookmoore out. Who knows what transpired between them, but the fact that she went with a loaded pistol suggests her intent."

Brookmoore deserved to be shot after seducing, impregnating, and abandoning the girl.

"What will happen to her?" Though Jessica had every right to be furious with Lilith, only compassion colored her words. She bit her lower lip. "Her poor parents. Especially her mother."

Crispin could sympathize with Mrs. Brighton. Her overbearing husband had bullied her for as long as he could recall. To have her only child commit another crime, this one a hanging offense, the woman would be beside herself.

He, however, wasn't as benevolent as Jessica. Brighton was partially responsible for his daughter's plight. The controlling bugger had manipulated and coerced Lilith her entire life. Perhaps she'd thought she loved Brookmoore, and when he tossed her aside like an old shoe, her mind had snapped.

"I expect she'll be committed." Sutcliffe offered. "Brighton's pockets are deep enough, and he'll likely be able to arrange for a private facility."

"What of the baby?" Jessica asked.

"It's difficult to say." Her sister looked pensive. "If she carries it to term—and she may not—then I suppose her parents will determine whether they take the child in, foster it out, or put it in an orphanage."

"Even though her part in what she did to Crispin and me was unforgivable," Jessica shook her head, her earrings swaying with the motion, "I cannot help but feel pity for her."

"As do we all. Though, I confess I cannot muster anything but contempt for Lilith's father," Crispin admitted.

"I take it we aren't leaving for Scotland, after all?" Equal parts disappointment and relief shone in Jessica's eyes.

No, the need no longer existed. He shook his head. "There's no reason. There can be no question of Brighton attempting to enforce the betrothal contract now." He smiled, feeling more at ease than he could ever recall. He was free to marry the woman he loved more than life itself. "It's up to you whether you want the banns read or if you'd like to marry by special license."

Jessica's gaze dropped to her hand, and she slowly turned the band around her finger. "I'd rather not wait." Her cheeks pinkened, and when she brought her eyes up to meet his, he knew full well why she didn't want to delay.

By damn, neither did Crispin. Too blasted bad Brentwood hadn't acquired the special license. He'd wed her today, and tonight, he'd introduce her to passion as he showed her and told her in a hundred ways how much he adored her.

The duchess hugged her sister. "I'm happy for you, Jessica. It's obvious to anyone with eyes in their head that you and Bainbridge care deeply for each other." She turned that penetrating stare upon Crispin. "Make my sister happy, Your Grace."

"Indeed, Bainbridge. You must, for if you do not, then *my* lady will not be happy, and that is unacceptable." Sutcliffe extended his hand, and Crispin seized it at once in a firm grip. "Congratulations, my friend."

"Thank you." Crispin drew Jessica to her feet, something which might very well be giddiness cavorting about his middle. "Is three days too long to wait?"

"No." She shook her head, her eyes luminous with love. For him.

Still holding her hand, he turned to Sutcliffe.

He held his hands up, palm outward. "I know. *I know.* You wish to be alone with your intended." Winking, he bent his elbow and held it out for his wife. "I haven't been married so very long that I've forgotten what it was like to be betrothed."

Jessica colored prettily as Crispin drew her into his arms before her sister and brother-in-law made the doorway. The door closed with a soft *snick*, and he buried one hand in her hair and placed the other at the small of her waist, pressing her to him.

He nipped her ear. "I vow, the next three days are going to be the longest of my life, waiting to make you mine."

"Who says we have to wait?" Her voice husky with desire, she peeked at him through her thick lashes.

God help him resist this siren. *Three days.* He had the willpower to resist for three days before he made Jessica his in every way.

"I do, minx." He tweaked her nose.

She stood on her toes and entwined her arms about Crispin's neck. "Well, then I suppose I'll have to persuade you otherwise."

And by God, she almost did.

Almost.

Epilogue

Pickford Hill Park
August 1810

Jessica laughed as she guided her docile black mare, Midnight, around a boulder between the copse of towering oak trees. These past four months had been the happiest of her life. Months of being the Duchess of Bainbridge. Of being Crispin's wife.

At first, she'd been afraid to learn to ride, but as he'd promised she would, she'd taken to the saddle like a duck to water. Pickford Hill Park now boasted eight ducks, four geese, another half dozen hens, two goats, two adorable spaniel puppies—gifts from him—and a very pregnant barn cat.

No donkey. Yet.

She fully expected to add more animals to her beloved menagerie, but he never complained. He had laughed, quite jubilantly, when she'd insisted on knitting cardigans for the kid goats. A few fervent kisses had shushed him quite effectively. That had led to an interesting bout of lovemaking before the hearth in the drawing room.

What was undoubtedly a dreamy smile curved her mouth. She did rather like that lovemaking business.

"Let's rest here in the shade," Crispin said over his shoulder. The summer's heat yet remained, and their morning ride had left Jessica a trifle overheated.

A small, musical stream meandered along the meadow just beyond the tree stand they'd sought sanctuary within. She just might be persuaded to wade in the chilly depths.

"I've had another letter from Thea," she said as he helped her dismount. He held her against him, permitting her to slide down the length of his sinewy body. When she encountered a familiar swelling, she grinned. She cupped his groin, earning a low growl and a smothered oath. "My, what do we have here?"

"I suppose she's asking us to visit Ridgefield Court again?" He'd buried his face in her neck, muffling his voice. He nuzzled the sensitive spot at the juncture of her throat and shoulder, and it was her turn to moan.

"Yes," she agreed, a trifle distracted when the lump against her hand began to swell. They'd only seen baby Amber twice since her birth. "Nicolette is back from her honeymoon and has promised to spend a week at Ridgewood." Jessica stood on her toes and kissed Crispin's jaw, relishing the faint brush of his clean-shaven skin against her lips.

"I seriously doubted Nicolette would ever marry. And to Westfall, no less." He snorted and shook his head as he tethered the mounts to low-lying branches.

"I know," she laughed and patted Midnight's shiny withers. She'd come to adore the beautiful mare. "And I can scarce believe Rayne and Ophelia have wed, too."

"At this rate, all of my friends will be married within a year," he muttered, not nearly as disgruntled as he pretended. Married life agreed with him.

And with her.

She met her husband's hungry gaze and gave him a seductive smile. "We've not made love outdoors yet."

His eyebrows dipped low as he slowly scanned the area, his intense gaze coming to rest on the boulder she'd skirted earlier. "Are you suggesting I've been remiss in my husbandly duties, Duchess?"

She giggled then licked her lips. Crispin had always been able to turn her bones to jelly with one look from his quicksilver eyes. "Perhaps just a trifle negligent."

"Then, I must remedy the oversight at once." He stalked toward her, his strapping legs eating up the distance between them, and she retreated, enjoying the chase as much as being captured.

She continued retreating, until she bumped into the dratted boulder, coming up short.

"Oh."

It wasn't large enough to pass for a bed. Scanning the area, she spied a grassy spot, still relatively secluded by the trees.

Crispin was upon her now, passion already sharpening the angles of his dear face. "Turn around, lady wife."

"I thought…what?" *Turn around? Whatever for?*

Oh. She complied and wiggled her hips when she felt his hands settle on either side of them. Of a sudden, she was shy, worried they'd be seen. "Crispin, are you sure this is private enough?"

"Quite sure." Air caressed Jessica's legs and then her bum as he raised her riding habit. "Trust me, darling. Spread your legs."

"Always, my love," she murmured as she complied.

"Let me make up for my negligence, sweetheart," he breathed into her ear.

"If you insist." She sighed breathlessly as he slid into her.

And he did. Most satisfactorily.

Duchess of His Heart

Prologue

Colchester, England
September 1802

Standing in the apple orchard, a short walking distance from the village of Colchester and All Saint's Priory—his father's parish—James Brentwood gazed overhead. Ribbons of sunlight threaded through the thick, verdant foliage heavily laden with crisp, crimson fruit.

Closing his eyes, he inhaled the familiar scents from his childhood: rich, warm earth, ripe apples, freshly cut hay, and an occasional whiff of honeysuckle drifting by on the capricious fall breeze.

Nearby, industrious bees hummed as they went about their work, and songbirds trilled while flitting from branch to branch. In the distance, his sister's chickens cackled, and a horse neighed in the adjacent pasture. He missed the peace and freshness of the English countryside when in London.

Before letting his mind wander once more, he cast a puzzled glance down the dusty, rutted lane. Regine was several minutes late. Unusual for her. Typically, she was as eager for their clandestine meetings as he, and she often beat him to their rendezvous.

Regine. Just thinking of his beloved tightened James's chest as overwhelming emotion tunneled through his veins. God, how he loved her. Since she'd been a toddler and he a young lad, he'd adored the raven-haired beauty with eyes so blue, they put the summer sky to shame.

If not for her father's recent and unexpected death, he would've asked for her hand in marriage this visit even though two years of his solicitor's training remained. He'd have to bide his time a jot longer, blast it all.

Scratching his temple, he grinned with unchecked happiness. Regine had agreed to become his wife over a year ago. They kept the agreement a secret but often spoke of their future residing together in London—him a successful solicitor and she, the mother of his four—*no five*—children.

Neither aspired to wealth or position nor coveted possessions. Each only needed the other, and they would be happy and content for the rest of their lives. Or so they'd vowed between passionate kisses and promises of eternal love.

Tomorrow, he'd return to London, but he'd savor these last few hours with Regine before bidding her farewell—after tasting her sweet mouth and breathing in her apple and spices fragrance one final time. Finances wouldn't permit him to return for at least a fortnight, and he craved memories to savor until her lush form was wrapped in his embrace once more.

At last, he heard muffled footsteps approaching, and he turned, excitement and expectation vying for supremacy. At eighteen, Regine Edenshaw was a vision, even in her somber, black gown. Her unbound silky, ebony hair swayed as she walked, her eyes downcast and neck bent as if deep in thought.

She was his. *His.* Or would be as soon as her mourning period ended. James would have to harness his impatience for a few more months before asking Mrs. Edenshaw for her daughter's hand. Pray God Regine's mother wouldn't require them to wait an entire year to wed as mourning protocol dictated.

Regine stopped a few feet away and reluctantly brought her gaze up to meet his.

His heart stalled at the intense sorrow and regret pooled in her eyes. Eyes sparkling with unshed tears.

Her lips parted, but no words came forth.

"Darling, what is it?" He moved to gather her into his arms, to soothe away whatever had distressed her, but she shook her head and held a palm up to ward him off. Torment ravaged her delicate features.

Alarm took root, spiraling outward from James's stomach and sending a chill washing over him. By God, if someone had dared to harm her.

"Sweetheart?" He brushed a fingertip across her satiny cheek. "What has you so distressed? Tell me." Somehow, he'd make whatever troubled her right—anything to put a smile on her bowed mouth and erase the sadness shadowing her azure eyes.

"James…" Shoulders slumping, she clamped her lower lip between her teeth, and her lashes fluttered downward to caress her pale cheeks.

His trepidation kicked up several notches, and dread engulfed him. The instinct that made him a damn good solicitor fairly shrieked. He wasn't going to like what she said. Not at all.

"James," she murmured again, her voice a mere thread of sound—a soft, spine-tingling entreaty in the now eerily silent orchard. Then she opened her mouth, gulped in a deep breath, and thrust her chin upward as if bracing herself.

Against what, for God's sake?

He swept the area with a swift, apprehensive glance, before settling his attention uneasily upon her once more. Something akin to terror knotted in his throat at the defeat and devastation he detected in her startlingly blue eyes. It stripped the air from his lungs and squeezed his heart in a ruthless, unyielding vise.

"I…" she drew in a ragged breath. "I am to be married," she finally said in a rush, dropping her focus to her hands, repeatedly wadding her black skirts.

What? Married? No. No. You're mine. Mine! My dearest, most precious love.

"Pardon?" he whispered stupidly, his lips stiff and voice gravelly with disbelief and pain. "Married?" He shook his head. He couldn't have heard her correctly. But he had. Her tense posture and waxen pallor revealed the truth.

"To who?" Or was it whom? What the hell did it matter? His thoughts raced, pell-mell, around his befuddled mind, all ability to reason calmly having flown. *You cannot marry another. You cannot! You said you'd be my wife.*

"To the Duke of Heartwaite," she replied, her voice flat and devoid of emotion.

A bloody duke? He fisted his hands until the nails cut deeply into his palms.

How could he, a poor vicar's son with scarcely two coins to rub together and in training to become a solicitor, compete with a sodding duke? Moisture blurring his vision, he choked out a single, strangled syllable, "When?"

"Next week." Her throat working and her hand trembling, she touched a bent knuckle to the corner of one eye. "I'm so sorry, James."

"Why?" He tenderly grasped her slender arms, peering into her anguished eyes awash with tears. "Why, Regine? I love you. You love me, too." Didn't she? Yes, else why would she be this miserable? "Please, I beg you, don't do this to us."

Eyes wide and tortured, she silently gazed at him, and the truth slammed into James with the force of an over-loaded grain wagon. A duke could offer her everything he couldn't: position, power, prestige, and wealth.

Evidently, love was a trifling insignificance compared to those *necessities*.

James stumbled backward, shaking his head, the pain eviscerating him so excruciating, he almost doubled over. Almost roared aloud against the knives carving and cleaving unmercifully into his heart and soul. And he did what any animal mortally wounded did. Reacted with primal rage and the urge to protect itself.

Curling his upper lip into a sneer, he raked his contemptuous gaze over her. "I've been so damned stupid." A complete and utter idiot. "I believed you were different. That money and position didn't matter—"

"They don't, James. Not in the way you think." She held a delicate palm out to him, beseechingly. "Please let me explain. I owe you that much." Her voice broke, and when he didn't take her outstretched hand, she let it drop to her side. "I am sorry," she murmured again, her face ashen, and her eyes wounded pools.

Sorry? *Sorry?* He didn't want her God-damned apology. He wanted her!

Something inside him splintered, fracturing into a million pieces, and where his heart had once been, an unfeeling stone replaced the mangled organ.

He threw his head back and laughed, harsh and cynical. "*You* don't owe *me* anything, Regine." With that, he turned his back and stalked away, resolutely disregarding her sobs, her vows that she loved him, and her pleas for him to listen to her.

Never again would he be taken in by a beautiful face or pledges of love and promises of forever.

1

London, England
Late January 1811

Pulling the folds of her woolen-lined, velvet mantle snugger, Regine Maberly, Duchess of Heartwaite, shivered as she picked her way around several inconvenient puddles. Perhaps she ought to have accepted the coachman's offer of a ride when he'd collected her packages, though the glover's shop lay but one street over.

Desiring the exercise, she'd opted to walk while completing her errands. But the gunmetal-gray sky sported a canopy of pouting clouds. She feared, much like a petulant child, they were about to make their displeasure known. Only in this case, in the form of an ugly downpour.

Her bonnet's scarlet ribbons flapped against her neck, both from her brisk pace—her boot heels rhythmically clacking and splashing her soggy progression—as well as the sulky wind's stubborn resolve to finagle a means inside her cloak.

The wind seemed determined to subject her sensitive nose to the mélange of foul odors, inevitably wafting about the city, too. Coal smoke, the dank aroma of The River Thames, as well as piles of waste and rubbish lining many of the streets all contributed to the fetid stench.

Compared to the Borderlands, where she'd lived these past two years, London's crisp, damp weather proved much milder. And yet, though she wore a redingote beneath the mantle, she couldn't entirely prevent the shudder the biting chill caused to ripple the length of her spine.

How she missed the warmer climes of the countries and islands she'd spent the first six years of her marriage visiting and exploring: Spain. Italy. India. Greece. Egypt. Even the Caribbean with its powdery beaches and vibrant rainbows of flowers.

After Heartwaite's death nearly two years ago—she'd always addressed him by his title at his behest—she'd considered living abroad permanently. She'd left England directly after her marriage and then had taken up residence in the country promptly upon returning. Thus, she'd eschewed an introduction to the *haut ton* all these years. A small and very welcome blessing, that.

She'd never coveted a title and all the finery, trappings, and expectations that accompanied the position. Oh, she could play the part of peeress to perfection—Heartwaite had insisted upon it—but beneath the silks and lace and jewels, the finely coiffed hair and practiced politesse, she was a simple woman at heart.

Plans to toddle back to the Continent had given her something to aspire to during the lengthy, lonely months of Heartwaite's decline and the expected mourning period afterward.

Unfortunately, fate—the willful, unrelenting force determined to up-end her life and plans—had interfered and decreed otherwise. *Again.* Blast Providence. Destiny. Fortune. Chance. Even blast the divine powers.

Flattening her lips into a thin line, she wrestled her frustration into submission. Railing and complaining were futile and served no purpose other than to cause further discontent. *Chin up, old girl,* she admonished the minuscule rebellious part of her that seldom made itself known anymore.

Resolutely reining in her melancholy musings, she lowered her head against the haranguing wind. The glovers was her last destination this afternoon. Within the hour, she'd be trotting up the steps to her cozy townhouse and enjoying a piping-hot cup of coffee while her sister sipped tea heavily laced with milk and sugar.

The cold wind nipped at Regine's cheeks, making her all that more eager for a cup of coffee to warm her. She'd acquired the taste for the rich brew during her travels and now preferred coffee to tea.

More proof she no longer belonged in England. Nonetheless, she must endure. For now.

Rather than join her on the outing, Juliet had begged to remain home and create valentines. Which, in truth, was a poorly constructed excuse to avoid venturing into public with her new spectacles.

For Juliet's sake, until her dearest younger sister made a match, Regine tarried in England. Or, if Juliet didn't choose to marry, then to travel with her if that was her sister's preference.

Which it very well might be, given the cool reception they'd received in London so far. Few invitations had seen their way to the sisters' rented Grosvenor Square doorstep since Regine had set up home in London. She suspected curiosity had prompted those half-dozen or so invites. A young, widowed duchess who'd managed to escape *le beau monde's* watchful eye was a novelty.

To be fair, however, she must concede it wasn't the height of the Season.

As she marched along, Regine permitted her mind to wander.

Not so long ago—eight years wasn't so very long, was it?—she wouldn't have believed the numerous extraordinary places she'd have visited. And yet—*yes, it is true*—she'd forfeit every single adventure, every monument, museum, great wonder of nature, and grand marvel of man, to have been permitted to select a different path for her life. The route she'd yearned to take with all of her heart, mind, body, and spirit.

If she'd only had herself to consider.

Two laughing boys—arms wildly waving—darted past, drawing her back to the present and earning them a tolerant smile.

Children. The one thing Heartwaite couldn't give her. Involuntarily, she pursed her lips against the scrape of disappointment such reflection always produced. She'd known that was the case from the beginning, but that didn't render the sting any less sharp.

As she passed a coffeehouse, a dapper elderly gentleman and a petite lady of middling years, attired entirely in flamingo pink with copious pink and white feathers adorning her bonnet, exited. Regine couldn't help but inhale the heady aroma of coffee, escaping the establishment through the open doorway.

At once, the familiar smell transported her to Spain, and the delicious coffee she and Heartwaite had enjoyed there. She preferred hers heavily dosed with milk, while her husband had enjoyed his black with four sugar lumps.

Pausing, she inspected the charming frontage, making a mental note of the coffeehouse's name: *Royale Roast Coffee Shoppe and Café.* Perhaps she'd return another day and bring Juliet with her. Once her sister became accustomed to her new spectacles, and to seeing clearly, she'd welcome more outings. *Hopefully.*

Regine cast one last appreciative glance over the quaint building. With its bright blue shutters and white gingerbread fretwork, it reminded her very much of something from a storybook. Her attention snagged on a man engrossed in a newssheet on the other side of a sparkling, clean window.

No. It cannot be. Her heart stuttered to a halt then resumed beating with the swiftness of a winded Ascot racehorse. *Heavens above.*

She pressed her fur-lined, ruby kid glove-covered fingertips to her mouth. A half-gasp, half-exclamation of distress lodged in her throat upon recognizing familiar auburn hair with an endearing, unruly mahogany lock flopped over a high brow. His hair had always done that. How many times had she smoothed the silky strands of coppery-brown from that noble forehead?

Head slanted in the manner that always bespoke deep concentration, he casually rubbed his thumb and forefinger over his chin.

I'm not ready.

She'd never be ready. Not if another eighty years came and went.

Feet rooted to the wet pavement, she gawped, forcing people to skirt around her.

James Brentwood. Good Lord.

Even after all of this time, he had her at sixes and sevens.

She hadn't seen him in over eight years, but she would've recognized him anywhere. He looked much the same. Same straight blade of a nose, square chin, lips perfectly fashioned by God, and eyelids lowered over what she knew to be vibrant blue-green eyes. Intelligent eyes. Kind eyes. Eyes, which had once looked upon her with devotion and love.

Such tender, reverent love.

Followed by hurt. Confusion. Betrayal. And finally—the most wounding of all—disgust and antipathy. Even after all of this time, Regine's lungs and stomach cramped with remembered pain, as if it had only been yesterday that she'd watched him stalk away from her.

I'm sorry. So, very, very sorry.

Swallowing reflexively, she lowered her hand from her mouth as she caught sight of herself reflected in the window. Blue eyes round and stunned and face pale as milk.

And, devil a bit, if her smart, port-colored half-boots, didn't carry her inside of their own volition. Even as her common sense and self-preservation ordered her to walk on.

To forget James Brentwood. To protect her fragile heart.

Piffle and twaddle. Regine wasn't a shrinking violet. Never had been. A swift *Hello* and, *How are you?* ought to suffice. After all, to ignore him would be the height of poor manners. Hadn't they been neighbors for over fifteen years? They'd been much more, as well.

He probably doesn't even know I've returned to London.

He would soon enough.

2

Regine slipped inside the cozy eatery, her attention riveted on James, and filled her lungs with the welcoming aromas. Robust coffee beans, heady tea, sweet chocolate, baking spices, and other delicious smells met her nostrils. Her tummy gurgled, reminding her she'd forgone her midday meal, and her light breakfast had consisted of coffee and toast.

She half-wished he'd glance up and see her and half-hoped he wouldn't. An urge to turn around and flee so overwhelmed her, she felt almost faint. Or perchance hunger made her light-headed. More likely, trepidation did.

After sweeping a glance around the room, she returned the smiles of a pair of twinkling-eyed, apple-cheeked matrons nattering in one corner. A precocious towheaded boy, sitting on his knees and dragging a spotted toy horse along the back of his chair while making neighing noises, grinned at her, revealing a missing front tooth.

A pair of gentlemen—bankers perhaps given their somber black suits—paused in their animated discussion to turn and boldly inspect her, their appreciative smiles and slightly inappropriate gazes, making her uneasy. Edging her chin upward, she focused on James—the man she'd once loved with all of her heart.

How could a gentleman turned out entirely in black, save his starched shirt and confection of a cravat, be so hopelessly attractive? So sculpted? Splendid? *Virile?*

Heat suffused her. *Good God.* What had prompted *that* particular thought?

He'd stretched his strapping legs beneath the table and crossed his ankles. Though the chair was of average size, his tall, powerfully built frame and preposterously broad shoulders dwarfed the sturdy piece of furniture.

Like a woman long-starved, Regine permitted her gaze to feast upon him and his sheer male essence. Memories flooded her: his breath whispering across her cheek; his strong fingers threaded through her hair; his solid body pressed to hers as he showered kisses upon her face and mouth.

Oh, James.

Of a sudden, Regine became aware she stared at him like a calf-eyed ninny. Her cheeks flamed hot—probably as ruddy as her shockingly bright mantle. Nothing like gawking in the manner of a gauche schoolgirl instead of a mature, widowed duchess. A world-traveler, woman of independent means, and guardian to a fifteen-year-old girl.

Regine refused to peek from beneath her lashes and determine if any of the patrons had noticed her uncouthness. Better not to know. Ignorance being bliss and all that.

In a few short heartbeats and an equal number of surprisingly steady steps, she stood indecisively beside his table. Her stomach wobbled with a whorl of emotion, and her pulse quickened, the blood sluicing through her veins at an alarming speed.

Approaching him was a mistake. She should turn and leave. *Now.* That would be the wise thing to do. Yes, but she was well and done with doing what was wise and expected. Hence her unfashionably loud attire.

Unfashionable for England, perhaps, but quite acceptable in the foreign places she'd stayed. She'd always preferred bright colors, and as a widow, she felt no compulsion to conform to Society's expectations.

Absorbed in his newssheet, James Brentwood didn't glance up but shook his head while lifting a lean, staying finger.

Remorse buffeting her, Regine permitted her gaze to brush every dear angle and plane of his face. How many times had she run her fingertips over his angular jaw? Kissed his slightly too-strong chin?

"No more of your delicious coffee for me, Mrs. Delaney," he murmured, distractedly. "Sleep will elude me until the wee hours if I indulge."

She closed her eyes for a long blink.

Lord. His voice.

The mellow timbre had haunted her dreams for years. Her daytime reveries, as well.

Sometimes, when she was in a half-awake, half-asleep fog, she'd believe James spoke her name. She'd come fully awake, calling his name, tears leaking from the corners of her eyes. And when she realized it had only been a dream, overcome with fulminating regret, she'd bury her face in the lavender-scented, satin-covered pillow and let sorrow have its way.

Dragging in a ragged breath and with her stomach flopping as frantically as a beached trout, she laced her fingers together. And squeezed. Tightly. Outwardly, she appeared serenely composed and unaffected, but inside she was a tumultuous, careening wreck. An apt description of her life for almost a decade now.

"I'm not Mrs. Delaney, James," Regine managed, through a throat too taut for speech and cursing to herself for the revealing, tremulous tenor. Consternation scuffed against gladness as she awaited his reaction.

He went rigid, his jaw, neck, and shoulders noticeably tensing beneath her scrutiny. Not a doubt remained that he hadn't recognized her voice.

Gradually, as if bracing himself for an assault or battle, he brought those startling aquamarine orbs fringed with sooty lashes to meet her gaze. He'd always had the most memorable turquoise eyes. Eyes a woman yearned to dive into and explore their mesmerizing, enigmatic depths and mine the treasures within.

And now that she'd seen glistening tropical oceans, she knew exactly what shade his eyes were—the sea surrounding the Isle of Crete just after dawn. And every time she'd looked upon that glittering water, she'd thought of him. Wished it was him at her side. Him watching her from across the breakfast table or with her as she exclaimed over another marvel of man or nature. *Always and forever, James.*

For an instant, unrestrained joy shone in his unflinching gaze. Then, his blistering eyes pierced her with withering scorn before a bland expression masked the emotion with the alacrity and might of a lightning bolt strike. Shutting her out as effectively as if he'd slammed and secured shutters or battened down the hatches of a ship.

Were his teeth clenched? Aye, indeed. A muscle definitely ticked in his jaw.

Regine dropped her focus to the hand resting on his thigh. *Balled tight.* Her treacherous attention shifted ever-so-slightly to the lump his fitted pantaloons couldn't hide. Latent desire took root in her belly.

He'd always affected her thus. Whereas once she'd gloried in her attraction to him, now it was a burden.

"*Your Grace.*" Harsh. Cold. Unwelcoming.

Rejection and pain scissored sharp and lethal, shredding her initial exhilaration at seeing him after all of this time. Scooting her gaze to the floor, Regine took a second to marshal her composure and arm her battlements. Definitely not a greeting one would welcome from the man she'd almost married. A man she'd wanted to wed from the depths of her soul, but circumstances had forced her to take a different road.

If only—

One could not live one's life reminiscing over if-onlys and what-ifs. The past was the past, and it was best left behind. Except, she'd never forgotten him. Never purged him from her aching heart or wrenched him from her soul.

Without waiting for an invitation, and somewhat astonished at her brashness, given he was not at all as happy to see her as she was to see him, she slipped into the chair beside him. She pointedly pretended not to notice the battle-hardened glower he leveled her.

She could collect Juliet's gloves another day. And bring her sister with her. They were for Juliet, after all.

This meeting with James was more important and long—so very long—overdue. A swift, subtle glance around revealed the other patrons had returned their attentions to their companions and refreshments.

With abrupt, efficient movements, he wordlessly folded the

newssheet into a neat rectangle. After laying it aside, he turned those brooding, hooded eyes upon her. He'd grant her no quarter, then.

Had she honestly expected any different?

After slipping her reticule off her wrist—the letter within making it a trifle stiff and poking out the top a bit—Regine placed the purse atop the table and offered a ghost of a bittersweet smile as she removed her gloves.

It truly was good to see him, but also heart-wrenching.

Being with James felt like coming home, and she realized just how homesick she'd been. Much like a person deprived of the sun for too long, he warmed her, comforted her. She wanted to sit and soak up his presence.

"You are well?" she asked, searching the striking planes of his face, half-hidden in the shadows. He was the same, but also different. Gone was the lean, jovial youth with sparkling eyes and quick smile. In his place was a somber man, full-grown. And impossibly even more devastatingly handsome.

Had he married?

3

The unbidden thought made Regine want to retch and sucked the previous pleasure from her spirit. But why shouldn't James have found someone? He, above all others, deserved to be happy after she'd broken his heart. Despite that unforgivable truth, knowing full well what her choice would do to him and how it would appear, she'd accepted that she had no other recourse and had done what she must.

My heart was broken, too.

Familiar anguish and guilt lanced her, and she curled her toes in her boots. *I had no choice. None.* She hadn't, but that didn't ease the torment or the regret. Regret, which nearly destroyed her during her first year of marriage to Heartwaite.

A woman wearing an austere black gown and a neat-as-a-pin apron bustled to their table. "What is your preference today, my lady?"

"It's *Your Grace,* Mrs. Delaney." James's voice dripped sarcasm as heavy as clotted cream as he gave a disinterested, flippant wave. "Her Grace, Regine, the Duchess of Heartwaite, to be precise." Each clipped syllable, a deliberately executed blow. As lethal and painful as an arrow striking her bruised heart.

Actually, it was dowager duchess now, but James didn't know that.

Excitement rounded the proprietress's acorn-brown eyes to plate-sized, and a thrilled smile commandeering the entire lower half of her face, the plump woman dipped an awkward curtsy. After rising, she folded her hands, gazing at Regine expectantly.

The heat of a blush licked her face, no doubt turning her cheeks fiery, too. *The dratted man.* She tamped down the urge to tell James exactly what she thought of his manners. But she didn't want to quarrel. Not when she hadn't seen him in so long.

Besides, she'd vow every avid gaze in the *Royale Roast Coffee Shoppe and Café* had swung to their table at Mrs. Delaney's groveling. Regine would rather not have an apt, earwigging audience observe their less than cordial reunion. On James's part, that was.

The bothersome man needn't have shared her title with Mrs. Delaney. She hadn't a doubt he'd intentionally reminded Regine of the differences in their stations now. Not that she needed her memory refreshed regarding the matter.

Every day for the prior nearly three thousand days, she'd castigated herself. But what else could she have done? Nothing.

She supposed it was too much to hope he'd have forgiven her after eight years. Nonetheless, she *had* hoped he could. Prayed that time had healed him of the wound she'd caused and that he could forgive her and find happiness.

Whoever said time healed all wounds was a monumental, blathering fool. People might move on, but wounds, just as joyous events, left indelible marks that never, *never* completely vanished. Could never be wholly vanquished from the soul.

Her thoughts turned inward.

Did she deserve James's forgiveness?

No. Because, she'd never forgiven herself either.

Nevertheless, if she had to do it all over again, given the circumstances of eight years ago, she'd have made the same choice. For it hadn't been just hers and James's futures at stake.

Marrying the Duke of Heartwaite, a man nearly fifty years her senior, had been the only means of providing for her ailing mother and three younger sisters after Father's sudden death and learning of his mountain of debt and angry, demanding creditors. He'd left his family homeless, destitute, and drowning in the aftermath of his irresponsible choices.

In truth, she counted herself fortunate the duke, Mama's third cousin twice-removed, had offered for her. He might've set her family up in their own household without requiring her hand in marriage, but George-Arnold, the fifth Duke of Heartwaite, wasn't quite that benevolent. A vain man, full of self-import, he'd coveted a pretty young wife on his arm.

Regine had always wondered if part of his motivation for wedding her was to spite his five greedy-guts children, too. Each of his progeny was quite horrid: pompous, opinionated, haughty, and unrepentantly scornful and disdainful of her.

As agreed, Heartwaite had paid Papa's debts, established Mama and the girls in a comfortable house, and provided a generous annual allowance for their living expenses. In exchange, at eighteen, Regine had married him, breaking her unofficial betrothal to James.

Shattering both of their hearts, as well.

"Trip over love, you can get up. Fall in love and you fall forever. Anyone can catch your eye, but it takes someone special to catch your heart."

Her heart contracted painfully behind her ribs as a Shakespeare quotation popped to mind.

No, indeed, time didn't heal all wounds.

And Heartwaite's five children only added to her pain. Each several years older than Regine, Heartwaite's three sons and two daughters hadn't attended the ceremony. And each, bitterly resented her and every pound Heartwaite spent on her with their every spiteful breath.

Not once had they visited when she and the duke returned to England, though she'd written them that their father lay dying. The moment he'd cast off this mortal realm, before his funeral, in truth, she'd received orders to vacate the ducal estate. She hadn't even been offered the dower house, as was her right.

Her husband must've anticipated his children's animosity and pettiness, because Heartwaite had the foresight to provide her with a substantial annual allowance, a house in Brighton, a coach and team, as well as had named her owner of a cargo ship. All of which, his solicitors had drawn up in a tidy legal document, much to the new duke's and his siblings' consternation.

In point of fact, the letter in her reticule was from the current duke, threatening to take legal action against her. *Again.* Oh, how the pudding soft, jowly George-Curtis, Sixth Duke of Heartwaite, had stormed like a recalcitrant child over the endowment. Swore he'd challenge her inheritance, claiming his father hadn't been in his right mind when he'd designated the bequeathment.

What a load of fustian blather and codswallop.

Heartwaite's mind had been as sharp the day he died as the day she'd met him. His body eventually wore out, but his intellect had never gone soft.

"Your Grace?" The proprietress gently urged, bringing Regine back to the present.

Regathering her thoughts, she offered a nascent smile. "Coffee with warm milk, please." Regine adopted what she hoped was a pleasant, nonchalant mien.

She'd become quite adept at disguising her true feelings. At the beginning of her marriage, it had taken a great deal of practice and self-discipline. Her sisters, mother, and husband had never known how bitterly unhappy she was.

Although, she suspected Juliet might've guessed. For all of her youngest sister's inability to see without her spectacles, the girl perceived much that went unspoken.

Regine wasn't the sort to make others suffer because she was miserable. She'd chosen to find the good in her life, and Heartwaite had turned out to be a considerate friend. More like a doting uncle than a spouse.

"At once, Your Grace." Mrs. Delaney bustled off, a broad smile wreathing her lined face.

"Coffee? I'd have thought a proper English duchess would only drink tea." James wrapped his long fingers around his cup but didn't bring it to his mouth. Though his nails were neatly trimmed, faint callouses and ink stains marred the fingertips. His words still held a harsh edge, but his features had softened a trifle, his eyes competing with the sea for magnificence.

"I still enjoy a cup of tea, especially India tea." Regine lifted a shoulder, refusing to feel chagrined for something so trivial or to take to heart his acrimony. She understood his rancor and couldn't fault him for it. "I acquired a taste for Turkish coffee while abroad."

"Ah, yes. Touring the Continent, seeing the sights, and all that with your husband." He made a pretense of searching the coffeeshop and then the damp street through the window. A hawkish eyebrow cocked, he asked, "Where *is* good ol' Heartwaite, by the way?"

4

Wrapped in death's slumber.

One hand in her lap, the other resting atop the table where she traced the bumpy ridges of the crocheted table cloth, Regine murmured, "He died, almost two years ago."

Eyebrows lashing together, James had the grace to look repentant. "My condolences."

"Thank you." She wasn't a bereaved widow, but she'd come to like and respect her husband. He'd been kind in his way.

Angling her head while fingering her reticule, she studied James. Fine lines etched the corners of his eyes, and his firm, well-formed mouth had a harder cast to it. She'd wager with his keen mind that he made a brilliant man of law. Yes, she'd made the right decision.

Steering her thoughts to other avenues, she asked, "How are your sisters? Your parents?"

At one time, their families had been the greatest of friends.

He directed a lengthy look onto the street again, the muscle in his jaw working once more—a clue to the vexation he secreted. "My parents are in Australia. Father is shepherding a flock of convicts there."

Her bewilderment must've shown, because he rolled a shoulder. "It's a long, rather scandalous tale."

One he, obviously, didn't want to share with her.

"And your sisters?" She smiled at Mrs. Delaney as she set the milk and coffee spiraling with steam before her. "Thank you. It smells wonderful."

"Turkish coffee. There's nothing quite as flavorful. May I get you anything else, Your Grace?" She looked hopeful.

Regine's stomach took that moment to spasm. A small repast wouldn't go amiss. "Have you any maid of honor tarts?" She'd never been able to resist the treats, always a favorite of hers. Greek, melomakarona came a close second, however.

"I do." A toothy smile splitting her dumpling cheeks, the proprietress gave an exuberant nod before hurrying into the kitchen.

A thick silence hung heavy in the air after her departure, like low fog rising from the Thames, and for a minute, Regine believed James meant to ignore her question about his sisters.

Hooking an arm across the back of his chair, he eyed her, slowly raking his focus from her tasteful bonnet to her bright boots, then making the reverse trip and lingering on her mouth for a jot too long. A nuance of something, evocative of when they'd been sweethearts, hooded his eyes.

Sensation pricked behind hers, and it took all of her forbearances to hold her tears at bay. Regret was an awful thing.

"My sisters have all married. Theadosia and Jessica to *dukes,* and Althea to an *artist.* Each is blissfully happy." Rancor tinged his words.

We might've been blissfully happy, too, his unrepentant gaze seemed to accuse.

He was wrong, however. Regine couldn't have—wouldn't have—seized her happiness at the expense of others. His included, though, he might never understand or acknowledge that truth.

At two and twenty, in training to become a solicitor, he hadn't had the means to support five women. He'd have been compelled to leave his position for better-paying employment and would've been obliged to take on a burden and responsibilities that weren't his to bear on his young shoulders.

James had never wanted to follow in his father's footsteps and enter the ministry. Since he'd been a lad of ten and she a wee lass of six, he'd chattered on about becoming a lawyer. Such a prestigious future lay ahead of him. He would've had to have relinquished his life-long dream to provide for her and her family.

So, she'd done the only thing she could do. James might despise her for marrying the duke, but her motives had been pure. He mightn't ever see it that way, however. Oh, she knew full well he thought she'd married for position and wealth. That pricked her pride more than a little.

Believing the chance quite remote, Regine hadn't considered what to expect if she encountered him. Point of fact, solicitors—he *had* become a successful solicitor, hadn't he?—and vicar's sons didn't regularly hobnob with the peerage.

Drawing her brows together, she bent her mouth downward. Well, he might do so now that his sisters were duchesses. *Good, Lord.* That made her sound like the worst sort of snob.

She wasn't. Not in the least. Why, she didn't even interact with *le beau monde.*

In her heart, she was still and would always be, the barefoot young girl from Colechester, sneaking kisses with James in the orchard not so very far from Reverend Brentwood's parish. They'd held each other, pledging their love, and planning their future. Together.

"Althea has quite a brood, and Thea's daughter is four or five months old." He rubbed the right side of his nose. Just like he always had when pondering. "Or mayhap six? I'm honestly not certain. I anticipate the news Jessica and Bainbridge are expecting any day, as well."

"I hadn't heard." Not secluded as she'd been, first nursing her husband, then observing the mourning period after his death. And then a mere six months after Heartwaite's passing, she'd buried her mother and assumed the care of Juliet. "I'm happy for them," she said quietly, not missing the emphasis he'd placed on *dukes* and *artist.*

His way of jabbing home his point once more. Though he needn't do so. His condemnation and censure were paltry compared to what she'd conferred upon herself.

"Have you any children?" His wasn't the casual question it appeared.

She shook her head while smoothing her gloves atop the table. "No."

Regine wasn't explaining Heartwaite's impotence. He'd told her from the beginning theirs would be a marriage in name only, and she'd known she'd never bear his children. In truth, that wasn't entirely accurate. Heartwaite had waited until they were married to inform her, denying her the right to refuse his suit for that very significant reason.

Father to five, he felt no burden to produce more offspring and had selfishly kept his physical incapability a secret until it was too late for her to deny his suit. She wouldn't have. Her mother and sisters had no means of support, and James must finish his training.

Neither her family nor James knew the depths of sacrifice she'd made for them. They never would. That brought her some small satisfaction. Not that she considered herself a martyr by any means, but she'd spared those she loved angst and worry.

"How fares your family?" Politesse required him to ask the obligatory question.

"Christiana and Marian are married as well. Mama died just over a year ago, and Juliet lives with me now." Unwilling for him to see the grief in her eyes from the loss of her mother, she stirred milk into her coffee.

Initially, resentment and anger that her mother could've so readily agreed to Heartwaite's suggestion had hardened Regine's heart. Eventually, however, she'd had to confront the indisputable truth.

Mama had been at her wit's end and without recourse. If she could protect her three youngest daughters by sacrificing the oldest, she'd do so. And she had. But, as Regine had learned while her mother lay dying, remorse and guilt had plagued Mama. She'd regretted depriving Regine of the life she might've had with James.

Mama had known they were in love.

If Christiana hadn't just seen her fifteenth birthday, she might've become the duchess, but Mama wouldn't wed a child to George-Arnold, Duke of Heartwaite. So she, too, had done what must be done. Such was the way with women, always at the mercy of men and society.

A tangled knot of emotions, almost impossible to separate, had paraded through Regine. Remorse. Guilt. Resentment. Forgiveness. And finally, after a long while, acceptance and healing.

"I am sorry, Regine."

Did he realize he'd used her given name? The sound on his lips was a consecration to her ears.

"I didn't know about your mother." James laid his warm hand atop hers, and she wanted to weep at his attempt to console her.

The compassionate gesture came so unexpectedly, she shot him an astonished look. She yearned to turn her hand over so that their palms lay against each other, to entwine their fingers as they had hundreds of times prior. A lifetime ago.

His sympathy and touch were her undoing. Fighting the tears burning behind her eyelids, she summoned a brave, if somewhat wobbly, smile.

She still loved James. Always had. Always would. Her heart would forever and always be his. But she'd lost her chance for a life with him.

"Have you married?" Blast and damn her tongue.

5

Though James's hand covered most of Regine's small one, he knew the fine-boned appendage as well as he did his own. Her fingers were delicate, not overly long, and the right forefinger had a scar from knuckle to knuckle where she'd cut herself when she was eight.

He shook his head and withdrew his hand, his palm burning with sensation. "I have no wife."

"Oh." Her pretty mouth compressed into a ribbon and color bled into her cheeks as her raven eyebrows, an exact match to the midnight tresses mostly hid by her bonnet, swooped together. "I see."

Did she? Really?

Bloody unlikely.

The only woman he'd ever loved had married another. He'd begged Regine not to. Would've done anything to make her his. In the end, she'd chosen the wealthy, titled, decrepit old duke over him, slashing his heart to shreds.

So much for true love, happily ever afters, and all that blasted fairytale rot and rubbish.

She took a careful sip of her coffee, an expression of bliss softening her features. The mole to the left of her mouth teased James, as it had all those years ago. Begging him to kiss the beauty mark as well as those soft, cherry red lips that tasted of apples and cinnamon and Regine.

Firmly tamping down the incipient feelings attempting to burble to the surface, he gulped a mouthful of cold coffee, barely concealing a grimace as the bitter brew slid down his throat.

"I didn't realize I'd grown so chilled completing my errands," she said, conversationally.

Yes, let's discuss the weather as if we're mere acquaintances. Not a man and a woman who'd vowed to love one another for eternity.

After slicing a glance outside—much wiser than making a colossal ass of himself gaping at the beautiful woman across from him—he brought his brows together. Scowling at the undeserving ashen sky, he jabbed a thumb toward the street. "It's freezing out there, and those look like snow clouds. Don't you have a coach or carriage?"

Pinching his lips tightly, James cursed inwardly. He sounded worried—concerned for Regine's wellbeing. She was nothing to him now. Merely a woman he'd once given his heart to, and she'd annihilated the organ before casually tossing it in hell's flames. Now only cinders remained.

She took another sip of coffee as Mrs. Delaney delivered the pastries. "Here you are, Your Grace. I took the liberty of bringing enough for you, too, Mr. Brentwood."

God. He nearly rolled his eyes. As if he could swallow food, with his mouth dry as dust.

"Thank you." Regine's sable lashes widened as her hydrangea-blue eyes lit with pleasure. She took a dainty taste of the pastry. "Delicious," she declared to the anxiously hovering proprietress.

After another awkward curtsy, Mrs. Delaney hurried to assist patrons at another table.

"I asked my driver to wait with the coach two streets over," Regine said, in answer to James's inquiry. "I wanted the exercise. I often take long strolls."

He remembered that about her. She loved to take lengthy, meandering walks and always discovered something that excited her. A bird gliding overhead. A flower waving in the breeze. The sound of the leaves brushing against each other, or a pretty rock.

Regine had been so innocent back then. So unpretentious and

unaffected. He'd never known her to covet fancy gowns or jewels or fallalls. That was why her abrupt decision to marry Heartwaite hadn't made any sense. Still didn't after all of these years, in truth.

They settled into silence—perhaps not companionable, but not stilted either—as she nibbled the pastry and sipped her coffee. A crumb balanced upon her lower lip, and she darted her tongue out to swipe it away.

Bloody hell.

James lowered his attention to his cold coffee, lest she see the desire flaring in his eyes. Though he'd only ever tasted her lips, she'd always had the ability to send his lust soaring with a tilt of her head, a twitch of her bottom, a look from those blue eyes, both innocent and seductive at once.

Regine was more delectable than she'd been as a fresh-faced girl of eighteen. She possessed a woman's refined features and curved form now. Impossibly more exquisite and alluring than the last time he'd seen her, tears streaming from those mesmerizing eyes as he turned his back, refusing to listen to her reasons for marrying Heartwaite. *The paunchy, old geezer.*

James damn well knew the why of it…

Prestige. Wealth. Position. None of which he could've given her. *Then.*

Why settle for an impoverished vicar's son? A man newly hired as the lowest ranking employee in a solicitor's office? Well, there had been two clerks who ranked lower.

And now, James was a partner in that same firm, and if he didn't say so himself, a damned exceptional lawyer, to boot. His clientele was very exclusive, and his fees very expensive since making partner.

Except he also offered his services *pro bono*. Often enough, truth to tell, to raise the grizzled eyebrows of his senior associates. Once a month, he opened the office on a Saturday and dispensed free legal advice.

If Regine knew, she'd approve. At least the Regine of old would have. He wasn't sure about the richly garbed duchess sitting mere feet from him.

A thousand questions he wanted to ask her tapped at his tongue. A thousand things he wanted to say. Things he'd said to himself at least a thousand times these past eight years. Things he'd raged at the heavens a time or two or a hundred, as well.

And yet, he remained silent, unlike the garrulous ladies in the corner who kept sending inquisitive glances his way. Hopefully, their idle tongues wouldn't carry gossip about Regine. She really oughtn't to have sat with him. It gave the appearance of a lovers' clandestine *tête-à-tête*.

At one time, he and Regine talked so effortlessly about everything. Now an awkwardness existed between them. Eight years in which the chasm had grown ever-wider and filled with uncertainty. Pain. Distrust. Loss. *Unbearable loss.*

He'd barely functioned the first few months after she'd married and left England. Only by pouring all of his energy and focus into becoming a solicitor had kept the heartbreak from snapping his reason. Well, after he'd stopped drinking himself into a stupor each night. He never wanted to experience that agony again. He wouldn't survive a second time.

A clock on a shelf near the door chimed the hour, and Regine glanced over her shoulder. "Is that truly the time? Gracious, Juliet will be fretting. I promised to be home with her new spectacles in time for tea."

She swiftly patted her mouth, and after fishing around inside her reticule, withdrew a letter and a timepiece before locating the coins she sought and placed them on the table.

Did she think he'd expect her to pay? What kind of a cad did she believe him? "I intended to see to your refreshments, Regine."

She raised her uncertain azure gaze to his. Her eyes had been the first thing he'd noticed about her, as a young girl of perhaps three or four. Wide and round. Clear and bright and an impossible shade of pale blue. Like a frosty morning sky.

Then she'd laughed. Giggled that infectious, unfettered way that was Regine's alone, and his little boy's heart had landed at her tiny, waving, chubby feet—hers to do with as she pleased for all time. And for several years, he and Regine had been the best of friends, sharing everything. Then later, they'd become sweethearts. They'd eagerly made plans to marry and spend the rest of their lives together.

But her father had died, and she'd entered mourning. So, he'd tempered his impatience. Only, a month after old Edenshaw's death, she informed him she was to marry Heartwaite. A week later, she'd become the Duchess of Heartwaite and left the country.

James hadn't even permitted himself to follow reports of the Duke's and Duchess's of Heartwaites travels in the newssheets or gossip rags. He'd resolutely put Regine behind him and faced his future. Without her.

"I thank you, James, but it wouldn't be proper."

Now she considered propriety?

She tucked the feminine watch inside her bag before collecting the letter. A shadow flitted across her face, and her lips thinned the merest bit as she returned the folded paper to its nest, and then donned her gloves.

Bad or unwelcome news?

"Thank you for permitting me to interrupt you." She slipped the reticule on her narrow wrist and rose, all elegant grace. One hand cradling the handbag, she skittered that blue gaze over him, hesitancy and a question brimming within. Something shifted deep inside those azure pools, and she dropped her hand. "Please say hello to your family for me the next time you see them."

Trivial stuff. Polite, nonsensical pleasantries that acquaintants might exchange—not a couple once passionately in love.

James sought his feet. He might not be a lord, but no gentleman remained sitting when a lady stood. He should say something. But what?

I missed you? Every day. Every hour. Every second.

Had she missed him, too?

How long would she be in London?

Yes, that would do.

"Are you in Town for long? Most people escape to the country this time of year." He used to go down to Colechester regularly, but since Theadosia and Jessica had married, he didn't make the trip as often. There wasn't a reason to anymore.

Not that he wasn't always welcome in either one of their homes. Or Althea's, for that matter. The truth was, he struggled in the company of such happiness, knowing he'd never experience the same. Of course,

James was glad for them. His three sisters had all endured varying degrees of difficulty before wedding, but in the end, they'd married the men they loved.

The woman he'd adored had married someone else—a bow-legged, bald-as-a-cue-ball, snaggle-toothed decrepit smelling of camphor and stale pomade, and crippled by bunions and carbuncles, too. Fine, that last bit he'd made up. The rest wasn't so very far off, however.

Though James had never actually met the former duke, a few questions in the right ears had painted a fairly accurate depiction. He'd also learned that although Heartwaite had long-since bid his youth behind, he was regarded as a decent chap.

That brought him a degree of relief, for although she'd crushed his spirit, he'd not have Regine unhappy or abused by her husband.

She busied herself, retying the ribbons of her bonnet. "We've only been here for ten days. I've let a house in Grosvenor Square. Juliet has some vision issues and is seeing a specialist."

"Nothing serious, I hope?" he said perfunctorily while collecting his coat.

She shook her head. "No, but she's not keen on wearing her spectacles. Without them, the poor dear can scarce see a foot in front of her. I've promised her we might visit several of the attractions and landmarks, even though it's the dead of winter. She's been rather bored in the country since our sisters married, and there was our mourning period, of course. I'm hoping her curiosity will help her forget she's wearing spectacles and make her less self-conscious."

He shrugged into his caped greatcoat, then gathered his hat and gloves. "Allow me to escort you to your coach."

"That's not necessary. Truly." Her cupid's bow mouth arced, but no joy lit her eyes. "I don't wish to inconvenience you further, especially if you have somewhere you need to be." They reached the door, and she stepped aside to permit him to open it.

Such a natural expectation for a peeress. Did she even realize she'd done so?

Eight years ago, she'd have pressed the handle herself and dragged him out the doorway by the hand. Where had that exuberant, buoyant girl gone?

God. How he'd missed her.

This serene—too poised and composed—woman lacked the spark, the vitality her younger self could barely restrain. Oh, there was no denying she was stunning. Exquisite in her radiant crimson ensemble, the color a perfect complement to her alabaster skin and ebony hair.

But where had she hidden the real Regine? Or, was this who'd she'd become? Had wealth and riches and position turned her into this dignified shadow of her former self?

Once on the pavement, he lightly took her elbow. A frisson jolted up his arm at the contact. Well, that hadn't changed a jot. One touch, and lust burrowed through his veins, almost making him forget her perfidy. For surely, desire was all this sensation was. After the way she'd discarded him like a holey sock, he couldn't retain any feelings for her.

They received several curious glances, many quite brazen, as they strolled along. The wind had gathered momentum and tugged furiously at their garments. James was no admirer of London's tempestuous winter weather. Someday, he hoped to travel and spend the winter months in more temperate locales.

"Just there." Regine jutted her softly rounded chin to a polished ebony coach. The Heartwaite crest, painted in silver and crimson, glinted brightly on the door. A few heartbeats later, they stood outside the conveyance.

The driver had lowered the steps and stood a respectful distance away.

As Regine turned to climb into the conveyance, James touched her elbow. "Regine, wait." He'd never get used to addressing her as *Your Grace.* She was now, and would forever be Regine.

Fool. Stop. She'll break your heart again. Turn and walk away and don't look back.

She looked up at him, those wide eyes soft and inquisitive. "Yes?"

"Perhaps you and your sister would like to visit Bullock's Museum of Natural Curiosities tomorrow?" *Bloody hell.* He sounded like a smitten swain eager for his lady's attention. "Or if that's not enough notice, perhaps the next day?"

She cut the driver a short glance before facing James fully. "You'd escort us to the museum?" Her guileless gaze searched his, uncertainty and yearning in hers. "Don't you have to be at your offices?"

He rubbed his nose and chuckled, delighted when she also grinned. "That's the advantage of being a partner. I can take an afternoon off if I wish to."

And I wish to. Very much, in fact.

"You're a partner? How splendid." Pride shone in her clear blue eyes, the outer ring a deeper, navy-blue. "I always knew you'd be a magnificent lawyer." *She had?* "Well done, James. I'm so pleased for you."

And she was. Her smile and the approval in her eyes weren't affected or merely politesse. Her reaction was, perhaps, the first authentic thing he'd detected since she'd tilted his world on its end and violently spun it around and around thirty minutes ago. The rest she kept hidden behind that carefully constructed façade of decorum.

If James hadn't known the carefree, vivacious girl of his youth, he might've believed the coolly poised, elegant woman before him had always been thus. She'd certainly taken to the role of a duchess with admirable aplomb, hadn't she?

The churlish thought left a foul taste in his mouth and a prick of guilt as well. He'd convinced himself he didn't care, and his bitter ruminations proved him a liar.

"Well, do you wish to visit the museum or not?" he asked, irritation with himself giving his tone a cryptic edge. Damn it all, she'd think he was angry with her.

Regine blinked twice then slowly nodded.

"I should be delighted to." A becoming flush tinted her ivory cheeks, whether from pleasure, the brisk breeze and frigid temperature, or his sharp question he couldn't determine. "I'm sure Juliet will as well. She's ever so fascinated with displays and antiquities."

The latter seemed an afterthought, and the notion pleased him more than it ought. Blast, but he must guard himself against Regine. One winsome smile or joy-filled gaze, and he was practically throwing himself at her feet. Again. *Fool!*

"Shall we meet you there at three of the clock?" she asked, her head tilted at an endearing angle. An angle ideal for kissing her sweet mouth. For tasting the soft, velvety pillows.

He tore his gaze from those tempting lips.

What had she said?

Ah, yes. Three. Museum.

Perfect. If James arrived at his office by six, he'd still put in a full day's work before he left at half-past two. "Yes, that will suit."

"I shall look forward to it," she said. "And I'm sure Juliet will be beside herself with excitement."

He handed her into the coach, and long after the door clicked closed, with the wind battering him from without, and his cracked heart buffeting him from within, he watched the conveyance. When the equipage turned a corner, he heaved a gusty sigh.

You, James Abraham Evan Brentwood, are out of your sodding mind.

One outing, he sternly admonished himself. *One.* And then he'd have Regine out of his system once and for all.

Like hell, he would.

6

Regine's stomach churned, tangling in worse knots than the time Juliet's cat had frolicked in the embroidery threads. She placed a gloved palm on her abdomen, certain she'd feel her belly rolling over itself. Breathing deeply, she checked her timepiece before tucking the watch inside her reticule once more—the fourth time since leaving Grosvenor Square.

It was precisely five minutes to three. Not so early as to seem overly-eager, but not late either. She abhorred tardiness and, similarly, disliked waiting on others—both bespoke a lack of consideration and respect. Heartwaite had maintained otherwise, and she swore while he had lived, they'd arrived *fashionably* late to every dratted function.

Fretting James might change his mind, she'd not told Juliet they were to meet him. Her sister would ask questions Regine wasn't prepared to answer.

"Bullock's Museum of Natural Curiosities," Juliet breathed, practically pressing her turned-up nose to the glass as the carriage rumbled to a stop before two and twenty Piccadilly. "So many marvelous novelties from around the world. All in one place." She gave an excited little bounce upon the seat as if she were six years old and not fifteen. "I'm ever so glad you agreed we might visit."

Bestowing an indulgent smile on her, Regine gave silent thanks to James for having made the suggestion. Had he recalled Juliet's fascination with nature even when she'd been a little girl? How often she'd find a feather, a rock, an insect, or something else, and insist on sharing her *treasure* with anyone who would listen?

"I've heard there are fossils and many preserved birds." A wrinkle appeared between Juliet's dark eyebrows above the thin metal bridge of her spectacles. "I confess, I think it's quite barbaric to kill creatures simply so humans can gawk at them. But I also acknowledge it would be difficult and cruel to keep live species in cages and such."

"We'll not visit any exhibits you object to, dear." Regine patted Juliet's arm, her stomach tumbling over on itself upon spying James standing, tall and confident, outside the museum's entrance. His beaver hat and a midnight blue caped greatcoat bespoke quality without being ostentatious. He might easily pass for a lord of the realm.

Her blasted, traitorous heart leaped with anticipation. She had no right to the gladness careening through her upon seeing him. Unwittingly, she clenched Juliet's arm, and then catching herself, withdrew her hand.

Foolish, foolish goosecap. The carriage bounced as the driver descended, giving her a minute to gather her equanimity and disguise her rattled state.

Juliet—her head cocked like an inquisitive sparrow, her rounded blue eyes assessing Regine much too astutely from behind thick lenses—formed her mouth into a small *moue*.

Before her inquisitive sister could ask whatever probing question had formed in her mind, Regine fashioned an artificial smile luminous enough to light Seven Dials. At midnight. During a winter storm. Truthfully, she felt somewhat like she grinned in the rigid manner of a grotesque gargoyle.

She scrambled for a topic to distract Juliet. "I forgot to ask if you need any more materials for the orphanage's valentines?"

When they'd first arrived in London, Juliet's despondency about the recently diagnosed need for spectacles had her sulking about their house, woebegone, and in a state of the blue devils. Regine had hit upon the notion of her artistic sister creating valentines for those less fortunate as a way to help her understand her circumstances weren't as doleful as she believed.

After procuring a list of charities for her to choose from, Juliet had selected the Shephard's Haven Home. A small but well-run foundling home and orphanage operated by two unconventional spinster sisters and their few, equally unique staff.

Juliet shook her head, her pink bonnet bobbing. "No. I believe I have plenty. In fact, I'm nearly finish—" She stopped abruptly and tapped her chin, a contemplative expression on her face as she gazed out the window to where James approached; he strode directly toward their conveyance with the swaggering long-legged stride and assurance of a peer.

"Although…" Juliet slanted a sly glance toward Regine, wrestling to keep her mien completely unaffected.

Her sister must not suspect her interest. It would only complicate matters.

"I suppose a bit more lace and red ribbon wouldn't go amiss," Juliet admitted.

As the door swung open, Regine gave a brisk nod. "It's settled then. When we pick up your gloves tomorrow, we'll stop at the haberdashery, too. You can purchase any other items you might be short of, as well."

"Hmm." Juliet made a soft, suspicious noise in her throat. "And *why* is it you didn't collect my gloves yesterday?" She made a pretense of examining the perfectly acceptable gloves encasing her fingers. Peeking at Regine over the rim of her eyeglasses, a distinct teasing glint shone in her eyes.

An exasperated groan throttled up Regine's throat and pressed against the back of her lips. Juliet was too dashed astute by far. "I explained already, dear. I ran into an old friend I hadn't seen in a great while. You know I was away from England for six years, and Heartwaite's failing health and the mourning periods for him and Mama kept me from London for another two."

She made to scoot from the seat and descend the conveyance. Gracious, her sister was becoming a busybody.

"Would that *friend* be James Brentwood?" False innocence laced Juliet's sing-song voice.

Pausing at the door, unprepared for Juliet to have mined that morsel so easily, Regine swung her gaze to her sister. She furrowed her brow. "You remember him?"

Regine hadn't considered that. Juliet had been seven, and she had assumed she'd long ago forgotten about her oldest sister's young and attentive beau. She sliced a glance to the object of their discussion, waiting patiently no more than six feet from the carriage.

Likely eavesdropping on their conversation.

James's expression didn't reveal one way or another whether he'd heard every word.

Juliet snorted and waved a hand as if most offended. "*Of course* I do. I was just seven, but I do remember you adored him." She leaned forward and touched Regine's shoulder, a maturity glowing behind those new lenses, far beyond her fifteen summers. "I know you only married Heartwaite to assure Mama and we girls were provided for."

Heart cramping from renewed pain and no small degree of astonishment, Regine closed her eyes for a blink. Hovering, half-crouched, she was at a loss for words.

Juliet knew? How? Was I that obvious, after all?

The question must've shown in her eyes, because her sister's mouth curved into a fragile little smile. "I'm near-sighted, Regine. Not stupid." Angling another considering glance toward James patiently standing outside, his hands behind his back and his head at a slight slant, a speculative gleam entered Juliet's eyes.

Her acute gaze swung to Regine and back to James three times.

Back and forth. Back and forth. Back and forth.

"Wipe that speculative look from your face, Juliet Minerva Francis Edenshaw." Regine pointed a narrowed-eyed gaze at her sister. She could practically hear the cogs grinding away in her youngest sister's mind. "There's nothing between us now. It's too late."

"Uhm hum." Juliet gave her a gentle shove as she giggled. "Regine, you look like a great, startled bird, hovering there. A purple martin, to be exact." Another discovery from Juliet's recently purchased *Fascinating Birds of the World Handbook and Field Guide*.

Today, Regine wore purple trimmed in black velvet. Not a demure lavender or heather, but rich, luxurious violet with equally sumptuous ebony velvet. Heartwaite had preferred she wear dulcet shades and pastels. The minute she'd tossed off her mourning weeds, she'd indulged her taste for vibrant hues—emerald, crimson, sapphire. Gold and silver, too.

Her way of rebelling.

Against what?

She wasn't precisely sure *what*. The social system that rendered women possessions? That kept them restricted and without rights, and most of them reliant upon men for their every need? Against fate, for forcing her down a path she'd never have chosen?

The coachman cleared his throat, and Regine directed her focus to the street once more. To the man from her past standing there, as handsome as ever, who would always own her battered heart.

James had closed the distance and now waited, hand outstretched, to assist her from the vehicle. Once her feet were safely upon the pavement, he reached to help Juliet descend.

She grinned at him, quite the most animated Regine had seen her since—well, since Mama's death. "Hello, Mr. Brentwood," she fairly chirped, dipping a bouncing little curtsy. "You are looking well."

She searched past him.

Whatever did the minx seek?

"Your wife's not with you?" Juliet asked.

Lord. Bold as brass, and without a jot of remorse.

"Or haven't you married?" She blinked up at him innocently.

Groaning inwardly, Regine purposely remained imperious to the crafty glance her sister slid her. *The little hellion.* They'd have a serious conversation when they arrived home. Nay. On the carriage ride home, and she'd disabuse her littlest sister of any misplaced romantic notions.

"Alas, I remain a crusty old bachelor." He chuckled and bent at the waist as if greeting royalty.

"Crusty? I should say not. Why, you're even more handsome than I remembered," Juliet quipped without any apparent regret for her impertinence. "Or, perhaps you've always been thus, and I can finally see you now." She flitted her fingertips near her spectacles.

Jaw slack, Regine blinked, undecided whether to chastise Juliet for her impudence or cheer that she had taken so to James and could jest light-heartedly about her hated eyeglasses. Where had her reserved, well-mannered sister gone? The one so embarrassed by her spectacles?

"And you, Miss Edenshaw, look quite fetching in your eyeglasses." He dipped his chin and murmured in a velvety voice, "Very *élégant*."

Pinkening under his praise, she tentatively touched the left temple two inches before where it looped behind her ear. She stood a little taller and confident. "Thank you."

Regine could've hugged him for his kindness.

"Thank *you* for accepting my invitation. Shall we?" James extended his elbows, and Juliet promptly latched onto his left arm.

Juliet shot her an, "*Ah ha! So that's the way of it,*" glance.

Casting the proffered arm a dubious look, Regine vacillated. Touching him again would be an enormous mistake. Her palm still tingled from when he'd handed her down from the carriage. But she yearned to feel him beneath her fingertips. To caress that firm, sinewy flesh.

Her life had been bereft of touch and affection for so long. Oh, Heartwaite had given her an occasional fatherly peck on the cheek, and naturally, she and her sisters had hugged to console each other when their mother died. But she'd missed—no, craved—a virile man's touch.

Not any man's. James's.

An acorn-colored eyebrow quirked in challenge at her continued hesitations, and by George! Did his lips tremble? *Blast the rotter.* He knew how he affected her, though she'd vowed to remain impervious to his disarming smile.

Setting her jaw, and dredging up the remnants of her resolve, Regine gingerly laid her finger inside the crook of his elbow.

He bent his neck, placing his mouth near her ear. "I've had dog hair cling to me with a firmer grip."

What? She blinked like a ninny. *Dog hair?*

He chuckled again, the contagious baritone resonating in his chest, and her traitorous lips twitched.

He's acting charming for Juliet's sake. Don't forget that.

326

"Relax," he said out the side of his mouth as they passed through the entrance, Juliet in her eagerness rushing ahead. "I shan't bite. Unless...you want me to." That last emerged a throaty purr.

Good God.

She glanced upward, searching his face for the hostility so apparent yesterday. Leeriness yet lingered in his marine eyes but not the frosty rejection he'd first turned on her at the coffeeshop. Regine raised her chin and summoned a smile. She'd enjoy today. For Juliet's sake.

"You might not bite, James, but your gaze can unshell a nut with a single, searing look."

A shadow fell across his features, and his attention shifted to Juliet, jaw slack, and slowly turning in a circle. "Truce for today?" he murmured for Regine's ears alone. He lifted his square chin toward her enthralled sister. "For her sake?"

"I wasn't aware we were at odds," Regine quipped, instantly regretting her playfulness when his eyelids slid half-closed, and he swept that hooded, sultry turquoise gaze over her.

"Make no mistake, Regine, we are."

She couldn't misunderstand the undertone of steel in his voice. Nor the lingering resentment.

"I've not forgotten," he murmured.

Her amusement fled, promptly replaced by self-recrimination.

See? You were greedy instead of wise. Fool!

Regine had known it was imprudent to accompany James on this outing, but she'd been unable to say no yesterday. Now, he obviously regretted his impulsiveness for asking as much as she did for accepting. If she'd possessed an ounce of wisdom, she'd have turned her back and walked away yesterday. Now, because she'd been weak and feckless, they both suffered from her impulsiveness.

"Oh." Dropping her gaze to block his scorn, she wet her lower lip. "Perhaps, it would be best if we didn't—"

He took her elbow and drew her aside, all the while making sure Juliet was within view. "I am perfectly capable of acting the gentleman in order for your sister to enjoy herself. I trust you are as well?"

"Of acting the gentleman?" *Good Lord.* There she went again. Why did she continue to jest?

Because, in truth, she wanted to see his beautiful smile. That flash of teeth and the humor dancing in his eyes. Like the James of old. The man who'd looked at her with adoration rather than derision in his beautiful gaze.

A sound very near a growl escaped him. "*Regine,*" he warned.

"Truce. Yes." She nodded emphatically. "A truce is just the thing."

Not possible. But she pasted on a pleasant face for her sister's sake. There could be no peace between them. Too much wounding, too many misunderstandings, and much too much time had passed.

His expression dubious, James gave a curt nod and guided her to her sister. "Miss Edenshaw, do you have a preference where we begin?"

7

Four days later, cognac in hand, James chatted with his brothers-in-law, Crispin, the Duke of Bainbridge, and Victor, the Duke of Sutcliffe, in Sutcliffe's drawing room as they awaited dinner's announcement. Though most of Society hadn't returned to Town after the Christmastide holiday, business had required Bainbridge's and Sutcliffe's presence in London.

Naturally, neither would consider leaving their brides behind, nor would their duchesses ever have agreed to the separation. Since wedding, they'd clung together worse than lint on velvet.

As such, Theadosia, James's middle sister, and the one most fond of entertaining had invited a few of their friends for dinner. Mathias, Duke of Westfall, conferred in low tones with Maxwell, Duke of Pennington before the frolicking crimson and orange flames flickering in the gray and white marble fireplace.

Pennington's wife, Gabriella, sat upon a royal blue brocade settee with James's youngest sister, Jessica, now the Duchess of Bainbridge, and their mutual friend Justina Farthington. The trio nodded at something Miss Farthington's aunt, Emily Grenville, was saying.

"Thea always manages to collect a crowd for any gathering," James said before taking a long swallow of the superb spirit. "It's the off-season, yet—" He angled the glass toward those already assembled. His sister had fallen into the role of a duchess as naturally as birds fly and fish swim.

Conferring a fond look upon his wife, Sutcliff nodded. "She does have a way. She's happiest when hostessing something or other." His gaze swept the tastefully decorated room. "And I believe we are expecting a few more guests as well."

No sooner had he uttered those words than the butler announced, "Her Grace, The Dowager Duchess of Heartwaite."

Equal parts excitement and dread kicked an unrelenting rhythm behind James's ribcage.

Exquisite in a midnight blue and white gown, with a filmy lace overskirt, Regine looked ethereal, like heaven had descended to Earth in human form. Angelic and impossibly seductive, too. In the years since she left him, she'd become preposterously more beautiful. A touch of rosy color tinged her high cheekbones, but other than that telltale sign, she remained supremely composed.

She must've suspected he'd be in attendance tonight. After all, his sister played hostess, which meant Regine didn't intend to avoid him as he did her. He hadn't considered that.

After eight years apart, this was the third time in less than a week he'd seen her. James didn't know how much more his heart or composure could take.

The old treacherous sentimentality he'd convinced himself he'd annihilated had resurfaced, bubbling and scorching and dangerously near to breaching his self-control. He'd convinced himself he'd put Regine out of his mind and heart years ago.

What about your soul? Taunted that persistent voice that refused to let him deceive himself.

Go to hell, he silently retorted.

Concentrating on the molded plaster ceiling details, he brought his stampeding pulse to a fairly normal pace and waited for the sickening clenching in his gut to ease.

Blast Thea. James had no doubt whatsoever that his sister had learned Regine was in London and decided to meddle. More on point—play matchmaker. He speared her a reproachful glare, but she merely winked as she rushed forward, hands outstretched, to greet Regine.

He'd bet his law firm he also found himself seated beside the alluring

Dowager Duchess of Heartwaite for dinner, too. Rage and jealousy and disgust roiled within him. Heartwaite had caressed her pearly skin. Trailed his perpetually wet lips on that gloriously silken flesh, and James had only ever tasted her sweet mouth.

Before evening's end, he'd have a word with his sister and tell her to cease her interfering. He'd plodded down the road in pursuit of the delectable Regine once. Only a beef-witted, bacon-brained, codpated fool would do so again. He was none of the aforementioned.

A partnership in a successful law firm and a handful of prosperous investments didn't now, nor would it ever, make him her equal. The girl he'd fallen in love with no longer existed—*if* she ever had. Mayhap, he'd only seen what he'd wanted to see. His eyes were wide open now, however. The key to his heart, firmly secured away.

Regine gracefully angled her head toward him in a restrained, yet regal greeting. A hint of disquiet dulled the brilliance of her black-fringed, azure gaze.

James doubted anyone else noticed the discomfit that compromised her smile and had her midnight lashes sweeping her cheeks, she masked her unease so skillfully.

Showing a modicum of wisdom, Theadosia guided her newest arrival to the seated women and made introductions.

God's teeth, this was going to be a devilishly long and exacting evening.

James downed the last of the amber spirit in one gulp, earning him a scold from Bainbridge. "That's no way to treat a superior cognac, old chap. I suggest ale if you don't want to savor the flavor and simply wish to gulp your spirits like a cup-shot sailor on leave."

Sutcliffe caught Bainbridge's eye and gave a discreet shake of his head while cutting a pointed glance toward Regine.

Ah, hell. Theadosia had told him. The last thing he wanted was pity from his indecently happily-wed brother-in-law.

"What?" Eyebrows knit in puzzlement, Bainbridge shifted his attention to her and then back to James. Twice. He flexed his eyes, narrowing them a fraction as comprehension took root, and they went platter wide and soft around the edges.

Not him too? *Blast and damn.* A fellow could only tolerate so much unsolicited commiseration.

"I take it you're acquainted with the duchess?" Bainbridge drawled, a good deal of amusement and incredulity dripping from each word.

"Which one? The damned room is overflowing with duchesses," James snapped. He regretted his sarcasm at once. Particularly since they well knew he was acquainted with the other ladies. "I apologize, Bainbridge. That was uncalled for. I'm a bit off my step tonight."

Since a certain lady with ebony hair the midnight sky would envy, and eyes of the palest shade of blue disrupted the rhythm of his heart.

"Think nothing of it." Bainbridge swept a glass from the tray of a passing servant. Thrusting the brandy at James in exchange for his empty glass, he said, "Feel free to quaff the entire contents. You look as if you need it."

Thank you. Just what a chap likes to hear.

Bainbridge deposited the empty glass upon the tray, and the footman moved on.

No. James wouldn't use spirits to numb his senses. He'd done that every night for six months after Regine's marriage. He might've wallowed in self-pity longer, but his law-firm partners had taken him firmly in hand and told him enough was enough. Either get off his arse, pull himself together and move along with becoming a solicitor, or see himself to the firm's door.

He owed much to those two curmudgeons. Both avowed bachelors, with high expectations, treated him like a beloved son. But they'd refused to coddle him or allow him to continue to muck about, feeling sorry for himself. They'd given him the kick in the rear he'd needed to pull himself up by his bootstraps and move on with his life.

He'd be damned twenty times to Christmas if he'd ramble the convoluted path of courting Regine again. *Really? And that's why I must keep reminding myself of that?*

Another covert scrutiny of the room revealed more guests had arrived.

So absorbed in his musings, James hadn't heard the butler announcing them.

"James?"

"Pardon?" He hauled his attention from the woman whose memory had tormented him these many years.

"That's the third time I addressed you." A distinct devilish twinkle brightened Sutcliffe's eyes, and by God, Bainbridge hid a chuckle behind a raised fist and feigned cough.

Devil take it.

Devil take them!

James realized with an unpleasant jolt, he was the only person present, lacking a title. Heretofore, he hadn't given a strumpet's virtue about his common birth, but surrounded by this lot, most of whom he considered friends, for the first time he felt—

What?

Not inferior or inadequate. Just not quite up to par. The sole plow horse amongst thoroughbreds at Ascot's racecourse or a Tattersall's auction.

The dinner gong rang, and everyone trailed to the doorway. James held back, aware he was the lowest-ranking male present. There were no lower-ranking females, which meant some unlucky peeress would find herself accompanied to dinner by an inferior. His sister, Jessica, came to his rescue, looping her gloved hand through his elbow.

"Are you well?" Concern darkened her eyes, the hue so similar to his own. "I remember Regine. That is, the Dowager Duchess of Heartwaite." Her sympathetic gaze swept his face. "I remember the two of you together."

She'd been—*what*—twelve? And Theadosia thirteen to Regine's eighteen?

Thank God, Jessica didn't remind him she also remembered how broken he'd been. Or how, even as a little girl, she'd fretted about him. Her sloppily-written, rambling letters those months after Regine had left England had said all those things as she'd innocently attempted to comfort her older brother.

James patted her hand. He counted himself lucky to have three affectionate sisters. "I am fine. Tonight isn't the first time the duchess and I have encountered each other since she came to London."

He'd not mention Bullock's Museum. That afternoon had ended pleasantly enough, but as he'd determined to do, he'd bid Regine an indifferent farewell—*liar*—with no intention of rekindling their relationship.

Though he might be a successful lawyer, he couldn't offer her the lifestyle, position, or comfort to which she was accustomed. Besides, when she'd married Heartwaite, she'd made her priorities clear. Familiar bitterness and envy, tempered by a jot of regret, throttled up his throat, and he swallowed against the burning.

"You should know that Thea also asked me to extend an invitation to her grace for the Valentine's Day ball Crispin and I are hosting." Jessica angled her head, studying him much too intently for his comfort. "I shan't invite her if you don't wish me to."

Did he want her to?

8

Jessica hesitated, worrying her lower lip. "It's just that we've heard she's not been well-received. And since our families were friends..." She hitched a shoulder. "We thought to ease her into Society."

Ever kind, were his sisters. How could he begrudge Regine and Juliet an invitation or two?

"By all means, invite her." He was capable of governing his emotions. At least he had been until she'd whirled into his life like an out-of-control dervish a few days ago. "I ask that you include her sister in the invitation as well."

At his request, she arched her eyebrows high but nodded. "I'd intended to."

"Good." He couldn't think of a more ingenious response since his musings had already leaped forward to next week.

God's ballocks. He was out of his bloody mind. Attending a Valentine's Day ball. The one day of the year set aside for romance and love and ridiculous tokens of affection. Poems. Odes. Sonnets. Sweets and flowers.

And he, like a lack-witted imbecile, had agreed to attend, knowing the woman who'd spurned him would be there. Another thought brought him up short. Would Jessica expect him to dance with Regine? No, by damn. A man could only take so much.

If James took her into his arms, he would never be able to let her go again.

Mayhap he could arrange to be out of the city. There was that ailing client in Bath...

As he and Jessica entered the dining room, he barely stifled an oath. His mouth thinned into an uncompromising line, he scowled at the table. His manipulating sister *had* placed him to Regine's right, exactly as he'd suspected she would. Leveling her another accusatory glance that promised retribution, he filled his lungs with a steadying breath.

And—damn it all—inhaled Regine's subtle perfume.

Apple blossoms. She always smelled of fresh apples and spice. Her shiny dark-as-a-raven's-wing hair was piled high on her head, exposing her nape and the downy hair there. He itched to brush his knuckles down the graceful column and across her bare, gently sloping alabaster shoulders fringed with the finest blue silk.

For an extended breath, he shut his eyes against the maelstrom of unwanted sentiment her scent heralded. Jaw clamped, he clenched the back of his chair. His teeth might crack from the force of subduing his desire. Lungs cramping with longing, he took his seat and breathed in Regine's tempting scent while spearing Theadosia a just-you-wait look.

She tipped her mouth upward at one side while rolling her shoulders.

In contrition or dismissal?

James snapped his napkin open and, after placing it on his lap, cleared his throat. He felt as awkward as he had at his first formal dinner. Taking a long sip of wine, he willed his awareness of the woman to his left to dissipate. Her warmth beckoned, and God help him, he could not dispel the aroma of apple blossoms from his nostrils.

Without conscious thought, he found himself leaning toward her, drawing in her essence. He fought not to close his eyes as the familiar scent wrapped around him, coiling through his gut and entwining his heart. Ah, her fragrance elicited such sweet memories. Sweet, tormenting memories reminiscent of another time.

For all of her affected poise, Regine seemed as uncomfortable as he, for she also sipped her wine and had yet to look at him. If they kept staring straight ahead, like dolls attired in the first stare of fashion on display, they'd soon garner the attention of everyone in the room.

Theadosia caught his eye and pointedly steered her attention to Regine. Always a superb hostess, she wouldn't tolerate any of her guests feeling self-conscious. If he didn't heed her silent warning, James would receive an ever-so-polite, but thorough tongue-lashing.

With a sideways, almost shy glance, Regine broke the silence first, "I thank you again for escorting us to the museum. Juliet hasn't stopped talking about the excursion."

"I appreciate she enjoyed herself." He relaxed a trifle, some of the strain seeping from his shoulders and spine. Dining beside her wasn't all that bad. He could manage for an hour or two. He signaled the footman to refill his wine glass.

At once, the well-trained servant poured him another glass of superb cabernet.

How many courses had Theadosia planned for dinner?

Things marched along quite nicely, almost comfortably, for the next half an hour until Westfall, seated to Regine's left, commented, "I ran into the Duke of Heartwaite at White's this afternoon. Surprised me, I must say. He's not usually one for London in January."

Heartwaite had five and twenty years on Regine. No wonder Westfall hadn't referred to him as her stepson.

Every bit of color leeched from her face, and she carefully set down her fork. "Indeed."

A trace of something James couldn't quite identify, but which raised his hackles, rendered her voice husky.

"You are correct, Your Grace. He prefers the comfort of his country estate during the winter months." Her tongue peeked out to dampen her lower lip. "And by chance, did he happen to mention why he'd ventured to London?"

Rather than look at Westfall, she raised stricken eyes to James. Lost, hopeless eyes.

By God, what went on here?

Westfall shook his head as he forked a bite of horseradish crusted roast beef. "Not specifically. Said he had a legal matter he sought counsel about."

"I see." If possible, she paled further, her attention fixed upon her plate. The delicate pulse at the juncture of her throat fluttered wildly, her chest rising and falling swiftly in agitation.

She was well and truly upset. Why?

Seated on Westfall's other side, Miss Greenville spoke to him, and, with an apologetic smile, he directed his attention her way.

"Regine? Is something amiss?" James raked his gaze over her. She was upset. Distraught even.

She met his eyes, and his stomach sank upon comprehending the fear pooling in hers. She bit her lower lip, her attention skipping over those seated nearest them before she edged closer.

"James, I know I have no right to ask, and I'll understand if you cannot. But perhaps you can recommend another solicitor then. I know this isn't the place, either." She looked around the table, again, blinking slowly and appearing somewhat dazed.

Her anxiety had something to do with what Westfall had said. But what?

Apprehension and worry had replaced the poised façade she'd presented at the coffeeshop and museum. And even here, earlier this evening. He'd never seen her like this, and every protective instinct he possessed surged to awareness.

She might've tossed him aside as easily as burned bread, but James would unhesitatingly guard her with his life. The realization sucked the wind from his lungs. From the very room itself.

His focus narrowed, blocking out the sounds and sights surrounding him until it was just the two of them. A tiny island in a sea of guests.

Comprehension slammed into him.

He still loved her. He'd never stopped.

Fool. Fool. *Fool.*

He'd but buried his feelings, repressed and denied his hopes and dreams for a future with her. Love—resilient and potent—had remained, and now it pulsed through him, as steadily and as forceful as the blood in his veins.

"I'd hoped it wouldn't come to this, but I am at a loss as to what else to do—" Faltering to an abrupt halt, she inhaled deeply, the movement threatening to spill her ample bosoms from her gown's respectable, but much-too-low-for-his-comfort-neckline. She flexed her fingers around her fork's handle as if preparing to guard herself.

James had never seen Regine like this. Afraid. Uncertain. And needing him. He lightly touched the back of her stiff hand. God, she was genuinely distressed.

"What is it, Regine? I'll assist if I can."

She swallowed audibly, and hand shaking, lifted her wine glass.

More fool he, but he could no more deny her request than he could cut out his own heart.

"May I pay a visit to your offices tomorrow, James? I fear I require legal counsel, as well." She raised those breathtaking pale blue eyes to his.

Forget-me-nots. That was the shade of her eyes. And he hadn't ever forgotten her. How could he? He'd given her his heart all those years ago, and he'd never been whole since.

"My stepson seeks to overturn my bequeathment," she whispered, brokenly. "Without the inheritance Heartwaite settled upon me, I have no means to provide for Juliet. No home. Nothing. I'll be destitute again." The last word immerged a tortured, husky rasp weighted with despair and hopelessness.

Again? Had she...?

An inkling took root. Did Regine mean what James thought she did? That she'd been in that place before? After her father died? Why hadn't she told him?

Even now, she fretted about her sister and not herself. And how dare that fribbling dumpling, Heartwaite, challenge his father's will? Admiration for her, as well as fury toward the duke, pounded in his blood.

"Of course. Come by my office at eleven tomorrow, and bring every pertinent document you possess with you." Mindful, they weren't alone, yet needing to offer her comfort, he touched her elbow. "Never fear. If the documents were legally drafted and witnessed, he has no case."

Giving a short nod, she reached beneath the table and clasped his hand. "Thank you. I realize I'm asking much after I—"

"You are not alone." He squeezed her slender fingers. *Darling, Regine.* Instinctively, he knew she needed to know that this time, she could count on his help. "I shall always be here for you."

A tremulous smile arched her plump lips, and her eyes softened. "I don't deserve your friendship, James. But I am ever so thankful for it."

Friendship? God's teeth.

He didn't want friendship. Or gratitude. Or appreciation. He wanted her. *I do.* Even after all this time. Even though she'd cleaved his heart from his chest and ground it into powder. He wanted Regine.

You're a damned fool.

Yes, he was. And he couldn't claim a whit of regret.

9

At promptly eleven the next morning, clutching a slender leather portfolio against her side, Regine swept past James and into his office. Deciding the reason for their meeting called for a more conservative gown, she'd donned a navy-blue and pearl-gray walking ensemble and matching redingote. Elegant and unquestionably respectable. Just as a *haut ton* duchess should appear.

Ah, but her heart was that of a flamboyant gypsy wanderer.

A curious mixture of amusement and devilment played about the edges of his eyes and mouth. As if he were privy to a great secret which bubbled behind his breastbone and danced impatiently on his tongue, waiting to be revealed.

A hint of the carefree young man he'd been, hovered over him. It sent her heart to flopping about, and she couldn't suppress her smile. He'd been so very young and charming. So eager to please her. The tiniest bit awkward, but endearingly so.

Before her mind took her down a path that was sure to cause more discomfit, she examined the tidy room representing so much of his life. He'd placed his desk so that his back faced a duo of tall windows, allowing him the most light to conduct his work as well as face the door. Two comfortable-looking, unpretentious, deep burgundy armchairs paralleled each other before the shiny, black walnut desk.

After tucking the file beneath her elbow, she removed her dark blue gloves and took in a pair of bookshelves. The leather-bound, scholarly tomes neatly arranged from largest to smallest on their shelves, claimed most of the west wall. A walnut-brown leather sofa and rosewood end tables graced the opposite wall.

Masculine, attractive, and sensible, through and through. A room very much like the striking man waiting expectantly for her beside one of the tufted burgundy armchairs.

"Regine?" He splayed one large hand across the top of the chair, a smattering of silky dark, whisky-colored hair atop the back. "Won't you have a seat while I examine the papers you've brought?"

"Yes. Of course." She nodded, and gloves clutched in one hand, and the documents in the other, crossed the earth-toned Turkish carpet.

Today James wore a royal blue superfine wool coat and an ivory jacquard waistcoat. Refined and elegant, but not ostentatious. His black pantaloons hugged muscular thighs. All in all, he was a splendid specimen of manhood. And he could've been hers for all time.

Yes, but at what cost to him?

She ought to tell him why she'd married Heartwaite. Oh, she'd tried that awful day, but James had been too wounded to attend her pleas. Mayhap now that his position was secure, he'd listen. Perhaps, just perhaps, he could forgive her, and her soul might be at ease.

Scanning the office again, Regine pushed aside her redolent thoughts. She harbored no doubt that James wouldn't be established in this comfortable office, a successful solicitor—*no, a partner*—in a law firm had she followed her heart.

The knowledge ought to console her. It did, but it didn't ease the perpetual ache in her breast. His success had been as important as her family's survival. As she slipped into the chair and set the documents atop his organized desk, she offered a grateful upward sweep of her mouth.

A heartbeat later, he sat across from her. Drawing the file near, he asked, "May I?"

"But of course. That's why I am here." She welcomed any excuse to be in his company, even if her reason today was alarming and unnerving. Her stepson, George-Curtis, was a slimy maggot.

If James found anything questionable in the papers, she didn't know what she'd do. However, she sought comfort in the knowledge that Heartwaite hadn't been frivolous when it had come to business matters. Confidence that James could offer valuable legal advice, should she require it, also soothed her frayed nerves a trifle.

In all honesty, Regine had no right to impose upon him, but he'd been so unbearably kind last night. Almost as if the past wounds had been erased, and he still cared for her. *If only that were true.* The unexpected news that George-Curtis, a podgy, pallid turnip-of-a-man who craved creature-comforts almost as much as he lusted after money, had ventured to London had rattled her composure.

No, the news had been as frightening as if a violent earthquake had shaken the Sutcliffe's home, stripping the ceilings of their decorative plasterwork and the walls of their gilded frames. She'd been overwrought, and she'd sought succor from the person she still trusted most in the world. She wasn't ignorant of the manner in which James had stiffened when she arrived for dinner, nor the starchy glances passing between the Duchess of Sutcliffe and her austere brother.

When Regine and Juliet had visited the glovers the day after their museum outing, they'd run into Theadosia and Jessica. How unusual that three misses from their small country hamlet had all become duchesses.

It hadn't taken much persuasion on Theadosia's part for Regine to accept the invitation to dine. Naturally, she'd known James would be there. But she couldn't stay away, now that she'd seen him again.

He remained in her blood, in her aching, wounded soul. His presence brought her such exquisite torment. It hurt to be near him, knowing she'd ruined the rare jewel they'd shared. Yet, she couldn't deny herself the opportunity to see him either.

On the Continent, she'd never fretted about an unexpected encounter with him. But since she'd seen his dear face in the coffeeshop window, she searched every street, every window, and every coach and carriage for his auburn hair and blue-green eyes.

Regine couldn't eschew an opportunity to see him. Even if he never spoke to her. How very pathetic she'd become. Pining for a man who, if perhaps didn't revile, certainly disdained and condemned her.

Nonetheless, other than their initial meeting, he'd been kind and courteous, and she believed, perchance, she detected a glint of primal protectiveness in his eyes last night. A distinct feminine appreciation for gallantry thrummed in her. And now, hopefully, he'd be able to advise her how best to proceed with George-Curtis.

Through her lashes, she observed James, a forefinger resting on his upper lip and head bent as he perused her documents. That stubborn forelock of bronze hair had fallen forward as it was wont to do. She wanted to smooth it back in place, and cup his chiseled cheeks between her hands and kiss him.

A crease drew his arched eyebrows together, and only the ticking of the mahogany bracket clock on one of the shelves interrupted the silence.

He flipped to a previously read page, marking it with his finger as he riffled forward and studied another. At last, he sat back, and fingers steepled, twisted his mouth into a half-smile. "These appear to be in order, Regine. I've found nothing in my initial inspection that gives me cause to believe the Duke of Heartwaite would prevail in court."

So great was her relief, she almost sagged against the chair. Except, duchesses didn't sag. "I cannot tell you how relieved I am." Leaning forward, she placed a palm upon the desk. "He cannot seize my ship or home? Freeze my funds?"

"He threatened you with that?" A fierce scowl lined James's face, and he balled the hand resting atop his desk as if he'd very much like to smash it into George-Curtis's bulbous, red-veined nose.

"He did. And more." Unless she made him welcome in her bed, the vile wretch. He'd also vowed to confiscate her horseflesh, furnishings, jewels, and even her clothing. Vengeful and vindictive. Resenting every penny his father had spent on her.

It wasn't as if George-Curtis or his siblings hadn't been provided for. Heartwaite had been generous with his children, bestowing estates on the younger sons as well as enormous dowries on his daughters. And yet, they begrudged Regine…everything.

The genuine fear she'd end up in the same position she'd been in eight years ago had niggled incessantly. No funds. No home. No means of provision.

Except things weren't the same at present as they had been then. Regine had only the one sister to fret over now, and if worse came to worse, Christiana or Marian would take Juliet in, albeit reluctantly. They'd married for love—one a rector and the other a professor—and each had children. Neither had an abundance of room or coin.

Simply knowing she wouldn't have to impose upon her sisters if George-Curtis chose to be obstinate about the matter and cut off her funds as he'd threatened until a court decision was rendered, felt as if a loadstone had been removed from her shoulders.

"I feared he might have had a case against me, and I would have to prevail upon one of my sisters to take Juliet in," Regine admitted, attempting to disregard the flush creeping from her neck to her hairline.

Something indiscernible flashed across James's features but disappeared in a heartbeat. "If you'd permit, I'd like to keep these to examine at my leisure." He tapped the papers with his forefinger. "Only to be certain I didn't overlook anything."

"Certainly." She gathered her gloves, prepared to depart, but reluctant to do so. Now was the time to tell James. Explain what had driven her to accept Heartwaite. To ask for his forgiveness.

Except the words wouldn't come, wouldn't form on her tongue. As a young girl of eighteen, her reasoning had seemed so sound, but had it truly been?

Hadn't James had the right to know the calamity that had befallen her family? To be a part of the decision she'd made that had so disastrously affected both of their lives?

In truth, these past few days, she'd begun to doubt the wisdom of her girlish decision. And still, the words remained stuck in her throat, her mouth dry as sand, and fear of further rejection rendering her mute.

Since when had she become a coward?

He scraped his fingers through his hair in a disarming manner, leaving a few strands tufted and endearingly boyish. "Ah, would you care for coffee?"

Already in the process of donning one glove, she brought her gaze up to meet his.

Warmth and masculine approval shone in his eyes.

"I would, in truth." Regine would've accepted an offer of cold tea or pond water. Anything to spend another few minutes with him. It was not wise and could only lead to more heartache, but she couldn't resist.

James flashed her one of his captivating smiles of old, and her mouth went impossibly dryer. "Excellent," he said, rising in an agile, smooth movement. He gestured toward the sofa. "Make yourself comfortable while I request refreshments."

He strode to the door, and she took the opportunity to take in his impressive form. Fine, to ogle, undetected. For certain, he hadn't gone soft from sitting behind a desk. She'd wager he still rode neck or nothing and mayhap boxed.

Unlike the mincing pups and foppish dandies she'd encountered on the Continent, James possessed an impressive physique. Well-muscled, his face a healthy shade, rather than pasty, and his fingers ink-stained and slightly calloused.

As he opened the door and poked his head out, she made her way to the sofa. She dropped her gloves and reticule on the table centered before the manly piece of furniture and then on impulse, removed her navy-blue bonnet. After placing it beside her other possessions, she flattened a palm over her fluttering stomach and sank onto the unexpectedly comfortable cushion.

Stop it, Regine Daphne Philippa Maberly! she scolded herself. *You aren't a green schoolgirl.*

James turned from the door and giving her another incandescent smile, he winked. Roguish and charming, and wholly unexpected. But oh, so very welcome.

Her ragged heartbeat quickened into a gallop, and the sun itself seemed to ease into the room, filling the space with golden warmth and radiance.

Instead of taking one of the chairs across from her, he settled beside Regine, his sculpted mouth kicked upward at the corners.

Why did James have to have such a lovely mouth?

She glanced downward, only to have his defined, muscular thigh

346

catch her attention. A groan almost escaped her. The carved marble and stone masterpieces she'd viewed in Grecian temples had nothing on the virile man inches from her. So close, in fact, his sandalwood and shaving lotion aromas wafted past. She curled her toes against an overwhelming urge to bury her face in his corded neck and breathe him in.

Duchesses didn't sniff men.

Nay, but country lasses might.

"James."

"Regine."

They spoke simultaneously and then gave a short laugh.

"Ladies first," James said with a gallant dip of his head.

However, before Regine could tell him what had been burning in her heart, a quiet rap preceded the entry of a fresh-faced clerk bearing a tray.

His ears glowing red, the young man very carefully paced to the table, and ever-so-slowly bent and deposited the tray. He breathed out an audible sigh of relief when he straightened.

"Thank you, Bentley," James said with an encouraging smile.

"Will there be anything else, Mr. Brentwood?" Bentley slid Regine a side-eyed, inquisitive glance.

"No, thank you." Hilarity colored James's denial, but in no way did his expression reveal his amusement.

After bending into a stiff bow, Bentley let himself out.

"I believe, Your Grace, you have conquered another male heart." Rubbing his nose with his forefinger, James chuckled. "I'll wager there is a long queue of males from pimply-faced youths to doddery decrepitudes awaiting a kind word or a smile from you."

Regine flashed him an astonished glance. "There is no such thing."

Would she have noticed if there were?

No, for though she might've been married to one man, her heart had remained faithful to another. It always would.

More because she needed something to do, or she might stupidly blurt her feelings and embarrass them both, she examined the refreshments. Her eyes rounded, and she shot James an astonished glance. "Maid of honor tarts?"

And shortbread and Naples biscuits. All of her favorites.

"Yes." His eyes twinkled with familiar jollity.

Oh, how she'd long to see that gleam there.

He'd planned this, and joy sluiced through her.

"James." She waved a hand over the tray, her smile a trifle unsteady, and a sheen of moisture blurring her vision. "You remembered."

His eyes darkening to the shade of the deepest sea, he gathered her hand in his and then astounded her by firmly pressing his mouth to her knuckles. "I've not forgotten anything about you, Regine." Huskiness tempered his tone, and she was nearly undone.

A spark of hope ignited, so minuscule, she was afraid to breathe lest it die.

He edged closer until his thigh touched hers, and she could see the cobalt ring circling his iris. His manly scent encompassed her, his heat an almost undeniable, magnetic pull. "I remember how you feel in my arms," he said throatily as he drew her to his solid chest.

Good God above.

"I recall the sensitive place behind your ear," he breathed against that exact spot. "Just here." He placed a hot kiss there, and she couldn't quite smother a moan of pleasure.

"James," she whispered shakily into his neck. "What…what are you doing?"

He leaned away a couple of inches, a tender, enigmatic smile bending his mouth as he brushed a knuckle along her cheekbone. Rather than answer, he pulled her onto his lap.

She gave a little yelp and grabbed his lapels, all too aware of the hard length of his thighs beneath her bottom and another insistent lump straining against his falls. He wanted her. A delicious thrill heated her blood. Sweet Lord, her beloved James, wanted her.

"James, Bentley might return," she managed between gasps as he continued his sensual onslaught on her neck and throat.

"Not if he values his position, he won't," he fairly growled. "He was directed to see that we are not disturbed."

Mortification scorched her face. *Good Lord.* What must the nervous clerk be thinking? Did he suspect what went on inside his employer's office? She gave a mental shrug. Let Bentley think what he would. At last, she was in James's arms again, and nothing else mattered.

"I realized something last night," James said, nuzzling her neck and making her head spin. All thoughts of propriety flew to the four corners of the Earth.

"You did," she murmured breathlessly, somehow finding her fingers threaded in his silky hair, and her neck arched to permit him easier access. "And what…" She moaned as he nipped her throat. "What…what did you realize?"

She could barely cobble together two words, she was so aware of him. Of every sinewy, hard contour as he wreaked havoc on her senses.

"That I still love you." He pressed her palm to his chest, and she felt the steady beat of his heart. "You are now, have always been, and will always be the duchess of my heart."

10

James hadn't meant to blurt his feelings. He'd intended to woo Regine, to break down her defenses and reservations first. But the words had played non-stop, a monologue in his mind since the realization had struck him with the force of a lightning bolt at dinner last night.

I love her. I love her. I love Regine.

Elation and trepidation and a myriad of other sentiments roiled within him in a cacophony of confusing feelings and emotions. But rising to the top was one indisputable, all-consuming truth: he loved her.

Regine's past didn't matter. Why she'd married Heartwaite didn't matter. She was here, in his arms, where she should've always been. Where he'd have her stay for as long as he drew a breath.

He loved her. And by God, from the doe-eyed glances coming from her gorgeous, guileless azure eyes, she still loved him. Their love had endured, despite everything.

"You love me?" Wonder and awe rendered her voice sultry as her eyes flicked back and forth, looking into one of his and then the other. "You *truly* love me, even after—?"

Such hope glimmered in her gaze that moisture stung the back of his. "I do, darling."

"Oh, James." A teardrop trickled from the corner of one eye and then the other.

His gut wrenched at the sight, making him recall the last time he'd seen her hugging herself, hunched over and sobbing as if in agony. When he'd left her without letting her explain. "Regine, I—"

"I love you, too." She sucked in a shaky breath and sniffed against the crystal-like droplets making a slow path over her smooth, ivory cheeks. "I never stopped." Her expression grew serious. "Please believe. I *never* stopped loving you, and it almost killed me to marry Heartwaite."

He pulled a handkerchief from his coat, and a heart-shaped slip of paper adorned with red ribbon and lace dropped onto her lap.

A frown turned her mouth down, and she stiffened before raising stricken, inquisitive eyes to his. "A valentine?"

He scooped up the valentine and waved it under her nose, grinning all the while. "This is from your imp of a sister."

Regine blinked at him as she patted at the moisture upon her cheeks. "Juliet?"

"Certainly not Marian or Christiana." He winked roguishly.

Her nose wrinkled in that adorable way it always had when she was perplexed, and the tempting love mark beside her mouth practically pleaded with him to kiss it. "I didn't realize she fancied you."

He chuckled and tucked her close to his chest. "She doesn't. The minx signed *your* name. She also vowed undying, eternal love." He waggled his eyebrows. "She mentioned my muscled chest and irresistible eyes, too."

"She didn't!" Regine jerked her gaze to his before groaning in chagrin, and her sooty lashes fluttered to brush her pink cheeks. Her eyelids popped open a moment later. "Wait. How did you know it wasn't from me?"

Eyebrow cocked, James looked askance. "I told you, I remember *everything* about you. It's not your handwriting. I'd recognize yours anywhere. I still have the love letters you sent me, including, if you recall, three valentines."

"You saved them?" Her voice had grown raspy from suppressed emotion.

He rolled a shoulder. "How could I not? They were all I had left of you."

She fingered the silky crimson ribbon. "I saved yours, too. Heartwaite never knew, of course." Fresh tears threatened, welling in her eyes, and she averted her gaze. "I want you to know why I married him, James."

He wrapped his arms tighter around her and brushed his lips across her temple then her forehead. "Sweetheart, it isn't necessary."

She laid a palm on his chest. "Please. I need to." Her gaze roamed his face, such earnestness there. "I need to make you understand. I never cared about his title, or money, or the things he could give me."

James had accused her of all of those. Thrown the words like daggers, each finding a target in her unselfish heart. A wave of shame washed over him. After last night, he guessed why she'd married the duke, but she'd asked to explain, and he owed Regine that and much more. And so, with a long, resigned sigh, he settled against the sofa's back, and after arranging her so that she lay cradled against his chest, he said, "Go on, then, love."

The telling was short. Regine spared herself no mercy. And with every softly uttered word, his love for her blossomed more profoundly and grew impossibly deeper. "So, you sacrificed yourself for your family and to ensure that I became a solicitor."

She met his gaze, straight on. "I did. I honestly thought it was the only way. Since then, however, I've wondered if I made the wrong decision. But by then, it was too late."

"I would've made it work, somehow, Regine." He firmed his embrace, almost as if by holding her to him so close he could erase the past. "I confess it wouldn't have been easy, but I *would* have."

"I couldn't fathom how, James. And Heartwaite only gave me a week to decide. I think he knew if he allowed me longer, I'd refuse him."

"Bloody sod."

She shook her head. "He was kind to me. More like a doting uncle." Her cheeks suddenly flushed bright pink, and she bit her lower lip. "He never...ah, that is. We never..."

"Never what?" Eyebrows drawn taut, he tried to discern her meaning.

Her shoulders rising and chest expanding, she inhaled then said in a rush. "We were never intimate. He couldn't perform the act."

"Sweet Christ on Sunday." Of all the things she might've said, James would never have expected that. Eight years of frustration and anger and resentment melted away as he took her mouth in a reverent kiss.

She responded, matching every slash of his tongue, every sigh, every moan. At last, his groin pulsing from need and fearing that if they continued, he might very well take her on the sofa, and despise himself afterward, he reluctantly lifted his lips from hers.

"Marry me, Regine." He said into her hair. "Marry me, and we can begin again."

Joy blossomed across her face, and she gifted him with a radiant smile. "Yes." She took his face in her hands and kissed him. "Yes. Yes. Yes."

Bainbridges' Valentine's Day Ball
One week later

Regine smiled into her husband's eyes as James whirled her around the sanded ballroom floor in perfect time to the waltz's lilting melody. They'd been married this morning with only Juliet, James's sisters, and their husbands in attendance.

She sent letters to Christiana and Marian, announcing her nuptials, but hadn't invited them to the ceremony. Neither she nor James had wanted to wait to learn if they could make the journey to Town.

Regine was, in a word—or two actually—blissfully happy. Ecstatic. Fine. Three words.

Juliet had become accustomed to her spectacles, and thanks to James's encouragement and kindly attention, she wore them like a badge of honor. Dimpling at him and Regine, her eyes sparkling with mischief and mirth, she'd made a very pretty apology for sending the valentine on Regine's behalf.

George-Curtis had taken himself off to his country seat after a brief meeting with James and his partners at the firm. James assured her that her nemesis would harass her no more.

And now, Regine danced in the arms of the man she'd loved for her entire life.

"I love you, Mrs. Brentwood," he whispered in her ear, edging her closer than propriety permitted. Though she was entitled to keep her title, Regine made it very clear, she preferred *missus* over *your grace*.

She, once so conscious of decorum, pressed into him, not giving a whit that the gossips' tongues would wag all over London tomorrow about the Brentwoods' scandalous behavior at the ball. Tilting her head, she said, "I love you, too. So very, very much." And then to give the tattlemongers *on dit* to bandy about, she touched a wisp of a kiss to his mouth.

A low growl rumbled in his throat. "Wife, if you keep that up, I'll cause a scandal that will be on the *ton's* tongues for the next decade." His smoldering gaze lowered to her décolletage. "I might, in any event."

The smile she gave him held a promise. She'd chosen her gown to please him, and not *le beau monde*. Designed by a very exclusive French modiste, the gown's fabric was a shimmering iridescent crimson. The color appeared to ebb and flow as she moved.

Regine had wanted to see the heat of desire in her husband's green-blue eyes. She'd succeeded. Peeking up at him from beneath her lashes, she wet her lower lip. "We don't have to stay, if you'd—"

Before she'd finished her sentence, he'd seized her gloved hand in his and, with one arm around her waist, guided her from the glittering ballroom. "What say we start our honeymoon, early, sweetheart?"

"I'd say that was a very fine idea, indeed."

Epilogue

Isle of Crete
9 June 1816

James squinted against the early morning sun cloaking the patio and stark white stucco buildings. Below him, the turquoise Cretan Sea sparkled, a myriad of diamonds against the pristine, powdery sand.

Regine hadn't exaggerated the island's beauty nor its charm. Since marrying five and a half years ago, they spent a month here every summer, and each time, it became harder to return to London.

In truth, more and more of late, he'd contemplated living half of the year in Greece. After a few additional wise investments and conferring with Stapleton Shipping and Supplies as to the best use of her ship, he and Regine were in a financial position where he wasn't required to work as a solicitor any longer. Well, at least not to charge a fee for his services. He'd continue his *pro bono* work for those unable to afford to hire a lawyer.

There'd be time to discuss those contemplations when they returned to England, for they must leave on the morrow. Regine expected their third child within the month and, call him old-fashioned, he wanted their baby born on British soil.

Yawning, he stretched his arms overhead and tipped his lips upward when slender arms slid around his middle from behind. Regine flattened her palms against his naked chest and pressed a hot kiss to his shoulder blade, her scantily clad breasts brushing his back.

Desire promptly hardened his groin.

"What are you doing awake so early?" He turned and gathered his sleep-rumpled wife into his arms and kissed the crown of her head. The fragrances of apples and spices met his nostrils.

Her hair lay in a tangle of silky raven curls about her shoulders and waist, and she smiled up at him, trailing her fingers across his collar bone in a seductress's invitation. "I missed you, and I'm hungry." She patted her swollen tummy through her gown's gossamer-thin fabric.

James cocked an eyebrow and lowered his mouth to her shell-like ear. "I have *just* the thing to satiate your hunger, my sweet." He rotated his hips until his groin brushed the apex of her thighs.

"I'm sure you do." A winged sable brow shied high on her forehead as she glanced at the distinct bulge straining against his pantaloons. "I fear you'll have to wait, darling. I've already ordered coffee, melomakarona, and bougasta. I truly am quite ravenous."

"Ah, pastries to break your fast again, my love?" Her appetite for food and *other things* had increased as the babe grew within her. She wasn't the least jot shy or timid about satisfying either.

Thank God.

He lay a palm over her distended tummy and, bending low, murmured. "How are you this morning, little one?"

She chuckled and covered his hand with both of hers as the baby gave a sound kick. "*He* is determined to let his mama and papa know he's ready to come into this world."

"*He?*" James grinned as the baby kicked again. "You're certain it's a boy this time?"

She nodded and shoved her ebony hair over her left shoulder. "Yes. *He.* The girls were never so rambunctious in the womb, nor was I constantly famished." She'd been terribly ill the first three months of this pregnancy, too.

"No, our daughters' waited to be born to display their high-spirits," he said, drawing her to his side and nuzzling the sensitive spot below her ear. "Much like their mother."

She drew back, an affected pout upon her plump mouth. "I beg your pardon? I am, at all times, the epitome of decorum."

He looked pointedly to the mussed bed and made a low, dissenting sound in his throat.

A delightful blush turned her cheeks pink, but she only nestled closer. "I didn't hear you complaining about my *high-spirits* last night, husband."

"Never," he murmured against her satiny throat before kissing and licking a trail to her high, firm breasts. Every day, he thanked God for bringing Regine back into his life, and every day, he grew to love her impossibly more.

Arching her neck, she gave a soft moan, then whispered breathlessly, "Perhaps I might delay breaking my fast—"

Before she finished the sentence, he scooped her into his arms, and in a half-dozen strides, laid her atop the tousled sheets. Bracing one elbow beside her, he rested his head in his hand while he leisurely explored the delicious cleft between her bountiful breasts with the fingers of his other hand. Leaning to graze his mouth across hers, he murmured, "I love you, Regine."

Her brilliant blue eyes softened at the corners as answering adoration shone from them. Cupping his face with her hands, she stared straight into the depths of his soul. "And I love you, James. Now, forever, and beyond eternity."

USA Today Bestselling, award-winning author COLLETTE CAMERON®
scribbles Scottish and Regency historicals featuring dashing rogues and
scoundrels and the intrepid damsels who re-form them. Blessed with an
overactive and witty muse that won't stop whispering new romantic romps
in her ear, she's lived in Oregon her entire life, though she dreams of
living in Scotland part-time. A self-confessed Cadbury chocoholic, you'll
always find a dash of inspiration and a pinch of humor in her sweet-to-
spicy timeless romances®.

Explore **Collette's worlds** at

www.collettecameron.com!

Join her **VIP Reader Club** and **FREE newsletter**. Giggles guaranteed!

FREE BOOK: Join Collette's The Regency Rose® VIP Reader Club to get updates on book releases, cover reveals, contests and giveaways she reserves exclusively for email and newsletter followers. Also, any deals, sales, or special promotions are offered to club members first. She will not share your name or email, nor will she spam you.

http://bit.ly/TheRegencyRoseGift

Dearest Reader,

Thank you for reading SEDUCTIVE SCOUNDRELS SERIES BOOKS 4-6.

I hope you spent many hours, escaping to Regency England with the heroines and heroes. I've introduced you to several other characters, and their stories are coming soon.

Although I strive to be as historically accurate as possible, I do take a bit of creative license with my romances. After all, they are historical romance with the emphasis on romance rather than historical fiction, where the emphasis is on the historical aspect.

Please consider telling other readers why you enjoyed this book by reviewing it. I adore hearing from my readers.

I so appreciate you reading my stories. I never intended to be an author, but once I dipped my toes into the writing world, I was hooked. I don't plan on ever retiring.

Many blessings to you!
Hugs,

Collette Cameron

Never Dance with a Duke

Seductive Scoundrels Series, Book Seven
A Historical Regency Romance

The cost of trust is more than she's willing to pay. But he'll do *everything* he can to change her mind...

A scandal ruined her future...

Nicolette Twistleton delights in thumbing her nose at Society. After all, becoming the Spiteful Spinster was what helped her through being jilted by her betrothed. Putting her faith in another man? Impossible. But there's something about the entirely too handsome and charming Mathias Pembroke that makes her wish she was the kind of woman who could learn to trust again.

A secret can destroy his...

Mathias, Duke of Westfall, wants nothing to do with his inherited title and all the public scrutiny it brings. He has dark secrets to protect, and can't afford to be distracted by the trappings of Society. What he apparently can be distracted by, however, is the lovely Nicolette. He understands her pain and knows he could help her heal...if only she were willing to open her heart to him.

Can love save them both?

When ghosts from the past emerge and threaten the fragile bonds they've begun to build, Nicolette and Mathias find themselves caught between their feelings for each other and devastating scandal. Will love be enough to protect them—or was their happily ever after doomed from the very start?

Enjoy the first chapter of
Never Dance with a Duke
Seductive Scoundrels, Book Seven

1

Hyde Park, London
Morning, 15 May 1810

Nicolette Twistleton puffed out a soft, poignant sigh as she strolled the sun-dappled footpath along the southern bank of the Serpentine in Hyde Park.

Bella, her pug puppy, frolicked about, yanking on her leash in an energetic attempt to investigate every single thing she happened upon: leaves, sticks, insects, rocks, worms, people— and their shoes. She had a particular penchant for the latter, which she thoroughly enjoyed ruining with her needle-like teeth.

Thus far, a trio of Nicolette's slippers and a pair of half-boots had met a gruesome end.

A pair of brownish-gray mourning doves swooped across the pathway, landing beneath a flowering cherry tree's heavily laden branches. Cooing softly, they touched bills, in what almost appeared to be an avian kiss.

Several feet behind Nicolette—enough to permit a bit of privacy but not so much as to cause raised eyebrows—her maid, Jane, carried Nicolette's parasol and hummed softly to herself.

A distracted half-smile curving her mouth, Jane twirled the plump pink peony she'd plucked from the front flower bed when they left the house an hour ago.

Jane was madly in love.

She and Jack, one of the Twistleton grooms, were to wed next month. Her dreamy expression and wistful sighs were beginning to wear on Nicolette's tattered nerves, however. As happy as she was for the loyal servant, she couldn't prevent the reoccurring twinge in the region of her heart.

Oh, the pang most assuredly was *not* envy.

No indeed—God forbid such a wholly ludicrous idea.

The familiar ache was a bitter reminder of Nicolette's absolute humiliation and devastation two years ago. Her then betrothed, Alfonse Bremerton, the Duke of Kilbourne, had jilted her a mere four hours before they were to have exchanged vows at St. George's Church. After the odious churl had danced with her thrice at a ball the night before, pretending to be the doting soon-to-be groom.

When his note had arrived the morn of their wedding day, she'd eagerly opened it, expecting a love note.

Nicolette,
I cannot marry you.
Forgive me.
K

Kilbourne hadn't even deemed her worthy of an endearment.

Seven words.

Twelve short syllables.

Thirteen if you counted Alfonse's initial, which she did not.

That was all it took to destroy Nicolette's life, her plans for the future, and make her determined never to trust a rogue again. Or even marry for that matter.

How could she possibly ever trust her gullible heart again?

By the time she'd received her former betrothed's cryptic note calling off their wedding, the cowardly cur was already half-way to Gretna Green with Maribelle Grosenick—a vulgarly rich heiress hailing from America.

Even more mortifying—salt in an already festering wound—Kilbourne's heir, a healthy male child, had entered the world a mere six-and one-half months later. Irrefutable proof that the blackguard had been playing Nicolette false during their courtship.

And he'd dared—*dared, by God*!—to plead with her to consummate their vows the eve of their wedding. After all, they were to exchange vows on the morrow, he'd cajoled, and all the while, Kilbourne had been plotting to scorn her.

Scapegrace. Hog-grubber. Jackanape.

Typical man—controlled by that *thing* between his legs and not the brain in the head atop his shoulders. And most assuredly not governed by any sense of decency, honor, or chivalry.

"Contemptible, maggot-patted bounder." She snorted, loudly and most indelicately, earning her a curious look from Bella's big brown eyes and also sending the cooing doves to wing.

"No, I wasn't talking to you, my precious darling," Nicolette told the sweet little dog, she acquired the purebred pug in Colechester two months ago. Bending, she patted Bella's soft head, earning a doggy grin in return. "Are you having fun?"

Tongue lolling, Bella gazed at her adoringly and promptly tried to nip Nicolette's gloved fingers in an attempt to play. Everything was a chew toy for the teething pup.

Thank goodness for this little dog who'd helped ease the sadness and loneliness Nicolette hid from the world behind a carefully constructed contradictory facade: part carefree flirt and part coldly aloof spinster.

She donned her mask of gay coquette and pretended to all of the world that she didn't have a single care. That being jilted hadn't affected her in the least. Until a man became too familiar or forward, then she retreated into an icy shell.

Men never knew which she'd be, on any given occasion, and she preferred it that way. It kept them slightly off-balance, which meant they couldn't ever get close to her. And if they couldn't get close, she ran no risk of heartbreak again.

It also kept the gentlemen from presuming too much. And Nicolette's caustic tongue deterred even the more daring of the bucks from over boldness. She'd once overheard two matrons declaring Nicolette's tongue was sharp enough to scrape barnacles from a ship.

Bah, she scolded herself for allowing her mind to wander down these melancholy paths on such a lovely day.

She *was* better off without Kilbourne.

That, she now knew to be an unqualified fact. For a man who'd stray while betrothed would assuredly do so once vows had been exchanged.

Had Maribelle considered that when she'd dallied with another's affianced?

She ought to have.

For if the rumors were accurate—and there was generally a tidbit of truth in all tattle if one dug around enough to find the nugget—he'd recently become romantically entangled with an Italian opera singer.

Another sound of disgust echoed in Nicolette's throat.

That made his fifth mistress since marrying.

Perchance, the lure of a title had sufficed for Maribelle, and after providing the requisite heir, she was content with her lot. Gossip also had it that the Duchess of Kilbourne was in the Americas for an *extensive* visit.

So perhaps, she'd come to her senses, after all.

Nevertheless, from that fateful day onward, at twenty years old, Nicolette had relegated love and all of the other flimflam associated with the useless emotion to a fusty, secluded corner of her heart. Where, in time, she hoped to forget she'd ever entertained such foolish, fanciful notions.

Pragmatism had replaced romanticism—reality instead of girlish daydreams.

Her desire for love had been exchanged with a passion for adventure. At least that's what she believed this restlessness besetting her was. She'd approached Mama and Ansley about the possibility of traveling to exotic foreign destinations. But both had looked at her with such incredulity, she might've sprouted a pair of wings upon her shoulders or feathers in her hair.

Her mother and brother *did not* share her enthusiasm for exploring other cultures and places. They were perfectly content dividing their time between London during the Season and Fawtonbrooke Hall the rest of the time.

Oh, an occasional short holiday to Bath or Bristol, or even a jaunt to France or Scotland for a few days, *might* be acceptable. But nothing so dramatic or distant as exploring ancient cities or other antiquities.

However, for a spinster facing a boring, *lonely* future, the notion of visiting faraway, mystical places had taken the place of her desire for love, marriage, and children.

Or so Nicolette told herself. Repeatedly. Daily.

However, as contradictory as it might be, she was sincerely glad for her married friends. Several had recently fallen in love and were happy as grigs with their very own dukes. Just because love hadn't worked out well for her, didn't mean she begrudged them their happily ever afters.

She, alone, seemed to have been Cupid's failure.

Puzzling her forehead, she bit her lower lip and skirted a fallen branch, a remnant from last night's windstorm.

The whole being jilted ordeal still hurt. Awfully. Encompassed Nicolette with a desolation, she only acknowledged when lying in her lonely bed at night. When all of the day's activities were behind her, and her mind was, at last, permitted to contemplate the reality she stoically ignored otherwise.

Nicolette faced a solitary and purposeless future, and when she'd grown tired of proving to *le beau monde* that she didn't care about being tossed aside, what would she do?

Upon spying a twig on the path, Bella yipped and tugged upon her leash. She pounced on her unwitting prey before clamping her little jaws around the eight-inch long stick and marching along proudly for a few steps, her curled tail in the air.

Only in the last couple of weeks had Nicolette's training Bella to walk on a leash met with enough success that the puppy could accompany her the entire length of her morning walks.

When an immense long-haired black dog loped by on the adjacent green, she promptly deserted her toy, dropping it to the pathway and trying with all of her might to chase the dog. The runt of her litter, Bella had no notion of her extra small size, even at almost four months old.

In the distance, an impatient male voice called after the large dog. "Sampson! Stop."

Oh, dear. Had he escaped his owner?

Undoubtedly, and one snap of his big jaws would severely injure Bella.

"No, Bella," Nicolette gently admonished.

The biscuit-colored pup was still learning appropriate leash behavior. She strained against her restraint, her sturdy little body visibly quivering for another moment before Bella reluctantly resumed her version of strolling.

These early morning promenades, when Mama was still abed, were the only times Nicolette claimed for herself. She raised her face to catch a ray of sun feathering through the bright green foliage.

Its warmth soothed and rejuvenated her.

It was a glorious spring morning, and she breathed out a deep, cleansing breath.

Typically, the weather would've invigorated Nicolette and helped prepare her to face whatever social fracas Mama had decided she must endure for the day and evening.

Always—*always, dash it all*—with the ultimate goal of seeing her happily wed. Mama wasn't ready to quit the field just yet regarding Nicolette's nuptials—*more's the pity*. She still dreamed her only daughter would find a suitable husband and eventual contentment.

And live *happily ever after*.

Pshaw. Nicolette wrinkled her nose.

As if that was ever going to happen now.

368

She'd given love a chance once, and with a few exceptions—her brother Ansley, Earl of Scarborough, being one—she'd henceforth concluded men were toads. No, toads could be cute, intriguing creatures, and it was unfair to make the comparison.

Surely she could do better than that.

Cockroaches.

Yes, men were cockroaches—the lot of them.

Most especially handsome dukes.

Well, excluding her friends' husbands—the Dukes of Sheffield, Sutcliffe, Bainbridge, and Pennington—who were decent enough chaps, she supposed.

Fine then, not *all* lords were devil's spawns. Just most.

Mindful of her propensity to freckle,   Nicolette lowered her face, and her pink bonnet's brim blocked the soothing sunshine once more. A smile tipped her mouth as Bella spotted a squirrel and made to charge after the small creature.

However, this particular squirrel, nearly as big as the pug, wasn't having any of Bella's bravado. It sat upon its haunches, scolding the puppy soundly for her impudence.

"*Ruff.*" Bella hopped on all fours. "*Ruff. Ruff. Ruff.*"

Hop. Hop. Hop.

She bounced on her sturdy little legs again, whining fretfully in her attempts to reach the taunting rodent.

Why, the little gray wretch appeared to grin tauntingly at Bella. It's small, sharp, yellow teeth clearly showing, it even made little chirping noises, which sounded distinctly like squirrely chuckles.

The dog that had raced by earlier must've heard Bella's frantic barks for it came tearing across the green straight toward them. Nicolette's heart faltered before kicking into double time.

A liveried footman charged after the creature, but he couldn't possibly catch the animal before he was upon Nicolette.

Good Lord!

Was the enormous beast friendly?

She wasn't waiting to find out.

She'd just scooped Bella into her arms when the rambunctious, hairy dog plowed into her. Panting and drooling, it reared onto its hind legs.

Heaven's above!

Releasing a startled squeak, Nicolette staggered under the creature's weight. Resting his enormous paws on Nicolette's arms, all the while rooting about with his broad muzzle, the brute tried to sniff Bella.

"Miss Nicolette!" Jane screamed, dropping her flower and rushing forward, wielding the parasol like a saber. She whacked the mongrel on his haunches, but she might as well have used a feather for all the good it did.

"Get away from them!" she cried.

Thwack.

"Leave her be, you great, hairy brute!" Jane ordered.

Thwack. Thwack.

Nicolette well knew Jane didn't possess the gumption to strike the dog hard enough to hurt it. Not that it would feel much through the thick pelt covering its large frame.

Her heart stampeding and Bella growling a warning low in her throat, Nicolette wrapped her arms more securely about the outraged, wriggling puppy. Shoulders hunched, she turned her back to the other dog, still persisting in trying to snuffle Bella.

Why must dogs always greet one another with intrusive, and sometimes rather embarrassing, sniffing?

Nicolette feared that at any moment, she'd feel sharp teeth shredding her flesh or hear Bella shriek in pain.

What manner of owner permitted their dog—a dog *this* large and intimidating—to run wild in Hyde Park for pity's sake? In truth, the circumstance might send a woman with a less robust constitution into histrionics or a swoon.

Nicolette wasn't prone to either. She wasn't that sort of woman and didn't plan on becoming one.

The dog hadn't growled or bared its teeth, and therefore, she deduced it wasn't vicious. But the sheer size of the beast made standing upright almost impossible. Under the creature's weight, Nicolette stumbled forward a pair of steps. It certainly felt as if the dog weighed almost as much as she.

A shrill whistle rent the air a fraction before a stern male voice ordered, "Sampson. Down."

Sniffing loudly and giving one last determined lunge toward Bella cradled in Nicolette's embrace, the dog succeeded in knocking her off balance. She didn't even have time to cry out before she tumbled forward.

Printed in Great Britain
by Amazon

55334759R00217